**Frank P. Ryan** is a multiple bestselling author in the UK and US. A writer of the year for the *New York Times Book Review*, his books have been translated into more than ten different languages.

**Other titles by Frank P. Ryan**

# THE TWINS OF
# MOON

## FRANK P. RYAN

**SWIFT**
PUBLISHERS

# A SWIFT BOOK

## First published by Swift Publishers
## 2019

*1 3 5 7 9 8 6 4 2*

Copyright © Frank P. Ryan 2019

A catalogue record for this book is available from the British Library
ISBN 978-1-87-408282-8

e-mail: enquiries@swiftpublishers.com

Cover art by Mark Salwowski
Typeset in Garamond by Word-2-Kindle

*I would like to thank my editor, Hilary Johnson, for her diligent correction of my numerous peccadillos. My thanks are also due to my friend and artist, Mark Salwowski, for his magnificent cover art. And finally, I would like to thank my friend, Derek Bradbury for allowing me my first glimpse into the inspiration for the Valley of the Raptors.*

# Contents

# THE OLD WOMAN

Her eyes are pools of darkness in which splinters of silver whirl, like a starry night seen through the blur of tears. The focus of her mind is no longer clear. She cares little for the fact she might miss events, a day, a century. Time for an Undying does not run in the linear fashion it does for humans. Time immemorial has been passing her by and still every single moment ravages her, her senses all-seeing, all-feeling, a never-ending torment of consciousness. Yet still her fists are capable of clenching until the bones crackle. Passions rage within her being. In her grief she lifts an arm, provoking the clanking of chains.

*In darkness was I born? So they would have me believe. And it would seem that the very moment of my birth provoked conflict. Thus was it my lot to be meddling in the conflicts of this warrior and that. Death would have appeared to swirl about me, coming in the shapes of serpents, or ashes, or the ripping of the beating heart out of my chest. Even now would I deny my guilt in any of this, even though all that would prove me innocent has long wasted away. Yet in the face of a single new accusation, I would contest it – contest it all – and all over again. If Mechi had not met with his death, those serpents would not have grown, and the land would not have been blighted by chaos. I might have prevented such a dreadful metamorphosis – I might still end it. In such furtherance must I constantly seek the light! Who then dares to call up the enchantment that enchains me?*

A sigh – another meaningful barb that pretends to offer promise. Yet a communication perhaps from somewhere distant?

A voice speaking as if in wonderment. 'There is not a hero in him, lying as he does in the shadow of the Mórígán . . .'

*More lies!*

Another sigh, and from that same source. It provokes the closing of her eyelids. A meniscus of inner light within those old, old, eyes – a sigh? All that a sigh might suggest . . . would it be too much to extrapolate to hope?

She bows her head, closes her eyes, as if to refocus her thoughts.

Yet then – a third sigh! And then a whisper: *'A boy . . . '*

What could this mean?

The two words have inserted themselves into her ruminations. She has fixated on them, their possible meaning: *a boy?*

Again the sigh, and again a whisper: *'Truly a boy . . . '*

It becomes more intriguing.

Could it be that a door is opening?

Her eyes blink open again. No – *no!* Hope is impossible on the Beach of Bones. She hears her own scream tear the fabric of a sky that is a lurid ultraviolet, shot through with spearheads of blood red.

*A boy! My hope is with a boy . . .*

'YOU MISERABLE WRETCH, SCRABBLING AT
SCRAPS!'

His voice – truly his voice for the first time in the aeons of her banishment! Yet why would he bother to communicate in this moment? What hope is there to be extinguished? Could it be that he has detected something new . . . the possibility of change?

She draws upon her being, upon her ancestry, upon her anger, upon her hope, then . . . then she refuses to be baited by his angry words. She returns to the interesting suggestion of a boy.

She must focus everything on those two words of hope . . .

*A boy!*

Should she blot it from her consciousness? Was he capable of reading the tiniest tremor of hope in her mind? No – she must not think along such lines. Indeed if there was to be any hope at all she must focus all on what it might mean. She must implant and then protect that tiny splinter of hope. She must cherish it so deep that malice could not possibly discover it. And from here play whatever role was left to her on the slightest possibility of redemption.

She must be careful.

The old woman climbs to her feet with groans of pain as the tide washes the stony beach in the revealing moonlight.

There is no hero hiding in the shadows. Her eyes focus on a tiny detail in her ravaged flesh: a hermit crab crawling out of the ruin of her left calf. She gazes down upon it with kindly eyes, as if from a great distance. She sees every detail of its scrabbling feet, the unwieldy rocking of the borrowed shell.

Yet already her mind is responding to this newfound whisper. She must focus all her cunning on what it promises while concealing all traces of hope from him: she must force herself to relocate in time! But she can only turn backwards. The future is not hers to see. She finds herself fluttering over some ancient battlefield in the shape of a heron with neither

side below her knowing, in the swirling fog of mist and
blood, who is friend or foe. But the thought will not go away.
The whisper still insists on breaking through:

*'A boy! A boy . . . yet one unusual in spirit!'*

The old woman turns ponderously around, then holds
her figure still as an unyielding reef in the freezing waves of
the incoming tide, gazing back up the Beach of Bones to
consider the only respite that is on offer. It looms before her,
a brutal hut, black as midnight, constructed of monstrous
slabs of rusting steel. There is neither door nor window, yet
into its grim shadow she now wills her miserable spirit to
retreat, with the tardy tread of a prisoner returning to her
cell.

# THE STEPPING STONE

'Stop fidgeting!'

Magio hesitated at his sister's words. He had been spinning around and around within the den, using his upraised bare feet pushing against the wall to propel himself, using the big rounded stone as an axle. He should be so happy. Here, on occasions beyond counting, he had been lost in wonder, his ears filled by the beloved thunder of the sea. The world was magical. All you had to do was to sense the magic and let yourself go with the flow.

He chortled with glee, muttering, 'Eefa – see ya – see ya – Eefa!', delighted with his discovery of how the words rhymed.

'Flibbertigibbet!'

'I'm not fidgeting.'

Eefa sighed. 'Yes you are, Gio. You're fidgeting with your feet. And it's distracting me from thinking.'

Surely she couldn't blame him for feeling nervous? The magic was gone. It had abandoned them both when Gran died just ten days ago. It just seemed impossible that the magic, the happiness, had been taken away from them. The shock of that had stunned Magio. He just hadn't anticipated it, even though Gran had been careless with her health for a long while. It had turned his world upside down. He ignored the guillemots overhead, attempting to understand how it was that he and Eefa were sitting here, in their rocky den, pretending things were still britzy. Neither of them could escape the memory, just those same ten days ago, when, here in this same den, there had been the flapping sound of sandalled feet approaching over the baked sand. Magio had found his startled self staring up at Quimbre's bronzed bewhiskered face, with his thick mane of grey hair pulled back into a pony tail, and there had been no escape from the look in those coal-black eyes. Magio was still haunted by the sympathy in those eyes and by the words coming out of Quimbre's thick-lipped mouth, those terrible words, 'Gran – she's gone, kiddo.'

There was a depth of feeling in Quimbre's brown face. But right now Magio's head was turning slowly to gaze up out of the den at his sister, Eefa, as if demanding she contradict it. He just wanted her to tell him it hadn't really happened. He wished that Quimbre's message had been another of his daydreams. But Eefa was no longer looking back at him. She was sitting, side-saddle, on the rocky perimeter above the den, her eyes gazing out onto the incoming tide rushing between the rocks.

'I don't know where I am any more. I'm lost – I'm lost, Eefa!'

Her eyes continued to follow the crashing waves.

Gran gone – really gone. Gone forever! Dead! That was some kind of a stupid word, dead! He just hated that stupid word . . . dead!

Magio was finding it hard to swallow. He wanted Eefa to hug him. For days now he had wanted somebody to hug him. But what he really wanted was a magical hug, the kind of hug that would bring Gran back. There were no such magical hugs. He was fidgeting again, spinning his body around with his legs.

Why had Eefa brought him back here today? Was it because she needed something magical too? Because this place, their den, was the closest thing they had ever known to real magic?

Magio swallowed against a hard, dry throat.

It was magical. Or at least something about their den really was magical. The feel of it, the memories they had shared in it. Sun. Sand. Blue sky. The sea . . .

*The sea!*

That was the real wonder, the real magic of it. How many times had they run barefoot here, to sit ankle-deep in the pure white sand, and stare at the Sea of Stars, listen to it, feel its salty moistness on their skins, inhale it into their lungs? The neverending roar of it, the demand and wonder of it, the love of it in every fibre of their beings?

That was all that he, Magio, had ever lived for. It was all he dreamed about, all that occupied his mind every morning when he woke up. But now he was trapped in a confusion of panic and disbelief. The magic had forsaken him. It had left him in the strange and disturbing situation where there was no more Gran to go back to. He had struggled to come to terms with it. How could it be? Yet still there was no escaping the horrible memory of Quimbre burying her in a hole in the sand like she was carrying some kind of plague.

*Oh, Gran!*

Why did she have to be buried the very next day after she died? Quimbre had insisted on it, even though it didn't give Magio or Eefa time to understand it. Even now he had no idea what it meant. There was nobody to wake him up in the morning, nobody to tell him to wash behind his ears. Nobody to feel the bristles of the worn-out toothbrush to make sure it was wet and he had cleaned his teeth with it.

Nobody to care about them any more! Why couldn't he have sat there by Gran's body and howled his rage? Why did adults do such incredibly stupid stuff like burying her straight away like that?

'Jinxy! Jinxy! Jinxy!'

'Hush,' Eefa said. 'You'll draw people's attention.'

*What people?* There wasn't another soul around.

'I don't know if I can bear it!'

'Hush!'

He climbed out of the den and sat down, cross-legged, next to his sister. 'You know it isn't fair!'

She put her arm around him and hugged him.

It was the mitziest thing, her hugging him. How had she guessed that he wanted it so much? He felt a shiver run right through him.

'What are we going to do?'

'I don't know.'

It was so unlike his sister to say that. She should be saying, '*It's okay. There's nothing to worry about. We'll think of something.*'

Gran hadn't been all that old – not for a grandma. Sixty-two years and nine days. He'd drawn a birthday card for her just nineteen days earlier. Then, when he saw her lying there . . . when he had felt the coldness of her skin and he knew for certain that Quimbre wasn't lying . . . that she really had died . . . Oh, jinxy! He let go the breath he had been holding with a tremble. He had blamed himself. Somehow, he hadn't tried hard enough to look after her. Somehow, he had let her go. How else could you explain that first your parents – he didn't even feel able to think of them as his mum and dad because he had no memory of them – but just the same he had managed to lose them too.

Magio joined Eefa in staring at the incoming tide.

How many times had they come to this beach to watch the first rays of the sun glimmering over the misty ocean immediately below their den in the black rocks? The early light was kind of pearly, as if the glimmer of the sun on the sea had brought steam out into the air. But it was no good thinking about that sort of thing now. Nothing really mattered now. This morning he had woken and just lain there on his mattress on the boards of the loft and listened to the racket of the birds in the trees nearby, and he had stared and stared at the smoky light creeping into the loft space through the cracks in the roof. He had exclaimed what he had been thinking, for about the millionth time.

He whispered it. 'I hate that name, Magio!'

'It's what Mum and Dad called you.'

He shook his head.

*Magio! Like some . . . some baby flibbertigibbet!* It would have been typical of Gran to have called him something like that, maybe . . . maybe when he was little and getting into mischief.

'Well, you don't mind being called Gio!'

No, he didn't mind Gio.

He felt Eefa hug him again.

He had to blink stuff away because it was too much to think about. He could hardly recall getting here today. His mind was blank for a moment or two before he recalled the memory of running. It had been Eefa's idea that they race here, to the den, again – just like always . . . His mind had been blank as he was running through the dust-baked streets. He had run like the wind, panting for breath as he arrived at the beach, his lungs fit to burst. But still Eefa had beaten him to the boulder. He had hated her for that, hated her just for a moment, then felt the hate turn back to love. Back here again, the sun rising over the incoming sea – it had felt so britzy. He so loved it all, this paradise of feathery pine trees, and the black rocks poking up out of the white sand. The boulder that was the first step onto the beach, warmed by the rising sun . . .

The anger rose in him again until it enveloped him, making it difficult to think. He knew he was fidgeting with his feet. He just couldn't stop himself fidgeting. It was so frustrating that he couldn't stop things happening.

Eefa had climbed onto her feet while he was preoccupied with his thoughts. She was out of sight now, exploring the cinder-like outcrops that had spewed out of a volcano a long time ago. The crater was close by, one of several dirt-covered mountains with hollow tops that surrounded the town. He tried to imagine it. The crackling earthquake roar of the thing going off, the spewing rivers of flame-spitting rock . . .

'Oh, for goodness sake!' Eefa was back, peering down at him with her face in shadow, a vexed expression. 'Stop twittering. You keep asking me questions. I'm trying to think and you're distracting me.'

'What am I distracting you from?'

'I – I don't fully know.' She shook her head, as if she, too, was baffled by something, but she sat down beside him again.

Magio sniffed. What kind of an answer was that? What was the point of spying out the land? It was just sea and rocks and seaweed and tide pools – the same view they had looked out over every time they came here.

He said, 'What is it you're really thinking about?'

'You're such an idiot.'

She was the smart one, so insistent when she was in this kind of a mood that he fell silent. All he could hear was the crackling detonations of the incoming tide through the porous black rocks and the sound that came between, like the cry of a bird – or like a human baby – that was hidden between the surges.

Gran dead . . . That was all he could think about.

Magio sighed, just looking around their den in the basin of volcanic pumice. During the run down to here, through the sleeping menace of Scogtown, he had almost felt the normal thrill, the joy, of the race. He had been no more than a few yards behind her, their bare feet taking the steps two at a time before she declared herself the winner, her feet astride the boulder.

'Race you again – to the den!' She was already running, looking back at him over her shoulder.

Thoughts of Gran had made him hesitate.

But already her lithe figure was a blur of movement, her flashing feet throwing back cascades of the powdery white sand. He had followed the trail of her footprints between the pine trees, with the rosy glow of the dawn captured in the myriad drops of dew among their leaves. Their feet had discovered a better purchase on the stony slope up to the headland, their eyes narrowed against the sand-whipping wind. With screeches and whoops, they had mounted the hillock of black tufa, weaving to avoid stepping on sharp stones, or carelessly discarded glass. Eefa was shrieking again, in celebration of having beaten him to the hollow in the cindery rock right at the edge of the headland, its roof open to the sky.

Their den . . .

She was already ensconced on the smooth rounded stone within it, ground to a giant egg-shape by its rolling around with past high tides, probably, they had both reckoned, for millions of years. They had figured that the stone, rolling about within the soft black pumice stone, had actually carved the den, which now provided them with a lookout over the rock pools and, as now, the incoming waves. On arrival, Magio had pressed his shivering body against hers on the stone, their warmth mingling where they made bony contact. He had drawn his knees up to his chest, his ears drowned by the roar of the tide through the pools and cracks and crannies of rock, and beyond it the rhythm of the onrushing breakers.

Her voice had shrilled in his mind: *My win, your forfeit.*

'Stop talking to me like that.'

It was supposed to be secret: their shared secret.

'No – I won't. And for your forfeit you must answer my question: what colour are my eyes today?'

Eefa and her stupid questions. What did the colour of her eyes matter from day to day? He shrugged. 'Pink.'

She inhaled, pleased to have confirmed that her eyes reflected the rosy hues of the dawn.

In Magio's mind, girls were strange. There was no figuring them. All those mornings when he had looked in on Gran before leaving her, her damp grey hair stuck to her scalp, attempting to rearrange the tousled blankets and sheet in an effort to keep her warm. There had been no bread to toast, not so much as a crust. Only after her death had he looked with more questioning eyes at the ruin of breeze block and boards where his grandmother had raised them.

Now, watching Eefa squint out at the waves, Magio squirmed. Maybe he should stop thinking altogether in their situation. Thinking wasn't such a good idea. He shifted his limbs to find a more comfortable position, staring out into the gorgeous vista of shore and sky. He wondered if he could glimpse the fading belt of Orion the Hunter in the lightening sky, which was between night and morning. The sky was the next best thing to the sea here . . . Here – this place – as he now imagined it, must be somewhere close to the end of the world.

*Jinxy!*

He was doing it again, thinking about things. Tears moistened his eyes. A shiver of fear ran through him as he recalled Gran's explanation of the weirdness of the world, they were living in.

*'The world,'* she would speak in her husky smoker's whisper, taking Quimbre's self-roll cigarette from her lips, *'has changed.'*

But what did she mean? Magio didn't believe, for a single moment, that Eefa understood what this meant any better than he did. Once upon a time kids went to school. School had been a place where the kids had gone to learn about the world before the calamity changed everything. Magio gazed again at the vista of rock pools and enormous arch of dawn-glowing sky.

*The world has changed . . .*

That was why he and Eefa had never been to school, why they had ended up living here on a desert island called Moon and in this ruin of a town called Warren. But Warren had changed, just as the world had changed . . . and it made no more sense than anything else. Magio snuggled closer to his sister on the spongy black rock.

'Don't you wish we'd gone to school, Eefa?'

'You'd have hated school.'

'Why?'

'You'd have broken the rules, every day, and in every way.'

'Why?'

'Because you're such a flibbertigibbet.'

'Aw!'

Magio flicked a lock of fair curly hair out of his right eye, where his untrimmed fringe had fallen down. It was so hard to stop thinking about things. How could you stop trying to figure out what was ordinary from what was . . . was something else? He squeezed his eyes shut. He couldn't bear to think of bad things any more. It made him feel more fidgety than ever. When he opened his eyes again, Eefa was back on her feet and frowning.

'Time to get back.'

Right now, Magio didn't want to go back home. He kidded himself that he was intrigued by the figure in the rock pools. But the truth was he just didn't want to go home, with its memories of Gran's death. 'Hey, look!' he whispered. 'There's somebody looking at us from the rock pool.'

Eefa spun round to peer at a woman, who was up to her thighs in the water, dipping and clutching at things. Neither she nor Magio had noticed her arrival. 'What's she doing?'

'Shrimping maybe – I don't know.'

Magio rubbed at the side of his knee, which felt raw from rubbing it against the rough side of the den. He thought he recognized the tall, skeletally thin figure wading through the pools encircled by the black spongy stone.

'Quimbre calls her Bird Woman.'

Eefa laughed at the notion.

Magio whispered, 'He reckons she's mad.'

'A mad bird woman!'

'She looks like she's mad. Have you seen her hair?'

'What about it?'

'If she let it down, it would dangle to her waist.'

Together they continued to watch the half-naked figure wade out into a pool, then bend down so her face entered the water, staring down into the shallows before pouncing on something that she hauled out and dropped into the canvas bag at her waist.

'She's not shrimping. She's scavenging.'

'You and your scavenging!'

Eefa liked to make fun of his interest in scavenging and hunting. 'So, what's she supposed to be scavenging?'

'I don't know – maybe crabs.' Magio peered down at the figure in the tide. 'Hey – I think she's looking straight at us.'

'No! She's looking at you.'

Magio grimaced at his mistake. Eefa so hated to be reminded that she was invisible to anyone other than her twin brother.

'Look – she's getting out of the pool.'

'Gio – we need to go!'

'Not yet.  I just want to watch her for a little longer.'

'Don't be stupid.'

'Quimbre says she talks to birds.'

'That's it!'

'He does. He says that she talks to the birds.'

Eefa grabbed hold of his arm. She was yanking him onto his feet. 'C'mon! The Scogs'll be up by now. We'd better hurry!'

# Too Late

They really were hurrying by the time they got to Scogtown. This had until recently been a wilderness of sand dunes full of rabbit holes. But now the Scogs had made it their peculiar home. In just a matter of a few weeks, the rumpled wasteland of hillocks, spiky grass and wild flowers had been transformed by a proliferation of Scog mounds.

Eefa moaned, 'I told you! They're already awake!'

'They don't scare me.'

'Well, they scare me.'

They hurried on, gazing about themselves in amazement at the towers of maroon sun-baked mud that were scattered, like grotesque anthills, on either side of the road. They were huge, anything up to thirty or even forty feet high, and utterly strange in their variety of shapes. As far as folks knew, the Scogs didn't actually live in the mounds. They lived in a maze of tunnels underground, a warren vaster and far more complex than anything the rabbits had constructed. People were increasingly fearful that the Scog tunnels would soon undermine the whole town.

Eefa whispered, 'I think we'd better run!'

'No! That'll only draw attention to us. Let's just hurry.'

But even as they hurried on through, Magio couldn't help thinking about the Scogs. The townsfolk didn't like them. People and Scogs just didn't mix. They mistrusted one another. Rumour had it that Scog's were cold-blooded, like reptiles. And that was if they had blood in them at all and not something more filthy and muddy. Some even claimed that Scogs were cannibals. They snatched pets for their cooking pots and, given the chance, were just as capable of baby-snatching. Others claimed the very opposite: that Scogs didn't eat meat. They were strict vegetarians. That was why they had such green fingers when it came to the plants that sprouted in abundance around their towers of mud. Some went so far as to claim that the Scogs must be part plant themselves and this explained the greenish tinge to their thick, bark-like skin. Some put it about that the reason why Scogs, though vegetarians, snatched pets and children, was to feed the roots of their jungles of plants.

Eefa muttered, 'I don't like it.'

'Me neither.'

It was because of the Scogs that Quimbre insisted on arming himself with his flintlock pistol and cutlass whenever he went into the town these days. Right now, Magio was also thinking of how Quimbre touched the talisman gold quarter moon he wore on a chain around his neck when talking of the grisly ones. Magio wasn't sure he really believed the stuff folks said about Scogs. As far as he was aware, nobody had ever seen Scogs doing any of these terrible things. In fact, folks rarely saw much of the Scogs since their mysterious arrival into Warren. They seemed to be more active at night, when folks were asleep. Magio assumed that it must also be during the night that they planted and harvested their gardens, since he had never seen them doing it in daylight.

'Hey,' he said, by now somewhat breathless, 'just look at their gardens . . .'

Even the nervous Eefa couldn't help but wonder. 'Oh, Magio – they're riots of colour. Look at how the bushes are blossoming!'

'Yeah!'

He really was looking – looking and wondering. How could the Scogs, who were supposed to be so wicked, grow such lovely gardens around their towering mounds of maroon-coloured clay in what had previously been desert sand?

There were wild grasses of a great variety, waving as the breeze blew through them, and mesmerising islands of wild flowers. How could monsters that supposedly devoured children take such an interest in flowers? In fact, the tide of blossoms shouldn't have been happening. Grasses and flowers like this just didn't grow in the dry sandy soil of Moon. And look at those trees . . .! What a strange wood was thrusting into life in Scogland, dense and beautiful – like . . . well, like the kinds of woods you found in fairytales. Magio would have so loved to climb those trees, make a den in their branches. Gran had agreed with the townsfolk when it came to Scogs. She had cursed their strange, wild gardens, calling them the witch forests of the lumpy folk.

*Witch forests . . . and lumpy folk!*

Magio just didn't know what to think about it all.

Folks said such unpleasant things about Scogs. Who knew if such things as magic really existed? But from the look on Gran's face when she spoke of it, it was clear that she had no doubt as to the nature of Scogs. She had grimaced as if even talking about them had brought an unpleasant taste to her mouth.

He spoke his thoughts aloud to Eefa. 'If you ask me, I suspect that the Scogs are not half as bad as folks think.'

'We don't know what they are. We just don't want to have to weave all the way round their mounds to get back home.'

How right she was! To skirt Scogtown entirely would involve a considerable additional trek. The only alternative was to run helter-skelter through the heart of the Scog warren.

He grinned. 'Let's run!'

'Don't be stupid.'

'Hey – most of 'em are probably still asleep.'

'I doubt it!'

'Race you!'

Magio was already running, forcing Eefa to follow on his heels. It was a thrill to hare it through Scogtown, following the curly tracks around the mounds, and knowing that under their feet the Scogs must be snoring in their burrows.

As they ran Magio couldn't help but notice how thick the tree gardens had grown in such a short time. Maybe the Scogs really did have green fingers. Eefa was already several yards behind him, though he could hear the slapping of her bare feet in the sandy ground, and her panting for breath. Then her loud shriek stopped him dead as they ran straight into what appeared to be a gathering of the huge lumpy figures, with their equally massive lumpy faces.

He took hold of her arm. 'Stop it, Eefa – stop shrieking!'

'I can't.' She shrieked again. 'We must turn around – go back. We have to! Come on, Magio!'

'Give over! They're behind us as well. They're all around us.'

Eefa grabbed hold of him in a clutch of terror.

'Stop panicking. They haven't hurt us. Look around you. They don't seem to be planning to hurt us.'

Now they were so close to them, the Scogs really were giants. Their hairless heads were turniplike, with huge dangling chins, deep-set jade-green eyes, and a tapering brow. One larger than the rest appeared to be addressing the others, who had gathered around some kind of lumpy sculpture, as tall as a two-storey house. Even more of them were now gathering about their leader, several dozens of them at least, with a rolling of their massive bodies and a curious side-to-side lumbering of shoulders even more massive than the boulder that opened onto the beach.

Magio grinned. 'Hey – maybe they're just come out to warm up in the sun. You know – like lizards?'

'Don't be such an idiot! They're dangerous, Magio. Look at their eyes. They're cold, like . . . like something that isn't human. And those nails are sharp as steel. That giant one – he's looking straight at us.'

'Uh-oh!'

Magio's eyes widened as he confirmed Eefa's fears. The Scog leader was gazing down directly at them with those baleful green eyes.

'Oh, jinxy! We've got to go back.'

But the other Scogs had formed a circle around them, moving surprisingly quickly, forcing Magio to be confronted by the leader, whose arms, as thick as the boughs of a large tree, were now flung wide apart, as if blocking any escape. Magio gaped at the enormously long, wide fingers, with thick flat nails, on hands shaped like massive spades for digging and shaping mud. His gaze lifted to meet those alien eyes, which were boring down at him. The others were shuffling ever closer, closing them in. The Scogs were making a growly sort of humming in their throats, which dawned on him as some kind of speech.

'What are they saying?'

Eefa shuddered. 'How would I know?'

Their speech was so slow and deep; it sounded utterly alien, like a wind blowing through a deep hollow or cave. But then he heard what might be their way of addressing Magio himself, with more and more of them calling to him.

'Boy . . .! Boy . . .! Boy . . .!'

Oh, jinxy!

The realisation that they really were speaking to him provoked even more panic in Magio. Then Eefa shrieked. 'Their leader – he knows I'm here. He's sniffing me out. He's got my scent.'

Magio stood frozen to the spot, his eyes wide with shock. The Scog appeared to be addressing him again in that strange low-pitched hollow voice. 'Boy – not want . . . Want she. . . Must have she . . . Give us she . . . Boy . . .! Boy go . . .! Boy go free . . .!'

'No!'

Magio shook his head.

This couldn't be happening. It had to be some cruel trick of his imagination. They couldn't possibly take Eefa. How did they even know she was there? Nobody other than he could see her. Nobody else, not even Gran, had ever been able to see Eefa. Never – not since she was born. Only he could see her, hear her, touch her.

The lead Scog was now tapping him on the shoulder with a finger that was as thick as Magio's calf. The taps felt like nudges from a sledgehammer. 'Boy . . . not want boy . . . Want she . . . Boy give us she . . .'

'Get lost!'

But the huge being, with its plate-sized eyes, insisted. 'Shee-warg . . . shee-warg wants . . . Shee-warg will have . . .'

'No!'

Had he truly understood the giant Scog's words? He was talking about something he called a shee-warg? Had this shee-warg, whatever that was, put some kind of spell on the Scogs? Magio knitted together the words of the giant Scog in his mind. The monster wanted Eefa. Could it be that the Scogs' only purpose in coming to Warren was to take his sister? But that was so stupid, so idiotic, it couldn't be true. How could the Scogs – or this shee-warg thing – possibly know that Eefa existed?

But somehow, they did.

Nobody other than Magio, Quimbre and, until her death, Gran, even knew of Eefa's existence. And Quimbre refused to believe in her very existence, putting her down to an invention of Magio's fertile imagination. How then could these horrible creatures even talk about taking Eefa?

'No! No – you can't take her!'

That deep voice replied, a growly rumble. 'Boy . . . not stop us . . . not stop shee-warg.'

'No – you can't!'

Eefa was screaming in his ear. 'We must run, Magio! They don't want you. They only want to take me.'

'No!' Tears erupted into his eyes.

The Scogs were all around them now. Paralysed by his own rising panic, he was at a loss as to what to do. His eyes, blurred with his tears, saw how more and more Scogs were coming out of the cave-like holes around the bases of the huge clay mounds. His ears were filling with the strangest clamour, a thundering cacophony of growls and moans. Then, suddenly, his vision was filled with a cyclone of wheeling shapes. At that same panicky moment, in the confusion of his despair, a new face confronted him: a tall, rangy woman with a weather-beaten face stretched taut over prominent cheekbones. A voice he did not recognise was shouting above the thunderous clatter of birds' cries into his ear.

'It is pointless to argue with them. Their communal mind is controlled by another.'

'I . . . I don't understand.'

'There is a terrible power at work here. More powerful by far than these simple beings. Yet by confusing the common mind, I may yet break the warg.'

'Who . . . what are you?'

'You saw me earlier from your eyrie among the rocks.'

'You're Bird Woman?'

'Some call me that. But this is no time for introductions or explanations. You must flee – you and your enchanted sister.'

Magio stared, blinking hard, at the strange woman, baffled at her words, but excited by the possibility they might somehow escape from the Scogs. He gazed up into her deep-set pale grey eyes, surrounded by wrinkles. 'Why should I trust you?'

'Who else can you trust?'

The Scogs were muttering urgently among themselves and beginning to edge closer to them again. 'I don't have time to explain, Magio, and even if I did, I doubt that I could explain to your satisfaction.'

Eefa grabbed Magio's hand and squeezed it hard. 'We have no choice. We must do as she tells us.'

Bird Woman was staring up into the sky. 'The Scogs are superstitious. And they are far more observant of nature than humans.'

Magio gazed up to where sea birds of every description were invading the morning sky, wheeling around them in gigantic circles.

'Now – while they are distracted – you really must run.'

'Run where?'

'As far away as you can.'

'What – you mean leave Warren?'

'Decidedly, yes.'

'Where would we go?'

'I shall direct you.'

'We can't just leave. Leave Gran's, where Eefa and I grew up? Leave Warren, leave the beach . . .?'

'I'm afraid that you must!'

Magio exploded. 'Why?'

'Warren is no longer safe for you.'

'Why – why, isn't it safe?'

'Look around you.'

He looked around at the circle of Scogs, who appeared for the moment to be transfixed with the encircling birds. 'Why – why are you helping us?'

'Would you delay even a moment longer, merely to ask questions?'

Eefa was tugging hard at Magio's reluctant hand. All of a sudden, they were running again, with Bird Woman pressing them to run even faster.

Breathless as he was, he just couldn't stop himself demanding answers. 'But what does it all mean? Why me – or Eefa?'

'You must head north – to the wild lands, where those who would hurt you will not find you.'

'Quimbre looks after us here. He'll stop the Scogs from harming us.'

'No one can protect you if you stay.'

Magio stared back at this tall, lean woman, with her wrinkled leather face and her calm, smoke-grey eyes. 'But . . .'

'No more buts, dear Magio.'

Eefa, who was now as breathless as Magio, spoke. 'But we can't just run away. We live here. Warren is our home.'

'Your enemies have sensed your importance. Now they know you exist, they'll never give up. They will come for you again.'

Magio, too breathless even to shriek, couldn't believe what he was hearing. Bird Woman had spoken to Eefa. She had even heard her speak.

## Strange Words

Magio whispered, 'Listen – they're talking about some kind of an adventure. Like the stories Quimbre used to tell us.'

'Don't be stupid.'

'I'm not. You can hear it for yourself.'

They were supposed to be asleep. But Magio and Eefa were too excited to sleep. At this moment, Magio was peering down, through a gap in the threadbare blue curtain that acted as a door to the loft space that was their bedroom. He was perched on a single bare foot, holding on with his right hand to the top of the rickety ladder that led down into the tiny hall and beyond its open door into what had been Gran's living room,

'Grow up, you idiot,' Eefa whispered. 'They're arguing over whether we stay or leave, because they know it's going to be horribly dangerous whatever we do.'

'Dangerous?' The idiot grinned.

Eefa shook her head. Magio and his silly notions of adventures! She couldn't believe that he was giddy with excitement. He didn't seem to understand what any such adventure would really entail. And this was happening after they had barely escaped by the skin of their teeth from the Scogs. She had no such giddy notions. What Quimbre and Bird Woman were really talking about was running away – fleeing Warren. They were expecting Eefa and Magio to abandon their home.

She felt his hot breath on her neck, whispering, 'What do you think is going to happen?'

She felt like slapping him back to reality. 'Never mind what's going to happen. We need to figure out what really did happen back there.'

'I know. I keep going over and over it in my mind.'

'It really frightened me, that stuff with the Scogs.'

'You reckon the Scogs really could smell you?'

The very thought terrified Eefa. 'Shush!' she muttered, needing more time to think about what was happening. 'Keep your voice down.' But the reminder of what had happened scared her so much she brought her hand to her mouth. 'I can't bear the thought that those . . . those horrible creatures could . . .'

'Could somehow see you?'

'They didn't see me. They smelled me.'

'But surely if they could smell you – at least it means that you're real.'

'I know that I'm real.'

Magio sniffed at her to see if he could smell Eefa, like the Scogs, but she pushed his sniffing face away from her.

'You're always complaining that you can't be real because nobody can see you, or hear you, or touch you? But – hey – if even the Scogs can smell you – you're real. They said they were sent to get you . . .'

'Shut up!'

Eefa's eyes sprang wide open with the thought. 'It's not that simple. I just don't even begin to understand what's going on.'

They shared a look: neither of them really wanted to think too much about what it might mean.

'Oh, Gio! You know, don't you, that it was Bird Woman who saved us?'

She was so nervous she was calling him by his kid name, something she had never done in years.

'Yeah! I know.'

'But how did she do that? Why did she save us?'

'I don't know.'

Eefa remembered the bizarre circling of the birds in the sky. Wow – all those birds, wheeling in circles. She had never seen anything like that before. It was as if they were obeying some . . . some enchantment.

'She really did it,' she whispered. 'Bird Woman somehow frightened off the Scogs by calling up those birds. I know – oh, I know it just seems so incredible, now I think about it.'

Magio whistled softly. 'You're not kidding.'

'Hsst!' She made a face. 'We'll find out what really happened. We'll ask Bird Woman about it later. But right now we need to listen to what they're saying down below.'

'They're talking about you, Eefie.'

His kid name for her! His was Gio and hers was Eefie! Eefa, who hated to be hugged, curled her taller figure round his to snuggle up to him at the parted curtain, listening to the conversation rising up out of Gran's living room. Quimbre's voice sounded argumentative, broken with the sucking pauses that she knew meant he was drawing on his pipe. 'Why run away? What protection is Magio going to get out there?'

Eefa bridled. *It's us . . . not just Magio!*

Then it was as if Bird Woman had read her mind. 'The boy isn't the only one we need to protect. Both the twins are in danger – they are in greater danger than you could possibly imagine.'

They heard the sounds of Quimbre's sandals pacing the bare earth floor. 'What you so worried about, woman – ghosts and phantoms?'

Bird Woman said, 'Do not nudge against me!'

'I beg your pardon, gentle lady.'

Magio and Eefa grinned at each other. 'Quimbre up to his old tricks!' They couldn't help giggling.

Bird woman appeared to pause. 'I'm no gentle lady. And I wish you wouldn't smoke that filthy thing. It pollutes my mind as much as it does my lungs. I don't know what you put in it, but it surely isn't tobacco?'

'There! I stop from puffing.'

'It would appear that you doubt Eefa's existence.'

'Pah!' Eefa and Magio could imagine how Quimbre's shoulders were now shrugging. 'Why would you say such things to me?'

'I've heard Magio talk about you.'

'Magio's a very imaginative boy. I have lived for quite a while with him and Gran. All this time and I come across no invisible sister. This twin exists only in Magio's head.'

'Your scepticism is understandable. Indeed, it is comforting! It means that Eefa's invisibility is working. You can't see or hear her. But she's real. You heard what those creatures said about her.'

'We only have Magio's word for that!'

'You, sir! You just nudged me again! Must I remind you not to do so?'

'Sorry – sorry, gentle lady!'

Eefa and Magio grinned.

'The twins are threatened. Now that the Ursascogans have confirmed Eefa's existence, that danger has greatly increased.'

Magio was now squirming with excitement. His hand, in squeezing Eefa's shoulders, was shaking. 'Hey, did you hear . . .?'

'Hush! I want to hear what else Bird Woman is saying.'

'What is this danger you speak of?'

'Since the Chaos,' the calm, determined voice of Bird Woman rose into the loft, 'there has been much going on that would otherwise appear strange. You must believe me that Eefa is real. What is more, she is special. We must do all that we can to protect her.'

Magio squeezed her. 'Wow, Eefie!'

'Shush!'

Quimbre's tone remained sceptical. 'How then? How are we to protect somebody we cannot see?'

'Well, I don't believe that we can possibly protect Eefa – or Magio for that matter – in this ramshackle ruin.'

Quimbre's voice fell to a growl. 'Here – this is Magio's home. What do you want him to do – to abandon his home? I don't fear those stupid Scogs. I see no good reason we run away. We shore up the windows and doors. If the Scogs come here, we make ready for them.'

Magio rattled his right foot on the top step of the loft ladder with excitement.

But Bird Woman's voice remained determinedly calm. 'Use your brain, man. The Scogs tried to abduct Eefa in the open street. They won't give up. It's possible they can detect her scent.'

Magio heard Quimbre snort aloud.

'It doesn't matter that you don't believe in Eefa. What matters is that she's real. I have reason to believe that not only is she real, she is important to the powers-that-be.'

There was a loud slap. Magio guessed it was Quimbre slamming the flat of his hand down onto the bare wood of the table.

'Be petulant, if you like.' Bird woman exhaled a sigh. 'I'll not argue with you. It's clear to me that the Scogs are determined to take her. They have located Eefa, are capable of sensing her, and they *will* come for her.'

Eefa's hand was reaching up to her mouth again, aghast.

Quimbre's reply was equally urgent. 'Four walls are safer than taking our chances out there.'

'You're mistaken, Quimbre. Gather up your weapons by all means, but meanwhile get ready to run. It doesn't mean we won't fight. We'll run and we'll fight, too, if it proves necessary. But I must warn you, this situation is more complex than you could possibly know. There are many unknowns. Here Magio and Eefa cannot hide. How would you protect them if and when a giant hole appeared from under our feet to swallow them up through the Scogs' tunnelling?'

Bird Woman seemed to wait to hear Quimbre's reply. But there was no reply. Magio assumed she had him thinking about the frightening notion of Scogs tunnelling under the house.

Bird Woman spoke again, but now her voice was softer. 'You're right to worry. Out there, we shall enter wild lands – but this is country familiar to me. We can hide from Scogs, or any other pursuers. This surely offers us a better chance of keeping them safe, and even then, only if we keep on the move. Heed my words. We have so little time.'

'You know these wild lands?'

'I know them as well as any. I have travelled them widely and am familiar with some of their resources, and their entrapments.'

'Hmph!'

'Consider this. It would now appear that the Scogs came here for no other purpose than to abduct Eefa. They found her through Magio. They were so bold as to openly admit it. It now appears that this was their sole reason for coming here to Warren.'

'You know I have never seen her – she is not there. Don't you see – Magio is now alone.'

'Then help me to save Magio.'

They heard the grunt that surely came with a shrug from Quimbre. They heard the puffing of his relighting his pipe. 'Woman – you're right to think Magio matters to me. But surely I need to know what is happening. I will not risk any danger to Magio. I need to know what's really going on.'

'My dear Quimbre – I don't pretend to know what it all means myself! The Scogs have a long history in these islands. They are easily underestimated and they are possessed of a vicious cunning. But I doubt that even the Scogs themselves are cunning enough to plan what is going on here.'

'Hmph!'

'They mentioned a being they called a shee-warg.'

'Superstitious hokum!'

'Call it what you like. Are you denying that a determined attempt at abduction took place in this town today?'

'What are you saying? We face attack tonight?'

'I doubt it will come tonight. They have identified and thus located what they want. The Ursascogans are slow thinkers. Moreover, they appear to want Eefa alive. If I am right, and Eefa is so important to them, they will do nothing immediately. Rather they will report back to whoever is directing them. They are not quick-reacting people. But it's my guess that a much more planned and purposeful attack will follow. That gives us a window of time to prepare our escape. We should be out of here by dawn.'

Listening to all of this discussion by the adults, Eefa and Magio couldn't help but hold onto one other's shoulders and stare, with looks of utter astonishment, into each other's eyes.

'Hey! Don't just grab at my sleeve. You're pinching my skin.'

'I'll hang on to your ear with my teeth, Magio, if you don't calm down. Stop getting excited like that. You heard what Bird Woman told us to do. This isn't a sprint to the boulder on the beach. We have to pace ourselves.'

Magio took a deep breath to calm himself, waiting for Eefa let go of his sleeve. He whispered, 'Sorry. I'm too mixed up to think. Do you suppose we'll ever come back to Gran's house again?'

'Do you think I don't hate it too? But you heard Bird Woman. We have to get away. And then, if I guess right, we need to hide.'

'Easy for you!'

She ignored the barb. The fact was she was worried about what he felt. She could see that he was white-faced with the shock of leaving home. He had been forced to abandon all of his beachcombing treasures. His prized collection of shells, starfish and sea urchins, and weird driftwood shapes. She knew how much he cherished those things. But it wasn't easy for her either. Neither of them had been able to catch a wink of sleep last night. And now, barely an hour after dawn, the company must have already covered five or six miles after sneaking out of Warren. They were trekking fast between tussock-clad sand dunes in an enormous sweep of bay, ignoring roads, even the winding goat tracks, always keeping the sea to their left. Bird Woman had been their guide from setting out. She had insisted that they travel northwards, into a bleak landscape in which they must appear, to any potential spying eyes, to be tinier than a sprinkle of ants against the vastness.

Magio was more excited by it all than Eefa was. All of his life he had longed for some great adventure, like the tall tales of the sea spun round the fireside by Quimbre. Well now he was setting out on an adventure of his own. Lucky Gio! But Eefa wasn't keen on any kind of adventure whatsoever. She was too shocked after the frightening events of yesterday to feel other than she was trudging in a daze. But they could hardly complain. Quimbre and Bird Woman hadn't had the opportunity to sleep at all. They had spent all night preparing for the journey, making up backpacks that would carry as much food, water, change of clothes and blankets, as well as weapons.

*Weapons!*

Quimbre was armed with his heavy flintlock pistol and his cutlass and Bird Woman had a long bow, which she was using as a walking staff.

'Hey,' whispered Magio, 'do you recall how Gran used to call Quimbre a pirate?'

'Yes – I do!'

It had seemed just a silly insult that Gran would hurl at Quimbre whenever she was annoyed with him. He would merely turn his back to her and say nothing. Recalling poor old Gran's irascibility, Eefa swallowed against a lump in her throat. In her heart she didn't know what to think of yesterday – it had all seemed so unusual. Things appeared to be changing about her with disturbing speed. Eefa shook her head, plodding on, deep in thought, a few feet behind the impatient Magio.

There had been something else that had astonished her last night. Bird Woman had talked as if she had no qualms that Eefa was real. She had even hinted at the possibility that she was special. It was as if she were somehow special – as if this was what had brought the Scogs to Warren. They had come here just to capture her and take her away. Bird Woman had also used that curious word 'enchanted' in relation to her. She had spoken to Magio about his 'enchanted sister'. Eefa wasn't altogether sure what that could possibly mean. On the one hand, wouldn't it be wonderful if this was the reason she had been born invisible? Wouldn't that be the most fantastic thing if it explained why she had to be invisible?

Could that possibly be true? Oh, could it?

But, now in the cold light of morning, she was inclined to doubt it. That same word, enchantment, had other connotations, other implications. She had spent her entire life being invisible, unseen, unheard, untouched – unvalued! She had felt like adding the word 'unloved'. But to be unloved you had, at the very least, to be visible.

Eefa trudged and trudged through the resisting sand and rock of Moon, while the wind-whipped sand excoriated her invisible legs and whistled through her non-existent hair
The fact that she was invisible didn't mean that she didn't feel things. She felt everything. If anything, she felt things more deeply than visible people felt them. And now she sensed that things were not merely changing: things were already so terribly, convulsively, changed that her life was never going to be the same again.

Why was all of this happening to her? Why had those stupid creatures – those monstrous, lumpy-faced Scogs – come to Warren just to look for her?

She kept thinking about it over and over and she just couldn't figure it out. It made no sense at all. Yet that the horrible Scog leader, chewing on words with that inhuman rumbling noise, had not only sensed her, he had insisted on taking her, seizing her, like – like she was an object! What in the world could that mean? Eefa had never thought herself as being of the slightest importance to anyone. Quite the opposite! She had thought of herself as being nothing to everybody. And that meant that the very notion that she was running for her life from these horrible Scogs was all the more baffling and, so, all the more terrifying. In her daze, she lifted her head and noticed something that seemed truly enchanting.

There were birds immediately ahead of her that appeared to be suspended, motionless, in the air. The sight of them stopped her dead.

Skylarks!

She stopped walking, falling a few yards behind the others, feeling such a powerful impulse just to observe them. As she began to walk on again, softly, quietly, between them, the larks ignored her presence. They were hovering in mid-air, in twos and threes, frozen in space, just as she had seen fish hold still in a current of river water. It looked wonderfully impossible, so much so as to appear magical. Looking about her, she realised that she was climbing a rise, where currents of air were wafting in from the sea. Maybe the larks were being held aloft by those air currents. But now, in passing through them, in gazing at them more carefully from close quarters, she saw that their eyes were fixed other than on her, as if entranced. They were completely unaware of her nearness to them. The birds were trembling slightly, as if responding in some very fine way to their hovering with tiny oscillations and adjustment of their plumage. Somehow, she had to presume that this allowed them to glide in the air, as if they were weightless. But they were not gliding. They weren't moving at all. They were . . . caught, entrapped – and then another word entered her mind – *entranced!*

Her hands clasped her mouth in shock.

At a call from Quimbre, she came to. She had allowed herself to become mesmerised by the birds. It had caused her to fall far behind the others, forcing her to hurry to catch up.

What did this mean? Had it been some kind of a message? Or some sort of clever trap aimed at separating her from the others? A thrill of fright caused goosepimples over her skin. She couldn't help looking back at the still suspended larks even as she hurried on to catch up.

# Seduction

Eefa woke to a peculiar state in which she was still half asleep but also strugglingly half awake. As evening was falling at the end of the second day after fleeing Gran's home, Bird Woman discovered a surf-washed bay with a crumbling blackstone tower. When they explored it, they discovered a single underground chamber that would provide shelter for the night. For Eefa, this musty repository felt less than comforting. But what comfort could one expect when you were invisible to all except an annoying brother and a strange woman with a thing for birds? Finding herself overcome by restlessness, she woke early in this murky dungeon, only to discover that she was still half lost within a dream. But the feel of spiderwebs about her face shook her awake and she now wished she was back in her dreams. The events of the previous two days so overwhelmed her that she felt like screaming.

The whole thing – this setting out into an unknown and hostile world, with nothing other than the packs on their backs – seemed foolhardy. All because the Scogs had cornered her and Magio as they were returning the beach. Perhaps Quimbre had been right in his arguments with Bird Woman? Eefa had thought hard about that when attempting to go back to sleep. But now that same unsettling feeling made sleep impossible. It caused her to climb up out of the shabby basement, and then further, up the broken steps of the spiral staircase within the ruined tower, bringing her up to the level that must once have held the flame that had protected ships out there on the inky blackness of ocean.

Sleepy as she was, she still tried to imagine it: a stormy night, lashed by gales and rain, the men living in this tower firing up the brazier that had once stood atop this level. They must have been hardy and brave. People who anticipated bad things and tried to stop them happening. That thought comforted her. She took a deep breath, keeping that comfort in her mind. It reassured her that there were good folks in this crazy world – folks who strived to save the lives of others. It wasn't just full of Scogs and cobwebby spiders.

She held onto that thought: it helped to calm her fears.

Eefa found herself sitting, straddle-legged, on the cold flagstone floor of the lighthouse platform, dressed only in her nightdress, gazing out onto the great bowl of charcoal sky with its myriad stars casting their light over the ocean. It really was beautiful. How lovely to think it must have been sights like this that had caused folks long ago to call this small piece of the ocean, with its many islands, The Sea of Stars!

Stepping back down the spiral stone staircase, Eefa emerged onto the beach, from where she gazed up once more into the night sky. They said that stars were other suns, perhaps some of them with other worlds around them. How wonderful the universe must appear to those who were visible, ordinary folks with normal lives, normal hopes and desires! Why, oh why, was she condemned to the terrible loneliness of being invisible?

*Gran – oh, Gran, how I miss you!*

Gran would have known what to do. She would have put her foot down, grown angry and very likely produced a few telling words that would have stopped this mad flight into the wild lands at the very beginning.

But Gran was no longer here to take care of them.

Panic at the thought caused a flutter in Eefa's heart. She must take a grip. She must close down those fears before they overwhelmed her.

She clenched her eyes and her fists tight shut. She took the deepest of breaths and then reopened her eyes and looked about herself once again in the moonlight. She was standing on a gravelly embankment looking down onto the wide cove that surrounded the stone tower. A tickle in her throat caused her to cough into her hand. A freezing onshore wind gusted against her, flattening her nightdress against her body, making her feel colder than ever.

She thought, *I am not alone!*

The others, Magio, Bird Woman and Quimbre, were still close by, huddled in sleep in the chamber at the base of the tower. They had all walked themselves to the point of exhaustion over those two days, with only the briefest naps in place of sleep before arriving at the cove with its ruined shelter.

Was there no lookout? She hadn't come across anybody. Yet the night before she recalled how Quimbre had sat it out as lookout over their first nocturnal shelter. Eefa and Magio had been put to bed, utterly exhausted. But surely tonight must have been Bird Woman's turn? That provoked another anxious flutter in her heart. Had there really been nobody looking out for them as they slept? Overhead, now, as she turned her face up once more to gaze at it, the sky appeared altogether cold, colder than the ocean, despite its lovely twinkling stars.

*'Eefa!'*

She recognised the voice, even though it was the gentlest of whispers in her mind. She felt Bird Woman's hand touch her shoulder. She turned to be comforted by what looked like the ghost of the tall, thoughtful woman who had brought Eefa a blanket that she was now wrapping about her shoulders.

*'Trouble sleeping?'*

Eefa nodded, glad to be proven wrong about the lookout – and as astonished as ever that Bird Woman was able to see her.

*'I expect that you were too anxious to sleep.'*

'Yes.'

Bird Woman's arm enfolded her shoulders over the comforting blanket. Eefa hadn't realised how much she'd been trembling until now.

'I'm scared.'

*'Your feelings are understandable. So much has happened in just a few days. It must be very confusing for you. Come – let's sit and admire the night.'* Bird Woman wrapped the blanket tighter around Eefa's shoulders as they sat down together, cross-legged, on the shingle.

'Thank you!'

*'My purpose is ever to protect you and Magio.'*

Bird Woman's voice was not really in Eefa's ears. Rather it felt like it was coming directly into her mind. Perhaps she wasn't really awake after all? Perhaps this was still a dream: a comforting dream.

Eefa sighed. 'I just can't get my head around any of it. Why we have to run away – the fact you really can see and hear me. I don't understand right now why I am hearing your words inside my head.'

*'It must be very confusing. We both appear to be communicating from what would appear to be a common dream state.'*

Eefa shook her head.

*'I sense that you resent your invisibility.'*

Eefa stiffened.

*'Perhaps, if my senses are correct, you have struggled to understand why the burden of invisibility was placed upon you?'*

Tears dimmed Eefa's eyes.

*'To be subjected to such a fate from birth, it must have felt unrequitedly cruel. But appearances can be deceptive.'*

Eefa was electrified by Bird Woman's words. What did she mean?

Bird Woman hesitated, as if she were about to explain further but decided against it. She maintained her hug around Eefa's shoulders.

'Can you really see me?'

*'Ah!'* There appeared to be a momentary hesitation. *'From your lovely flaxen hair to the storm-crossed turquoise of your eyes.'*

Was that the real colour of her hair and eyes? It was a question that had tormented her all her life.

It was such a comfort for Eefa that Bird Woman's arm now hugged her so powerfully. It was the only human touch she had ever felt other than Magio's in her entire life. Her shoulders rocked with her sobbing.

*'Come now! Dry your tears. Let us take a stroll in the starlight. Perhaps you are ready this night to open those beautiful eyes, and that determined mind, to the mysteries.'*

'The mysteries?'

*'Is not that ocean of stars not the greatest mystery? Oh, I promise you that there are myriad such mysteries in the everyday*

*world about you. You, Eefa – you, in your very being – are such a mystery.'*

'How am I a mystery?'

*'Did you not wish yourself to come here tonight, though you should be sleeping after such an exhausting journey?'*

'I . . . I think I must be sleepwalking.'

*'It is natural that you should attempt to explain an enchantment. Why else would you come here, when not yet awake? Does that not suggest that something attracted you here?'*

'I don't know.'

Eefa wiped her nose on the edge of the blanket and stared out to where the neverending wrinkles of waves caught the moonlight, as if, somehow, the whole scene, ocean and starry sky, were part of some wonderful whole. Now that she listened more carefully, she could hear the roar of the waves behind the bluster of wind.

*'Perhaps we can take advantage of the situation to learn something about your mystery? Would you like that?'*

Eefa nodded.

*'I would help you to explore it – that is if you are not too tired?'*

They walked, barefoot, down onto the cold white sand of the beach, then further out into the bay, to an area that was dotted with large, rounded stones.

*'What do you see, Eefa?'*

Eefa hesitated. 'I can see patterns in the rocks.'

*'Good! Now – take your time – see if you can decipher the patterns.'*

'Does it matter?'

*'Let's just treat it as a game.'*

Eefa asked herself, is this really Bird Woman talking to me in my mind? If it wasn't, the implication was terrifying.

She couldn't avoid the new tremble in her voice. 'It isn't easy to make things out in the moonlight.'

*'No, it is not. But if my eyes do not deceive me, these stones were meant to be read not in the bright glare of the sun, but in the moonlight.'*

'Who do you think made the patterns? Why did they make them?'

*'Those are interesting questions. Judging from the lichens that coat the rocks, I would imagine that, whoever made them, it was surely a long time ago.'*

In spite of the dread that was now invading her being, the notion that she was reading a message from people from so very long ago intrigued Eefa. A thrill crept over her goose-fleshed skin.

'I think I can see a spiral.'

*'Clever girl! You're right. And quite a big one, at least fifty paces across, and with a great many coils.'*

Eefa was about to walk on further but the touch on her shoulder suggested that she should stop.

'What is it?'

*'Observe the pattern of the wind within the spiral.'*

It wasn't easy to make it out in the moonlight, but when she knelt down on the sand and watched the pattern carefully, Eefa saw that the sand was blustering within the spiral, as if following its contours. She hauled the blanket even closer about her shoulders, trembling even more.

'What does it mean? Do you think we are expected to walk around inside it? To follow the coils to the centre?'

*'That's a brilliant insight!'*

Out of the side of her vision she saw that a shadowy figure squatted on the sand to one side of the circle. The figure nodded as if expecting her. She had the terrifying notion that it had been this shadow speaking to her in the words of Bird Woman. It spoke. *'Why don't you follow the pattern right now, just as your instincts direct, while I watch over and protect you?'*

Eefa hesitated, now deeply uncertain. That voice was a little too friendly, the hugging a little too close for Bird Woman. Was she really speaking to Bird Woman at all?

*'Don't worry. As far as I can see, there appears to be no threat. Though I strongly suspect that the people who created the spiral danced as they followed its coils – and very likely their dance would have been accompanied by music . . . by song.'*

Eefa hesitated again. She was increasingly uncertain about this dream journey. 'I don't think I could dance my way round it.'

*'Why not?'*

'I'm not very good at dancing. To learn to dance, you must have others, at the very least a partner. Dancing wasn't on offer to me.'

*'One does not need a partner to dance. Merely the inspiration. Take your time in doing so. Let the lullaby of the sea provide your music.'*

The lullaby of the sea!

Seductive words! Eefa hesitated at the entrance to the spiral. She wondered if every word in her mind was a lie.

She twirled and fluttered her way through the coils, all the time with the sounds of the sea in her ears and under the glorious ceiling of the stars. In truth, it felt glorious to do so. She had to control her sense of exhilaration as she danced around every coil until she reached the whirling sand at the centre of the spiral.

The voice whispered, *'Now you must tell me exactly what you feel.'*

'I feel that I'm one with the ocean and with the sky.'

The shadow chuckled, a gentle, almost self-conscious sound. '*It would appear that you have solved the mystery of the spiral.*'

Eefa felt emboldened by her own resolve. 'Thank you! Whoever, or whatever, you are. You've somehow made me feel special for the first time in my life.'

'*Your gift goes beyond that, Eefa. You didn't just wake from sleep, in spite of your exhaustion, and come to this beach by accident.*'

Eefa stared at the shadow, her breath catching in her throat.

'*Oh, come now! Let me truly hold you. You so belittle yourself that you cannot see your own potential, your wonder of being.*'

Eefa left the spiral and approached the shadow, reluctantly allowing herself to be held. The shadow embraced her, hugged her much too fiercely. But Eefa didn't feel love in the hug. She was increasingly alarmed. But at the same time she needed to know what this was all about.

'*Is it not a wonder that you have interpreted a communication from people so long ago, from nothing more than a collection of stones on a beach?*'

Eefa steeled herself, refusing to be flattered. 'Was this the mystery you wanted me to see?'

'*The mystery I would show you is the mystery of yourself. Look upon it as an initiation of sorts. Shall we continue our stroll?*'

Reluctantly, Eefa nodded.

They walked on for a short while, moving out towards the tide, entering a section of bay that sloped out into nearing surf. It was full of stones.

'Oh, my!'

'*You sense another communication from long ago?*'

'What is it?'

*'I cannot interpret it. You must discover the mystery by yourself.'* The figure squatted down again, straddle-legged, and lowered what appeared to be a cowled head. *'All I ask is that you tell me what you are experiencing – not merely the vision in your eyes but in the totality of your senses.'*

Eefa gazed for several moments at the cross-legged figure, caught by moonlight as if etched in silver. She took a deep breath and then she stared at the strange patterns of the stones in the glaringly white sand.

'The stones – they're glowing.'

*'You're right.'*

'Why – how could they be glowing?'

*'I don't know. But, perhaps, when the big tides come, they are under water. Are there not beings in the oceans that glow?'*

Eefa walked among the stones. 'I'm seeing stones piled up on other stones to make little pyramids. Big stones on the bottom and then smaller and smaller to the peak at the top.'

The voice was silent.

She stood erect and gazed about her. As ever, the fact it was night made it difficult to see anything clearly. 'I can't see a pattern. Only the fact that they seem go on forever in all directions. Maybe I should walk a bit more.'

*'Have a care. Keep me informed of all you see, hear, sense . . .'*

The wind strengthened. It struck her body, causing her to stagger, almost knocking her over. Eefa tightened every muscle, her elbows hugging her chest until it blew over and then she looked about herself again.

'The pyramids are in lines.'

*'Is there a pattern to the lines?'*

'None that I can see, other than the fact the lines spread out over a big distance . . . and there are huge numbers of them.'

The shadow appeared to hesitate. *'Perhaps we have explored enough.'*

Eefa thought that, perhaps, she was winning in this confrontation of thoughts and words. 'No. I'm going to follow a line back to its source.'

*'I'm not sure that you should explore any further.'*

'I'll be careful.'

The shadow climbed back onto its feet. *'Stay close to me. Tell me all you sense, even as you sense it.'*

Eefa stopped walking. She was staring down at the nearest pyramids, which reached as high as her knees. 'I'm looking into the distance along a single line. But as I do so my vision seems to blur.'

*'It senses that you are resisting it. Perhaps you should lower your resistance. Allow it to enter your senses.'*

Eefa shook her head. What was this strange place? Was it the focus of some religious gathering, long ago? People from before the Chaos?

*'You are now so close to answers to the mystery. Please keep talking to me. Do not allow your mind to wander.'*

She shook her head. There was a new voice inside her head, a more powerful voice, one that was rapidly rising in strength. It appeared to encourage her.

*'Go on! You are so near!'*

She began to walk again. Her legs appeared to be performing the motion all by themselves. The urge to hurry was growing so strong within her that she could not help it. She took several more steps.

'I can see the pattern more clearly now. The lines are coming together. As far as I can see, the pyramids are laid out in lines radiating from a single focus – something like a great eye. The eye is at the very edge of the shore where the beach meets the incoming tide.'

*'Go on! Do not hesitate . . . Come . . . Come to me!'*

The topmost stones, the cap stones, on the pyramids were somewhat rounded and flat. The sound she heard was the capstones vibrating in the wind. It was a beautiful if eerie sound, like a legion of tiny organs humming . . . and then a new, much deeper, voice. It sounded urgently guttural.

*'Come! Come! Here you will discover what truly awaits you . . . Something very special . . . a mystery of vital importance to you.'*

She so wanted to believe . . .

Eefa gazed at the nearest line and she took her bearing from it. She walked in that direction without taking any notice of what was happening about her. But a jolt of fright caused her to hesitate.

'I . . . I'm afraid.'

The two voices were competing in her head. But the powerful voice was drowning out the kinder, weaker one. *'Do not be afraid. The eye is beckoning. It is calling you . . .'*

Eefa could not stop her feet from picking up pace. She was now running, despite her tiredness, her every sense reaching out to the furthermost limit of the converging lines. They were leading her to the incoming ocean. There, at the very pupil of the eye, something hungered for her arrival at the meeting of ocean and sky . . .

'No!' This was a different voice, a clear voice, one in her ears rather than inside her head . . .

*'Heed your instincts, girl . . . The answers you crave are so close now . . .'*

'Don't listen to them, Eefa.' This really sounded like Bird Woman's voice. But it was half strangled, as if she were hurling it through a malevolent gale.

Eefa was no more than half a dozen paces from the surf. Here she sensed the closeness of the more powerful voice, the malevolent spirit that had seduced her to this place. A raw terror blocked her throat so she could no longer breathe.

'Don't take another step.' Bird Woman sounded breathless, as if she had been struggling to break free from some terrible constraints . . .

The urge to walk into the tide was overwhelming. 'Please . . . Please, help me!'

'I am here to help you, Eefa. You must resist its suggestion. Step into the cynosure and you will lose my protection.'

Eefa looked back over her shoulder at the first of the two shadows, the one she had believed her protector. The face within the hood was charcoal grey in the moonlight, around which a cataract of white hair fell to her waist. Eefa felt a wave of dread sweep over her. It was as if a malevolence was enveloping her, attempting to take possession of her. With every last ounce of her will, she forced herself to turn around. She resisted the instinct that pressed her towards the eye.

'Oh, Eefa – I am here.'

She threw herself into Bird Woman's arms.

'I'm so confused.'

Bird Woman hushed her. Eefa had the impression that even Bird Woman was trembling, shivering.

'There was . . . what seemed to be your friendly voice in my head.'

'It wasn't my voice – and it was no friend.'

'I . . . I don't understand.'

Eefa's entire body shivered with cold. She was still dressed in no more than her nightdress. There was no blanket around her shoulders. 'It pretended to be you. It pretended to care for me.'

'Hush, hush!' Bird Woman was wrapping a real blanket around her. Bird Woman was leading her away from the surging tide.

'There was a voice – a voice telling me to walk into the sea.'

Bird Woman, who seemed a little out of breath herself, halted on the inner edge of the great sweep of bay. She had fallen to her knees onto the sand and stones. 'It so nearly had you . . . Oh, so very nearly!'

'What was it?'

'A shade of place! It took advantage of our exhaustion. Even I was overcome – lulled into slumber – when I should have been guarding you.' Bird Woman took a deep breath, then climbed back onto her feet. 'Come,' she said. 'Let's get you dressed and warmed with a hot drink. It would appear that this crumbling ruin is no refuge. We must wake the others. We need to get you and Magio away from here.'

# An Unexpected Comfort

He never speaks, but she can read him – she who has long been intimate with every twist and turn of his pitiless and labyrinthine plotting. On this occasion, she holds herself utterly still, every sense alert. There has been a change, a shift in the quality of the light, in the blows and eddies of the air, in the very crash and thunder of the sea. This would appear to herald a cutting change of mood, sharp as the severing of flesh by a honed blade. Her mind spins. It is no surprise that the weather, the angry seas and livid skies, reflect the darkness of his moods. There are invisible movements about her, hostile sensations that alert her to the likelihood of a renewed attack. His brooding presence is nearby – so close by now she positively feels the weight of his malice. She is sensitive to myriad minuscule perturbations, the most significant of which is an overwhelming, rancorous weight upon her heart. She takes to striding the stretch of stony beach, making a show of dragging her chains. But this is a duel she is not equipped to win.

He suspects!

Very well, he inevitably suspects. But what can he possibly know of what is already afoot?

She can hear her own laboured breathing in her ears, the pounding of her own heartbeat. She can predict his response: some new, and even more terrible indignity. She must strike first.

'*Think you that through such torment you are become the object of my thoughts, my fears, my hopes? Though it grieves me in so many ways, you are mistaken! My thoughts are elsewhere. My desires, my hopes, my deeply offending loves . . . all of them deliciously elsewhere. How much must this offend my Lord of Pain that I remember them, all of them, with such precision and indeed an effusion of joy! You will, perhaps, find this questionable? Yet I would assure you that it is this simple – I know you put little value on truth – yet still I refuse to kneel before your capacity to inflict pain. In this you are undoubtedly the master. Yet still have I learnt to sleep, when sleep should have been denied me. Oh, I have learnt many other lessons. I have discovered the bliss of unconsciousness, even through the manifold punishments you have racked me with. Does this affright you – this spurning anew?*

*I dearly hope so.*'

In answer there is a monstrous downpour of rain. Lightning crackles in the navy sky overhead. A vision of monsters of the deep invades her mind, creatures of nightmare that provoke fright even in one inured to such visions. How vital the fact that he can invade her mind, but he cannot read it.

'*Have you not asked yourself why darkness so readily drew you in? You could have chosen the light? The killing of Mechi might not have condemned you. My love might have saved you.*'

She senses another violence of mood, which is reflected in the growing maelstrom of wind and sky and ocean. Amid the lashing storm, something quite terrible comes into being and then hauls itself out of the ocean and up along the battered shore to hover before her. A wraith of reptilian coldness, vicious jaws, claws of monstrous violence, eyes as pitiless as quartz.

She laughs.

When you are tormented, the instinct is to curl up and attempt to hide. But she has never been inclined to do so. It feels more as if she were metamorphosed to a falcon, sitting astride her perch in the glimmering light of morning, hooded from the world she once existed in. She flexes her talons. Then, at the first lunge, she hurtles headlong into a dive of rage, clawing, then wheeling and changing direction, aiming always at those quartz eyes, ripping and tearing apart the apparition.

In this she has taken her persecutor by surprise. For a split second her soul spirit is freed, clear of chains, the enchantment suspended. It surely is a rare opportunity to signal to her beloved Woll. She signals just three words:

*'An unusual boy!'*

As abruptly as she sends the message, it is extinguished – before her persecutor, in his startlement, has the opportunity of noticing the communication. Yet still she worries that she might not have been speedy enough. She cannot breathe until she knows, from the ambient mood, that she has succeeded. Even then, knowing she has succeeded, she hesitates. She must not let slip her advantage. Yet she cannot resist further distracting him with a gloat:

*'Change is coming.'*

He employs silence.

She has become familiar with the dreadful truth of change in the very fabric of her being. Change is acid to the Undying. Even so, she is familiar with the fact that even in the world of the Undying change is just one more measure of the unstoppable, unalterable measure of existence, overwhelming feeling, overwhelming ambition, overwhelming hope and love . . . and most especially pride. There is no escape from it.

Even to struggle against it would appear to be futile. But such logic would be insufficient to alter his indomitable ambitions.

She whispers the word into that cold but listening ear, *'Change!'*

She allows herself the lament, *'How sweet my solace within a word! Yet words surely are the expression of ideas. And ideas are the very core of thought, and redemption, and your incongruous punishment of me.'*

Was there more she could have said? Much more. She hesitates for a moment, or a year, she knows not in human terms.

Her tormentor, as ever, is silent.

Yet it would seem fruitful to concentrate on what clearly irritates him, all the more to distract him from the glorious truth.

*'I give nothing away in addressing such thoughts at you. For I know that you have sensed them and scowl in response. You fear change as much as I long for it. My fault, if fault it can be construed, was to welcome the wonder and delight of love, to give my heart gladly to one who touched my heart, to cherish that feeling of love within me. That was something alien to you, a blessing you could never understand since there was never love within you.'*

No response.

She goads him. *'Am I wrong in sensing your pause for thought? Surely even you must consider the possibility that we may be wrong in a decision, a behaviour, an ambition? How else but through the admission of fault do we find understanding? Consider then, offensive husband, there might be the possibility that you have got everything wrong'*

*'In all that deals with feeling I am your mistress. I am aware of the irony that I am the antithesis of that. Even the*

*terrible punishments you judge condign are flawed through your inability to misunderstand the meaning of love.*

*'You buried me here on the rim of the ocean so the wild creatures could feed on my flesh. You chained me, and so drowned me, in the neverending ebb and flow of the tide. You employed storm and rage of wind and ocean to tear open wounds in my flesh, being further food for the creatures of tide to gorge on. Thus would you torment me, anticipating that I would beg for mortal death!*

*'So would a petty mind devoid of love imagine victory!*

*'Even so, how stupid you were to choose the sea. You failed to realise that the sea was my first love. It was upon its shores that I was brought into being, to revel in sight and smell, and exult in the glory of the strange creatures and forms that abound in its bounteous depths. Perhaps it was that same old jealousy that so provoked you to torment me thus? Do you really think that revenge is everything? There are deeper passions.*

*'I cannot believe that you have forgotten our love. But then perhaps you imagine you have discovered a better avenue of passion, some sly intercourse, which extenuates your pleasure of tormenting me? Be careful, my former darling. There might be danger in seeking a darker love.'*

She hauls at her chains and barks a laugh; her tormentor is capable of shortening or lengthening them, even to eternity. She is obliged to remind herself of the gathering peril. She has a secret to conceal through such distractions: a boy – a mortal boy! One she must be careful not to reveal.

She must give nothing away.

*'Do you remember a day of glorious sunshine when we walked by a river, with trout rising, and the birds and insects busy in the air and sky about us, the same day you took me in the wild flowers and made tender love in the shade of a blossoming*

*cherry tree? And remembering this, do you feel even a morsel of compassion for me?'*

Silence in return.

℘

For some time the old woman glares at the storm-ridden sky over the ocean as she struggles to recall the distant emotions, the enveloping darkness, that her reflections have brought back to mind. She must find courage in a new hope, no matter how in this moment she is bewildered by its promise, even as her tormentor lashes at her all the more, lashes at every aspect of her being. But even he cannot quench the rising hope, any more than he can halt the flow of time and tide . . .

*The flow of change . . .*

Her senses are filling up with the disturbing sense of change, of change unstoppable . . . But even as she does so something else intrudes, a newcomer lurking at the periphery of her vision, something altogether darker than usual.

She gazes again into the shadow world and she sees there the spectre that newly accompanies him. Then it would appear that he has truly wedded darkness! And with it, the game has taken a lurch into new danger. He has ratcheted up the screw.

The old woman abandons her obsessive ruminations about herself and her torment. She signals, taking care to conceal it behind a blurry camouflage of thought, a noisy distraction: and her call is answered.

*'Give me hope!'*

She is presented with the vision of a boy – but now it would seem that he is a twin. There is a sister. Immediately she quenches the signal and closes her mind as if to sleep.

Why would her allies place the repository of her hope in such innocents? It is not safe to dwell on such a question.

# A BRUSHWOOD FIRE

'Hey – Evie!'

Magio's voice! His pet name for her!

'I'm sorry to have to wake you up! But we have to hurry up and get dressed and out of here.'

He was sitting up in the gloom of the chamber at the base of the old tower, his eyelids blinking away the stickiness of sleep.

'What is it? Why are you wearing a blanket? Is something wrong?'

'Everything's fine. We just need to get going again.'

Bird Woman had urged her not to frighten him. But the fact was that Eefa had difficulty hiding her own fears. But she needn't have worried. The expression on his face was his usual bright, wide-eyed silliness.

'You've been up and out there without me.'

'No, I haven't.'

'Don't you go having adventures without me!'

She stared back at him, for the moment speechless.

Adventures! That was all it ever was with Magio. It brought back the many times when Gran had scolded Eefa for failing to stop him doing something silly. What Gran had failed to realise was that verbal chastisement of Magio didn't work. He'd just switch from reckless to childish. He'd adopt his hurt look. He was doing it right now. And, after the fright she had just had, she had no time for Magio fooling around.

Eefa ignored him, throwing her clothes on, and stuffing her blanket and whatever else was left into the backpack.

His doleful eyes kept glancing her way.

'Stop it, Magio.'

'You know what I was dreaming about?'

'No. I don't want to know. We've got to hurry.'

'I dreamed about Mum and Dad."

'Hush, now!'

'It seemed so real. I thought I could see their faces.'

'Oh, Gio!'

She saw that tears had come to his eyes.

They had questioned Gran a thousand times, but she had been unable to explain what had happened to them. Gran, with her ever-present glass of Quimbre's juniper juice, had been unable to come to terms with anything whatsoever. Eefa and Magio had pined over the loss of Mum and Dad for so long. It just made it worse when they were given no proper explanation. It wasn't enough, as Gran did, to explain it all away as the result of the Chaos.

'We've been there a thousand times. You know it does us no good at all fretting about it.'

Magio ducked his head down. Now it was his turn to be in a great hurry to go, leaving Eefa paralysed with frustration and worry.

She just couldn't imagine what it would have been like to have a mum and a dad. And then she couldn't help but assume that, maybe, the loss of her parents had played some part in the fact that she was invisible. That maybe her invisibility had been a punishment because she had, somehow, failed to deserve parents.

'Hey – c'mon, kiddo!'

Quimbre's shout from overhead. *C'mon, kiddo!* Kiddo – not kiddos! Because Quimbre didn't believe in her existence.

'Hey, I'm coming!' Magio shouting back up to Quimbre, leaving her without even attempting to give her time to accompany him.

Eefa was forcing herself to stuff what remained into the backpack. Forcing the backpack closed, the strap tied about it. Her eyes blinking shut, as if also packing away the terror of last night . . .

*Oh, Mum and Dad, please come home! I'm lost without Gran and worried to death about Magio. There are things I . . . things I don't understand. Things I don't know how to do right. Things I worry about. I worry about everything, all the time. I worry that bad things are going to happen and I can't do anything to stop them.*

Magio was laughing up there at the top of the steps. Quimbre must be tickling him, getting ready to set out.

She had to make herself put her foot on the first stone step. Then the next . . . There were times when she imagined she really did recall Mum's pallid face as she bade them goodbye. She had imagined her apologising for leaving them with Gran but declaring she had to go find Daddy. *'The world has changed, darling. I need to find out what is really going on – I'm so sorry to have to leave you to take care of Magio.'*

The third step . . . The fourth . . .

How much of this was her imagination? How much was true?

Eefa had no idea.

She just could not bring herself to give up hoping. That would feel like a betrayal. She would be betraying not only Magio, but also Mum and Dad, in spite of whatever had happened to them. She thought again about those terrible words:

*The world has changed.*

Oh, how she heard those words go around and around within her head. But what did they mean? Something dreadful, she now imagined, something so dreadful that people like Gran and Quimbre didn't know how to explain them. She was at the top of the steps, hurrying out of the shadow of the cobwebby old tower. Out now, into the light, she could see that morning was breaking. Eefa's eyes lifted to gaze at the ruin, with its tumble of black stones, seeing more evidence there of a world that had grown tired and old, a world crumbling away to chaos, to nothingness.

'Eefa!' It was the voice of Bird Woman. She was looking down into Eefa's face, with a sideways twist of her head. 'You look tired. Are you recovered from last night? You missed so much of your sleep.'

'I . . . I . . .'

Bird Woman's hand rested firmly on her left shoulder, as if willing her strength. 'Would you like me to give you something? A potion that will help?'

Eefa was dying to ask more questions of what had happened on the beach during the night, but she read Bird Woman's shake of the head. Magio was still close enough to overhear.

Eefa whispered, 'What would this potion to do me?'

'It will keep you awake, lend power to your limbs.'

'I *am* feeling so very tired.'

Bird Woman shook some white powder into a small pottery cup of water, then bade her drink it. She drank it all down, then passed the cup back to Bird Woman. She heard the whisper, close to her ear. 'It will also help calm you. Fear is understandable. But it cannot guide our actions. You and I, we're about to set out. First close your eyes a moment or two, take a single deep breath. And then, as we take our first step forwards, we shall abandon fear in our wake.'

As they set out walking once more, a dozen paces behind Quimbre and Magio, Eefa felt stronger, less anxious, with every step. 'Who are you, really, Bird Woman? Why are you helping us?'

'Who I am does not matter. What matters is that I am here to protect you, and Magio.'

Eefa shook her head. 'Neither Magio nor I understood what's happening. You keep telling us you are here to protect us. To protect us from what?'

Bird Woman shrugged. 'In truth, I do not know the whole truth of what is to be. Only what I am entrusted to do.'

'That doesn't make sense.'

'It might make sense of a sort – if it were dangerous at this juncture to know too much.'

'You say, entrusted? Entrusted by whom?'

'Again, I do not know.'

'How then are you instructed?'

Bird Woman smiled, then shook her head. 'Not through these!' She indicated her ears. 'Not even thus!' She indicated her head, her mind. 'But through here!' She indicated her heart. In that same moment Bird Woman's lean and creased face relaxed, as if aglow.

They continued to follow in the wake of Quimbre and Magio for several more minutes before Bird Woman spoke again. 'It's hard to explain. But you deserve an explanation. Have you ever sensed something – felt something that was of the utmost importance – but not in words. A message, perhaps a wordless command, not in your ears, or your mind, but in your spirit?'

'I . . . I don't know.'

'Let me try again. You love your brother, Magio. I have seen how you try to take care of him. Did anybody tell you – instruct you – to do so?'

Eefa thought about that. She was unable to answer Bird Woman's question. She was feeling less tired, if also slightly giddy. It must be the influence of Bird Woman's potion. 'Back in Warren, on the beach – you were staring up at us from the rock pools. Magio saw you. You were watching us.'

'I was watching over you.'

'Why? Why do you protect us?'

Those deep brown eyes in Bird Woman's leathery face beheld Eefa with a calm resolution. 'It would take some explanation – and at the end of it you will no more believe it than now, when you are so sceptical. I can sympathise with your need to understand. But I'm afraid that I do not have the explanations you seek. You want to know the why of things. I cannot explain the why of it all, only the how of it.'

'But you must know something of why you are taking care of us?'

'Oh, Eefa! I'm sorry if I sound so vague. But of one thing I am quite certain. You and your brother Magio are in danger.'

'What danger?'

'I think you must surely sense it yourself, if you but allow yourself to do so.'

It was true. She sensed something, at the very extreme of her sensibility. It made her shiver. Something that raised the hackles on her neck. As if some hostile thing lurked at the very extremity of what she could see, hear, reach.

'Where are we heading?'

'Further north. I am directed to a place that will provide the ultimate respite. A place in the high mountains at the very centre of Moon. Our destination is the Valley of the Raptors.'

'Why there?'

'I do not know.'

'You really don't know?'

Bird Woman crossed her arms over the centre of her chest, over her heart. 'I sense it here. I sense it very strongly. That's all I can tell you.'

'How far away are the high mountains?'

'Perhaps a week's journey – if we encounter no delays. So, let us put our best feet forward and stride out in the lovely cool of morning!'

CR

They had travelled for hour after hour through soft, foot-sinking sand dunes of a great up-slope and now they were treading awkwardly through the same foot-sinking sand on the down-slope. Magio had set out with obvious excitement at the notion of high adventure, but after the first three or four dunes even he had slowed down enough so Eefa could catch up with him.

'What's up? I expected you to skip over the surface like a hare.'

'I'm worried about you.'

Startled by his reply, Eefa said, 'What do you mean?'

'There's something wrong. I can tell from your face. What were you and Bird Woman talking about, back there at the tower?'

'Nothing much. She was just telling me where we're heading.'

He didn't believe her. He could see from her eyes that she was keeping something from him. 'And where's that?'

'Someplace in the high mountains.'

'Hey – britzy!'

'No, it's not britzy!'

Boys were bonkers, inexplicably so. Next thing he'd be excited by some tracks in the sand, the footprints of a scuttling insect, or the flip-flop curves of a winding snake.

'Don't you get it, Magio? We're running away. Away from home and heading for some strange destination in the mountains. Bird Woman calls it the Valley of the Raptors. But even Bird Woman doesn't know why we're heading that way. It will take us a week, or possibly more, of trudging to get there. And we don't have the slightest idea what we'll find when we get there.'

'Wow!' His eyes lit up.

Eefa snorted. She was so annoyed by his inability to realise the danger of their situation that she almost told him about her terrifying experience back there on the beach. But she gritted her teeth and plodded on.

They were beyond exhaustion when Bird Woman discovered a rocky overhang where the company could dump their backpacks and flop down in its shelter. There was still an hour or so of daylight left and Magio was excited by some scratches on the roof of the shelter. There were spirals and criss-crossing lines and what might have been humanlike pudding figures, with stretched out arms and legs, and green masklike faces. They were surrounded by zigzags that looked like lightning. Magio called Quimbre over to take a look at the markings.

'They look ever so strange. Who do you think did them, Quimbre?'

Quimbre put his arm around Magio's shoulders. 'Hey, kiddo – just the doodles of some old folks from long ago.'

'But how did they get so high in the rocks to do them?'

Bird Woman interrupted their conversation. 'Those are Scog markings – signs demarcating a clan, if I'm not mistaken. And that also answers your question as to how they got high enough to score them. They merely stood on their feet and reached up with a stone point.'

'Scogs? But Quimbre said they were old – some old folks who lived here on Moon long ago.'

Bird Woman nodded. 'Quimbre is right. Scogs call themselves Ursascogan. In their language it means 'the First Folk'. There are signs all about Moon that point to the Scogs being among the first to colonise the island. They buried their dead in stone tombs out there in the desert.'

'Britzy!'

Eefa punched Gio's shoulder. 'Stop staring at the scratches with your mouth hanging open. We've got to be practical. It's going to be cold during the night. We've got to make some kind of a den here.'

'Eefa is right,' Bird Woman said. 'Hush now – all of us, we need to keep calm. Enough talk about the pictures on the stones. As Eefa says, we must be practical. We need to eat. I must go find some fresh meat.'

'Hey – can I come with you hunting rabbits?'

'Not this time, Magio.'

'Aw . . . jinxy!'

'Eefa is tired and needs to rest. Besides, you heard what that Scog leader said. They will still be looking for her. You must keep those sharp eyes of yours on the lookout for danger until I get back.'

'Ooo-kaayyyy!'

'And while you're keeping a lookout, perhaps Quimbre could gather some brushwood for a fire.'

Quimbre was looking askance at Magio's fallen face. 'You ever lit a brushwood fire with a flint?'

# The Blood Sacrifice

Queen Pittaquera gazed about herself in the vast underground Chamber of Wrath, where her husband, King Wirgnatha, stood tall and stately before the gathering of his people. There would be no flowery introductions to his speech. 'We, the Ursascogan people, know who and what we are. Our very name proclaims us as the First Folk, claiming natural hegemony of these lands.'

A great cheer shook the pillars of rock that supported the ceiling of the gargantuan space within.

'Through such divine precedence do we claim the mountains that soar above the plains, and the oceans that encircle them.'

The cheer was even louder than before.

'Who but we could justifiably call the very air and even the blue sky above the air as our birthright?'

The cheers now rose to a crescendo, amplified by the echoing walls. Feet and weaponry were hammering in a thunderous but hymnal rhythm against the rocky floor. The cheering grew so enthusiastic that the king was obliged to halt his speech to allow the bedlam to settle down. And even then, growing impatient at the continuing din of cheering, he slammed the Lance of State against the stone floor.

Wirgnatha's deep rumble of voice continued, steady, rhythmical, insistent. 'Long – long – have we skulked beneath the earth, we whose labours constructed towns and cities of stone for those who flaunted themselves our masters. Today that subservience ends!' He raised his hand to quell the cheers before they could become too enthusiastic again. 'Yes, indeed, my beloved Ursascogan people! Thus do I deliver you, on this prophetic occasion, the liberation we have longed for through ages of subjugation and ignominy! The time has come for the Ursascogan people to assert our rightful hegemony!'

The ground vibrated again as the choir, two hundred strong, began the sacred litanies in sonorous plainchant. Pittaquera could not suppress a spurt of pride as her husband stood majestically erect, then turned to face the huge diamond-shaped rostrum that stood at the very lip of the pit on which the sacrifice would be offered. With a surprising daintiness for one of his enormous stature, he invited his wife, the queen, to join him on the rostrum.

She saw, this close, how her acquiescence secretly delighted him. Indeed, the glower on his heavily tattooed face as his eyes met hers was a revelation. Had she really imagined, as she plotted in league with their eldest son to usurp him, he was fooled even for a moment? He made no attempt to conceal the tooth-clenched leer of triumph as the sacrifice was dragged onto the rostrum in chains.

The king addressed the gathering once more. 'Here, with heavy heart, do I present to you my very own son, Igorpogra – my first born – who in cognisance of his infamy, will now go down his knees before you.'

Pittaquera's eyes misted with tears as Igorpogra fell, somewhat uncertainly, to his knees, his tormented body supported by his guards. The glare of the pit was reflected in the sweat that fell from his lowered face. The horror of it overwhelmed her mind, her spirit.

Wirgnatha knew that there was no danger that Igorpogra could plead for his life since his tongue had been excised. Taking care of such matters was routine for the monster that was her husband. He had even considered the possibility that their son might open wide the bloody cavern of his throat and bray, like a wounded animal. Wirgnatha had ensured that this did not happen. The crowds would hardly notice the stout wires that tethered Igorpogra's jaws shut, sewn into the bloody gums. Pittaquera could only watch, even as her heart was breaking, Wirgnatha's nod, signalling the twist of the dagger inserted into her son's belly, all conducted carefully out of sight of the people, but effective in making the prince bow before the pit.

The queen glanced at her husband, her voice lowered to a whisper. 'Please stop this now! Has he not been denigrated enough already? You might show magnanimity and end this torment!'

The king hesitated. She thought, perhaps even still there is time? Surely there were lesser punishments, dreadful enough in themselves? Wirgnatha's gaze moved from his son to his wife, whose shoulders he now embraced, crushing with his brute strength the rebellious tension he found there. Then he spun on his rostrum, his arms lifted wide above his massive shoulders, and bellowed, 'My son, the traitor – yet would I show him the mercy of allowing you, my people, to decide his fate.'

There was a pause, surely a flicker of astonishment, among the multitude before the roars rocked the chamber once more.

'Fire of Wrath!'
'Fire of Wrath!'
'Fire of Wrath.'

It was just another cruel trick. For the heartbroken queen it came as no surprise. Fire was ever a favourite in the sacred ceremonies of the Ursascogans.

Wirgnatha took hold of her hand, and forced her arm up high with his own, as if in perfect agreement, but meanwhile squeezing her fingers to near breaking point in his enormous fist. He roared out a laugh of triumph before ordering, 'Let the choir of virgins sing as the sacrifice is made.'

The sea of expectant faces, greedy for blood, made Pittaquera feel sick to her stomach. Her tear-filled eyes could only follow the lances that were prodding Igorpogra to the edge of the pit, below which the lava spat a fiery red from the core of moiling silver. The evidence of torture was all too apparent now in the blaze of light, with so many bleeding wounds that scored his body from head to toe. But such was the hysteria of the multitude that none cared. Even now, Pittaquera took a mother's pride in witnessing how bravely her son accepted his fate. But even his stout heart could not resist a moan as his body plunged into the furnace.

The multitude roared.

The exultant Wirgnatha allowed himself to be drowned out in the new clamour of cheering and foot-stamping. He waited, on this occasion, without attempting to cut the din short with the lance. Indeed, he was patience itself, standing erect, until such was the silence you could hear nothing but the crackling and spitting from the furnace at the bottom of the pit.

'With what heavy heart have I witnessed the sacrifice of my own disloyal son. With the gods thus placated, can we, the Ursascogan people turn away from sorrow and lift up our hearts in celebration of our coming deliverance?'

CR

Queen Pittaquera, daughter of the House of Obenuf, was beside herself with grief. And yet had she not brought such brutality upon her own head? As a youthful and somewhat pig-headed princess, she had been foolish enough to fall for this brute, even though he bore the tattoo of the lowly clan of Yaliam, or Mudborn, on his prodigious shield of breast. Her attraction had, in part, come from his great stature and obvious physical strength. But even more egregious had been her allowing her youthful self to be taken in by his densely intertwined red eyebrows. Eyebrows were symbols of potency among Ursascogan males. Those eyebrows had proved prophetic. Potency Wirgnatha had in great measure. Offspring after offspring, in quadruplets and quintuplets, had been her lot. And so exhausting had this potency proved to be that she had been too consumed with the affairs of family to notice his conspiracies against the house of Obenuf, until it had been too late.

In her lust for him she had broken all too many historical taboos. Hierarchies that had been established, and dutifully followed, for millennia had been ignored, annulled, even banished.

*My fault*, she now acknowledged in her grief.

Igorpogra was hardly innocent of treason against his father. He had indeed plotted. But such plotting of eldest sons against fathers was so habitual among Ursascogan aristocracy as to be punishable, by and large, by nothing more dreadful than banishment. To condemn a son to the pit for such minor transgression! To sacrifice him before the multitude was ruthless to the point of wickedness. Pittaquera might console herself with the thought that there were fifty-three younger offspring, of which twenty-four were strapping sons and the remaining, and perhaps even more wily, twenty-nine daughters. But Igorpogra had been her favourite. And how many more sons might go the way of Igorpogra if further sacrifices were deemed expedient?

The king called forward the wizar, Khakhov, to conclude the ceremony. The aged magus trembled as he stood tall and bent over the lip of the pit, with his white beard cascading down almost to his waist and his domed bald head a landscape of orange freckles and hair-sprouting warts.

'His Royal Highness,' the wizar proclaimed, 'has demanded that the Ursascogan nation now serve him in a role that will prove both demanding and exalting. He would command the might of our armies and thus restore us to our rightful place as masters of this island, no matter that this means a new war with the old enemy, the humans. Who better to lead us in such a sacred venture than the mighty Wirgnatha!'

Another great cheer erupted from the multitude.

Queen Pittaquera's ears had turned to the wizar and his fawning words. They switched direction to harken to her husband's bellicose reply, growling curses about the accursed human kind. She frowned at those promises of crushing the ancient enemy, of casting aside their vaunted weapons, and the sport of hunting down the survivors. None, it seemed, were destined to survive.

Words, she thought, are cheap.

Her firstborn son had been burnt to death and she was forbidden to openly mourn him. In this moment of grief Pittaquera fervently wished that her husband was dead. But she was in no position to make this reality. The five armies were at Wirgnatha's command. But no more could he dispose of her, easy as this would be for him physically. She carried the rank of royal descendent. In the sacred lines of succession, he was no more than a general in one of the armies. He was only king through marriage to her. No doubt he was plotting how this obstacle could be overcome, much as she, however discreetly, was plotting in the opposite direction.

She was obliged to be discreet.

Pittaquera had grown up in cultured society, where vanity ruled in social discourse as much as tradition ruled in the mating obligations. She had broken such tradition in her marriage to her husband. Wirgnatha had risen through the ranks from mud to claiming a new line of royal succession. Where most of the aristocracy despised his low origins, the masses revered him – and especially the military.

Yet still, she asked herself, where had the old rules of aristocracy taken them? Were not her people the most despised race in this misbegotten world? The dominant race, the humans, had a wide variety of derogatory words for them. Molas, skunk diggers, Scogs . . . Oh, that horrible word, Scogs! There had been a time, after the humans had developed their vile weapons of fire, when they had hunted the Ursascogans for sport. They saw the First Folk, in the land they had originally ruled as their own, as degenerate monsters who deserved no better than to burrow underground. Who, then, could blame the masses for supporting a strong and fearless king who was determined on insurrection?

Should she not, in loyalty to her people, be supporting him?

Perhaps she would, despite the sacrifice of her firstborn, if she truly trusted him and his vaunted ambitions for the Ursascogan people. But the fact was she didn't trust him. Because of his fear of the fire weapons of the humans, he was taking her people down a dangerous path, one leading them in the direction of dark spiritual forces. It was a perilous

undertaking. All previous Ursascogan insurrections, and
there had been many, had been put down by the humans
with great slaughter. Their human enemy, numerous beyond
belief, were possessed of terrible weapons, far more powerful
than the Ursascogan tradition of brute strength, lances and
swords.

But then had come the cataclysm!

None, whether Ursascogan or human, had understood
its origin. But the changes it wrought had struck humankind
much harder than it had her people. Perhaps it was the sheer
good fortune of living underground, in their labyrinths, that
had protected them? Whatever the explanation, it had been a
blessing in disguise. No longer need the Ursascogans fear the
overwhelming numbers of humankind. But was it enough to
warrant open insurrection? How would Wirgnatha protect
his rebellious people from the humans' weapons of fire?

Pittaquera couldn't help worrying.

At this moment her reflections were interrupted by a
prickling intimation of . . . of something new afoot. All of her
senses registered some strange disharmony of being – some
extraordinary intrusion into their midst. Abruptly her ears
swivelled back to the towering figure of the king astride his
rostrum, with the Lance of State restored to his right hand.

'To this purpose,' Wirgnatha was grandiosely promising,
'I will have gathered about me new forces that will be put
under the command of my armies. We, the despised, will
become the conquerors of this world.'

Pittaquera saw that her husband was pointing towards the
pit. The eyes and the ears of the masses were also swivelling
in that same direction. The cheering halted to a complete
silence, causing Pittaquera to frown.

The wizar, Khakov, with his flowing beard and bald head, was still poised over the pit, as if waiting for something to happen. All that Pittaquera could hear was the crackling of the furnace deep below ground. It was so still now throughout the huge chamber that the wizar's words came through with the utmost clarity, even though he spoke in his customary soft and quavery voice. 'I should warn you, my king, that such victory does not come easy. The sacrifice has indeed been made. I am obliged to your command.'

The king brought down the Lance of State with a resounding crash against the stone floor. 'The time for dithering is over. Do what you must!'

What was the wizar really up to? What was the pair of them up to, Wirgnatha and the cunning old man, now bent forward over the pit? Pittaquera hung on the wizar's every word.

'In pursuance of His Majesty's determined purpose, I have taken spiritual counsel with The One.'

Pittaquera's senses reeled at the thought: *The One!*

But Wirgnatha's voice was huskily insistent. 'And what was His answer?'

A great silence froze the congregation as that quavery voice replied, 'The One has heeded our prayers. He has promised us deliverance. It will take the form of a being of supernatural power, one who will come to our assistance in the new war with the humans for hegemony of our homeland.'

His words provoked an avalanche of whispers.

The king barked, 'Are you all so craven that you fear our very saviour? Where has our dwelling in mud brought us? Where is the indomitable heart of the Ursascogan people? Get off your craven knees and fight.'

There was, Pittaquera reflected, an admirable indomitable quality about her husband. That much she had predicted rightly from his eyebrows. Yet still she worried that his vaunted ambitions might not be the answer to her people's woes. She felt the weight of responsibility on her shoulders. Her people must at all costs be protected. If her arrogant husband proved to be right, then she could but applaud him. But what if his arrogance should prove to be a disaster?

Khakhov was humming, a deep resonant enchantment, from the depths of his wrinkled throat. 'Come, then!' he addressed the crackling furnace. His face, suspended over the lip, was now reflecting the moiling red of its flames. 'One life, the firstborn prince, have we offered Thee, The One. One life, a royal life, did we offer in supplication, and in return we implore you to grant us the promised gift. One who would gather the darkness of your almighty will to abet us in our struggle. A being empowered by your grace, who would smite and destroy our enemies! As the great king, Wirgnatha, has sacrificed his firstborn in your honour, grant us, we beseech you, O Great Lord of Darkness, a spirit of your eternal being, a darkling force of the night.'

The wizar's words caused a chill to enter Pittaquera's heart. She hardly dared to watch, yet was unable to avert her eyes, even to blink.

The wizar took a step backwards, then two more. He almost tripped over his clumsy feet, as if startled by his own handiwork. And now Pittaquera could see that there was something emerging from the pit. It was hard to make it out through the thick vapour of sulphurous yellow. The very stench of the pit was rising with it, assailing her nostrils. Then she caught her first glimpse of what was emerging and she emitted a shrill, heart-stricken cry. In shape it was tall and slender, strangely vaporous still, its flesh squirming within itself, like a throng of writhing serpents. Yet still it glowed and spat sparks and charcoal-like embers, as if still drawing out its being from the broiling magma. But moment by moment, a more tangible figure was taking form, its surface cooling, its inner being shimmering with every shade of the rainbow. Two serpent eyes, of emerald green, blinked open and confronted the astonished sea of faces.

'Welcome, O Great One!' cried the wizar's quavering voice. 'We venerate The One who sent you. How should we address you?'

Those terrible eyes focused on the elderly figure with his bald pate and his cataract of white beard. The maw that was its mouth parted, stretching wide open in an exploratory yawn, provoking fangs of glistening ivory to extend from the jaws. A mewling sound, like that of a newborn cat, caused the hackles of every neck to spring erect. A mass of hair, as red as molten copper, sprang from its scalp, long and flowing about its head and shoulders.

Surely female, thought Pittaquera.

But that thought was hardly reassuring. The being reached out an astonishing stretch of arms, overly long even for her stature. Claws, as sharp as the fangs, extended from every digit. It purred its reply, the words chilling the hearts of the astonished multitude, a deep, strangely seductive whisper.

*'I will answer only to he who is king.'*

Wirgnatha hesitated for a split moment, his eyes wide. 'Then you will answer to me. I am Wirgnatha, King of the Ursascogan people!'

*'Then to you will I reveal that I am known by many names. But the name I choose as duly representative of this pact of*

*sacrifice is Lustfera, which in the language of the ancients is the Star of Mourning.'*

At those words, a fist of ice closed about Pittaquera's heart.

# A Close Call

Magio couldn't believe his luck. He was taking part in a real adventure. In a real adventure you found yourself running for your life. And that was exactly what he was doing. He was running for his life. What was more, he was doing it in moonlight. When you were running for your life you expected to hear the contact of your feet on the ground. But in the soft desert his feet made no noise that he could hear. He'd have loved to hear the slap of his running feet against the ground. That would have made it feel even more like a real adventure. All the same, he didn't dare to stop running. He didn't dare even to turn around to look behind him. Something told him it was the wrong thing to do. The sand was so deep in these endless dunes that he had to yank one foot after another out of it with every step. This was not only denying him the satisfying slap of his running feet on the ground; it was slowing him down.

*'Run!'* he shouted to himself.

'Quieten down!'

Eefa's voice. But he couldn't see her anywhere near. It didn't make sense that he couldn't see her nearby. Now that he looked about himself, he was entirely alone. There was also this stupid panic rising inside his chest. And at the same time, he had this notion that if he could just heave himself over the top of the dune, he'd be able to slither and slide his way down the other side on his bum. But when he tried to get to the top, his feet kept sliding back, so he made no progress.

He moaned with fright.

'Keep quiet!'

*Oh, Jinxy! That really was Eefa's voice.*

Trust Eefa to spoil his adventure. She didn't believe in adventures. But still he wanted to know she was safe. The trouble was, he couldn't see her. She was just a disembodied voice, which struck him as strange. Eefa was never invisible to him. He had to figure this out. She must be deliberately concealing herself from him. The realisation shocked him. She had never hidden herself from him before.

A whole bunch of things were no longer making sense.

Then, for some utterly nonsensical reason, his sister began to sing. Her voice became eerie as she sang, hauntingly strange and beautiful in a way that froze his blood. He glimpsed her waiting for him up ahead, on the top of the dune in the smoky moonlight. Her hair was fair, lighter than his own, but maybe a shade or so too light. It looked almost white. On this wild windy night, it also looked out of control, spraying about her head like smoke caught up by a whirlwind. She had her back to him, framed against the junction of sea and starry sky, twirling a lock of wispy strands around her long slender fingers.

He cried out, 'Oh, Eefa . . . is it really you?'

'Hush!'

The figure was slowly turning around. At first his heart leapt to recognise his sister. But even as she continued to turn, a change began to invade her features. The face became longer and the mouth opened wide, revealing two rows of wicked fangs. And then she – it – hissed.

Magio shrieked with terror.

'Be quiet!'

A hand was shaking him roughly. He opened his eyes and saw Eefa's face very close up to his own. She whispered, with her lips pressed right up to his ear, 'You've been dreaming. But don't call out. Don't even talk.'

His voice trembled. 'Did you hear?'

'Yes! I heard it.'

'Then it wasn't just in my dream. There was somebody chasing me. I thought it was you, Eefa. And then . . . and then it turned . . .'

'Hush!'

He whispered, 'But it can't have been just a dream. Not if you heard it too.'

She whispered back, 'I don't know what to think.'

'I think we're being hunted.'

'What?'

'We're being hunted, right now. And whoever, or whatever, is hunting us, it can hunt us here in the moonlight, and it can hunt me in my dreams.'

'But that's impossible.'

'Weird – I know!'

'Oh, for goodness sakes, Magio!' Eefa was shaking her head, peering up out of the hollow crevice where they had rested for the night, her eyes darting about the landscape under the night sky.

'What is it? What are you looking for?'

'Hush! There's something coming.'

She pressed her finger against his chattering lips and then dragged him down again so they were both flattened to the ground. 'I'm beginning to think you're right. Something is chasing us.'

'Oh, jinxy!'

Eefa put her arm around his shoulders, in that rough way she did when she was frightened herself.

'It felt so absolutely real. I was trying to climb to the top of the dune. Somebody, or something, was hunting for me. Then my feet kept slipping. I got really scared. But then your voice spoke to me. I thought I could see you, up ahead, waiting for me. It was something that looked like you from behind. But when you turned around . . . '

Magio's heartbeat was pounding in his throat as they fell on all fours, their heads lowered but all senses alert, as a shadow swept low across the air overhead, travelling at such speed it was gone in an instant. He began to whisper a question, but Eefa put her hand over his mouth and held it there.

'What did you see?'

He whispered, 'I don't know. It might have been some monstrous night bird, but if so its flight wasn't like any bird I've ever seen.'

Its flight had been flapping and heavy like that of a bat. But no bat that he had ever seen was remotely as large as that. For several minutes he didn't dare to move. He stayed down, skulking close to the ground, waiting for his heartbeat to come down out of his throat, and hoping that the shadow would not return.

'Oh, Gran!' Eefa sighed. 'Why aren't you here to protect us?'

Magio was still blinking, and breathing deeply.

Eefa whispered close to his ear, 'We need to warn Bird Woman. She needs to know everything that has happened.'

It seemed to take an eternity for Eefa and Magio to crawl along the crevice to where Bird Woman was posting guard over the sleeping figure of Quimbre.

'There's something wrong,' Eefa whispered to her. 'There's something horrible out there, and Magio thinks it's looking for us.'

'It's up there – in the moonlight,' Magio added.

'Hush, Magio, and let me explain.'

'I won't hush.'

'It woke Magio up from sleep.'

'It didn't just wake me. It came right inside my dream.'

'Stop – *stop!*' Bird Woman raised her hands in an attempt to placate their fears. 'Let's sit down and talk about it calmly. What do you mean, Magio, when you say it entered your dream?'

'I saw it – I mean I saw it in my dream. I thought it was Eefa, but it turned around and I saw it wasn't Eefa at all. It was a monster.'

'Shut up, Gio! Bird Woman doesn't want to hear about your dream.'

'Oh, but I do, Eefa. I very much want to hear about Magio's dream.'

So Magio told her all her remembered. How he had found himself struggling to gain the top of a dune, while all the time slipping back down again. How he had heard Eefa's voice calling to him.

Bird Woman interrupted his recounting to turn to Eefa. 'Could it be that Magio called out in his sleep and you really did tell him to hush?'

'Yes, I did.'

'So – the voice he heard was really your voice. And then that would explain why it sounded so true to Magio.' Bird Woman nodded. 'Carry on, Magio.'

'Then she began to sing. Or at least I thought it was Eefa singing.'

'As if I'd sing to you!'

Bird Woman smiled at Eefa. 'So – now we know it wasn't Eefa singing to you. Tell me all you can recall of this song?'

'It was sort of . . . ghostly.'

'A haunting song?'

'Yes. Haunting – but also beautiful. I know it sounds weird, but it was like a song that was so beautiful it made me feel a chill inside.'

'Ah! So it frightened you?'

Magio nodded, his lips clenched pensively. 'And then I saw her – or at least I thought I saw her. She had her back to me, but she looked like Eefa.'

'How?'

'Eefa changes her looks at times. But often she chooses fair hair, just as I saw in the figure. And she was twirling a lock of her hair round her finger, like Eefa does.' Magio hesitated. 'And then she turned. What I saw –'

'It wasn't me.'

'No – it wasn't Eefa. There were staring eyes, unblinking eyes. And a mouth full of fangs.'

Bird Woman stared at Magio for a second or two, deep in thought. 'We have little time. First we must wake up Quimbre. We're all desperately tired. But we cannot rest here, not a minute longer.'

Quimbre was exceedingly truculent when woken. And he was reluctant to subject young Magio to a flight without rest. 'Surely the lad can get a little sleep? Can't we rest until first light?' Quimbre argued. 'It can only be a few hours away.'

'A few hours are time aplenty for this new enemy to discover us.' She gave him no comfort. 'We are faced with several vital questions. What evil is now headed in our direction? What if you but settle into sleep when attack arrives? Would you take that risk?'

Quimbre's head fell. Bird Woman was right. They just couldn't afford to take those chances.

'And, though you doubt it, Magio is not the only target. We must presume that Eefa is their prime target. But perhaps – though having listened to the extraordinary story of Magio's dream – I find myself wondering if we are truly focused on what is really happening here. Perhaps Magio might also prove our saviour?'

Magio, intrigued, muttered a tired, 'How?'

'Because of both the focus and the reality of your dream.'

'I don't understand.'

'It all goes back to the confrontation with the Scogs in Warren. I've been replaying that confrontation in my mind. I believe that they at least suspected that Eefa was there. But that didn't take a lot of figuring out since they were most likely informed that she existed and that you two always did things together. I wonder now if the Scog ambush wasn't really an ambush at all. I've seen Scogs fight and they don't stand around and allow any escape. They are immensely strong and, when called for, equally aggressive. My guess, therefore, is they were merely probing. They suspected that Eefa was there. But, for some reason, they needed to confirm it. And, given your reply, Magio, we can assume that they did confirm their suspicions.'

'But I said nothing.'

'Think back to your actual words.'

Magio recalled that extraordinary confrontation. How the Scog leader appeared to be addressing him in that strange low-pitched voice. 'I think he said: "Boy – not want . . . Want she. . . Must have she . . . Give us she . . ."'

'And what did you say, in reply?'

Magio shook his head. 'I think I said, "No!"'

'"Give us your sister – boy go home," he said.'

'I said, "You can't have her."' Magio shook his head. 'But the stupid thing wouldn't take no for an answer. He tapped me on the shoulder with that huge spade of a finger and he said, 'Boy . . . not want boy . . . Want she . . . Boy give us she . . ."'

'And you told him he couldn't have her?'

'Yeah!'

'You see, Magio! You didn't say, "I don't have any such sister." You implied, yes I have such a sister, but you can't take her.'

'Oh, jinxy!'

'What's done is done. But the Scog leader said something else, something quite curious at the time, did he not?'

'Yes. He talked about stuff I never heard of. Like something or somebody had sent them to look for us. Somebody else who wanted Eefa.'

'A shee-warg.'

'That was it – yes.'

'I believe that a shee-warg is a soothsayer.'

'What's that?'

'A kind of witch-adviser. Various magical beings, from wargs to shapeshifters, are commonplace in spell-casting and soothsaying in Ursascogan legends.'

Magio's eyes widened. 'Scogs have legends?'

'Never mind that for now. There must have been more. Tell me what you remember about that confrontation with the Scogs.'

'I admit that I panicked. I remember how my mind was invaded by a sort of dark cloud. I felt lost, trapped.'

'But still they let you get away. Oh, I know that I distracted them by causing the birds to wheel in the sky. But even I was surprised at how readily we escaped. From what I know about Scogs, they are not so easily cowed.'

'Why, then, did they let us escape?'

'I'm not sure. But the more I think about it, the more convinced I am that none of them could actually see Eefa. How could they? Their eyesight is no better than Quimbre's.'

'Nothing wrong with my eyes!' Quimbre retorted.

'But you have never seen Eefa. You have always considered her a figment of Magio's imagination.'

Quimbre snorted. 'With good reason.'

Eefa spoke up. 'What are you thinking, Bird Woman?'

'I'm wondering about how curiously the Scogs behaved. They're not as smart as humans. But no more are they as stupid as humans imagine them to be. And they would never back down from a fight. I think they were told what to do by somebody smarter than themselves. Indeed, I am now inclined to believe that the ambush wasn't really an ambush at all. They were probing. They simply wanted to confirm that Eefa was there. And this they did discover.'

Eefa blurted, 'So what does it really mean?'

'It makes me wonder afresh. What if the local clan were emboldened because there's some kind of a bigger plan in the wind?'

'What do you mean?'

'For some time the Scogs have appeared restless over the whole of Moon. Their strange towers, with their dense proliferation of plant life, have been springing up in many different places, some invading the ruins of townships, others appearing in parts where there was no history of human habitation in recent times. Such a change in behaviour surely heralds something?'

'What something?'

'There have been numerous Ursascogan rebellions in the past.'

'Scog rebellions?'

'Rebellions against the hegemony of humans.'

Quimbre bristled. 'They're a degenerate race, devoid of civilisation.'

'I'm not so sure about that. Civilisation is in the mind of the beholder. Moreover, when has that kind of attitude hindered rebelliousness in the downtrodden?'

'Downtrodden?' Magio said, agog.

Bird Woman smiled, but it was a pained smile. 'Yes, Magio. Moon is but a dot in the ocean of our world. Many were the different races of ancient ones that first populated the Sea of Stars. And many more were the cruel wars that raged between them.' Bird Woman nodded. 'But now we face a new danger. We must change our route. The original plan was to cut diagonally inland, following the highland route through the Jarro Mountains. But now I think we'll be safer travelling the coastal route. The going will be harder. But, hopefully, it will offer more opportunities to hide our tracks over rock than on soft sand, and better chances to discover respites in caves and rocky overhangs.'

Quimbre snorted again. 'If you're right, and this spy of theirs is hunting us right now in the very sky, then a nightmare journey into dawn it will prove to be, keeping wherever we can to the cover of shadows, even when the difference between starlight and shadow is the slightest shade.'

◌◈

Quimbre's words proved to be prophetic. A nightmare journey it proved to be. They managed to creep through ten miles of desert, wet with sweat, despite the cool of the moon, and all four cramped with exhaustion. And then, to everyone's horror, they heard that terrible hiss again. Magio felt Eefa's hand grip a tight hold of his own. Petrified, they stopped hurrying. They were overtaken by Bird Woman's urgent whisper in their ears, 'Down! Everybody down! Flat to the ground!'

'What is it?' Quimbre whispered, equally urgent.

A strange cloud obscured the stars.

Magio coughed; the air was so full of dust it got down into your throat and made it too dry to breathe. He peered up again until he saw what was causing it: a darkness, like a whirlwind, and the spout appeared to be moving about, as if searching . . . Almost immediately he felt several spots, like hailstones, strike over the length and breadth of his body.

'What is it?'

'Moths – monsters of moths!' muttered Quimbre.

'Desert Emperors!' Bird Woman confirmed.

'How peculiar!' Eefa whispered.

Bird Woman agreed with her. 'This cannot be a normal phenomenon. Their flight appears frenzied. Something is driving them into such bizarre behaviour.'

Quimbre muttered, 'Think, woman!'

'I'm racking my brains. What could possibly link the bizarre behaviour of moths to our purpose?'

Quimbre emitted a curse. 'Scogs are renowned for their closeness to nature – to natural phenomena.'

Magio replied, 'But in our entire lives, Eefa and I had only had that one meeting with them.'

Bird Woman entered the conversation. 'Yes – oh, Magio! You are absolutely right. It has to be somehow related to that single confrontation.'

'But what?'

Bird Woman asked, 'Did any of them do something to you?'

'The lead Scog was the only one close enough even to touch me.'

'Yes! He touched you. You mentioned it last time we talked about the confrontation in Quarry. You mentioned how the Scog leader touched you with his finger.'

'Yes! He did. When he was demanding to take Eefa! He touched me on the shoulder with his finger.'

'Which shoulder?'

Magio tapped against his left shoulder. 'This one.'

'Touched you – light, or hard?'

'How could it be light? He had a hand as big as a rock and his finger was as thick as my leg.'

'Then he pressed you hard?'

'He practically pushed me over.'

'That has to be it.'

'What?'

'If I'm not mistaken, you're wearing the same garment that covered your shoulder – I can see it under your travel coat.'

'It's my favourite shirt.'

'Did I not warn you that the Scogs are cunning? They have a far deeper lore of nature than humans.'

'What is it?' Eefa demanded.

'We have so little time.'

'But what are you thinking?'

'The moth swarm is male. They are drawn by a scent that calls them to the female. The male moths are said to sense it from surprising distance. They are driven mad by what humans might describe as desire. In his single touch, the Scog marked Magio. He smeared the scent that comes from the female moth on your brother's shirt.'

Magio said, 'What?'

'You must take it off, Magio – immediately.'

While Magio was struggling out of his coat, and then his short-sleeved shirt, Eefa still pressed Bird Woman. 'But even so, what would that matter? Moths, even Desert Emperors, cannot really harm us.'

'The moths are no direct threat. But the scent is attracting whole swarms of them, which descend towards us, with Magio as their fulcrum. It is locating where we are as precisely as a beacon.'

Eefa recalled the heavy shape that had flown over them, the loud flapping of huge bat-like wings. 'Oh, now you're frightening me.'

Bird Woman nodded. 'You are right to be frightened. But now that we understand a little more of what is going on, perhaps we can circumvent their plan. Quickly, Magio, pass me your shirt.'

Magio threw the balled-up shirt to Bird Woman. In the shadowy light of the stars, Bird Woman wrapped Magio's shirt tight around a long arrow. 'Well now, the Scogs thought to track us with this through the wilderness. Let us turn the trick on them.' She fired it high and far in the opposite direction to which they were headed. Then she stood back in the pallid light of the stars to observe its potential effect.

Magio, his voice quivering, asked, 'Is it working?'

Bird Woman called out to the company. 'Look for yourself. The moth cloud is moving.'

Magio climbed to his feet and stared up into the sky. As if by a miracle, the swarm of moths rose high into the air and followed the flight of the arrow.

Bird Woman breathed a sigh of relief. 'What cunning rogues the Ursascogans are! But we have averted their trap! But let's not get overly confident. Adversity has been turned to opportunity. While our hunter follows the moths, we can make haste.' She gazed up into the sky full of stars. 'There's the first glimmer of approaching dawn.' She looked around them, her eyes pools of darkness. Then she lifted up her face to sniff toward the east. 'I smell ocean. I think we are but a mile or two from the coast. We can make it within the hour if we abandon all pretence of concealment and run.'

# The Hunter

The statuesque flame-haired being who strode through the rubble-strewn remains of Ashtree, former capital city of the island nation of Moon, was unruffled, though much of what greeted her vision was offensive. Humans were an abomination upon the natural world, willed as it was to beauty and form by the Undying. Now it would appear that she must endure not only the insult of adopting this ungainly human form, she must also come to terms with the human concept of time. Lustfera halted for several moments, her flowing turquoise gown settling in the dust motes evoked by her passage, as her emerald eyes examined the shattered façade of what would likely have been the civic centre, with a tottering colonnade of pillars supporting what remained of a balcony on the second floor where some dignitary, no doubt puffed up with self-importance, would have addressed the governed. Today it was the abode of scuttling reptiles and web-weaving spiders. She permitted herself a moment of exultation: how the havoc of the Change had reduced hubris to desolation!

The One would be pleased.

With that agreeable thought she willed her transference into the maze of gloomy tunnels that proliferated below ground. Those who knew of its existence assumed that it had been excavated in the response to the violence of the Chaos. In fact it was far more ancient, an abandoned labyrinth mined out by some forgotten clan of Ursascogans. This created yet another problem for her striding presence: the clan had been surprisingly short for Ursascogans, so the tunnels, carved out of the foamy black brimstone, were not designed to accommodate her. She was compelled to traverse its stygian depths with stooped shoulders and with her elegantly long neck bent horizontal.

Judging by the stink, the labyrinth now served an underclass of humans. Dim-witted as the Ursascogans were, they would never have allowed the accumulation of filth that she encountered in exploring the winding tunnels, to be repeatedly accosted by all manner of human garbage. Had any one of them been sober they might have been forewarned to observe that she cast no shadow. A vexatious example insisted on irritating her with his attentions. When he took possession of her arm, she was pleased to be led into a stinking cloacal cubicle, from which, following a single scream, she alone emerged to continue her exploration.

She halted her perambulation when confronted by a sign dangling on a chain of bones outside a darkly-lit cavern.

THIS HEER IS BASTOS PLACE
IF U AINT SCUM U MAY FREELY ENTER

Her target was sitting in what appeared to be an inebriated state on the serving side of the liquor-puddled bar in the cavern within, chewing abstractedly on a chunk of green-veined cheese. It was hard to credit that this was the hunter she was looking for.

Lustfera took her time in appraising the proprietor, who appeared to be wracked by the throes of misery. He was so massively broad-shouldered that, sitting slumped over the ale-dripping wood, he resembled a horizontally-expanded dwarf rather than the formidable figure she had expected to find.

She perched atop one of the three-legged stools opposite him and made a closer inspection, confirming a motley collection of scars across the ruin of his face.

'Bastos Kull?'

'Oo's asking?'

His voice was very deep and, given his present state, very wet – with a peculiar sing-song effect that caused her to study him even more closely.

'I am.'

The penetration of her own voice appeared to provoke a mental start in the man. If man, indeed, he happened to be.

Judging from appearances, she decided that Kull was unlikely to be wholly human. He was so inebriated it took him several seconds to acknowledge her presence. But now that he did so, he underwent a transformation. He swung around, clambering awkwardly off his stool, and stood up to re-examine her. His stature, which was only half a foot shorter than her own, now confirmed her earlier supposition. He was large enough to be at least a quarter Ursascogan. Like her, he had to bend his neck to accommodate the ceiling. And now that he leaned down so he could confront her face-to-face across the bar, his two bulging amber eyes were on a level with her own. There was something in those eyes, a surprising intelligence, coupled with extreme malice, that interested her.

'We ain't met?'

'I think I'd remember if we had.'

'Hmmm!' He lifted a half-consumed cigar from the wet surface and took a second or two to relight it. 'You don't mind?' He appeared to struggle to find the word he was searching for in his drunken brain, instead waving the smoking ruin of the cigar.

'Oh, I heartily approve.'

'Maybe — Bastos likes your style!'

He sat down again, scratching his black-stubbled chin with a spade-like hand. Then, impulsively, he threw wide open both his arms, to embrace the gloomy cave that surrounded them. 'Welcome to me humble art!'

Lustfera gazed about the poorly-lit chamber through the smoky gloom. His art, as he called it, was a display of heads in a variety of niches cut into the bare stone wall. They included just about everything of any importance that moved: large species of predatorial animals, humans, Ursascogans, and a variety of other beings she had never had the pleasure of meeting. Some peculiar entities had been pickled in jars to preserve the flesh, including hair that had turned a bleached white, while others had been boiled to leave nothing but the ivory skulls with grinning teeth, and where relevant, horns, antlers, tusks, fangs. The trophies took up every wall from floor to ceiling, including that behind the bar.

'Perhaps you might indicate items of particular interest?'

He shrugged those massive shoulders, then began to itemise the grisly trophies, one after another. It was a comprehensive litany, drawn from an epic variety of hunts, both human, animal and a deal of others.

'I'm impressed.'

'Yeah?'

'You would appear to be a formidable hunter.'

Another determined suck on the soggy remains of the cigar, through the smoke of which those rancid eyes bulged back at her with evident pride.

'Bastos Kull be the best.'

'That is why I am here.'

'Ah – so now we gets down to business!'

Kull took the cigar out of his mouth and squashed it within one enormous fist. He searched for a cloth to blow his nose, and failing this, he pinched his two nostrils with what looked like an expert manoeuvre, before hooting the contents of his nose into a bucket at his feet.

'Are we quite ready?'

'You got us ear.'

Lustfera was only belatedly aware that, contrary to every iota of logic, this obnoxious being was sexually attracted to her. She did not hesitate to part her cloak to reveal an ample cleavage.

He responded by grinning, revealing a row of tombstone green-furred teeth. 'What can ole Bastos do for Lovely Lady?'

'I wish to employ your services.'

Kull shuffled on his stool, attempting to right his drunken posture, then farted, loud and without any attempt at apology. 'Woss in it for me?'

'Whatever might you desire?'

Kull's eyes widened. He snorted a laugh down those massive, black-hair-sprouting nostrils, like a malevolent ogre.

'I take it that I have engaged your interest?'

'Bastos Kull at your command.'

'We should discuss terms?'

'Terms, it is.'

She leaned still closer to him, over the iridescently-glittering counter. 'What then is your heartmost desire?'

His eyes widened. 'Money, Lovely Lady. Lots of it.'

'Then let us barter!'

'An' wimmen! Lots of 'em too.' Those amber eyes squeezed tight shut with what she had to presume was some exceedingly vile innermost dream. 'Wimmen what has to give us everything we wants.' Those drunken eyes fell shut, enamoured no doubt with inner visions of bliss. 'All I wants - an' more.'

She sized him up in silence.

His eyes reopened. Drunk as he was, Kull was cunning enough to take a step backwards. 'I . . . I be obliged to apologise to you, lovely Lady. I mean, well you can see how rough a life I lead. You be a ray of sunlight shining into the darkness.'

'Then it would appear that we have the makings of a deal.'

Kull eyed her closely again. His lips grinned obscenely at her seemingly even more generous cleavage. 'My Lady . . . Them's the words what just springs into us mind. I think . . . Well, yeah, that's what we should call you. Just kinda funny how they jumped right into us mind.'

Her eyes widened in gazing into his even more closely. 'Let me explain my side of the deal. I need you to hunt down a party.'

'A party?'

She was observant enough to witness a slight movement of his ears in her direction, which rather confirmed her earlier suspicion of Ursascogan lineage.

'A party – a group of individuals! I need a skilled and ruthless hunter.'

'Uh-uh?'

His expression suggested he was still trying to figure how her name had somehow suggested itself inside his mind. But she had no time or inclination to explain. 'I have importane duties that otherwise distract me. Yet this is a pressing need. I don't have time to track down a party of four, two brats an old man and . . . and a conniving bitch.'

He searched under the bar for a new cigar, waving it in her face questioningly. 'No problem – huh?'

'Perfect!'

She watched him light the cigar. This time the fumes were so intoxicating she could not resist leaning across to get close enough to sniff every atom of the aromatic smoke into her long, pale nostrils.

'My Lady, you fancy a drag – I'll find another.'

'Tempting, but no, thank you. Will you, or will you not, agree to hunt down this party for me?'

He lifted his gaze from her cleavage to her face. He leaned forwards over the counter, until his broad, pocked and hairy nose was within an inch of that same cleavage, and forced her to withdraw several inches to avoid the inconvenience of the snot that was dripping from those nostrils.

'There's just the matter . . .'

'Of the fee – yes – I understand! Let me make you an offer. I want you to hunt them down, the two brats, a man and a woman. Hunt them,' she nodded towards the walls, 'and add them to your collection.'

There was a hesitation on his part, time enough to blink. But it didn't last very long. 'An' the small matter . . . My Lady?'

'You'll be amply rewarded.'

'A promise ain't spit compared to gold in the hand!'

'I thought it was women you lusted after?'

'Gold buys wimmen.'

She opened her left fist and a shoal of coins cascaded onto the bar surface to form a small mountain of gold, twinkling in the puddles.

Drunk as Kull was, he wasn't so stupefied he didn't know a fortune when he saw it.

'The faces is blank, with neither king nor queen.'

'Does it matter where the gold comes from?'

'Faceless geld is Scog gold.'

'The Ursascogans are the greatest miners on this misbegotten island. There is no purer gold to be found.'

He picked up one of the blank-faced coins between finger and thumb and licked at it with the tip of his tongue, then lightly bit into it with those tombstones of teeth. 'Tastes good enough . . . bites even sweeter!'

'Do we have a deal?'

Kull cackled, a squelchy eruption of a laugh that bathed the red-haired hirer in his spirit-laden exhalation. 'But what do I call you?'

'My Lady will suffice.'

He hesitated. 'This quarry . . . any of um likely to fight back?'

'No doubt the old man will fight, but I doubt he will prove your equal. The woman – she might prove tricky.'

'Tricky?' Those bulging eyes were now fixed on hers.

She gazed about the walls, with their collection of heads, and shrugged. 'The girl – well, let's say she might prove a different kind of challenge. One that might make it all the more interesting a chase. She's invisible.'

'Invisible?'

'You cannot see her. But take my word for it, she is there.'

Kull's amber eyes stared into her own. This was clearly a challenge he had never encountered before. His focus moved from her face to the small mountain of gold – then back to look her eye-to-eye again.

'You are the great hunter. I trust you to find a way. A scent perhaps? You can make use of the boy, her twin brother. He is never far from her.'

'Could be me gals'll come in useful.'

'Your gals?'

He grinned. 'Me hunting pack.'

'You can play what games you like with them. But the invisible brat – you must be sure to kill her.'

'What's so special about her?'

'Never mind what! Will you accept the challenge?'

'My Lady – we got us a deal!'

She snatched back the gold, provoking his eyes to move higher again, to confront those chilling eyes, which were by now appearing less drunk.

'Bastos Kull don't hunt for no promises.'

'Nor would I expect you to. No more would I reward promises that are not completely fulfilled.'

She tumbled a quarter of the gold back onto the counter.

'This is your advance, Bastos Kull. But I warn you that a bargain with me is a bargain in blood. There will be no foregoing it once struck. Complete the task and you will have all that I have promised you. But fail me and there will be a forfeit.'

'What kinda forfeit?'

'Blood for blood.'

Bastos Kull stared into those cold emerald eyes, no longer bothering to sniff up the snot that was gathering in his nostrils. He didn't even bother to wipe it off his upper lip with his filthy sleeve when it ran down in two shiny tramlines onto his scarred, thick-lipped mouth.

# THE CHAOS

Magio woke from sleep to notice that there was a shadow nearby under the shelter of pine branches. He could smell the fact it was Bird Woman. She had a kind of earthy smell, like smoke mixed with crushed leaves in your hand. When he dared to peer out at the shadow through half-closed eyes, he confirmed it was her. She wasn't even trying to sleep. She was watching over him and the sleeping Eefa.

'What's the matter? Why aren't you sleeping?'

'I don't really require much sleep. And I wanted to make sure that Eefa is resting. She had such a shock back there on the beach.'

'The beach?' Magio sat up, rubbing at his eyes, which felt sticky with sleep. Then he remembered the beach she meant. It wasn't their latest scare, with the moths and the thing hunting them. It was something right back there, that night when they slept in the cobwebby basement of the ruined tower.

He said, 'I tried to talk to Eefa about it. But she wouldn't talk to me. All she said was that it was scary.'

'That's true.'

Why in the world was Bird Woman so bothered about that stupid beach? As far as Magio was concerned, it was all of two adventures past. But knowing Bird Woman, there must be some important reason. 'Why? What really happened?' Bird Woman put her hand on his shoulder and she leaned towards him and raised her eyebrows, as if in apology. 'Magio – I have a confession to make. The reason it was such a shock to Eefa was that I failed her.'

'You did?'

'I'm afraid so. And ever since then she has been struggling to sleep. She really needs sleep and rest for the gruelling trek ahead. So, I gave her a potion to help her sleep. But, perhaps, that gives you and me the opportunity to talk.'

The notion of Bird Woman failing Eefa was alarming. The urgency in her voice astonished him. 'What's going on?'

'There's nothing that you don't already know about. I just need to have a little chat with you.'

'If this is a dream, I want to wake up. I want to go back home to Gran's. I want to race Eefa to the beach and run along the shore with her.'

'Oh, Magio! Please calm yourself – it's not a dream.'

Still, his head dropped.

'Would you like me to hold your hand?'

'I'm not a kid.'

'Indeed, you are not. You and Eefa, you're both remarkably mature for your age. It's just that I need to ask you some questions that might help me to understand things a little better.'

Magio pressed his lips together. Since the overnight stop at the ruined tower they had hurried on, travelling only through the night. Bird Woman wouldn't let them rest until they made it to a hilly wood of pine trees. Here, as dawn was breaking, Quimbre had rigged up this shelter with branches laid tent-like against an overhang of pink clay. Magio knew that right now daylight must be fading outside the shelter. Quimbre was still out there, mounting guard in what sounded like a blustery wind.

'I promise you, it's just a few simple questions.'

Magio blinked, then lifted his head so he looked Bird Woman straight in the eye. 'It's okay. Go ahead and ask your questions.'

'Magio, what you must understand is that I have received instructions from within my mind. I know how strange that will seem to you. Yet it fits with the reality that I find before me. I think there must be a reason why Eefa had to be invisible from the moment of her birth.'

'Why? It makes no sense to me whatsoever.'

'Think, Magio! If Eefa was making this journey on her own?'

'Don't be silly. She'd never go on a journey like this on her own.'

'Think theoretically, Magio. If for some reason, she did – she would require no hiding, no concealment. None would know that she was making the journey.'

'I still don't get the point you're making.'

'Magio – think about it! If you were a magician and you wanted to keep a girl safe – a girl, as I now am wondering, who had a very special purpose in life – what better way to keep her absolutely safe than to make her invisible?'

'Who would have done a thing like that to Eefa?'

She spoke softly, placatingly. 'That's what I'm trying to figure out.'

Magio was now sitting up and taking interest. He gathered his thoughts. 'What sort of power would want to make a baby girl invisible?'

'Well, now, that's an extremely important question. I think that we both would like to know the answer. But we'd better move away from Eefa, for fear of waking her. It's already evening outside, and falling cold. So why don't you wrap your blanket around you and let us go outside.'

'Hey – we can keep Quimbre company?'

'Yes, if you like.'

'I like to talk with Quimbre about hunting.'

'Very well, then. But we must huddle down so no one other than Quimbre can see us. No lighting fires. And we need to keep our voices low.'

They emerged, with Magio wrapped up warm in his blanket, though he noticed that Bird Woman had felt no need to wrap herself up to keep warm.

Quimbre had his empty pipe in his mouth. 'What's this – a delegation?'

'Magio wanted to keep you company and talk about hunting. But first we finish our conversation about his sister.'

Quimbre shook his head.

Looking up through the encircling trees into a cloudless evening sky, Magio wondered if he would ever get used to sleeping by day and travelling by night. 'Bird Woman,' he spoke to Quimbre while inclining his head towards the squatting woman, 'she thinks that it was, like, some kind of a deliberate plan that Eefa had to be kept invisible from the day she was born.'

Quimbre chewed on the end of his pipe, looking exceedingly sceptical. 'Some kind of magical plan, huh?'

'But you have to believe she's real, Quimbre.'

Quimbre ruffled Magio's unruly brown hair and grinned. 'Hey, kiddo – old Quimbre wants to keep you happy. If it makes you happy, I believe in fairies.'

'Bird Woman, she's trying to figure who would have some really important reason for keeping Eefa invisible.'

'Magic – juju kinda stuff, huh?' Quimbre's shoulders shook with laughter as he waved his hands in front of Magio's eyes.

Bird Woman exhaled. 'Magic of a sort, perhaps?'

'Magic – juju!' Quimbre began to belly-laugh.

Magio insisted, 'But Eefa is real, Quimbre.' Bird Woman nodded, then she, too, ruffled Magio's hair. 'Perhaps it was as necessary for Eefa to be invisible as a mother bird hides its nestlings from the sharp eyes of raptors.'

Magio was alarmed. 'What do you mean – nestlings and raptors?'

'Perhaps Eefa is of interest to more powerful enemies than the Ursascogans?'

'I don't understand.'

'Dark forces would appear to be searching for Eefa. This was surely apparent from the confrontation with the Ursascogans in Warren. I suspected then that the real enemy was unlikely to be the Ursascogans. From their conversation, it seemed likely that they were following orders from someone more powerful.'

'Yeah – I remember. That Scog and his talk about a shee-warg!'

'Indeed!' Bird Woman's hollow cheeks seemed to deepen in the low sunlight of evening. 'But, as I explained already, a shee-warg is just a soothsayer. The Ursascogans turn to soothsayers, seers, even witches, for advice. I doubt that any such being would have the power to make a child invisible from birth. And that brings me back to what happened on the beach, Magio. Back there, in the cove of the ruined tower, Eefa was confronted by something far more powerful, and dangerous, than a shee-warg or Ursascogans.'

Magio snuggled up next to Quimbre. He recalled how shaky Eefa had been after her experience on the beach. 'She must have been so scared she wouldn't even talk about it with me.'

'It was my fault,' Bird Woman confessed. 'I should have been more vigilant. But the same power that confronted Eefa seduced my mind to sleep. I woke with a premonition of danger and found her on the beach, at the very edge of the tide. From what she subsequently told me, she was guided by some dark spiritual force.'

'Poor Eefa!'

'She spoke of it – when I was helping her back. In that same moment, I sensed it. It was exceedingly powerful and malevolent.'

'What else did Eefa tell you?'

'I spoke of the eye,' Eefa answered Magio, emerging from the tent of branches. 'You woke me up with your whispered conversation.' She sat down among them, clearly irritated that they had been talking about her in her absence.

'What eye – what are you talking about?'

'What's going on?' Quimbre interrupted, staring wildly about himself.

Magio told him, 'It's okay. I know you can't hear her. But Eefa's come out of the tent to join us.'

Quimbre blinked, shaking his head. He couldn't keep the suspicion out of his voice. 'Well then – what are you asking her, Magio? What eye are you talking about?'

Eefa answered. 'I heard it as a whisper inside my head, a whisper that I felt I could not disobey:

*The eye is beckoning. It is calling you . . .*

Magio explained what Eefa was telling them to Quimbre, whose scowl only deepened.

Magio's voice fell to a horrified whisper. 'What did you do?'

'I couldn't stop my feet from picking up pace. I was running, even though I felt really tired. I was following a pattern in the sand of converging lines. But the awful thing was that they were leading me towards the sea.'

'You should have scarpered.'

'I couldn't disobey the voice in my head. I was in a half-asleep, half-awake state. I wasn't really in proper control of myself, any more than you are in one of your awake-dreams.'

'But what was it? What were you being led to?'

'Something the voice called "the eye". I had the impression that this eye, if it was an eye at all, was more like a being. A being of absolute power that was waiting for me out there, where the line of the ocean meets the sky.'

'You'd have drowned!' Magio spun to stare at Quimbre, who would have heard nothing of this conversation. 'Oh, Quimbre. This eye was trying to make her walk out into the sea. It was trying to drown her.'

Quimbre glared at Bird Woman. 'You were there. Did you see this?'

Eefa put her hand on Magio's shoulder. 'Magio, tell Quimbre not to blame Bird Woman. She saved me.'

Magio passed on her words.

Quimbre was becoming increasingly angry. 'I don't understand any of this. What in holy hell is going on?'

Eefa spoke in a husky whisper. 'I was bewildered. The most frightening thing was I no longer controlled my body, my legs. I couldn't stop myself taking step after step towards the ocean. And then I sensed it.'

'What?' Magio felt his muscles jerking with the tension of it.

'I . . . I sensed a presence. Something huge . . . terrible . . . So enormous, on rising, its presence blocked out the sky. . .'

Magio had become so jumpy he couldn't keep his body still. Quimbre comforted him with his bearlike arm around his shoulders. 'Hey, rascal! You need to lie down. Go back into the shelter and get some sleep.'

'I wouldn't be able to sleep. I need to understand what's going on. Hey, Bird Woman! What Eefa sensed – that presence that was drawing her into the sea – are you saying that's what is really chasing us?'

Quimbre turned in a fury to Bird Woman. 'What presence? What's Magio talking about?'

'This I cannot explain here and now. Suffice it to say that the situation is dangerous. I need to understand more. Eefa – please allow me this. Quimbre, you may take a walk, see if you can catch some food, if you don't want to hear this conversation. But there are things I must know in order to help the twins.'

'I'm going nowhere.'

'Very well! Then, please be patient while I ask Magio some questions about his relationship with his sister.'

Magio attempted to liberate himself from Quimbre's bearlike grip. 'Hey, Bird Woman! You mean that Eefa was made invisible because some enemy – some very powerful force – would have been looking for her from the day she was born?'

Quimbre snorted, but at a glance from Bird Woman he held his tongue.

'I just can't believe it. The very idea that poor Eefa has been forced to become invisible because of some . . . some horrible witch, or spectre!'

Eefa's voice fell, so it was barely audible. 'You weren't there, Magio. You weren't on the beach in that cove.'

'Maybe you were just sleepwalking? You've done it before.'

Bird Woman stopped them with an upraised hand. 'We shouldn't argue among ourselves. Eefa is still recovering from her shock.'

'Yeah. I'm sorry. I know she was really shocked when the Scogs wanted to take her, back in Warren. And then she was double shocked when you were able to see her.'

Eefa snorted. But Bird Woman hushed her. 'Let Magio speak. Tell us why Eefa was doubly shocked by that?'

'If you ask me, I think she was coming to believe that she wasn't just invisible but not really there at all. Like maybe she was just the results of my imagination. I mean, that's what Quimbre has always thought.'

'What do you mean?'

Eefa shouted, 'Enough!'

Bird Woman nodded to Magio. 'We shouldn't just focus on Eefa. Perhaps it is time we discovered more of who you both are. You must have fond memories of your childhood?'

Magio said, 'I do have some memories. But I can't be sure if they're real or I'm just imagining things from what I've been told by people like Gran and Quimbre.'

'Just tell me whatever you recall.'

'I have recurrent dreams of the sky lit up by flames, as if it were one huge bonfire. The ground was shaking from side to side. There were tall buildings whipping like they were caught in a great wind. Then the buildings began falling down.'

Magio began to shiver.

Bird Woman stopped Magio there. 'The wind is rising and we are all getting colder. Let's continue this conversation inside the shelter. If Quimbre wouldn't mind keeping guard a little longer?'

Quimbre seemed only too glad to be left to himself again as Bird Woman ushered Magio and Eefa out of the cold and wind. Then she carried on, in a soft voice, 'Do you recall anything of your parents?'

Magio shrugged. 'I recall bits – though again I could still be imagining things.' He hesitated, trying to think back. 'I have things that come back to me in dreams. Like going to places with a man that I think might have been my dad. There was some other island, definitely not Moon, where there were endless beaches. There were giant crabs that lived on land and not in the ocean. Fish of fantastic colours – I could see them swimming around a reef. I think my dad tried to teach me something about swimming under water.'

'Any memories of your mother?'

'The same – just bits and pieces. A tall woman with fair hair, like Eefa often imagines her own. She was wearing a blue swimsuit. I seem to remember her leaning back on a towel under the shade of palm trees and saying something like it was paradise.' Magio shrugged. 'But maybe Eefa is right and it's just me, hopefully dreaming.'

'Was Eefa always there, even when you were a child?'

'Always! We were inseparable.'

'Good.'

'We learnt things together. The way I figure it now is that whenever anybody taught me something – you know – the way people teach kids, she learnt from it by watching them teach me. And she's really clever. She's smarter than me. That's for sure. I'm the silly one, always getting into trouble.'

'You really cared for one another, I can see.'

'Yeah.'

'You're a very brave boy.'

Magio took a deep breath. 'Then tell me – who's this enemy?'

Bird Woman sighed. 'It isn't a person – not another person as you would be familiar with.'

'Who then?'

'Oh, Magio – there are forces you don't understand.'

'Then explain them to me – make me understand.'

'Maybe I will. When I have a better understanding of what is going on for myself. Now is not the time.'

'Hsst!'

Their conversation was interrupted by Quimbre, who was climbing to his feet. 'Stop all this blabbering! You're making too much noise!'

Quimbre was right. They had allowed themselves to grow overly excited, forgetting that they were still in danger. Over the horizon, that the sun was setting, lighting up the sky with spectacular livid mauves and splinters of silver. Even as they all peered up into the sky from behind Quimbre's bulky silhouette, the crepuscular shadows of evening were thickening. From Quimbre's stance he appeared to be listening.

'What is it?'

'Hsst!' He pressed a finger to his lips. 'Something . . .'

'The wind?'

Quimbre shook his head.

By now Bird Woman was also on her feet, joining Quimbre in listening closely, and then Magio and Eefa followed. All four of them turned from side to side, staring out into the gathering dusk.

And then they heard the howling, distant but unmistakeable, even against the noise of the wind.

Magio said, 'Wolves?'

'Not wolves.' Bird Woman shook her head.

'Wolf hounds,' Quimbre whispered. 'Hunters breed them. A cross between hunting hounds and wolves.'

'How close would you reckon?'

'A fair way yet. Maybe several miles.'

'You think they have our scent?'

'I reckon so, judging by the howling.'

'Quickly, Magio . . . Eefa! We must make ready to flee.'

'Aw, but we're so tired!'

'Sorry, kiddo. I know you're not rested enough.' Quimbre patted his head. 'But now you see that a good adventurer is always ready to run.'

Bird Woman spoke tersely. 'I have a potion that Magio and Eefa might share. It will help stave off fatigue. But there is no time to be lost. We must gather our blankets and tie up the bundles. Meanwhile, Quimbre, see if you can figure some way to divert those hounds from our trail.'

# The Die Is Cast

Khakhov, Grand Wizar of the Ursascogans, wandered with the aid of his gnarly walking stick through an extraordinary landscape, his mind weighed down with worrisome considerations. The Valley of the Smiths was elliptical in its geography, like a gigantic volcanic eye with the rim of an eccentric caldera forming the lids of the eye, while a pit of seething lava formed the pupil. Huge figures, stripped to loincloths of leathery pelt, laboured in this natural amphitheatre, their sweat-running torsos tattooed with the clan logos of the Six Smiths, which consisted of various artistries of hammers, pincers, eagles, stars, daggers, lances, swords and cannons. The elderly wizar's ears were filled with the groaning and clanking of the lifting machines, ferrying the cauldrons down into the magma and, when the ore was molten, ferrying them back up again. Smiths were pitching the floating slag out of dozens of immense cauldrons, themselves aglow with the same fierce intensity as the crackling broiling metal, before being gripped on either side by huge gauntlered fists and carried to the moulds. Elsewhere forges blazed around a variety of red-glowing metals, which were being hammered over the rounded curves of monstrous anvils. Khakov had to step aside as two burly figures – their tattoos identifying them as Clan of Brass – rushed past him ferrying a crucible of molten metal. With a series of loud clanks, they fitted massive pins to the waiting flanges on a scaffold, built of oak trunks, then hoisted the crucible above the waiting mould, and, all in a continuing ballet of movement, poured the molten cataract into the receptacle.

The wizar observed their efforts with close attention, his eyes narrowed against the sizzling and sparking flare. A frenzy of such activity had gone on through the night and it was nearing completion as the first light of dawn illuminated the pallid sky above the eye, mixing with the smoky mists of the smiths' labours. It seemed to Khakhov that there was a stranger magic here than even the Smiths took for granted. A magic beyond the lore of melting ore into a watery river of bright red and yellow flow that would reveal itself as glittering metal on cooling.

What he was sensing here, sensing more than seeing in the heavy labours in the hallowed valley, was the beginnings of a change – perhaps a very great change – and it filled his bones with foreboding. Conservative by nature, Khakov knew he could not predict the outcome of that change. So alarmed was he by that uncertainty that he had to pause to allow the racing of his heartbeat to settle. It had all begun with that unpleasant business of the execution-by-sacrifice of the royal prince, Igorpogra. A father of sixteen sons and grandfather of sixty-four, the wizar had been profoundly shocked by that sacrifice.

Khakov was so deeply immersed in his thoughts that he was almost run over by the Iron Smiths, rushing by with an enormous craft with eighteen wheels, fashioned of oaks and cased in iron. He read their clan from the tattoos, with wingspread eagles over their pectorals. Youthful Iron Smiths! The clan had a reputation for innovation to the point of foolhardiness. Khakov tapped his stick on the stone floor with irritation at the near miss as one of them, a coral-eyed god of size and muscle, bent on one knee before him and attempted to explain.

'Forgive us, Grand Wizar. The Clan of Wood has constructed this mighty vehicle for the transportation of the Leviathan.'

'You have built this great carriage for the Bronze Smiths, who are resurrecting the Leviathan of legend?'

'Yes, Holy Master.'

The lad's apology only slowly penetrated through Khakov's ire. His gaze only vaguely followed the rolling monstrosity as it travelled on, to be lost in the melee of forging, casting and construction.

*Could it possibly be true?*

The wizar was inclined to laugh with utter disbelief.

*The Leviathan of Legend!*

It was an insane notion. The wizar doubted that any such weapon had ever existed. It was a myth, such as the cognoscenti knew – a myth invented to give the masses hope and some semblance of pride during the troubled times. But the very notion of such a myth becoming reality was too much even to think about. King Wirgnatha had worked the masses into a fury of indignation and vengeance. His people had plenty of reasons for resentment at the hurt and indignity visited on them by the humans over many generations. He too was sensitive to that hurt. Wizars must be sensitive to the feelings of the masses. But what he was witnessing here worried him more deeply than any of the usual problems of illness, infertility, jealousies and intrigues. He sensed it again at the very core of his being: that unsettling sense of change. His people were entering a process of ambition so perilous . . . it arrested his perambulation, his heartbeat once again irregular, uncomfortably fast.

He thought, *This is more than the usual insurrection. It . . . it is war . . . open war between the Ursascogans and humans.*

He shivered with that thought. He must speak again with Wirgnatha. But would His Royal Majesty take any notice of his advice? A king who had sacrificed his own son contrary to Khakov's measured advice?

His thoughts were interrupted by another bedlam of thundering.

For several moments, through the flares of light and the hammering, Khakov reconsidered the plight of the queen, Pittaquera.

He was deeply troubled by Pittaquera's distress following the brutal killing of her firstborn son. Had the king taken her into his considerations when he gave the execution order? Though Pittaquera affected to disbelieve it, Khakov knew that the king was right in concluding that the prince had been plotting against his father. Even so, the wizar had counselled Wirgnatha against such drastic punishment. Pittaquera came from a distinguished lineage. Such shedding of royal blood would inevitably lead to division within the royal household.

But when Khakov had offered advice into the seated Wirgnatha's ear, the king had whispered the strangest explanation.

'There is a voice in my head, Wizar, and it instructs me as to what I must do.'

'A voice in your head, sire?'

The king had nodded. His bulging eyes had lifted to glance up at the holy man and in that moment Khakov had glimpsed . . . fear.

Even as he remembered that fateful conversation, the wizar had to protect his hearing with his cupping hands as another massive explosion of force erupted out of the pit, releasing a rush of hot foul-smelling air that singed his eyebrows. What was he doing wandering amidst this dreadful cacophony? He wiped his brow with the fine silken sleeve of his right forearm. And then, to his surprise, he heard a voice inside his own head:

*You are not alone. There are others who agree with you.*

Khakov stood where he was, his limbs paralysed. A voice had spoken to him inside his head. He didn't believe that voices could speak to him inside his head rather than through his ears. The unfortunate truth, and one he had been obliged to conceal for all of his vocational life, was that he didn't believe in supernatural forces. His entire life as Grand Wizar had been a lie – but he hoped it had been a lie mitigated by the fact that he performed his duty because he deeply cared for his people. He had made it his life's contribution to interpret the parables to condemn stupidity and crime, to extol kindness and caring, and by extension, to encourage his flock to care for and alleviate the omnipresent poverty, suffering and grief.

A voice in his head?

He halted in his perambulation, mesmerised, to discover that his stroll had brought him to the very epicentre of whatever was happening on this strange and disquieting morning. The king had just arrived. He was seated on a wooden platform, ringed by his court and protected by heavily armoured warriors. Wirgnatha appeared somewhat confused, like one who found himself waiting for something to happen – something perhaps that had been the subject of the voices in his head.

What could it be?

From around the wizar came the bedlam of hundreds of voices, all roaring out at once, and made worse by the echoing calderas of black rock that hemmed in the valley. It was impossible for him to hear his own thoughts. He reconsidered those perplexing words of that voice inside his head.

*There are others who agree with you.*

The wizar was feeling somewhat confused himself.

*What others?*

He asked the question even though he had no idea of what this mental conversation could possibly signify. Such was the confusion now raging within him that all he could do was observe what was happening.

There was no answer.

Somewhat panicky again, he closed his eyes, inhaled deeply, then exhaled as slowly as he could manage. Then he opened his eyes again and gazed about him at the expectant faces of all who were gathered in the valley about him. The first clear rays of sunshine were beginning to invade it from the great eye in the sky. The activity of the smiths appeared close to completion. But what great scheme was about to be revealed? What could be so special as to conjure up voices in the royal head? Was it really possible that some new lore, some forbidden knowledge, was about to be unveiled?

A shadow appeared before him, condensing to a tall being that was gazing down at him from a shrouded face. He recognized its form as quintessentially female. But her face was impossible to make out.

*You know me, Holy One?*

Here, without doubt, was the source of that voice inside his head.

Her form appeared to condense further from a kaleidoscope of colours until she appeared before him, effulgent with power. But her face remained hidden beneath a veil that concealed her face. All he could make out was those terrible eyes. In that same moment, an instinct told him that he should avert his gaze before he lost his soul. But he was unable to do so. He gaped into their glowing emerald, knowing that this was the same being that had risen from the sacrificial pit of fire in the ground, in all of her glory. She was Lustfera, the Star of Mourning.

'My Lady!'

She gazed down at him for several moments in silence. Then she spoke, little above a whisper, but her words penetrated his mind like the cut of a barber surgeon's lance. *'I have been observing you in your peregrinations. I have entered your mind and listened to your closeted ruminations.'*

The sounds of the blazing wells, the hammering, the roars of smiths, appeared to recede. It was as if his very being was enveloped by silence.

*'You, who affected to be spiritual counsellor to your people, would appear to have lost the faith. You no longer believe in the gods.'*

The wizar bowed deeply. 'I confess that my heart was troubled, my mind confused. But your manifestation among us has restored my faith. I am consumed with contrition and self-loathing. Would you have me kneel?'

*'I am not the one you should kneel before.'*

'Who then?'

*'I am the servant of the Master. He who is known as The One. He, indeed, who is now weighing you in the balance.'*

The wizar fell to his arthritic knees, attempting to suppress the wince of pain. 'Ask of me whatever you desire. What would your master have of me?'

CଛR

The Star of Mourning observed the old Ursascogan as he knelt on the stony ground, with his head bowed. She didn't trust him. How could one trust a wizar who no longer believed in the gods? And yet the Ursascogans had enormous faith in the old man.

*'You appear to be troubled by doubts and conscience. I hope you will not prove a disappointment. I should caution you that there are others who would delight in taking your place, should the need arise.'*

'My Lady – such will not prove necessary. I have endeavoured all of my life to be a true servant to the powers.'

She laughed, a throaty sound. Her laughter must have rung out like thunder in his head. *'Have a care, old man, if you would seek to play games with me.'*

'You see me as naïve?'

*'Naïve you most certainly are. You are Ursascogan after all, though wise in that company. The Ursascogans possesses unusual physical strength. Yet it is a strength that has ever led them nowhere. Be grateful to The One that on his most holy behalf do I offer to guide you.'*

'Guide us? How, My Lady?'

*'I would confer the wisdom and power you need to prevail against the human enemy.'*

A crescendo of cheering from the multitude interrupted her conversation with the wizar. Her attention shifted to the sweat-soaked giants, hauling their castings out of the templates. There were squeals from the winches as enormous weights were hauled out of the moulds. Then a renewed thunder of hammering, hot metal being doused in water, clouds of steam arising from the hissing metal.

The old man's mouth had fallen open and his eyes were opened wide.

*'Why so shocked? You have seen moulds emerge from castings before.'*

'Indeed, I have. But none so remarkable as this.'

He was familiar with casting cannons of bronze, which his people had produced for the humans in ages past. Yet, through his eyes, she read deep puzzlement in the emerging shapes, and even more so of their likely fitting together into one enormous construction.

*'You begin to comprehend?'*

'If it is what I can hardly dare to imagine, I am astonished.'

*'And what might you hardly dare to imagine?'*

'That you have brought into being the Leviathan of legend?'

*'I pity your small imagination, and its petty fears. Soon what you hardly dare to imagine will become manifest in the coming war with the humans. Then will you be in a position to judge for your timid self.'*

# A Breath of Gold

She has endured the latest storm and observed the movements of the sea as it settled, and even as she did so, morning turned to midday, and then to night and still she endures. She has endured in mortal terms as days turned to weeks and weeks to months, years, decades, millennia. She has endured an endless litany of winters so she could anticipate the arrival of spring. The seasons are limited here, in the barren heat. Yet winter inevitably falls and spring does come. She emerges from the rusting iron walls to gaze down on the first wild flowers, widely separated because of the desert climate, each diamond-encrusted with dew. It is ever her pleasure to study them closely, the drought-resistant leaves, the tiny petals; at times she is inclined to take pleasure in allowing her flesh to be penetrated by their lancinating thorns. So is she content to sit before her prison, in her clanking chains, to observe balmy summer days and the violence of winter storms, to become one with the shifting seasons of this world's moods, the extraordinary range of colours that glow within the core of its being, its love-hate intercourse with light and sky?

*'Did you realise that you allowed me these comforts?'*

She senses the anger her words provoke.

*'Some whispered, perhaps to comfort me, that you were defeated. But I was not so foolish as to believe it. Not with the depths of malice in you. Defeat would have required surrender. And you were never one to surrender, any more than you were*

*capable of forgiveness. So, I offended you. I offended you deeply. I created that anger in you. I do not contend that my sentence was unjust. Yet even such a deserved fate must surely come to an end? It was said that you found defeat in battle with Mechi, son of the Morrigu. I knew it could not be so. It was also said that the battle took place on the summit of mountains and moved to the deeps of the oceans, then in the air above the lights of ice, only ending in the blue-black wastes that hold the stars in their embrace. All lies. I recognised the lies even as they were spoken. It was said that after your defeat that you were buried standing erect in the core of the sun and that, once buried, there followed a period when day turned to night and night turned to day. None of this did I then, or do I still, believe.*

*'You are too deep, too formidably cunning, to place your fate in the whim of the great crow of battle, Mórígán.*

*'I know that you have infinite lores of survival. I know also that I have heard your curses in my ears, carried on the gale. I knew how obdurate you would be, from the very beginning. How even after your people were beaten in battle, you refused to bend the knee to the sons of Miled. You were obliged to run to Magrann, knowing he understood every enchantment, and would cloak your continuing existence within walls of magic. All this do I know, as I know that you had some part in Magrann's own downfall. How clever of you, coveting his lore of magic and ultimately stealing it for yourself.*

*'Why then should I be surprised at your enduring cruelty? Yes, I betrayed you. Was any betrayal more bitterly punished?*

*'If there was reason for my betrayal it was your unbearable arrogance and possessiveness. Your overweening jealousy at my popularity with others, and yes, at my growing list of admirers. Was your anger at my infidelity such that you must punish me*

*thus, she who professed to love you for eternity, to be tormented instead for that same duration?*

*'Very well – but know you that even walls of magic have their weaknesses. And even as I have endured you as my eternal enemy, so too will you come to endure me as that same foe. Some yet profess to love me – yes, they still exist – and as they grow stronger may they disturb your peace, as you surely have ravaged mine.*

*'Are you so arrogant as to assume that your subjugation of me has gone unnoticed? Do I not have family and beloved friends among the Undying, powerful allies who have never ceased to search for my release? Do you sense at this very moment the rising imbalance of the elements that herald apocalypse?*

*'Oh, so sweetly do I sense it even upon the comfort of the waves in the cold clear moonlight, those who love me, those who would comfort me with whispers of release and revenge, my comfort on the waves.*

She sighs.

*'And now, it would appear, you have attempted to tilt the game in your favour, entering the world of the mortals and thus breaking every rule of nobility.*

His answering voice is carried in a rolling thunder.

*'THERE ARE NO RULES. YOU WERE EVER THE FOOL, RELYING ON SUCH SENTIMENTALITY.'*

His voice . . . his overbearing voice once more tearing through her consciousness . . . yet still his voice only for a second time in the torment of aeons.

Has he she done something to arouse his fury anew?

How dearly she hopes so!

*'I have done with you. I have done with your torment, and perverted games. I shall bury my spirit in the depths of the oceans.'*

No reply.

But now she is sure that he is listening: has been listening to every tormented word.

Even so, despite the aeons of degradation and cruelty, she feels the rebellious soul rise in her.

*'I would die there, in the depths of the ocean, rather than present you with any further satisfaction.'*

No reply.

She needs none. He is listening, watching, drunk with the satisfaction of her torment.

She drags on the chains to allow her to move to the edges of the lapping waves. There she drags them further. She is rewarded by a slackening. He would witness her wade into the ocean. She wades further. Immediately her legs are awash and swarming with the little things, the crabs, and small fish, the sea urchins and starfish, which in a multitude nibble at her flesh. But she ignores these simple lives. She hauls some more, wading deeper.

Larger beasts are now gliding by her. Dangerous beings. She has no fear of them. She hauls again, to find her body immersed beneath the waves. She is descending into the depths of the ocean, knowing that here she will discover a ravine that goes dizzyingly deep. She has visited these parts before.

Is he still watching, laughing?

She knows that he is.

She wades on and on, until she arrives at the edge of the abyss, whereupon she steps into it without a moment's hesitation.

She has anticipated that he is lost in exultation at this new torment. And in his glee lies her opportunity.

As she tumbles into the utter dark of the deeps, she catches the glimmer she has been anticipating even deeper still. She gauges her arrival and then closes, tight shut, her eyes. Only at the perfect moment does she open them again, opens wide her every sense. She is drowning in a constellation of fairy lights, the sweetest of nature's own magic. And she knows that he sees this too: he will be lost in the wonder of it for that briefest of moments. In that same briefest of moments, the constellation of fairy lights emits a golden glow, which she captures as a whisper in her cupped hands, then takes it in a whisper to her heart.

*We have readied the Bree Salis . . .*

All in that same distracted moment, the fairy lights are extinguished, and with them, the whisper is lost to the ocean.

# HUNTED

Magio was woken up by the squeeze of his sister's arms about him in the dark of the cave where they had made camp. Her hair was in his eyes, wisps drifting between his teeth. She was crying aloud in a panic. He was close to panicking himself in response and had to pull her hair away to breathe.

'What is it?'

'Oh, Magio!' She was panting for breath.

'What?' He was still half asleep, blinking himself awake as the dawn filled the large chamber with a faint milky light.

'A nightmare!'

'Hey!' He shook himself free to kneel opposite her. 'A nightmare?'

'It was really terrifying – so frightening!'

'What . . .'

'I dreamt I was dead.'

'Oh – jinxy!'

'Yeah!' She was still trying to calm down her breathing. 'I . . . I was on a beach of stones. There was this place, this hut – oh, Magio, it was really horrible. It was built out of black slabs of iron. Like a prison made out of massive plates from some dead ship. Uggh!' She couldn't stop herself shivering.

'But that's my dream!'

'No! It wasn't like you described it at all. The sea was raging – in a terrible fury. Waves lashing me, and the . . . the iron thing . . . and then . . .' Eefa hunched up her shoulders. She began to tremble and shake.

'It's all right. You're here. You're safe.'

'The feeling . . . oh, Magio, the feeling was so awful.'

'It wasn't real – you're here in the cave.'

'Then a huge wave struck. I went under the wave, deep under the sea.' Eefa cried out. 'I went right down, deep down. I thought I was dead.'

Magio began to shiver himself.

Eefa sobbed. 'I had something in my hands. I was holding something golden in my hands. It was like an egg, but so light and glimmering, it could have been made of smoke. And yet I knew that what I was holding was my life. I was right down there at the bottom of the ocean and I was holding my life in my hands.'

'It was just a dream.'

'No!'

She was holding her hands out to him, right now, as if she were holding something invisible in them about the size of a gourd.

He didn't know what to think.

'Then, I was here. Here in my blanket, covered in sweat.' Eefa lifted up her eyes to meet his. 'But still the dream felt utterly real.'

Magio blinked his eyes, staring at Eefa's face, staring at her cupped hands and thinking about the old woman he had seen in his own dreams, the old woman shackled to an iron monstrosity on the beach.

Then Eefa's voice changed. It fell so it was deeper, yet gentle and soft. It really didn't sound like Eefa at all.

*'You must find it and bring it to me.'*

'What?'

*'You must find the Bree Salis – find it and bring it to me.'*

Magio shook Eefa's shoulders. 'What are you talking about?'

Eefa's eyes were blinking, her entire being trembling. 'I don't know what's happening, Magio.'

He took a deep breath. 'Hey – maybe Bird Woman might know.'

'Oh, Magio! The world is going crazy. Nothing makes sense any more.'

He hugged her and she let him do so. It was so unusual, Eefa who hated to be hugged or mollycoddled. But he could see what she was saying was true. As far as he could see, nothing did make sense any more.

They heard a hushed whisper from Quimbre, from just inside the entrance to the cave, where he had been setting some kind of a trap. 'Hey – kiddo. Keep it down! Remember – dawn is breaking and our hunter is out there, and he has those hounds.'

Magio took Eefa's icy cold hand and hauled her to the cave mouth, curious to discover what was really going on. 'Where's Bird Woman gone?'

Quimbre ceased from chopping at what looked like a blackened beam of oak that he must have found in the cave. In the vague light, it was possible to see that Quimbre had rolled up his shirt sleeves, exposing muscular forearms proliferating with tattoos of porpoises, whales, mermaids and sea dragons all over the nut-brown skin. He had been shaping the beam with hacks of his cutlass to fit into a slit he had cut in another beam. Quimbre put the sword and beams aside to stroke his moustache. 'I don't rightly know where she went – only that she was scouting things out. You can see for yourself what it's like out there. She told me this place is called Ayatini, which means "the misty marshes".' Quimbre wiped his nose on the rolled-up sleeve of his left arm. 'Me – I hope it's food she is scouting. My belly is rumbling.'

All of their bellies were rumbling. They had long finished off the two rabbits Bird Woman had trapped in the desert. And now that the sun was rising above the horizon, Magio could see what Quimbre meant. It was their first morning in Ayatini and it seemed that the place deserved its spooky name.

Magio whispered to Eefa, 'Hey – it's still light enough to explore the cave. There's a tunnel back there. We've just got to find out where it leads to.'

'Not if Quimbre says we shouldn't.'

He knew that Eefa was still too spooked by her dream to want to explore the cave. But at the same time, he guessed that she didn't want Magio to leave her on her own.

'Hey, Quimbre – I'm just going to explore the cave at the back.'

Quimbre had already returned to whatever he was constructing in the entrance and he didn't bother to answer.

'C'mon, Eefa!'

She reluctantly agreed. 'All right. I'm coming with you – but only to make sure you don't go wandering too far.'

'Maybe we can light a torch?'

'No torch!' Quimbre shouted out from behind them before returning to his trap-making.

'We just want to explore.'

'No lights, kiddo! Don't forget we have a hunter on our tail!'

'But it's too misty out there for anybody to see.'

'No torch. And you don't explore far. Bird Woman will soon be back and we could be heading out of here in a hurry.'

'Aw!'

'You promise me, kiddo?'

He sniffed. 'Ooookaaaay!'

'And no scarpering! You take your time. Stay all the while where old Quimbre can see you. Agreed?'

Magio was already off and running, with Eefa in pursuit. He was heading for a bend in the tunnel. Eefa just about got close enough to grab hold of his shirt before he got lost in deeper shadows.

She tugged at him. 'Stop! Oh, look! Wow – what is that?'

'What?'

'Look there! I think that's fossilised manure.'

'Oh – britzy!'

Eefa wrinkled her nose at it, even though it hardly stank at all.

Magio spun his head. 'You feel that? There must be another opening.'

'Feel what?'

'There's a draught. Can't you feel it?'

'Yes. I can.'

'I think the draught is really blowing this way. It must be coming from deeper back in the cave.'

'Don't you go exploring!'

'We've just got to!' Magio couldn't hide the excitement in his voice. 'It must mean another opening – a second way out, up ahead?'

'You heard what Quimbre told you. Don't you even dare!'

'Scaredy cat!'

'Oh, Magio . . .!'

'What?'

'Look here!'

Magio halted his impulse to explore further to join her in examining what looked like a heap of bones. 'I think those are feathers.'

Eefa halted. She brushed aside cobwebs to discover what appeared to be a giant skull. 'Yeah – and that's some beak.'

'It's huge.'

'Has to be a bird. Like some king of a giant bird.'

'Britzy!'

Even Eefa was impressed. 'It must have been like one of those giant birds Quimbre talked about in his sea stories.'

Quimbre had always been a mine of stories about the archipelago of islands, known as the Sea of Stars, of which Moon was only a single island, and according to Quimbre, rather a boring example. Quimbre had spent many a winter's evening regaling them with his adventures in sailing the Sea of Stars, ever since he was a boy on his father's sailing ship. Battles with giant sea creatures that had given him the scar on the side of his brow, or the ramming of a rogue ship that was blazing back at them with a solid wall of brass cannons – it was that battle that had left Quimbre with his slight limp.

She urged him, 'Let's go show him the skull.'

'Yeah!'

In his excitement about the bird skull, Magio forgot about exploring the deeper cave. They ran back to the cave entrance, hugging their newly discovered trophies.

Quimbre was looking their way, with an expectant grin on his face, alerted by Magio's excitement.

'Look, Quimbre! What do you think? Do you think it was one of those birds that were too monstrous to fly?'

'Well, now – we got ourselves a mystery, huh?' Quimbre shrugged those huge shoulders and he put aside his preparations. He laughed. 'Hey – you can tell me about your discoveries. The trap is just about ready anyway.'

'What trap?'

'Quimbre's little surprise for this hunter and his hounds when they come hunting for you an' me. There's only one way in, which is this here cave mouth.' He acted the scene, where a hunter, crouching low, encounters a sudden shock. 'I've prepared a little shock for him. But never mind. Tell us about your discovery.'

Magio and the invisible Eefa sat down next to where Quimbre had earlier gathered kindling to light a fire. In the flickering light, Magio handed him the strange skull.

'A skull – yeah! That's what it is for sure. But what a big one, huh!'

Magio whooped. 'A giant one! Like the giants you fought in your stories.'

'Could be – could most certainly be! Now that would be something, huh? Perhaps later, when Bird Woman comes back, and maybe we fill those hungry bellies around the fire, Old Quimbre will tell you another story about those birds.' Quimbre reached out to ruffle Magio's hair. But then he halted his arm, suddenly spun round, at the same time raising his hand to silence them.

'Hush! Somebody's coming!'

He was on his feet in a flash, the flintlock pistol in his hand, already cocked. He waved them deeper into the cave while he took up a position next to the opening.

The heard a single bird-call, like the cooing of a dove, before a shadow slipped through the cave entrance in the glimmer of imminent dawn.

Quimbre heaved a sigh of relief, standing aside for Bird Woman to pass him by, with a shiny trophy wrapped up in a handmade basket of river reeds.

'I see you struck lucky.'

'A good-sized rainbow.'

Eefa grinned at Magio. 'She's caught us a fish.'

⊗

Nobody talked about fossil bones or iron shacks or cave explorations. They were just too famished to think of anything other than food. Eefa and Magio watched every move as Quimbre – who had quickly blocked off the entrance to the cave, so the light of the fire would not show through – cleaned and then filleted the fish. They helped him fix a couple of makeshift tripods so they could barbecue the bloody meat. Quimbre seemed to have forgotten his earlier promise of a story; rather he immediately took his due portion so he could return to finishing his trap at the entrance; meanwhile Bird Woman came over to sit, straddle-legged, next to Magio and Eefa around the fire.

At length, when they had satisfied their hunger, the children told Bird Woman about their discovery of the giant bird bones.

'We were just exploring the cave, weren't we, Eefa?'

'Yes. But I didn't let him go in too far.'

Magio turned around to see why Quimbre was huffing and puffing, and saw him lift a big rock into the mechanism of his trap. He shouted out, 'We found some great bones, didn't we, Quimbre?'

'Sure, kiddo. But hush! Keep it quiet!'

Eefa elbowed him to make him aware of Quimbre's warning. But he was too excited about their discovery. He showed the huge bird skull to Bird Woman. 'Hey – take a look at that.'

Bird Woman laughed as she examined the skull. 'You're absolutely right. It is the skull of a very big bird. Also, a very old one, even if not quite old enough to be changed to stone. From the beak, I'd say it hunted fish and crabs in the shallows. Well spotted.' She nodded, but she seemed somewhat distracted.

'What is it?' Eefa pressed her.

'We must hurry. Eat quickly. Save some of the cooked fish for later. But get our belongings packed and ready to leave.'

'Did you see who's hunting us?'

'No. But I heard the hounds.' She reached out and patted Magio's knee in a comforting way, because of the expression on his face. 'Quimbre is right to set his trap. We must employ tricks to shake them off. There are ways that hounds can be led astray. But one thing we really can't afford is to let them get within sight of us.'

'Tell her,' Magio urged his sister.

'Tell me what?' Bird Woman was looking straight at her, those large grey eyes openly curious.

'We're probably being silly.'

'No, we're not,' Magio countered her. 'Eefa and me, we've been frightened by a dream.'

'A dream?'

'More like a nightmare in my case,' Eefa said.

'The strange thing is, like, we're having the same dream – or maybe different versions of the same dream.'

'A common dream – or a nightmare?' Bird Woman's voice was calm, but also insistent. 'You must tell me everything you remember – every detail!'

The twins did their best to recall all that they remembered of the dream of the old woman who was bound by chains to that forlorn iron hut. Bird Woman had climbed to her feet even as she was listening, packing for leaving. She was leaning on her long bow, using it as staff, when she looked down from one of them to the other, where they were still sitting, cross-legged by the dying fire.

'So – it does appear to be a common dream. A dream – or a nightmare – about the same old woman, who appears to be manacled to iron chains, or next to some sort of prison cell of rusting iron . . . And today, Eefa, you saw her for the first time? And she was reaching out, holding something in her cupped hands?'

'Yes.'

Bird Woman's eyes narrowed and she held up a hand to Quimbre, who had come back to get ready for leaving.

'You finished the trap?'

'Yeah. Primed and ready. We must go now.'

Bird Woman nodded to Quimbre. 'Just a moment, please. I must ask Magio and Eefa a single question. What was in the old woman's hands?'

'It looked like a big golden egg,' Magio said.

'No,' Eefa corrected him, in a subdued voice, 'it wasn't as solid as an egg. It was egg-shaped, and golden, but made of skeins as light as smoke.'

'Did she say what it was called?'

'Yes, she did,' Eefa said. 'She called it by a very strange name. She called it the Bree Salis.'

Bird Woman stiffened. 'The Bree Salis?'

'Yes.'

'What did you make of this, Eefa? What did you feel – sense?'

'I felt an intense urge, like something I could not ignore. I had to find it – find it and then bring it to her.'

Bird Woman's brow rose to a mess of wrinkles. Her grey eyes widened, reflecting the spluttering residual flame of the fire.

'What is the Bree Salis?'

'The Bree Salis – it's an ancient term, found in myths and legends. I doubt that folks these days would consider it anything other than fantasy. A power in myths that deal with resurrection.'

'Resurrection of what?'

'Oh, dear – it would appear that I have answered a puzzle with yet another enigma. During the metamorphosis of the butterfly, or the moth, such delightful beings begin life as an egg. That egg hatches as a caterpillar, so we already have a mystery. But then the caterpillar ends its existence by sealing itself away in a kind of shell we call the pupa. What you might not know is that inside the pupa the caterpillar's body melts. The ancients regarded this as a metaphor for death, since what re-emerges from the pupa is a transformed being, resplendent with its new capacity for flight through its beautiful wings, and its extraordinary compound eyes.'

'I still don't understand.'

'The emergence of the butterfly is a kind of rebirth, giving rise to an utterly new being – a mystical reincarnation.'

'It's just a story?'

'The ancients believed that death, for us humans, was a similar process. We entered a period of pupa-like quietude, returning to the dust we were born of. But then, when the Undying gods thought it appropriate, we might be reborn in a similar wonder of rebirth. That rebirth is the Bree Salis.'

They looked at her, transfixed.

Eefa's voice shook. 'But why would the old woman speak of this to me?'

'Therein lies the mystery.' Bird Woman appeared to take a big breath. She smiled and ruffled Magio's hair with playful affection. 'But I fear that we have passed too much time discussing the mystery. We must hurry now – get ready to go.'

Magio didn't want to just go right now. He wanted to understand. 'You think this Bree Salis is something to do with what the dreams mean?'

'This I don't really know. Oh, Magio, I wish that I fully understood the mysteries. But unfortunately, I don't.'

Just then Quimbre whistled to hush them. They looked in startlement to where he was waving them to silence. He had a hand to his ear, as if urging them all to listen hard.

When they did so they heard a howling.

'We have to run!'

Quimbre shook his head. 'We cannot go back out there. The wolf hounds will immediately pick up our scent.'

'What then?'

'You and Magio – go hide in the cave. Go – no more talking of mysteries! I'll make a stand to give you time.'

'No!' Magio cried. 'You can't fight them on your own, Quimbre.'

'Go now!'

Magio stared up defiantly into Bird Woman's face. 'It isn't right. There's another way. There's another way out of the cave. I felt the wind on my face.'

Bird Woman stared at him, eye to eye. She spun to face Eefa. 'Did you feel it too? A draught on your face?'

'I – I think so. Magio is much better at spotting these things. Quimbre used to play games with him. Hunting and exploring . . .'

Bird Woman grabbed several flaming branches from the fire to fashion into a firebrand. 'Quickly – take me to where you felt this draught?' She spun to address Quimbre before following Magio's running feet. 'Come with us!'

'I follow. You run!'

They were all running, Magio, Eefa and Bird Woman, through the twisting labyrinth of the cave in the spluttering light of the firebrand.

'Here – here! I can feel it – the draught.'

'You lead us, Magio!'

'What about Quimbre?'

'Quimbre will know what best to do.'

The firebrand burnt out as they ran on for what seemed a mile but was probably just a hundred yards or two before Magio felt the draught suddenly grow weaker on his face.

'We've gone wrong. We must have passed it by.'

'What?'

'We must have passed by an opening off this tunnel.'

They retraced their steps, now in the pitch dark, still hurrying, frantically feeling their way along the walls of the tunnel.

It was Magio again who found the fissure, extremely narrow, and off to one side. 'Let me try it,' he insisted, letting go of Bird Woman's hand, and squeezing through. Behind them they heard the barking and howling as the hounds found the entrance.

'Quickly! Follow me!'

Even as Eefa and Bird Woman squeezed through after Magio, there was a terrific crack and then the rumble of falling stones.

'Oh, poor Quimbre! I hope he's all right.'

But Bird Woman was not waiting to find out. They forced their bodies through another tight squeeze, with thick foul-smelling dust filling the air and clogging up their noses and throats, before they emerged onto the cold fresh air of the top of a headland, bathed in thick mist. Bird Woman searched in her pack for some plant to put off scenting hounds when a shadow burst out of the fissure behind them, causing their hearts to pound.

At the same time, they heard an anguished roar from the beach far below – a roar, followed by cursing, a deep-throated voice uttering threats over and over and over. It was accompanied by a dreadful howling.

The figure shook itself to reveal the grinning Quimbre, covered in the smelly dust and spiders' webs of the cave. 'Sounds like my trap was a success. I reckon there's one less of his mangy hounds.'

'Good old Quimbre!'

Quimbre extended his dusty fist so Magio could touch fists with him. 'What say you, kiddo – britzy, huh?'

Magio hugged him as, with a grin, Quimbre accepted a rag from Bird Woman to wipe the dust from his bearded face. He looked down into the mist and spoke thoughtfully. 'This hunter – he will not stop – just because he has lost a hound.'

Magio joined Quimbre in staring down into the thick mist. 'Oh, Bird Woman – what do you think?'

'Quimbre is right. So, we hurry on, taking every precaution. Our first priority is we find fresh water. We are on the banks of a small river, so we can wash off the dust off our hides, and out of our hair, and out of our ears and nostrils. Then we wade for a distance through water, heading inland against the stream. It will help to hide our scent from the pack.'

# No More A-Whinin

For several minutes Bastos Kull was still so bewildered with grief that thinking clearly just wasn't possible. He found himself roaring again like a mindless brute at the blocked-off entrance to the cave, squatting on his interlocked legs, rocking backwards and forwards, with the hound's broken body, still warm, across his lap, her head against his breast. He had been misled into thinking this hunt routine. An old man, a woman, and two brats! The green-eyed seducer had spun him a yarn about his quarry. It had led to overconfidence on his part and that had cost him in blood. Now he needed to control his rage and stop his useless roaring into the misty dawn. The quarry was, likely, on the run. Since there was no question of them emerging from the blocked-up entrance it suggested that there was a second opening to the cave.

Kull had stripped himself of his yew bow, placing it carefully against a ledge. He had also unburdened himself of the twin-headed axe, so he could squat more comfortably and examine the body he had hauled back out of the tumbled entrance to the cave. He retained his belt, and the sheathed daggers, though he considered it unlikely he would need them here. Maw and Claw were whining and growling, like they were impatient to be casting.

'The quarry will keep!'

Instead Kull gazed down onto the crushed and bloodied corpse of his firstborn cub, Fang. The pang of grief rose in him again until it was overwhelming. He had trained her from that first whiny ball of fur to do his bidding, and she had rewarded him by growing into a heart of furious purpose.

'Served ole Bastos well, you did, me fierce gal!'

His tear-misted eyes traced the damage done by the heavy fall of rock: the broken and distorted front legs and the crushed skull. That cunning keystone in the trap had done the damage, driving her huge canine teeth right through the grey-brown fur of her cheeks.

'Well, now – we be learning more o' this quarry!'

Kull took a long deep suck of air through dilated nostrils, then exhaled a noseful of snot with an expert squeeze of his thumb and forefinger.

That roof fall in the entrance hadn't killed Fang by accident. It was calculated through and through . . . The cunning resourcefulness of one of um!

Kull clenched his teeth at the thought of that.

'Gotto be at least one fighter among the four, more'n likely the old man.' He now corrected his mental image of the four: one experienced fighter for sure, the woman, said to be conniving, and the two brats, one of them said to be invisible! 'We gotto fix that into us head, so we don't make the mistake o' underestimating um again.'

The tone of his voice was exciting Maw and Claw, and their pitiful whining would tell the quarry their location. Correction . . . the enemy . . .

*The enemy!*

Well, now, that was a new consideration.

Was Bastos Kull, the greatest hunter in all of Moon, to stop thinking of a quarry as such and think of them anew as an enemy?

'Hush – hush now, me bootiful gals! We got to box clever! No more a-whinin' from you, and no more a-howlin'! What we gotto do is start over. We be taking no confidence for granted. We start again. Believe nothin' we been told about this particular quarry. And we trust nobody, least of all that liar what hired us in the first place.'

He sat back a few more moments and reconsidered the situation. Yeah – the enemy – and that rather than quarry was what they now was! And likely they'd be running even as he thought!

The logical course was to abandon Fang's corpse and continue the chase. But more personal instincts, family instincts, persuaded him otherwise.

'Fang was fambly – fambly comes first.'

Kull decided that he had no worries about catching up with the enemy. 'We'll track um down, gals. And when we do, we'll take us revenge.'

Kull rocked a final goodbye, hugging the great broken head, brushing his unshaven cheeks against her bloodied flesh and bone. Fang's body was big – the biggest of the three. Her head was as long as his arm from elbow to fingertips. A drip of snot dropped from his tear-filled nostrils as he hacked with his serrated knife through the bones of her chest.

He spoke softly. 'Gone you be, me darling – gone altogether. No more a-hunkerin' up to Papa, like when you whimpered and cried after I fed you the proud strong heart of your own mama.'

And what a bitch of a battle that had been!

'Your mama, she was fixed on tearing the throat out of Papa, even after I'd gone and put three arrows into her. She surely was a storm of fang and claw, more of a wolf than a hound. Papa had to put a lance blade clean through her unyielding heart to put her down. And all just to get me a hold a me three lovely gals.'

Kull closed his eyes in memory of what, in his reckoning, had been a sacred event.

'But now, Fang – you too be gone.' He couldn't prevent another snuffle of tears. 'And now, even though it breaks us heart, we can't do with no waste.'

Kull climbed to his feet and he whistled for Maw and Claw to come to him to be stroked.

'A dead un be a sore loss. It be a burden we got to bear. And dead, misfortunately, is meat. And we can't afford to be sentimental.'

The wolf hounds howled.

'According to fambly custom, bones go to ground and flesh to table. Them's the rules of the hunt. Even now, on this melancholy occasion, we got to be practical. The dead goes to feed the living.'

Wiping the tears from his cheeks with his sleeves, Kull severed the head from the body and he began to skin and butcher the carcass. But the tears flowed again when it came to the heart. It brought back the memories of butchering the carcass of her mother-bitch, when he was after her pups. Man alive, even when she was as good as done for, she had that final snapping at him, and added to the damage on his face. The acquisition of his gals surely had cost him – and that was fair enough.

That fight made him respect and cherish the courage and strength of the wolf hounds. And he had done his duty by the mama's cubs. He had reared her offspring – his three gals – becoming a proper papa to them, feeding them out of his own hands, looking after their every need.

'And now look at you – what booties you become!'

Eyes the colour of burnished steel. And at the core of their fierceness and faithfulness, in each and every one of them, a heart of darkness. A heart that matched his very own, a heart was what you got from the daughters of a she wolf.

'This is gonna be a hunt and a half, this un! A war!'

It was understandable that Claw and Maw were feeling that same grief he was feeling, howling and mewling all the time he was cutting up the meat. But they were also hungry. There wasn't much food to be found in these misty wastelands, with their quagmires and salt marshes. Bastos Kull should know since he was born here – if anybody wanted to know. But all the same he had come out of these ungiving lands not only as a hunter without equal, but just as importantly, a survivor.

His hounds hadn't had much the way of meat in several days. And yet they held back, just as he did, at the thought of what it was they were fixing to eat. But they all just had to get on with it. That special treat – Fang's heart – that must surely go to her sisters. It was what Fang would have wanted. So he would never deny them that. But it was such a difficult hunk of meat to hack out of all them rubbery giblets what attached the heart to lungs and stuff. He just hacked and hacked. And so, even now, taking a good hard look at the organ in his blood-soaked hands, it resembled nothing less than a hotchpotch of tubes and chambers, and stringy things that, so far as his tear-misted eyes could gather, looked like them fleshy things you found inside the shells of sea creatures. He just cut the messy thing into halves and he tossed the chunks of bloody meat into the dirt before the snouts of the two whining gals.

'Come on! Gobble it all up. We got us a task to finish.'

Grief was grief, and it surely had its place. But Bastos Kull hadn't earned the reputation as the greatest hunter in Moon for sentimentality. He lit a pipe of tobacco and put aside the task of further butchering for now. That could wait until he had the opportunity of examining the cave.

He had to be very careful in clearing the entrance if he was to take a good look inside. The enemy had spent time in there, resting and feeding. They had left in a hurry. What was the betting they had left some personal stuff behind? Stuff they had handled. Stuff that would provide his two remaining gals with a good scent. He puffed on his pipe as he set to, hauling rock after rock out of the congested tumble, gradually clearing the obstruction, all the while keeping an eye on the emerging crack that looked like an ancient problem with the roof.

'A rock fall – so that was what did for Fang!'

He shored it up with a careful re-use of the very scaffold of timbers that the enemy had used to construct their trap. Then, armed with a torch of intertwined twigs, he moved deeper into the main chamber of the cave and took his time in having a look around. He couldn't miss the ashes of their fire. It was positioned in the most hospitable place to take advantage of the breeze that seemed to blow through the cavern, a breeze that didn't come in through the entrance he had cleared. It confirmed his suspicion there must be another way out.

'Okay – so we takes a poke around this fire!'

There was a whine from the entrance. When he turned, holding the torch aloft, he saw the snout and bright reflecting eyes of Maw. She was the littlest of his gals, but also the most curious, and the smartest.

He whistled for her to come join him.

'What we got to consider,' he scratched her under her chin, 'is the possibilities – um as might hinder us and um as might help us. We got no reason to hurry. Not when Papa was born in these here misty marshes and knows um in bone and sinew.'

Maw rumbled in her throat.

Kull liked how each of his gals had their very own voices. He could tell their voices even in the dark. He patted her head as she cuddled up closer to him.

'What do you think?'

He took comfort in the fact that anyone who knew Ayatini's misty marshes also knew that you had to be calm and circumspect if you wanted to survive a journey through them. And for more reason than the mist and marshes! He laughed to discover that the silent Claw had also joined them. Probably missed her sister and followed the sound of his voice.

'Ole Bastos was begotten hereabouts. Here in what me ma called the Magical Lands of Forgetfulness.'

He guffawed with laughter at such a quaint understatement. His ma's notion of forgetfulness was a pearl of a joke.

'Taught me what you might call the hard facts of nature, did ma. And here I plundered, boy and man. I had such a time, preying on strangers. I could tell you tales as would make your hair curl. Ayatini was me school o' learning, so to speak, and here Bastos become what ma called her trouble and vice.'

Kull sat down before the ashes of the quarry's fire, leaning his elbows on his knees and cradling his broad, heavy-jawed face in his hands. He rekindled the fire with twigs and branches the enemy had conveniently gathered for the

purpose and failed to make use of. It tickled his imagination
that he was cuddling his gals exactly where the same enemy
had settled by the fire.

'Oh, such a time we had, ole Bastos and me bat-eared
brother, Cakkie . . . That was before I had to get rid of him
afore he spilled the beans on me enterprise.'

Kull laughed and he half cried at one and the same time
with the memories of his unloved childhood.

'Always had the edge on Cakkie.' He tapped his head,
with those big banana-sized fingers with their filthy black
nails. 'Always! Them as came sneaking around, probing and
searching, I arranged for um to disappear. So, you see, even
ma herself eventually found herself lost in her very own
notion of the Magical Lands of Forgetfulness.'

Kull guffawed with laughter, watching the fire splutter
and threaten to go out. He scrabbled around to gather up
what remained of the kindling, sprinkling it over the ash-
strewn embers. And still he was laughing.

'All of um none the wiser. Bastos ran rings around um,
one an' all.'

It took Kull a few minutes for his mind to settle back
down from his reflections and focus back onto the hunt.

'The thing we need to do now, gals, is to sit back and
figure this enemy out. The old man is smart – smart and
experienced. I figure that in now. So, what we gotto take on
board is we dealing with a. A smart old man an' a tricksy
woman!'

He tapped the ashes from his pipe against the sole of
his boot, took a deep breath, listening to the howling of
what sounded like a sea-to-shore gale building up in the
near distance. Typical weather for the Misty Marshes. Here
was he, ensconced in what had been their cave of comfort.

Meanwhile, where were they? Forced to flee this respite and exposed to that blowing gale. The thought comforted him. It helped to alleviate some of his rage and pain over the loss of Fang. Bastos Kull was in no hurry. But it was time now for him to formulate his plans.

He wouldn't bother to keep the fire going. What need when he could cuddle up close with his gals? He'd rest the while until the gale was over. Meanwhile he'd explore the cave for what might prove helpful in the hunt. Kull moved patiently through the dark interior with another flaming brand. With his head bowed to avoid the stony teeth that snarled at his head from the low ceiling, he picked up a fistful of grassy straw that they had likely used for a bed and he held it to his nostrils. 'Here, Claw gal. Get a sniff o' that.' He searched further, found an old skull of a bird, which he sniffed in turn. Was there a different scent here? 'This un's for you, Maw. You got the best snout.'

Maw snuffled excitedly around the old bones for several seconds. Then she lifted up her muzzle and she growled.

Kull grinned with delight. 'So, me darlings, after such a time of trial and grief, we got us a lead – a drag to follow.'

He whistled a new command. His gals whined, then lay on the rocky floor, and he joined them, entwined among the shaggy limbs, huge heads, slavering jaws and fangs, by the ashes of the fire of their quarry. As he settled down to sleep, he asked himself a question: was this new scent on the bird skull the drag that would lead him to the invisible girl?

# THE LIE THAT BELIES THE TRUTH

As dawn broke a powerful wind was howling about the latest makeshift shelter, constructed in a dip in the ground, surrounded by a ring of boulders with branches piled on top. A major storm was blowing in from the distant direction of the sea. The wind blew through the shelter and it hurt, like a cutting edge, where it found the exposed skin of Magio's face. Even when it lessened, it left him with a ringing in his ears. He wanted desperately to go back to sleep, hoping that when he woke up again it would be full daylight and the storm would have gone away.

Back home in Gran's he'd fall asleep as soon as his head hit the pillow. But here there were no pillows and the sense of omnipresent danger made it impossible to relax. That plus the fact that they were spending a least an hour every day wading through freezing cold streams, with their boots slung round their necks on their laces, and when it came to deeper waters, it meant wading through with most of their clothes tied up into packs carried on top of their heads. Sometimes the current rose so high that Magio and Eefa had to swim, holding their chins up so they wouldn't swallow water. Despite these difficulties, they had somehow managed to press on northwards and by degrees more and more inland. At least, now that they had put some distance between them and their pursuers, Bird Woman had decided that they could travel by day and sleep at night. Still, despite all of the discomforts, Magio told himself that it was all one should expect of a great adventure.

It was the threat of danger that hurried them onwards. But then, as any adventurer recognised, the journey was and should be filled with danger. The trouble was that Quimbre's tales of adventures sailing the Sea of Stars, which he would regale them with back at Gran's with his pipe aglow, the heroes knew what they were doing, and why they were doing it. But here, in the gales and rivers and freezing cold, Magio and Eefa had no real idea why they were running or what they were really running from. True, when they had set out, it was about escaping the Scogs. But now it seemed that they were being hunted by somebody they didn't know – and didn't even know why he was hunting them. What was more, it was somebody they could hear roaring like a wild beast, and he had a pack of wolf hounds.

When another shriek of wind blew through the shelter, Magio pulled his blanket over his head and he tried to block it all out and return to sleep. But he just couldn't. He ended up tossing and turning and peeping out, waiting apprehensively for daylight. All the while he knew that, since he couldn't hear his snoring, old Quimbre must be outside in that dreadful weather, standing guard over them. Bird Woman was likely to be out there too, hunting as she often did at night, no matter what the weather. In fact, now he came to think about it, she rarely appeared to sleep, and even when she closed her eyes and appeared to drowse, it was never for more than an hour or two.

*Jinxy!*

Thinking about it was just too perplexing for his tired mind, so Magio just gave up trying to sleep altogether.

Crossing the tiny shelter, congested with packs, he shook Eefa's shoulder to wake her.

'What is it?' she muttered sleepily.

'I can't sleep. I keep racking my brains, trying to figure it – what's really going on – and I can't.'

'Stop it!'

She turned over and attempted to get back to sleep, but he shook her again and insisted that she sit up and talk to him.

'It's just about dawn anyway, so you might as well wake up.'

'Ooooh, Magio!' Her voice was cross with him.

'We need to talk.'

She turned so she was lying on her back, smelling sweaty, blinking up at him with heavy eyes. 'I'm too tired to talk.'

'You know as well as I do that things aren't making sense.'

She shivered, sighed, then exhaled and sat up, blinking her disgruntled eyes at him.

'Maybe we can figure it out, if we really think it through?'

She flopped back down onto her back again.

'It's no good pretending you don't care, Eefa. You've got to help me figure it out. We need to find some kind of explanation for what is happening to us.'

She peered at him even though her eyes continued their sleepy blinking. 'What in the world is it you want? Just tell me so I can get back to sleep.'

'I've been going over things in my head. Even the stuff I didn't really want to think about, like that scary stuff in the desert with the moths and bats. But it's no good being a scaredy cat.' He shrugged, deeply pensive. 'Back then, before the cave, something else was hunting us. I don't think it was that horrible man with the wolf hounds. I think it was something with wings, something even weirder.'

She sat up properly now, though her voice was still slurred with sleep. 'Slow down a little to let me wake up properly. What is it you are really trying to say to me?'

'I don't know.'

She shivered, then hauled her blanket up and pulled it tight around her shoulders. 'Maybe it's nothing to do with us.'

'You're making no sense.' Magio stared at Eefa, who was twirling a lock of hair around her finger. Why couldn't she see what was worrying him? Why couldn't she feel it?

She shook her head. 'I can't explain it. I'm just as puzzled as you.' She hesitated, her eyes meeting his for the first time since waking up. 'Maybe it's something to do with the time before?'

'What do you mean? Like before the Chaos?'

There had only ever been two people in their lives who had survived the Chaos and so were in a position to tell them anything about the time before. These were Gran and Quimbre. But the problem was that neither of them had ever seemed to know much about it. They seemed reluctant even to talk about it. And when they did, they only seemed to remember bits and pieces of what had happened. Quimbre had cursed it and Gran had moaned about it. But neither of them had ever offered any real explanation as to what had happened, or why it had come about.

'I've been thinking,' Magio whispered, 'what if it was the Chaos that took our mum and dad?'

'Why in the world?'

'I don't know. But when I was thinking about that I asked myself, "What if the calamity that had happened to

Mum and Dad back then was somehow related to what is happening to us now?"'

'That's crazy!'

'Haven't you noticed – crazy things are happening to us!'

'Odd things are happening, yes. But saying it's to do with the Chaos . . . '

He spoke to her in a whisper. 'Nobody knows what caused the Chaos.'

'We know that it killed off most of the people who lived here on Moon and presumably all of the islands in the Sea of Stars.'

*Yeah,* he thought, *and maybe even further afield?* It astonished him that he had thought something as terrible as that. It was the first time in his life that he had thought anything as horrible as that. His voice trembled as he whispered again, 'Gran lived through it, but, if you ask me, I think maybe she didn't understand it.'

'More like she was too terrified to talk about it.'

Magio sighed. 'She only ever spoke of it when she had guzzled too much of Quimbre's juniper juice.'

'Yeah!'

Magio couldn't help but laugh at the memories. 'Do you remember her face when she talked about it?'

Eefa mimicked that face now – she had always been such a brilliant mimic. And she mimicked Gran's rasping voice as she described it. 'All that was left, child, was fear and hunger and discomfort of "every shade and description".'

Magio chuckled. 'I do so miss her.'

'Me too!' Eefa reached out to pull him to her in an awkward hug.

'Do you think she's gone to some place in the sky?'

He shook his head. 'I don't know.'

'Quimbre says she's still here, in you and me.'

'Well, in a way, she is.'

She spoke softly. 'Do you think she thought like that – that she wanted to go on living inside you and me even after she was dead?'

'I don't know. Stop asking me these questions.'

'I don't want her to be dead.'

'Me neither.' He sighed. 'Do you remember how she'd call Quimbre those names?'

Eefa shook her head. 'When he was pampering her all the while, looking after her every need!'

They laughed together.

Eefa dropped her head. 'He called the old shed his hammock, like he was still aboard ship. He didn't care about the smells from the privy.'

'She called him "Quimbre the trickster!"'

'But he could so make us all laugh.'

'Yeah!' Magio nodded. 'Do you remember how she hated that he had rigged up a ferret hutch on the shed roof made out of old crates?'

'He'd barter the little 'uns from his breeding pairs.'

'He had a hundred different tricks up his sleeve. Growing his own baccy leaves, and brewing his own juniper juice.'

'She also called him "Mister Fixit".'

'Yeah!'

For a moment Magio was back in the happy memories of Quimbre and Gran, when Quimbre would wink an eye at him as Gran was ranting on at him. It even continued while Quimbre was rigging up the makeshift rails all over the place after her stroke, so she could make her way around the home.

'Poor old Gran!'

'Do you remember the commotion when he was helping her manoeuvre her sticks to get her to the privy, with Gran moaning and groaning and cursing him every step of the way?'

Magio imitated Quimbre's cackling whisper. 'She lost the muscles of walking, but she didn't lose her tongue.'

They fell over one another, laughing.

Oh, there had been so many moonlit nights spent fishing on the beach with Quimbre, under the sky ablaze with stars. He could still smell the pungent self-grown tobacco that Quimbre would smoke . . . he could still hear the longing that would enter Quimbre's voice.

'We fishermen, we are really hunters. We track the creatures of the deep.'

In his mind's eye, he saw the distant look on Quimbre's face, as he paused, inhaling smoke. Magio was nodding with him, lost in those beloved memories.

'You understand, kiddo? I've got that great monstrous thing out there, that great blue and rolling ocean, in my blood.'

Magio understood.

But Gran didn't. She didn't even believe it when Quimbre said he was a fisherman. He had discovered what she thought one morning, as daylight was just breaking. He was hurrying home after a run to the beach. He had sneaked into the yard in the grey light and checked out Quimbre's breeding ferret, in her hutch – Feefo appeared to be sleeping. He had stuffed Feefo inside his T-shirt before clambering onto the roof of Quimbre's hut, from where he could sneak into the attic bedroom through the open window. He was careful not to wake Gran, who slept in her chair in the living room below.

It was as well he did so because today she wasn't asleep. He could hear her moaning through the curtain over the ladder.

'Oh, my poor knees!'

Gran had arthritis in her knees. Magio could hear it grinding sometimes, like stones grinding on stones, when she was getting up out of her chair. She had seemed to grow old fast after her stroke. Her skin had turned dry and scratchy and her hair was whiter and thinning over her head. He had hated that: he had hated what was happening to her, because it was making her life so painful and difficult.

'You scallywag, up there. Don't think you fooled me skulking off into the night and then climbing up over that roof.'

Magio's heart had missed a beat. Gran was standing at the bottom of the ladders. He poked his head out of the curtain to look down at her.

'Sorry, Gran!'

'Never mind sorry! You haven't brought in that flea-ridden pest?'

She was talking about Feefo.

'No! Honestly – I promise!' Even though he had.

'Filthy wild thing. I should never have let that scoundrel bring it home. Gets its teeth into everything. Takes me all day to put things right when it's set loose.'

The ferret was squirming inside his T-shirt right then as he attempted to lie his way out of his predicament. 'Feefo is in her hutch.'

'See that it stays there.'

'Yes, Gran!'

It was no good reminding her that Feefo was the source of the rabbits that she relied on for them to eat.

She merely continued to grumble. 'How did I let things come to this?'

'You shouldn't be so nasty to Quimbre. You depend on him, Gran.'

'No.' Gran's eyes rose to meet Magio's. There was a fury in those blue eyes, which had been increasingly invaded by yellowy white circles around the edges of the irises. 'Don't you get too attached to that man! He's a scoundrel – a pirate!'

Magio had been so astounded by her words that he had stopped breathing. Quimbre a pirate? It was as if all that he had assumed about his world had come tumbling down around him. Gran's words had so shocked him that he had never even mentioned them to Eefa. But then Eefa heard it for herself from the lips of Bird Woman when they had been getting ready to flee Warren.

In the time Magio and Eefa had been talking, daylight had arrived, at least in the form of the first morning grey. But for Magio, it was somehow unwelcome. It meant another day of running scared. He was struggling to breathe.

'Oh, Eefa!'

'What is it?'

Her eyes were now probing his. But he just couldn't bring himself to explain. He so needed to think more about things.

One thing was for sure: adventures weren't at all like they were supposed to be. What were they really doing here? As far as he could determine, there was no master plan. You just ran, and ran, with your heart in your mouth and you had to learn how to put up with the most desperate situations just to stay alive.

Magio was gasping for breath. He couldn't bear to sit in the shelter any longer. He crawled out, still dressed in his sleeping shirt, into a dawn of intense cold, silence and mist.

The cold caused a rash of gooseflesh to crawl all over his skin. But he didn't care. He wanted to see Quimbre. He wanted to just look at him so he could feel reassured that Quimbre was the same helpful old man he had always been. He had to be somewhere around, but Magio couldn't see him. All he could see was rock and shrub, covering rising ground. They had been climbing into some place that Bird Woman called the Foothills of Shadow. Magio forced himself to take deep breaths. Yet still the restlessness tormented him. It nauseated him in his gut. It twisted and turned within him.

*What if Quimbre isn't who I thought he was?*

Gran, he reluctantly decided, was cantankerous. Maybe she had lied about Quimbre? But why would she say such things about him? Did she just despise him for no reason other than he was dark-skinned and bearded? If so she had never mentioned it. Did she resent the fact that she was so dependent on him? That made no sense. And that changed the direction of Magio's thoughts entirely. Quimbre – where in the world had he really come from? How had be come to live with them in Warren?

Magio only vaguely recalled the occasion when Quimbre had arrived into their world. His first memories were of Quimbre as some kind of handyman, who would do jobs for Gran. For some reason or another that Magio didn't know, he had moved into the ramshackle shack in the yard, making it into a kind of den. It seemed that, once arrived, he never moved out. He would claim, during the endless altercations with Gran, that he couldn't move out because everywhere – not just Warren – had gone to the dogs. But Magio now sensed that this was an excuse. Quimbre had stayed because they needed him. Magio just sensed that so strongly that he judged it right. And, though she would never have admitted it, Gran must have realised it.

But even so, Quimbre – had he really been a pirate?

Pirates weren't the handsome desperados you heard of in stories. They were robbers who attacked ships and stole stuff. They hurt people . . . even killed people. A creeping feeling moved over Magio's goosepimpled skin.

What was the real truth?

*Stop it! Stop it! Stop it!*

He tried to quell his rising misgivings. Gran – Quimbre – they were in their ways equally peculiar, equally secretive, and equally kind and caring. Was it possible that they both knew something about the Chaos they didn't want to talk about?

He inhaled deeply, slowly, then released his breath in shock as he felt the weight of Quimbre's hand on his shoulder.

'You okay, kiddo?'

That was Quimbre's voice. Quimbre's shadowy bulk suddenly blocking out the light right in front of him. Had Magio let his imagination run away from him? Surely this was the really kind man who had taken care of him like a grandad?

Magio could hear his own teeth chattering.

Quimbre roared with laughter. 'Hey – kiddo! Maybe you better go back in there and get some warm clothes on!'

Magio dived back into the shelter and he got fully dressed. He told himself to stop obsessing with Gran and Quimbre and focus on the real mystery. It was nothing to do with Quimbre. It was all down to the Chaos. The Chaos had something to do with when everything had gone wrong; it was what had caused the wrenching loss of their parents, maybe even why Eefa was invisible. That's what he should be trying to figure out. He doubted that Quimbre knew anything about the Chaos, any more than Gran had. But what about Bird Woman? She was the kind of person who knew stuff, strange stuff, secret stuff – stuff that nobody else knew. She had known from first meeting her that Eefa was real. Nobody, not a single person Magio had ever met, had realised that. Did Bird Woman know what was really going on? Magio sat back down on the blanket he had slept on and he attempted to figure it out.

The more he came to think about it, the more likely he thought that Bird Woman was the most likely among them to have some idea of what was really going on. But, for some reason, she was keeping it to herself.

# THE SIEGE OF WART

For several days Ursascogans had been massing in the sand dunes and desert scrub outside the ancient stone walls of the port town of Wart. There could be no concealing their increasing numbers, any more than there could be any mistaking their intentions, given the thunderous chanting, posturing and rattling of weapons. Their arrival, accompanied by the Pachydonts, their gigantic beasts of burden, had provoked a predictable panic in the town residents, who had closed the arched gates in the buttressed gate tower. Judging from the busy sawing and hammering that had been coming from inside the walls, they had also been busy with reinforcing barriers all through the night. As dawn broke, the townsfolk were presented with the vision of Queen Pittaquera, ensconced alongside the king, Wirgnatha, on a throne fashioned from the solid trunk of a mighty oak tree some six or seven feet in diameter, which had been hauled into position in the centre of the approach road, though calculated to stay clear of cannon range from the town walls. Before the royal couple, laid out on the gravelly ground and fastened at its four corners by lumps of lava-rock, was an ancient map of Wart. Drawn out in sepia on stretched sealskin, it delineated the walls and organically meandering streets, with the deep and naturally protected arc of harbour decorated by tiny pictograms of boats, sea fairies and dolphins. This same map was a painful reminder of Ursascogan disgruntlement, since it harked back to the original construction of those same walls, and gate tower, by Ursascogan labour some two centuries earlier.

Wart had been Moon's most important port prior to the Chaos. But there was little in the way of commercial activity these days, with only the occasional sail-driven barque making the journey from the other islands, or more occasionally from the distant shores of the continental Tír. Even so, it was the fact that Wart still retained a functioning port that had led Wirgnatha to choose it for his opening salvo in restoring the birthright of the First Folk on Moon. Pittaquera knew that her husband planned some choreographed display in 'taking back' Wart. She was in no doubt that he had in mind a fury of battle, blood and fire. But she was equally determined that the conquest, however rightful, should be calm, even dignified, with as little bloodshed as possible.

'Please, Wirgi, let there be no slaughter.'

'Hsst!' he cautioned her, his voice lowered for just her ears. 'Do not refer to me in such terms before the assembled army!'

'A great king, confident in his righteousness and power, may show clemency.' She spoke softly, but loud enough for the aged wizar to hear.

'Are the humans now our friends? Why would we bother to spare them? They humiliated and enslaved us, compelling our ancestors into forced labour to construct such walls and towers, bridges, and harbours. The mystery to me is why we, the First Folk, allowed such puny upstarts to subjugate us in the first place!'

'Do not forget how calculating and organised the humans were, and still are. They have the writing of words, which we lack. And they have machines of war that we have never been capable of reproducing. Moreover, in ages past we have contributed to our own undoing, proving more inclined to fight among ourselves than against the common enemy.'

'Desist from making excuses for those who call us Scogs. They are obliged to put their words down on paper so they remember them. We do not need such feeble aids to remember what is important to us. In our sacred folklores, passed from tongue to tongue, we remember all we need to remember. Let the humans revel in the words on paper of how they battered us down into the dirt, where we were forced to live like rabbits. Yet our folklore recalls a different history – one that has no need for books of paper, but is graven into our very hearts and souls.'

'Yes, beloved, you are right. Ours is a proud history, one of a sacred enlightenment with the nature of the world around us, and also one of good judgement based on that enlightenment. If you, my husband, are to be seen as the inheritor of such proud enlightenment, you must take the town, by all means. But please, I beg you, without recourse to slaughter!'

Pittaquera could see from her husband's face that he didn't welcome the advice. Ever since he had sacrificed poor Igor to conjure up that snake woman, Lustfera, out of the pit, his head had been filled with notions of blood and vengeance. The queen dreaded what such bloodlust would lead to, coupled with resurrecting past injustices, inebriated celebration, and goodness knows what else. But any further debate between king and queen was halted by the intrusion of the shape changer, Iquotattle, who heralded his return by materialising, in his unclothed scaly skin, in the gravel immediately before the royal couple.

The wizar, Khakhov, who was seated to the king's left, hissed a seething resentment at such grandstanding.

But it didn't prevent the fawning Iquotattle from claiming centre stage, and lifting those repulsive crocodile eyes to those of the king, and addressing him directly in his wheedling voice. 'Great Majesty, I adopted the form of a lizard so as not to be observed. This enabled me to climb the pediments of the arch over the ancient entrance gate. From there . . .'

'Just tell me, plainly, what you saw, before I wrench your squeaking head from your shoulders.'

'A thousand apologies, Majesty. To grasp the significance of my observations it is necessary to imagine from where, and how, I made them.'

Wirgnatha could hear her husband's teeth grinding in frustration. But a nod from the wizar caused the king to hold his tongue.

'From such a vantage I saw that the enemy is convinced that a direct attack on the gate would be impossible.'

'Nothing is impossible to the Ursascogan army!'

'Indeed, sire.' The creature giggled. 'Almighty as you, and your great army, may be, the enemy is assured that even with such might you cannot hope to batter your way against a hundred tons of stone.'

'What do you mean?'

'The gate itself is flimsy enough – mere boards of oak, even if fully two feet thick. But the humans have gathered the stone ballast of a hundred ships to reinforce the gate on the town side. It no longer opens. Indeed, it cannot open. I would, with due respect, advise . . .'

The wizar spat, 'Do not presume to advise your king!'

The changer giggled again, a chittering high-pitched nervous sound. 'You hired me, Majesty, to so advise you.'

'I hired you to scout the defences of the human usurpers.'

'Once more, my apologies, sire. Yet, if I might presume upon your gracious patience . . . would it not be prudent to offer terms?'

'Make terms with the humans!' The huge figure of the king rose from his seat and he pounded the ground with a stamp of his right foot. 'Ursascogans do not offer terms with their enemies.'

'In that case, forgive my ignorance, Great King!' The changer prostrated himself on the somewhat shaky ground, yet still unable to suppress a chittering giggle that appeared perilously close to laughter.

'Never,' the king emphasized with a great pound of his other foot, mere inches from the squirming shape changer. 'Never!'

'Forgive me . . . forgive me . . . oh, my Great Lord!'

'Do you presume to imagine that it is fitting that we, the First Folk, should offer terms to an enemy that has so despised, subjugated and enslaved us, here in the very theatre of war?'

'But, sire – I have merely spied as you ordered. I merely report what cunning those human wretches have conspired at the gate.'

Abruptly, the king laughed, and all of his massed lead warriors laughed with him. Even the queen felt a hint of a smile creep over her lips. All, it would appear, other than the shape changer, knew a secret that suggested that, in spite of the human precautions, the gate and its surrounding tower was far from impregnable.

'Enough of this foolishness!' Wirgnatha thundered to his assembled army. 'It is time I addressed the mayor and his council.'

 C3

'What the devil are those rogues up to now?'

Urt Daquira, the mayor of Wart, was peering through a leather-bound telescope over the parapet of the great gate, which gave him the best possible vantage of the extraordinary host assembled in the near distance. Daquira, who was in his sixty-seventh year, had occupied the same office for the port town of Wart from his thirty-seventh birthday, following the death of his father. His attention was now drawn to the thunderous bellowing of what sounded like gargantuan rutting stags.

'Whatever in the world . . . ?'

'Pachydonts, sir.' Commander Vetlan spoke. 'They serve them as beasts of burden. They have elongated nostrils they use to transfer food to their mouths. The Scogs make use of these animals as living trumpets to signal in circumstances where we civilised folks would choose trumpets of brass.'

'What are they trumpeting?'

'A bellicose signal, I would presume!'

Daquira snorted disdainfully down his nose. An exceptionally tall, and exceedingly lean man, his mountainous nose, with its caverns of nostrils, was thrown into striking relief by the hollowed cheeks and cadaverous cheekbones. Even as Daquira considered this explanation, the trumpeting sounded out again.

'What do you make of that?'

Vetlan shook his head. 'I have absolutely no idea, sir!'

But even as the commander spoke, there was a movement among the horde of giants. Daquira returned the telescope to his eye to witness a single member of the horde detach itself from the tumult of drums and monstrous beasts to proceed towards them. Daquira kept a wary eye on the single mounted figure approaching in a slow and pompous plodding. Through his telescope he saw what appeared to be an ancient being, its face lined and sagging, but even at a distance of a hundred quells, huge in stature, three times or more the size of a human, with features as fixed as stone. It rode an extraordinary beast, massive, with a shield-shaped countenance, triple-horned, and a maw of enormous interlocked fangs. The beast's legs were as thick and rounded as tree-trunks, and the feet were equipped with dauntingly massive claws.

'What manner of a mount is that?'

'I believe they call it a fanghorn, sir.'

'I hope we have our cannons trained for when it comes into range?'

'Sir – I think we should desist from attack.'

'Why?'

'Because it would appear that they want to parley.'

Daquira followed the progress of the approaching figure astride the peculiar beast, which did not even hesitate as it came into cannon range, and then, flintlock range.

'By the gods, I hope you are right and this is an emissary.'

'I believe so, sir.'

'Is it likely to speak human?'

The commander shrugged. 'We must certainly hope so, sir, since none among us are likely to speak Scog.'

Daquira was both intrigued and dumbfounded by the appearance of this strange being astride its even stranger mount. The Scog grew enormous as it neared. Its head alone was half the height of a tall man. Its eyes, of the strangest azure hue, were now studying Daquira in turn. This close its features looked even more withered, the skin folded upon itself like centuries-old leather. Indeed, Daquira was inclined to think that the skin, so thick and ridged, and, where folded, so akin to that of an alligator, confirmed the being's utter alienness. As far as the mayor could see, it bore no weapons. At lease none other than the brute size and claws of the fanghorn beast it rode. Even as Daquira considered the problem of communication, his question was answered by the approaching figure, who spoke in a rumbling voice, deeper than any human could possibly muster.

'I presume that I am addressing Daquira, Mayor of Wart?'

'You are.'

'Then, sir, might I respectfully exchange words of greeting from His Majesty, Wirgnatha, High King of the Ursascogan People, First Folk of the Archipelago known to humans as the Sea of Stars.'

Daquira was at a loss for words to reply. He had never heard any such nonsense. Scog king indeed!

Commander Vetlan spoke on the town's behalf. 'And who, if I might respectfully enquire, are you, sir?'

'I am Khakhov – Grand Wizar and Counsel to Wirgnatha, and to her Highness, and Queen of the Ursascogan people, Pittaquera.'

The words, spoken slowly yet in perfect human tongue were far deeper in pitch than any human throat could utter, and with an alien strangeness of pronunciation. The Scog ambassador's words provoked a silence that lasted for several seconds before the astonished mayor was capable of responding.

'What in the world are you all doing here? What does your king, whatever-he-calls-himself, want from us?'

'His Highness, King Wirgnatha, has declared war on you. On behalf of the Ursascogan people, he demands our right as the First Folk to take possession of this town of Wart, and in due course, to recover this island you call Moon – to possess and to rule it in perpetuity.'

Mayor Daquira wasn't sure if he should laugh or be righteously outraged. 'Who the devil does he think he is, this purported king of yours?'

'My Lord and King, Wirgnatha . . .'

'Yes, you already told us who you represent. A . . . a filthy mud-dwelling Scog! Have you forgotten your place? What madness, in the name of the holy Undying, would provoke you clowns to threaten Wart with a siege? Have you forgotten that we have powerful weapons? Must I remind you of the history of previous confrontations with humans, which have been sorely ruinous to your kind?'

Khakov rumbled calmly on, unhurried in his reply. 'Such indeed has been the history of past confrontations between us. Even so, I would counsel you to reflect. The tides of power are apt to change. You may presently witness a power that supersedes your brass cannons. Yet even now, through order of the king, and through the intercession of Her Merciful Highness, Pittaquera, I am entrusted to offer clemency. You must surrender Wart to the king. Though I recognize that abandoning the town will cause dismay and consternation, you will be allowed to depart without slaughter. So, with these terms, His Royal Highness, Wirgnatha, demands that you now obey the royal command and surrender Wart with immediate effect.'

The mayor was now red-faced with anger.

'Sir!' The commander was tugging at his arm.

'What?'

'Sir – you should get your head down!'

Mayor Daquira was so outraged that he had forgotten his sense of self-preservation and was standing tall and erect above the parapet, a perfect target, his face blanching, his eyes blinking, and his tongue in a tangle with what words he was in too much of a fury to express.

The emissary, Khakhov, waited for his reply in silence. There was a stirring in the Scogs in the distance, but no attempt to attack.

Daquira no longer cared. These issues were too important to bother about his self-preservation. What was the commander doing, irritating him with his constant interruptions? But the commander, now tugging again at his sleeve, made clear that he had spotted something through the telescope.

'Sir – look for yourself! The enemy appears to be bringing into bear something . . . I wonder if it might be some armament.'

'What possible armament . . . ?'

The wizar rumbled on again in that same infuriatingly slow but insistent voice. 'I am commissioned to inform you that we come armed with a weapon of great power, one that in hallowed legend was known as the Leviathan.'

Daquira was not in the mood to be impressed by a weapon of legend. He shouted at the figure on the enormous beast. 'Let me tell you, perfidious creature, that we humans are not impressed by your mythical weapons. Let us not mince words. This is brigandage. What you intend is to rob us of our town!'

The figure on the beast appeared impervious to insults. Its countenance showed no change of expression.

'I'm afraid that you cannot win. Such is the power of the Leviathan that we will have the town. I would earnestly counsel, sir, that your people must abandon Wart. You may gather your possessions and go hence without injury or hindrance.'

Daquira was suffering a mental breakdown. 'Go hence! Go to the devil, do you mean? Go starve in the desert? Go throw ourselves into the sea?'

The huge figure astride his gargantuan mount shrugged. 'Would you have me repeat the terms?'

'Are you mad? Where are we to go? How are we to live? We have women and children. We have the deepest possible roots here. You can't just come along and demand to take our town from us like that!'

'We built it.'

'You were employed as labourers. You did not build it.'

'We were employed as slaves. And indeed we built it. We hefted every stone and shaped those stones into houses, and civic buildings, into bridges and temples. We waded into the sea and carried those stones from the sailing ships that could not get close enough to the shore to unload them. We built the town and harbour from the stones we had carried on our backs. And then what did you do with us when it was done?'

'What did we do with you?'

'You exiled us from what we ourselves had created.'

'You were duly paid for your work. When the work was done, we let you go. That was all that happened.'

The huge face, with its great drooping jowls, moved slowly from side to side. 'Not so, Mayor Daquira! Your ancestors forced us out of the town at cannonpoint. Indeed, you used the same cannons we hefted back out of the ships to the shore.'

'You had a reputation for drunken belligerency.'

'Drunk with the cheap alcohol that was our pay. Rot-gut rum that made us insensitive to our pain. That you calculated, and even that you terminated.'

'You became dangerous with your multitude of resentments.'

'There you touch upon it. Those resentments did not disappear during our wandering in the wilderness.'

'What wandering in what wilderness?'

'I have no desire to explain the trail of grief my people followed, wandering through all the islands of the Sea of Stars. The insults and prejudices, the lies and provocations, the pain and hurt. Such was our ignominy that we buried it under ground. We, the First Folk, who knew the land and every intimacy of its treasures of plants, and animals, and fowl and insects. In our suffering, we wept for justice, but no justice came our way. Such was our fate until our beloved king, Wirgnatha, called upon the very gods to redeem us. And in answer a spirit of darkness came to our rescue.'

The mayor heard these words, which appeared to him to be the usual complaints and wheedling one heard day-to-day from underlings. But it became clear that the multitude of enemies out there could also hear the wizar's words. There was a thundering of monstrous feet and clanging of weaponry, in answer to the wizar's last statement, that even from the distance that separated the Scogs from the gate tower rattled the very foundations.

'You, you poxy old wizard! Coming here on a monstrous beast and with a rabble at your back! What you're demanding – why, it's utterly laughable!'

'Surely, then, you must ask yourselves if it is worth dying for.'

'Dying for?' the mayor growled. 'I have already warned you. We have weapons – powerful weapons.'

'We remember your weapons. We do not fear them. And I, too, have warned you. We have a weapon more powerful than any you have ever witnessed. Yet still, we will show you a clemency denied to our ancestors. We will allow safe passage if you will but surrender Wart without a struggle.'

Commander Vetlan intervened. 'Surely you will allow Mayor Daquira time to consult with the town council?'

'His merciful Highness, King Wirgnatha, will grant you an hour.'

'An hour is not long enough.'

'It is all you are granted. Surrender and your lives will be saved. But let battle commence and that guarantee will no longer be valid.'

The mayor laughed mockingly. 'The gods preserve us.'

'The gods have no interest in your preservation. Heed my warning. You have but one hour.' So saying, the wrinkled figure turned his enormous mount around and began its plodding return.

Daquira's face was now flushed a beetroot red. Around him he was aware of cannons being primed through the ancient gun ports in the walls. 'What egregious impertinence! To be so addressed – castigated – by a stupid Scog!'

'Yet,' countered Vetlan, 'not so stupid as to encourage that horde to enter cannon range.'

'But there's one of them who remains in range.' The infuriated mayor stared after the receding giant, who rode slowly away, rocking rhythmically from side to side on his monstrous steed. 'What I'd give to fix a cannonade on the precise range and direction of that impertinent rump!'

ဆ

Pittaquera's head was filled with a thunder of drumming and the trumpeting of pachydonts. Through the flame-lit and colourful tumult, her husband rode his mount resplendent in a gown of purple silk and golden embroidery, prancing through the cheering multitude. The queen was only a trifle less resplendent in a gown of turquoise damask. Both were mounted on albino fanghorns, splendid with gilding and shouldered with the sacred emblems of Akri, the sacred beings of the creative beginnings of the First Folk legends. The returned wizar, Khakhov, disembarked from his mount and bowed down before them.

'Majesties – I offered them an hour to take their own counsel. But I am rather afraid that resistance is a forgone conclusion.'

Pittaquera wrung her hands and shook her head. 'But it defies reason. Why by the sacred Undyings would they refuse clemency?'

'They are human, Majesty – they assume ascendancy over all that flies in the air, walks on the ground, or burrows beneath it.'

Wirgnatha didn't share her misgivings. He positively glowed. 'Then it would appear that we should ready for attack?'

'Indeed, sire.'

Wirgnatha turned to Pittaquera and snorted. 'Wife – we offered clemency. Now will you desist from protecting these pompous turkeycocks?'

Dread filled her as a column of three dozen smiths of the brass clan whipped and guided the dozen pachydonts that towed the leviathan into the foreground. It provoked frenzied cheers from Ursascogans of every clan. Although there had been rumours, never had they, as a gathered people, seen the fully assembled apotheosis of legend. Sheening green, like a gigantic stick of asparagus, its huge barrel of forged bronze glimmered with runes. Such was its power and presence that any who dared to reach out and touch it fell to the ground in an apoplexy of adoration.

She saw how the wizar stood a respectful twenty paces to the left of the monstrous weapon, with his wand of ebony elevated. She also saw the shimmering shadow that towered behind him, and which now controlled its gathering charge.

'Your Majesty?' The Brass Clan Chief lifted his right arm.

'Prepare to fire!'

The great flower head of the weapon opened to reveal a maw of green flames, which whirled and twisted upon themselves.

Pittaquera could see that Wirgnatha seemed restless, anxious. She leaned closer to him. 'What is it?'

'We await the will of Lustfera.'

Terror gripped the heart of the queen. 'Oh, Wirgi!'

'I have already asked you – commanded you – to desist from so addressing me before my army!'

She had to bite her tongue and wait, with bated breath, as the mist of writhing serpents adjacent to the Leviathan materialised to take the form of the terrifying being. Those crystal green eyes seemed to discover Pittaquera's own and glower.

*I am at your command, King of the First Folk.*

'Fire the weapon!'

The explosion from the gaping mouth of the Leviathan carried the dreadful green fire of the Star of Mourning through the air, fizzing and sparking, and crashing straight through the gate tower of the town, which, together with huge sections of the walls on either side of it, was blown to smithereens. But it did not stop there. Through the yawning hole of former gate and wall, it raged on with unstoppable destructive power through every street and building in its path, laying complete waste to everything, all the way through to the towers and ship-loading structures at the very edge of the ocean, and then, unabated, it struck the very ocean, where it created a furrow of raging steam to the furthermost horizon.

Wirgnatha roared with triumph, his fists raised into the air, his eyes bulging with pride. The jubilant cheers and drumming of feet of the Ursascogans rose to a thunderous crescendo that went on and on for many minutes. Pittaquera stared at the devastation throughout all the celebration, her eyes filling with tears as she saw the smoke and flames now issuing from the ruined town. Then, blinking away her tears, she saw that raggedy spill of townsfolk, some with horses, donkeys and carts, who were fleeing the devastated port.

She pleaded with her jubilant husband. 'They have witnessed the power of the Leviathan. At least let them run – if only to spread word of your triumph.'

'If such is what it will take to please you, wife, so let it be. I shall on this occasion grant them clemency. Let them carry the tale of terror to all they meet. It will suit my purpose if the humans here on Moon will never dare to confront me again. Let all who hear of this cower and fall onto their knees in surrender to the might of the First Folk and their indomitable king.'

# ADVICE FROM THE SHADOWS

The company of four were climbing higher into the mountains, having left behind The Foothills of Shadow. All the while, and it really did feel so at every step, they were running from the howling of wolf hounds. They hurried on now even in daylight, for there appeared to be no strategy other than flight that would enable them to escape their pursuers. Another evening fell, with the sun setting behind a morass of dark grey clouds, broken at intervals by localised bursts of lightning. This really did appear to be a land of frequent storms. So bright were the flares of the lightning, they charted their evening passage as bright as day. Bird Woman informed them, during a brief rest, that they were climbing the lower spine of the island – as if Moon were some sleeping giant and the slopes and peaks were the bones of its back. The land between the craggy rocks was boggy, making progress slow. You had to be careful to avoid plummeting into a crevice in the marshy ground. Insects buzzed about them, many inclined to make a meal of their blood, so Bird Woman had coated Magio's face and arms with a smelly oil to discourage them biting. He found himself plodding on, losing himself in daydreams, only to be prodded back into reality by Eefa, who insisted that he remained sharp. That was a very difficult thing to manage in the boring plodding. Even at night he dreamed about those vicious hounds howling after him, knowing they had his scent in their nostrils, and that they were intent on tearing him to pieces if ever they found him.

'Be brave, kiddo!' Quimbre gave him a comforting pat as they plodded on.

*Be brave . . .* How was he supposed to manage that?

For a time, Bird Woman walked by his side, staying close to him.

He whispered, 'I don't feel brave at all.'

'Hush now! Don't allow yourself to be downhearted. If you but think about it, the shifting mists, even the bogs and fens, are our allies, helping to hide our tracks and impeding our pursuers.'

Magio nodded wearily, attempting to stay observant, while Bird Woman headed forward to take the lead. He could actually see the individual droplets of condensation in his eyelashes and his hair was clogged with it, so it was dripping down the back of his neck. In spite of the heart-warming words of Bird Woman, it seemed to him that the bogs with their freezing mists were more of a hindrance than a blessing. Then fate confirmed it when he plunged into a concealed pit that sucked him down like quicksand.

Bird Woman was too far ahead to rescue him, so it was left to Quimbre to haul him back out by his hair. Magio knelt coughing and spitting on the spit of sandy land, his eyes peering out of a mask of mud. Quimbre took one look at him and laughed. Magio was so outraged, he pushed Quimbre away from him, causing Quimbre to lose his footing on the slippery bank, so that Quimbre fell into the stinking mud himself, and with his hands still in Magio's hair, he hauled Magio back in with him. Magio screamed, going under again, his mind gripped by panic, until he found himself hauled back out once more by Quimbre, who was attempting to hold his slippery body erect on the bank by his shoulders.

'Don't do that again, kiddo!'

They were peering out of masks of mud at each other.

Quimbre roared with laughter. Then Magio, with eyes wet from weeping, roared with laughter too. Quimbre picked him up as if he were a small child, and found a place with a clear-running stream, where he simply plunged into it with Magio in his arms.

'Hey, better clean water than stinking mud!'

They lay down on the bed of the stream so the water was up to their necks, and they washed themselves, their clothes, and then Quimbre's weapons, freeing everything of the stinking mud. All the while Magio sat shivering, but he was unable to keep a smile off his face because of Quimbre's colourful cursing. Quimbre helped him back out of the stream, with water pouring everywhere from their soaked clothes and hair.

'Oh, you idiot, Magio!' Eefa stared at him, outraged.

He was shivering and jerking, his teeth chattering so he couldn't really speak a proper reply.

'C'mon, kiddo!' The burly man was still shaking with laughter as they stripped, dried themselves off and changed into dry clothes. Quimbre squeezed what water he could from the soaked clothing before sticking it into their backpacks. 'We'll dry the stuff out over a fire, when we get the chance.' Then they just carried on, meandering through the misty landscape.

To Magio it all seemed to have settled into a grim game of hunter and hunted, and the hunter was clearly winning. Whoever he was, their hunter seemed to be utterly determined and inexhaustible, despite the obstacles they had attempted to put in his way. The truth was that both Magio and Eefa were losing confidence in evading their pursuer. But Bird Woman clearly had no intention of giving up.

'For the last two, or possibly three, nights, we have sensed our enemy gaining ground on us. I know that you are both very frightened. You hear, as I do, the howling of the hounds in your sleep. But we can't allow fear to rule us. That is playing into the hunter's hands.'

'But what else can we do?'

Bird Woman paused, and lowered her pack. Though she must be exhausted herself, she never allowed it to show. 'If I gauge it right, we are close to a place of oracle that might offer some guidance.'

'What sort of oracle?' Quimbre demanded.

'The abode of a seer, said to inhabit the interface of the worlds of mortals and that of the Undying.'

Quimbre shook his head. 'A witch, you mean? You have faith in the scheming entrails of such a being?'

'I know where we must head in our journey. But I entertain the hope that she might help us.'

'Hey? A real witch?' Magio began to feel somewhat excited again.

'A seer! One possessing magical powers she uses to probe the whims of the Undying in their meddling with us mortals.'

Magio's eyes widened. 'Britzy!'

Eefa exclaimed, 'Never mind britzy! Bird Woman – is that what's really going on? Are the Undying interfering with us – with our lives?'

'I fear that it is possible.'

'You really think this witch-woman might help us?' Magio said, intrigued. Maybe at last he might get some answers to the questions that had been tormenting him.

'We shall see, young Magio, if first she can be persuaded.'

Eefa was unconvinced. 'Should we not better avoid her?'

'Perhaps we should. Yet I can think of nobody else who might be able to advise us. I sense that such a being is somewhat close. And we find ourselves in such a desperate situation. We have lost direction in our flight to escape the hunter. Perhaps we should be prepared to gamble?'

Magio bit his lip. 'What do you think, Quimbre?'

'I don't fancy the advice of witches.'

'She isn't really an evil kind of witch – Bird Woman says she's a seer.'

'Seer, witch – doesn't matter to an old tar like me. She'll take pleasure in casting her spells. And then you've got to watch out, kiddo – she's as like to cast a curse as a blessing.'

'Bird Woman seems to trust her.'

Quimbre grimaced, shook his head. 'Mayhap she does, but not me!'

Bird Woman snapped, 'Would you rather that we end up food for wolves?'

As it happened, the howling tore through the mists, louder than ever, and it caused all four of them to stiffen. It sounded no more than a few miles distant. It was so near that Magio couldn't help shivering. Quimbre put his arm around Magio's shoulders and nodded to Bird Woman. 'Hail her, then – this witch. We appear to be hopelessly lost. We need direction.'

Bird Woman's face was grim in the fading light. 'Then let us make a small circle.' She sat down, cross-legged, on the stony ground and bade Magio, Quimbre and Eefa to copy her example. 'We should really prepare a welcoming fire. But we cannot risk it since it would bring our pursuers down on our necks. Thus, I can but sprinkle the blessed chrism about us and attempt what little in the way of enchantment is left to me. We should all hold hands.'

Magio saw how Eefa had positioned herself with Bird Woman to her right and himself to her left, and he held the hand of Quimbre to his right and Bird Woman to his left. Her eyes were closed, her face uplifted into the falling night.

'I know you hear my voice, O Wise One of bog and moorland. We crave your assistance in this moment of peril. We seek what is just and right. Our pursuers seek only darkness. I beg you, in honest charity, to guide our path.'

The mists appeared to thicken, throwing the company into a still colder, darker gloom. It felt as if the very air about them were holding its breath.

Bird Woman kept her face elevated, her eyes tight shut, and she spoke again, huskily, urgently. 'Would you have our pursuer kill us for his sport? Would you have this innocent boy be torn asunder for the very crime of being born? Please hear me. Arise from your slumber.'

Yet still there was no answering comfort.

'Was there never a time when you were young, and the world appeared to be reasonable, and offering sweet possibilities of being? Those that hunt us wish to extinguish such possibilities.'

As if to add emphasis to Bird Woman's plea, the howling started up again, so loud now the hounds must be scrambling after their thickening scent, no more than a mile away.

'Oh, please protect us, O Wise One. There is a child who needs your protection, one wearied beyond exhaustion.'

The voice, when it came, appeared no more human than the whisper of the wind in Magio's ears.

'You confabulate, huntress of the air and clouds. There are two, not one, in your embrace. And it is the hidden one, she who

*cannot be seen, who is expected in the Land of Eternal Winter.
. .'*

Magio at stared at the smoky outline of an old and wizened female shape that had taken form in the centre of their circle. His voice shook so much, he could hardly express the words. 'B-b-but . . .'

Bird Woman hushed him with a sigh.

'With respect, O Wise One, I conceal no one.'

*'It is obvious that greater powers than I possess are conflicted with regard to your quest. Such peril is best avoided. Since the Chaos, so much has become confused. I sense a continuing disturbance in the harmony. There have been stirrings in powers long regarded as vanquished. The First Folk, long prostrate in subjugation, gather in open rebellion. And one both ancient and terrible has seen fit to encourage their rebellion. Thus, am I unwilling to involve myself in such a fearful paradox.'*

Eefa spoke. 'Please . . . I apologise that I don't know how to address you, but please listen to Bird Woman. She is our only protector. We are so very desperate for your help.'

*'You would entreat me – you, the unseen – and one, if I judge right, hardly in need of my help. You could fly away on the breath of the wind.'*

'I cannot abandon my brother.'

*'Needs must!'*

'Oh, please help us.'

*'How strange the twists and turns of fate! Know you, Woman of Birds, that there is one among the Undying who seeks to destroy you, and your charges.'*

'Whom do you speak of, O Wise One?'

*'I am not at liberty to divulge.'*

'But why, in the name of reason, would an Undying have any such malice directed at mere children?'

'*Are you so naïve as to imagine you inhabit a world of reason?*'

'Please – but a name, I beg of you?'

'*One such has come to power among the Undying. One who has taken the name of The One. One whose servant's heart is three serpents entwined.*'

'His – or her – a name, I beg you?'

'*I cannot speak of The One. But I can inform you that his servant claims the title, Lustfera, Star of Mourning.*'

Bird Woman's face creased with worry. 'But why would such a being concern himself with Eefa or Magio?'

'*I have told you all I dare, and perhaps more than I should.*'

'Oh, please,' Magio found his voice to ask, 'what caused the Chaos?'

'*A war among the Undying provoked such ruin – a war that continues still, among those who do not measure time.*'

Magio stared at the ancient figure, dumbfounded. He would have asked more questions. But Bird Woman hushed him before addressing the wizened creature that appeared to be made of little more than skin and bones. 'For the kindness you have shown us, we are profoundly thankful. Is there any practical advice that you can give us?'

'*The mystery you seek awaits you on the Sacred Mountain. You will find it in the Valley of the Raptors.*'

Bird Woman exhaled, then she bowed deeply.

'I thank you again, from the bottom of my heart.'

'*You owe me no thanks.*'

Bird Woman stared at the wraithlike figure as it faded to nothing with her eyes glazed, as if entranced.

'Strange words. But they may in time prove helpful to us. Quickly, quickly now – Magio and Eefa – we must flee before the hounds discover us.'

'Where – where are fleeing to?'

'We are headed to the high mountains – the land of eternal winter.'

# WHISPERS IN THE NIGHT

Magio had never felt so exhausted. Back in Warren, when he had heard that they must flee from the Scogs, it had sounded really exciting. But since then they had been running and running, with the howling of the hounds ever at their heels. No doubt it was good that they were close to their destination. But he had fallen so many times during the last few hours of daylight that poor old Quimbre had ended up carrying him piggyback for the last few miles. It wasn't turning out to be the adventure he had hoped for. Adventures shouldn't be this scary.

As darkness fell, they rigged up yet another shelter against the lee of some boulders. Eefa, who had been unusually silent since the meeting with the seer, had immediately fallen asleep. No doubt she was just as exhausted as Magio. But despite his exhaustion, Magio couldn't sleep. He huddled up against his sister's curled form, in a half stupor, aware of the hollow knocking of his heartbeat in his chest and at one and the same time feeling guilty that Quimbre and Bird Woman were abandoning sleep, with both of them standing guard out there in the dark.

And those shocking words kept going around in Magio's head: *A war among the Undying provoked such ruin . . .*

He didn't even try to resist the dream when it crept over him. It was the same dream as before, but tonight it seemed more real. He was back on the horribly barren beach, where the old woman was chained to her prison of rusting iron.

He had to stop feeling sorry for himself and force his mind to concentrate. It now seemed important to him in a way he had not realised before. A dream that kept on coming back . . . surely it had to mean something? Weird things were going on, like that stuff with Eefa on the beach below the dilapidated stone tower. Eefa had described that, too, as some kind of a dream, as if she had woken into her own nightmare. Perhaps dreams weren't what we thought they were? Perhaps they were . . . well . . . jinxy! The truth was that he didn't rightly know what to think. Could it be that he was getting some kind of a message that he was too stupid to understand? Maybe dreams were some kind of . . . of communication?

If this was a dream, it was a very peculiar dream. In a normal dream, you shouldn't be so fully aware that you were dreaming. You shouldn't be able to look about yourself and take stock of the location of your dream. The shock of what he saw, when he now did so, caused him to blink, over and over. The beach wasn't a very nice place, not like the lovely soft white sand like the beach at Warren. It was sandless, a cruel desolation of stone. There were no seagulls. There were no clumps of dune grasses, or wild flowers. A biting wind blew around it, coming in from the sea, whipping stones into strange clumps and shapes.

His eyes turned to the old woman, seated cross-legged before the iron shack. For the first time he saw that she wasn't wearing any clothes. What he had previously assumed to be rags were tatters of seaweed . . . seaweed and – oh, he hardly dared to credit it – torn flesh, tatters of her gaping skin. There were things wriggling about inside the holes in her skin, things devouring her flesh.

Tears rose into Magio's blinking eyes.

'You . . . you're really here, aren't you?'

*'I am always here, child.'*

It was such a shock to find himself talking to the old woman, he was close to panicking. But even calming down, he wasn't quite sure as to what she meant by that word – 'always'.

'Are you . . .' His voice was so husky from fright that he had to start again. 'Are you human?'

No answer.

He wondered if this meant she wasn't really human. Yet, now he came to think about it, how could she be human, tethered to that monstrous thing made of rusting iron, day in, day out?

'Who are you?'

*'I am a prisoner, as you can see.'*

Her smile, the desolate appearance of her face, with its bedraggled hair, tore at his heart. He struggled to find words to say, but took a breath and did so. 'I think it's really horrible that somebody did that to you, to chain you. Did you do something really bad?'

*'Perhaps I did.'*

'So, you're being punished?'

*'Mayhaps I am.'* Those eyes, blue as an evening sky, opened wide and Magio felt a strange calm come over him.

'Why are you here – being hurt like this?'

*'My sentence was to experience what it is to be mortal – but without the blessing of death.'*

'I don't understand.'

*'How indeed could you possibly understand the cruelty of such a sentence for an Undying. For a year, for a day, for eternity – it was to be the ultimate curse to one that was ever living.'*

Magio had to think for several long moments even to begin to understand what she was saying to him. 'That's . . . well, it's downright jinxy. How could anybody do this to you?'

*'I transgressed.'*

'How?'

*'I betrayed one I should have loved with all of my heart and soul.'*

'Why would you do that?'

*'Guided by our hearts, we make mistakes. Even we Undying – we are susceptible to entrancement . . .'*

'I don't really understand. You seem so gentle and kind. And what they are doing to you, it's so . . . so bloodywell cruel.'

*'You feel pity for me, child?'*

'Yes, I do.'

*'You would help me?'*

'If only I knew how.'

She laughed, and the laughter appeared to echo around the rocks and the mountains that lay back otherwise in silence.

*'Oh, but your pity – your sympathy – is such sweet solace. That an innocent might pity me, I, who once had such power in my fingertips!'*

'I don't know what I should call you. My . . . My Lady.'

*'What a strange, even wonderful boy you are. But I sense that you have an additional question?'*

'I have a sister.'

*'Ah!'*

'I want her to be real.'

She smiled again. *'Such an unselfish price to ask!'*

'Can you help her, My Lady?'

There was only silence in answer. A silence that appeared to fill the stillness of the dreadful beach, and the vision of the retreating vision of the chained figure by the iron shack, until it was gone from his sight.

The experience was so strange, so disturbing, that Magio woke from his dream. He spun his head, looking about himself in the shelter, to make sure he was truly awake. The wind of his dream was still howling outside. He shivered as he peered out through the cracks in the shelter at the filmy light of pre-dawn. He could barely make out the heavy shadows of the boulders against which they had made their shelter. Magio pulled his blanket around his shoulders, sitting up, cross-legged, rocking back and forth, his thoughts all of a jumble. For several moments he refused to open his eyes, so frightened was he by the sounds of what now appeared to be a growing storm outside. The wind repeatedly rose to a crescendo and then fell, as if it were the sea. Oh, how he missed his blissful mornings on the beach, the race to the rock, the first bare footsteps on the warm white sand, his vision filled with the waves and sun! Did they really have to go back out onto that creepy mountain path with those vicious hounds hunting them?

Just then he heard the sound of Eefa crying.

He opened his eyes and saw her just a few feet away, curled up on her side like a shrimp. He scampered across to her, wrapping himself around her and gripping her so fiercely she became instantly awake.

'What's going on?'

He whispered, 'You were crying in your sleep.'

'No, I wasn't!' She was attempting to distance herself from him, snuggling up into her own curve, but he wouldn't allow it. He clung to her curved form.

'Yes, you were. But it doesn't matter. You're awake now.'
He hesitated, not sure if he should tell her what he had just
experienced. Then he blurted it out. 'I had another awake-
dream.'

'I don't want to hear it. Please stop talking about it,
Magio. I just want to go back to sleep.' She jerked an elbow
backwards, as if to brush him away.

Her elbow hit him on the shoulder. He winced. But he
refused to stop talking. He whispered again, 'The dream was
about the old woman.'

'Stop it! Stop talking!'

'Bird Woman thinks that the Old Woman is important.'

'Sssh!'

'I asked her if she could help you become real.'

He felt her entire body stiffen. But all of a sudden there
was no more time for whispers. With a shout from outside,
Quimbre was calling them to get ready to run yet again. As they
broke cover, they encountered Quimbre breaking camp in a
great hurry. Bird Woman had returned with two game birds
strung over her back. As they scurried preparing to abandon
the camp, she told them that she had taken advantage of the
pre-dawn light to scout the territory immediately ahead,
so she could plot the route for yet another arduous trek, to
the pass for the mountain summit. Even as she spoke, they
heard the howling from what seemed perilously close. They
were instantly on their feet and getting dressed, with Bird
Woman's urgent prompting in their ears.

'Hurry now! We are but a few miles from the entrance to
the pass. We'll be there in little more than an hour if we can
elude those dreadful hounds.'

# Perfidious Chance

'We got um!'

Kull ignored the howling wind that was battering snowflakes against his bulging eyes. He whistled, two-fingered, sending Maw and Claw surging ahead, their nostrils no longer casting, their eyes now fixed on the quarry, jaws slavering at the promise of meat. And now he had his first sight of um: the cunning vixen of a woman, the old man and the boy. No sight of the girl. But then that was to be expected. The bargain was he kill um all, these three – and the girl. Invisible! So, he had been warned, but maybe not scentless. Not if his nostrils had caught her on that bird's skull in the cave! Invisible – let's see how invisible she was now to his gals' sharp-sniffing nostrils when she found herself within clamping distance of their sharp-toothed jaws. He could already feel the weight of that gold in his hands.

'After um, now! Go, me bootiful gals! Take um down!'

He couldn't keep up with Maw and Claw, not with their great strides. His chase was made all the more difficult by the weight of his wet fur coat, added to the weapons he carried: his bow and his twin-headed axe straddling his back, and the sheathed heavy daggers belted to his sides. But still he pounded after them, his long legs leaping through the snow-covered ground.

Wiping his running nose with the back of his hand, he raced onwards and upwards, whistling hard through his fingers so as to keep jollying the gals up. You got to keep control of the pack when they got this close. You didn't want um to get over excited. Didn't want Maw and Claw killing um off before he even got the chance to look um over. Get the business sorted for a start. That was the first priority. Confirm the tally. Only then, when you got the business in hand good and proper, did you get to savour the pleasure of taking your trophies.

Hounds alive! They surely could run! They had arrived onto a flat panhandle that led into the pass between two mountain slopes. On the level ground Kull was now thundering hell for leather between clumps of thick-stemmed dark green and violet tundra grass, poking through the virgin snow.

Up ahead, his gals had just about cornered the trio. The wolf hounds were fanning out, their bodies creeping through the snowy ground, jaws slavering, throats growling. Maw was in the lead, within thirty feet of the running figures. Kull could make out the smaller figure of the brat running ahead of the two taller figures, who were shielding him, heading towards a standing boulder that marked the path towards the soaring mountains. Maw had already outflanked them. Clever gal! She was now in front of them, cutting off their path, with Claw blocking um in from the rear. They had stopped running. The old man spun round to face Maw and the vixen facing Claw. The gals had adopted the baiting position, bodies hugging the ground, ready to spring, jaws agape with slavering fangs.

It was well nigh done.

Kull stopped running, breathing heavily from the exertion. In the thickening snowfall, he hefted his twin-bladed axe two-handed above his head, roaring with triumph.

But there was still the bother of the invisible brat. He was just pondering the problem when the boulder appeared to rear up out of the ground. Something huge struck Maw an almighty blow, knocking her thirty feet into the air. Claw was snarling, squirming closer to the ground. She was attempting to get around the new obstacle, shifting sideways and howling. Kull, perplexed, closed in on the conflict, trying to figure the situation out. Whatever it was, that thing was too big to be human! Kull's eyes darted to where Maw had landed. He saw that her snout was bubbling blood. Not dead then, but injured bad. He whistled twice to Claw, telling her to hold back.

He roared, 'Claw – Maw! Back to us – back!'

This situation was too dangerous for his liking.

Another shriek. The shriek contracted his heart. It was a hound shriek. 'Oh, Claw – me poor gal!'

That did it.

Throwing all caution to the winds, Kull raced ahead to the scene of battle, where he couldn't believe his eyes. A monstrous Scog sentry, a good twenty feet tall and covered in warrior tattoos, was rearing gigantic against the background of the mountain pass. The Scog had hauled Claw into the air by her back legs, and even still she was twisting and growling and attempting to snap back at the huge fist that was tethering her. They were still forty paces ahead of Kull, but from this close he could hear the Scog bellowing. The brute was stabbing at poor Maw with a huge crescentic blade of gleaming bronze.

Beyond the melee, the quarry was escaping.

'No!' Kull roared. 'Stop that! Don't you hurt her!'

Kull threw down all the extraneous stuff he was carrying other than his yew bow. In seconds an iron-tipped arrow thunked into the tattooed breast of the Scog. Without waiting to see its effects, Kull notched a second arrow and sent it into the same enormous body, this time seeing it thunk into the bulging neck. The Scog ignored the wounds. His focus remained the writhing and snapping Claw, who he threw to the ground and was attempting to trample with his foot, as broad as a tree trunk.

Kull grabbed his twin-headed axe from his belt and ran full pelt at the Scog sentry, roaring a mixture of grief and rage. But the giant stood his ground, holding the injured Claw under one foot and extending the huge blade towards him within an enormous fist.

Kull surprised it by speaking pidgin Scog. 'Let go me hound, ya stinking monster!'

The Scog pointed to the path ahead that curled upwards into the mountains, ascending towards distant peaks. Kull was just about knowledgeable enough to translate the Scog's low monotone of growly words.

'Hunting is forbidden on Dil Oonahaahaa.'

Kull shook his axe at it. 'Oo gives a shit!'

'Spilling of blood is forbidden.'

'Oo says?'

'By order His Royal Majesty, Wirgnatha, High King of the First Folk.'

Kull jumped up and down with rage. His quarry was clearly getting away from him, heading for the mountain pass. He kicked at the tree trunk that was pinning Claw to the bloodied snow. It was like kicking at the rocky mountain towering above him.

Kull spat a gobbet of phlegm onto the ground at his feet. He roared, 'Ya stupid bog-creeper! I don't give a rat's pelt for no stupid king. Outa me way or I'll take me axe to you.'

The Scog moved not so much as an inch. Its voice remained infuriatingly calm as it repeated the warning in a slow, calm drawl. 'No hunting, no shedding of blood on Dil Oonahaahaa.'

Kull leapt into the air and he buried his teeth in the Scog's neck, exciting a new maelstrom of conflict. Somewhere within the melee, a horribly injured Fang re-entered the fray, so they were all of a tangle, snarling, growling and howling, while the Scog roared and struck out in every direction, with no intention of giving up the fight.

From the corner of his eye, Kull caught a glimpse of the three figures, now a good hundred paces distant, his hopes dwindling as they scurried up into the soaring mountains.

Scog sentries! Who in the world heard of such a thing? Kull struck out at the impertinent giant, a piledriver of a punch in the middle of his enormous slab of a chin. All it did was to open wide the Scog's eyes with astonishment. But it left Kull dancing around, sucking on his broken knuckles. Then the Scog brought down a huge fist on the crown of Kull's skull. He felt his body bounce against the snow-covered rocks, as if a sledgehammer had slammed hard down on his head. He felt his skull splinter with the blow. And in the confusion, as the dizziness roared and swallowed him up, he heard the snap of his long bow.

Flailing wildly, Kull buried his axe in the nearest leg, below the knee. But the blade stuck in the knee bone of the creature, as if it had struck knotty wood.

'I be hurt,' the Scog grumbled. 'You hurt me!'

Kull heard his own voice moan, as if from some disembodied distance. 'I'll hurt you . . . hurt you a deal more . . . if ya don't let us pass.'

But the creature ignored his warning, lifting a big conch shell from where it was tethered around its neck and blowing out a strange, ululating call into the misty valley far below. It took Kull a moment or two to realise that he was calling for reinforcements. Even as the realisation was sinking into Kull's failing brain, a new blow yanked his right shoulder out of its socket. 'Noooo!' he roared, lashing out with his three still-functioning limbs. He was vaguely aware of the fact he was sitting astride one of the stupid giant's shoulders, sinking his teeth into its enormous nose. A huge hand, with the fingers thick as tree roots, ripped him off the Scog's face and that same hand tossed him thirty or forty feet away into the trampled and bloodied snow.

Kull struggled onto his hands and knees, glancing up at the mountain trail, where there was no longer sight of the quarry. 'Damn you! Damn you to hell – ya stupid monster!'

In that same moment a great fist descended for a second time onto Kull's head. It struck him like a falling tree, crashing him down onto the rocky ground underneath the snowy covering. His eyes were playing tricks with him, turning the entire rocky landscape onto a slant, so he was gazing into a dizzy spectacle sideways. His skewed vision caught a glimpse of Maw borne aloft in a gigantic fist, as if in preparation of being torn limb from limb.

He heard his own slurring voice. 'Stop! We yields – we yields! Don't kill me bootiful gal. Not me darling Maw!'

# The Valley of the Raptors

The company emerged from thick mists, as if they had broken through the curtain of a waterfall to find they were approaching the head of the twisting mountain path. They were confronted by a narrow cleft within a soaring mountain peak, completely enveloped by snow.

Magio turned excitedly to Bird Woman. 'What is this place?'

She surprised them all by saying, 'Back there – when that Ursascogan sentry saved us all – he used a term, Dil Oonahaahaa. I do not speak the Scog language well, but I recognised the term. It means the Sacred Mountain.'

Eefa felt a chill go through her as she thought she understood. 'This mountain is sacred to the Scogs?'

'It would appear so.'

Magio blurted, 'But why is it sacred?'

Bird Woman shrugged. 'I don't know. Perhaps we shall discover why in good time. Meanwhile we should press on just a little more. We need to find a haven where we can escape the bitter cold and rest. We no longer need to rush. Given what we have seen at the entrance to the pass, I doubt there will be anybody hunting us here.'

Eefa was just relieved at the thought of resting.

The confrontation down there at the start of the pass had been the most terrifying experience she had ever had in her life. Yet Quimbre was already back to his normal self, gathering snow to melt for drinking water. Magio appeared to sense the tensions in her. He came up close and whispered, 'Hey – Evie!'

He must see how she was trembling. 'Oh, Gio – I can't stop thinking about it. That terrible man! How his hounds came to . . .'

He squeezed her hand. 'I know! Me too!'

In her mind she was still screaming at the top of her voice as the wolf hounds were tearing through the snowy ground towards them, their jaws agape, covering the distance between them with great bounds. She recalled how Quimbre had taken up the rear, his flintlock loaded . . . And how Bird Woman had notched an arrow in her bow. She could still hear Quimbre's roar to Magio ringing in her ears. 'Run – kiddo!'

Next to her, Magio had been frozen with terror. He must have known, as Eefa did, that there was no outrunning those enormous hounds. But Quimbre had pushed him hard in the direction of the pass. 'Get going! Run like the wind!'

Eefa's mind was still back there running, hand-in-hand with Magio. They hadn't dared to look back . . .

'Now then, kiddo!' Quimbre interrupted her memory of terror. He grinned at Magio, his hat filled with snow to be melted.

'You wouldn't dare!'

'Wouldn't I?'

Magio shrieked as Quimbre emptied the hat over him.

Eefa couldn't believe it. Magio was now shrieking with laughter, hurling fistfuls of snow back into Quimbre's bearded face. He hurled himself at Quimbre, causing them both to fall into the snow. They were rolling about in it, hysterical with laughter.

'You idiots!' she cried.

Bird Woman put a gentle hand on Eefa's shoulder. 'Hush now! They are merely relieved to be alive.'

But Eefa couldn't readily shake those terrible images out of her mind. The huge figure of the beast master! There was something so horribly determined about him. He had looked like one of those scary figures in the tales of ghosts and ogres that Gran had delighted in telling them.

She whispered, 'If it hadn't been for the Scog!'

'Indeed! We've been fortunate. Let us not waste our good fortune!'

But Eefa couldn't help it. She couldn't stop the shudder that went through her. A fine but relentless pattering of snow continued to fall on them. She whispered, 'Hold me.'

Bird Woman stared down at her. 'What is it?'

'I don't know.' She shivered, but it wasn't from the ambient cold. 'I feel . . . I still feel so very afraid.'

'There is no need to be afraid. The hunter, and his vicious hounds, are long behind us.'

Eefa hesitated. Bird Woman's words were comforting. But the feeling just wouldn't go away so easily. 'It isn't just that. I've got such a strange feeling . . . I think it's to do with the fact we have come here. As if something is happening inside me.'

Eefa watched as Magio and Quimbre climbed back onto their feet and shook the snow off themselves, ready to trudge ahead as long as the light lasted. Eefa pressed on with the others for a mile or two along the rising path, but the strange feeling never went away. Bird Woman signalled a stop when they arrived at a gathering of caves among the hillocks of grass and lichens that grew thinly among the high-altitude boulders. Quimbre and Magio searched cave after cave until they found one clean and dry enough to sleep in; meanwhile Bird Woman tiredly slid off the gear that had hung from her shoulders throughout the journey and inclined her head at Eefa. It seemed to Eefa to be a comradely signal, outside of the vision of anybody else. In the fading light, Eefa gazed up about herself at the extraordinary valley that had opened off that narrow cleft in the mountain. Beyond the densely wooded valley floor, sheer cliff faces soared to either side of them, pocketed with a huge variety of holes and crevices. In many such openings she glimpsed movement: the fluttering of feathered bodies, or the glint of black predatorial eyes peering down in their direction.

Then, as if prompted by an unseen and unheard signal, the evening sky was invaded by raptors.

Huge bird shapes floated and swooped with ringing cries through the air above them. It was the most wonderful, if eerie, spectacle that Eefa had ever seen. Next to her, Magio was clapping his hands in open-mouthed awe, his eyes glittering. He began to cheer at the top of his voice.

'Hooray!'

Even Bird Woman gazed up into the sky in silent enchantment.

Magio, unable to stand still, was taking directionless steps here and there, tugging at Eefa, as if lost as to what to do.

'We must stay calm,' Eefa urged him.

'I can't!' His face was flushed with excitement, as if desperate to explore their immediate surroundings. 'C'mon!'

She didn't feel like coming on – whatever that meant.

Quimbre appeared to be the only one untouched by the source of their excitement. He was busy with setting up a new shelter in their chosen cave.

Magio took off, running away from Eefa, forcing her to follow him – if for no other reason than making sure he didn't do something stupid. She slid down a slope of snow over shale to discover a small, dark lake.

'What are you up to?'

'Don't be a spoilsport.'

'Please be careful, Magio.'

'Oh, I don't want to be careful! Don't you feel it here, Eefa?'

'Feel what?'

'Stuff – I can't explain it. Stuff like I never even dreamed of feeling before. Like there's a . . . a real adventure, a very great adventure, opening up right in front of us.'

'You're not making any sense.'

'I can't describe it any better. Just stop thinking about it. Just look at them – look up there, into the sky!'

Eefa followed his gaze, back up into the sky where huge winged forms criss-crossed the darkening maroon, rising out of or settling among the proliferation of openings – yet more caves that pocked the valley walls.

A hand on her shoulder startled her. She spun round to find herself confronted by Bird Woman.

'Pardon my startling you, Eefa. Yet I could not fail to observe that you were studying the valley. Tell me what you sense – it might be important.'

She said, simply, 'It's so high. I think it's probably higher than the clouds. And yet it's surprisingly thick with plants and trees.'

'Yes, it is. It's positively lush.'

Eefa, unnerved by her own observation, said, 'What do you make of it?'

Bird Woman was now gazing keenly about her, inspecting what little she could in the falling dark. 'I agree with what you were saying moments earlier. I feel it too. There is a distinct feeling of strangeness here.'

'What kind of strangeness?' Magio asked.

'Perhaps a magic of sorts. But I agree that this is no real answer, but rather it begs new questions. Night falls even as we speak. Quimbre has made ready a cave. We should rest for now. Tomorrow is another day.'

'Britzy!'

Bird Woman led Eefa and Magio back up the slope of scree, to where Quimbre was lighting a fire with brushwood at the cave. As they settled around the crackling flames, comforting themselves with the last few morsels of food to eat, Eefa reflected on Bird Woman's words about strangeness and magic. It seemed to her, gazing across to her deeply tanned and lined face, illuminated now by the flickering flames, that Bird Woman seemed somewhat stranger than usual herself. She just couldn't control her impatience any longer. She had to know.

'Bird Woman – is this where you belong?'

Bird Woman smiled, shaking her head. 'That's a very strange question.'

'But you haven't answered it.'

'If you mean, is this the place of my birth, or my upbringing, then I can assure you that it is not.'

Eefa spoke softly, thoughtfully. 'This is the Valley of the Raptors, isn't it? That was where you have been leading us to, from the very beginning. And it was what the old seer spoke of too. But yet you say you haven't been here before.'

'It is true! This is the Valley of the Raptors. But it is also true that I have never been here before.' Bird Woman sighed.

'I can see why you might struggle to believe me. Perhaps I should qualify that statement. I have never been here in the flesh. Yet I have been drawn to this valley in my dreams.'

Magio's head dropped. 'I don't know whether that's britzy or jinxy.'

'It's neither, Magio. We all have dreams. And some of us, as you well know, have the same special dream, over and over.'

Eefa nodded. 'You mean, like the common dream Magio and I have been sharing – of the old woman chained to an iron shack?'

'Yes.'

'But what does it mean?' Magio persisted.

'Like your longing for a great adventure, Magio, all my life I have sensed the existence of a place such as this. A place I would one day come to and discover my true purpose. It isn't easy to explain hopes, dreams – as both of you know. Perhaps I hoped that if and when at last I discovered it, I would discover a new sense of meaning . . . enlightenment?'

'A meaning for why you have always been interested in birds?'

Bird Woman hesitated. 'When you become so very interested in something, as I did with birds, you don't necessarily know the reason why.' Her face lifted and her eyes reflected the orange of the flames. 'From the earliest of my memories, I was enchanted by birds. I watched them, studied them, fed them what little I could. Even as a young child they would take the food from my hand. I felt what you might call a bond, deep in my heart. As I grew to maturity as a woman, my sense of the wonder of birds remained. It simply grew stronger, more . . . magical. If it came to a choice between friends and such magic, then I knew that I must learn to survive without friends.'

'Hey, like you mean, birds spoke to you?'

'Dear Magio! I don't claim that such communication was in the form of words. How can I explain . . . well, do we not feel communication through music, or the beauty of landscape, or a sense of being? Perhaps it was truly a sense of magic. If magic, then it was as if through the magic of birds that I was developing some otherworld reach within my spirit, my soul.'

Eefa gazed up into the circle of light that haloed the fire, observing that it had started to snow. She felt the first small flakes land in her open eyes, causing her to blink them away.

'Do all birds, then, speak the same language?'

'Animals do appear capable of communication. Have you not seen a look you recognise in the eyes of a dog, or horse?'

'You mean something closer to a feeling?' Eefa asked, fascinated.

'Like that, I suppose, but more complex than mere feeling, or instinct. Some very basic level of communication.' She hesitated, as if searching for words. 'I suppose that I felt that I had a great deal to learn from birds. Theirs is a cruel world, without the rules humans take for granted. And yet, perhaps, I did learn something about our human world from them, and from their behaviour, too.'

There was a silence then, lasting several thoughtful moments, during which it began to snow again, a spindrift of tiny flakes, swirling around in the light of the fire. During the same silence they were joined about the fire by Quimbre, who must have overheard the conversation. If so, he made no comment, merely lighting his pipe and then smoking it in silence. Eefa was inclined to smile as she noticed how Magio inched a little closer to Quimbre.

She knew it was going to be hard to sleep tonight. There were intermittent hoots, caws and shrieks coming from down out of the sky – sounds she associated with the huge beating wings. The Valley of the Raptors was a strange and scary place – and the strangeness seemed altogether as one with the presence of Bird Woman. There really was something very curious going on. Bird Woman had closed her eyes, she had crossed her arms tight about her breast, and her lips were moving, as if in prayer.

'What is it, Bird Woman?'

'I am seeking that same enlightenment, Eefa.'

'Who from?'

'From the forces that instructed me to bring you here.'

'What forces – what instruction?' Magio interrupted.

'My instruction was to find the special one – she who cannot feel the storm.'

'What does that mean?'

'I believe it means your sister, Eefa.'

Eefa shook her head. 'I don't feel so strong – so superhuman.'

'No – perhaps I chose the wrong words. Yet, in ways that you perhaps are unaware, you are empowered.'

'Empowered, how?'

'Soon, I believe, your question will be answered.' Bird Woman leaned sideways to gaze at Eefa face to face. 'You and Magio should take shelter in the cave now. We're all very tired, needful of sleep.'

Eefa turned to look at Magio: had he heard what Bird Woman had just said to her? Something was about to happen. And, if Bird Woman was right, it was likely to happen soon.

Perhaps it was time they took her advice and went to sleep in the cave. But Magio was too excited to end this conversation. He insisted, 'Why haven't you a name? You must have had a name, once – something different to Bird Woman?'

'You're right, Magio. Once I had a name. But when others spurned me, and called me the name you know me by, I decided I had no further need of my birth name. I accepted the name they taunted me with. I was proud to bear it.'

Magio looked across at the weathered face of Bird Woman. 'You really can talk to the birds up there in the sky?'

'I can make use of them – communicate with them.'

'That's magic?'

Quimbre laughed. 'Magic, kiddo?'

'Don't you believe in magic, Quimbre?'

'There's a deal of truth in what Bird Woman is saying. I do believe that birds will court one another, as would lovers. And the parent bird will lead you away from its nest by deliberately exposing itself to danger.'

Magio's voice fell to a whisper, addressed to Quimbre. 'But you don't believe in magic?'

'My daddy was a very stubborn man. He said that he would believe in magic when it struck him between the eyes.'

Bird Woman shrugged. 'Perhaps, Magio, it depends on how one defines magic. Here – when I first arrived into this brooding valley, I sensed that it changed me. I suspect from what Eefa told me, she felt something similar. Perhaps you sense it too? If so, you might call that magic.'

What Bird Woman was saying was very interesting. But Eefa was struggling to focus on it. She was falling asleep where she sat, in the fading warmth of the dying fire, staring up into the black of sky where spindrift snow now whirled and eddied like a swarm of fireflies. Where the tiny flakes landed on her skin, they prickled like icicle points of unmelting cold. When she lifted up her arm and tried to catch the snowflakes, she saw that her entire arm was sprinkled with them.

Quimbre had been saying something, in answer to Bird Woman. But abruptly he appeared to hesitate. And then a note of surprise had invaded his voice. 'Perhaps . . . by the very gods, I am coming to believe in magic!'

Eefa stiffened. She saw how Magio was looking at her, wide-eyed. Gazing down at herself, she saw how her entire being was covered with snowflakes. Her eyes darted back to Quimbre, whose was staring back at her, the pipe in the process of tumbling from his lips.

'Oh, no!'

Eefa struggled to her feet, wondering if she should run. But where could she run to here?

Quimbre was also climbing to his feet. Tears were dimming Eefa's vision, melding it into a blurry fog, as if the entire sky and landscape had become suffused with the falling snow.

She felt powerful hands take hold of her shoulders.

'You are real!'

She wept.

Quimbre's brawny arms lifted her bodily from the ground, as if she weighed no more than a feather. 'I can see you, feel you now. I can even make out the features of your face. Your eyelids are full of snow – I can see them blink.'

She shook her head. 'I'm so sorry!'

'Did you just speak? Did I really hear you say sorry! How is it that I hear you now? How is it that I see you and hear you?'

Magio said to Quimbre, 'You can hear her now because she's letting you. Only those she wants to can hear her.'

'All this time I did not see you! All this time I thought you a figment of Magio's imagination!'

Eefa spoke hesitantly, her words broken with tears. 'I had grown used to the fact nobody could see me – nobody other than Magio and Gran. Then . . . then you arrived. You were so big. And Gran said you were a pirate. I was terrified of you.'

'You were terrified of old Quimbre?'

'Yes.'

Quimbre lifted his fingers as if to touch her face, but held back an inch or two, then stood back a pace. 'How strange you are. How beautiful! Magio asked me if I believed in magic and I said no. But now magic has truly struck me between the eyes.'

'Please, Quimbre, will you forgive me?'

Quimbre laughed. 'Only on condition you give old Quimbre a hug.'

Her eyes moist, Eefa went on tiptoe to hug the great bulk of Quimbre and then kiss him on his grey bearded cheek.

Tears filled his hoary old eyes.

# The Price of Failure

It was like rising out of a suffocating pit of pain. Even when he managed to get a single eye open, he didn't recall who he was or what he was doing here, lying in what looked like a pool of blood. That just didn't make sense. Nothing about this made sense. Things that were supposed to work didn't work. He closed his single functioning eye, though even this simple act proved difficult because of the gritty feeling of what he presumed to be blood. His head was equally stupid. It took him several moments of slow and difficult consideration to realise that the blood he was lying in was his own. And he wasn't alone among the carnage. He was cradling the ravaged head of a hound in the crook of what appeared to be an arm that didn't feel like it really belonged to him.

This brought on a spell of fast breathing – in-out, in-out – snorting through what didn't really feel like his nose.

A feeling of panic rose in him, overwhelming his pain.

*'Love it.'*

It was a voice of command inside his head.

*'Stroke it!'*

Such was his terror he didn't dare to disobey.

Whatever it was that he was now stroking – and his fingers registered that it was something furry – he had been commanded to love it. This made no sense. The trouble was that his brain wasn't working the way it should be working so he couldn't tell why it made no sense. He swallowed, and even that was difficult. Shit! Piss! Monstrous hell! Somehow, he had to figure this out.

He exhaled a snort, spraying blood. The act involved him contracting his chest and this caused him to double up with agony.

*'Stop!'*

He stopped.

*'Look at what you are stroking!'*

He looked at what he was stroking, but his vision was blurred. Taking a breath through a single surviving nostril, he tried searching with his fingers . . . *One of the gals!* But which one?

'Oh, no! Broken, us be – me poor darling!'

*'Waking at last, are we? Good!'*

The shock of this – whatever this was – numbed his mind. He fell back into drifting in and out of consciousness. But it just wouldn't let him be.

*'Remember!'*

He did so – he remembered what he had no desire to remember . . . That fight with the stupid Scog at the climb to the mountain!

That was what had happened to him – and to his hound.

The renewed swell of pain caused him to roll over onto his back. Pain from innumerable injuries blotted out any reason in his mind.

*'You must continue to remember!'*

Bastos Kull didn't care to remember. He was trying to find a way to forget. There was no way he could merely rest on his back. There was no position he could find to stop it. He was too injured, too damaged.

*'Remember! Then assess the situation!'*

'Oh . . . aaah!'

From what he could remember, he and his single surviving hound, Maw, had fought with a gigantic Scog. They had lost the fight. He had suffered numerous broken bones. His blood was leaking out of myriad wounds.

Panic wheeled inside his skull. Why wasn't he dead? He'd seen less injured quarry that were dead as a stone.

*'Assess the situation!'*

Who was talking to him, inside his head?

*'You are mortally wounded.'*

Now there was an unnecessary reminder. He felt at the great rip in the skin of his abdomen. As he did so the same hissing voice crept into his head.

*'It isn't just a tear!'*

'What?'

*'The wound goes deeper than just the skin. The underlying muscles are ripped apart, your guts are torn apart.'*

He moaned with pain, then began to shove his intestines back into the gap in his abdomen. It wasn't easy with a single functioning hand. Just feeling their oily sausage shapes made him heave. The more he struggled with the nauseating task, the more he retched, and the agony of retching made him vomit. The repeated vomiting made him feel as if his single functioning eye was being pushed out of its socket.

The voice inside his head was brutally calm. *'You are broken, Bastos Kull.'*

The word 'broken' pierced him like the blade of a lance. How had he got himself and Maw into such a terrible predicament?

*'You are dying.'*

Yeah – so he was dying! Right now, he didn't give a tinker's damn. All he wanted was for the agony to end. But still there was a spark of stubbornness in him that made him turn his head and confront with his one working eye the tall dark silhouette, arms akimbo, against the sky. She looked different from the sexy female who had come to his bar to hire his services. Her figure was semi-transparent, as if serpents were coiling and twisting about one another within a gossamer shell. And the eyes gazing down on him were a green-glowing quicksilver, with serpent slits for pupils.

'Why . . . why torment us?'

*'I enjoy it!'*

It screamed against every instinct in him to beg, but he did force himself to do so. 'Tricked . . . Us been tricked by a scheming witch!'

*'I contracted you to provide a service for me. I offered you a fortune in gold. You agreed the contract. But you failed me.'*

The fact that she was right was now meaningless. There was nothing he could do about it. He might derive some satisfaction from hating her. But he doubted that his hating her would matter.

'Why keep us alive?'

*'It is fortunate for you that I don't have time to find an alternative hunter. Thus, am I obliged to repair you.'*

What was she rambling on about? He was snorting all the more now with his breathing. Death was hauling him in.

*'Your broken bones will be mended. Your failing heart renewed.'*

He didn't know what to make of nothing no more. If he was able to laugh, he'd have laughed aloud. He just didn't have the breath to waste. There was a dizzying sense of movement that made him fear the worst. He closed his single functioning eye.

*'Don't imagine you will be restored to your former self. Your former self failed me. You will be reconstituted to my requirements.'*

'Go to hell . . . witch!'

Pain rose so that he was flickering in and out of consciousness. There was a vague awareness that things were happening to him. Through the rising agony, he felt bizarre currents streaming through him.

'Whoooaaaa . . . !'

*'Be quiet!'*

He wondered if beyond the wall of agony, perhaps, he really was dead. His limbs felt torn apart, as if outside forces were controlling them. His mind was spinning, as if trapped in a whirlpool. The spinning stopped, but he was left disorientated, no longer sure where he was, or if he really existed any more. There was a roaring sound in his ears, a sulphurous smell in his nostrils, and then a rainbow blaze of lights.

'Oooohhhh!'

Kull gazed about himself through the single functioning eye and realised that he was no longer on the stony ground before the spiralling path up to the mountain. He had been transported to another place. He was suspended, upside-down, over a bed of blazing lava. He was close to the bottom of a pit.

He heard the command. *'Resurrect it!'*

The 'it' was him.

His lips fashioned the word, 'Shiiitttt!'

He heard guttural voices in a language that he didn't understand. His body was floating in a soup of strangeness. Winged goblins flitted about him. Their bodies seemed to burn at their core beneath a skin of charcoal, like the fissured lava in the pit. Then the capacity to breathe rushed back into his lungs. But his first breath was so agonising he couldn't stop himself from screaming.

'Stop . . . it . . . right now!'

*There is nothing to be gained from resistance.*

'Don't want it! Don't want to be resurrected!'

*The choice is not yours!*

Yet more vile things were being done to him. It felt as if every organ in his body was being torn apart and then melded back together again.

He whispered, 'Even I . . . Even Bastos Kull . . . showed mercy.'

*Demon bots are not given to mercy.*

Demon bots!

His body was being lowered into the blazing lava in the pit. The furnace was incinerating him, setting him aflame.

'Noooooooooo!'

*I would burn you to a cinder with pleasure. But a bargain was struck in blood. That bargain has saved you from death. But you were so far gone – you and the cur – that I am obliged to refashion you.*

Kull was too exhausted to reply. He was screaming his lungs out as he was hoisted back out of the pit. The demon bots rasped, and spat, and ground their sharp fangs, and hissed, but then they withdrew from him, as though in fear and awe of their mistress. His own fear was cut through by a terrible scream. For a moment he thought it was his own throat, screaming. But it wasn't him.

*Maw!*

The screaming went on and on. It brought tears to Kull's eyes. 'Stop it! Stop what you're doing!'

*The cur must also be remade!*

'Don't hurt her! Don't you . . .! Oh, me poor gal!'

She laughed. The voice was amused, light-hearted, an incongruous sound in this brutal landscape of fire and torment. How could anyone be light-hearted when committing such terrible torture on those who served her? In that moment he discovered that both his eyes were now functioning. He blinked them clear of grit to peer more clearly at the tall, shadowy figure, which now seemed to be nothing more than wreathes of black smoke.

She appeared to read his mind, addressing him in a voice that resembled the crackling of river ice. *'What you call pain will end. And when it does, you will not fail me a second time. If you do, I promise you that you will not emerge alive from my furnace.'*

He could only throw back his head until it was touching his spine and roar, roar again, roar and roar and roar.

He could hear her cold voice through his misery.

*'There is a word in the spheres of the Undying. That word is anord. Anord ruined this miserable world, as it ruined the world of The One I serve. You call it the Chaos. It is in both our interests that the anord should end. But this would demand the introduction of stern order. That is what I am tasked to effect – my instruction from The One.'*

Maw was still screaming in the background even as she spoke with that emotionless slithery voice. He wanted to rip her throat out. But he was worn down beyond screaming. He found that he was sitting in dirt under a night sky. He had no idea where he was, or how she had spirited him here.

He felt a creeping reawakening of his senses. It happened in the reverse order of which he was lost them: eyes, hearing, mouth and tongue . . . He was beginning to feel things, all over his body. His jaw, for example – the jaw that had been shattered by the Scog sentinel felt movable. He tested it, moving it up and down, and then round and round. It felt sound. It felt better than sound. He tried gnashing his teeth. He inhaled, opened wide his fingers, staring at them, then bunched them into fists. Tentatively, he felt about himself. He tested his arms. Both appeared to work. He climbed onto unsteady feet, staring about him. He patted at himself, unable to credit the return of strength and power in the parts of him that had been broken by the Scog.

'By the Powers . . . oooohhhh by the suffering . . .!'

*'You are more than restored.'*

'More than . . .?'

*'Must I remind you of our bargain?'*

He struggled to remember. 'What bargain?'

Then he heard a growl.

Maw!

He called out to her: he whistled for her to come to him.

She didn't come to him, not right away. But she whined and she side-tracked here and there.

Even so, how his heart leapt.

'Oh, Maw – me dearest Maw!'

*'My offer remains.'*

What offer . . .?

*'You must continue the hunt. The quarry now thinks you dead. They will abandon their wariness. The gold will yet crown your success.'*

The gold?

The memory trickled back into his mind: the bargain made back in his bar, surrounded by his trophies. That cascade of gold coins. Gold – enough to make Bastos Kull a lord.

# Frost-Glow

Eefa assumed that she was awake-dreaming again, imagining that she was standing barefoot in soft white sand and shivering in the crisp morning air of the beach at Warren. Then she discovered that she was not standing on the familiar beach; truly, it wasn't a beach at all. She was standing in a magical landscape in which every feature had been exquisitely captured in frozen crystal by a thick layer of hoar frost.

'Oh – oh!' she exclaimed in a mixture of astonishment and delight.

All around her, on various levels in the rocks and frost-painted trees, she saw minuscule darts of movement. She had to look really carefully to detect their origins, being astonished yet again by creatures with skin as crystalline as the hoar frost, but of a more greenish hue. They resembled humans, but they were only a few inches high, with slender bodies and willowy limbs, all seemingly made out of ice. The myriad eyes that were now uniformly staring at her were of the faintest blue. While Eefa couldn't help but swivel her gaze from one to another, she noticed that many had what appeared to be wings folded over their backs and spicules of ice over their bodies that was so fine it resembled hair.

'What's happening?'

Her reply came from myriad tinkling voices. 'We have come to welcome you!'

'I must be dreaming?'

'You are very much awake.'

'I can't believe I'm awake! Oh, you . . . you are too beautiful to be real!' Eefa's bewildered eyes swept the frost-coated landscape, and now that she knew what to look for, she was seeing the tiny ice-encrusted beings everywhere.

'We are not beautiful. We are survivors. As you must become, if we would serve the Lady of the Shore.'

Eefa's eyes widened at this reply. She also saw Bird Woman, seated cross-legged on a rocky promontory, where she must have mounted watch for the night. Then . . . oh, she must truly be awake . . . or possibly sleepwalking? Yet it looked and felt altogether real. Most unusually for Bird Woman, she appeared to be dozing, with her eyes slightly ajar. Her lean face, her entire skin, was coated with that same fine frost.

'What's happening – has she been hurt?'

'She is merely enchanted.'

'Enchanted?'

The ice-crusted beings ignored her astonishment. One of them, a female, taller than the others, caught Eefa's attention. She was sitting astride the neck of a snow hare on a nearby ledge of rock. She slipped from her mount in a graceful curve of movement and was now genuflecting before Eefa, her head bowed.

Eefa clapped her hands in delight.

The creature was so gorgeous, so magically constructed, as far as she could judge, out of hoar frost. Her skin was greenish, like all of the others, but her entire body seemed to be pierced with sharp spicules of what appeared to be ice. Eefa didn't know what to think. The poor creature looked as if she should be freezing cold and miserable with the spears of ice that ran through her figure, but on the contrary, she appeared to be full of life, and piqued with curiosity about Eefa herself.

'Oh, you cannot be real!' Eefa was so jittery she had to take a deep breath. It was so strange, and yet wonderful, it had to be another of those peculiar dreams.

'You would prefer it to be so?' The creature spoke with a quiet voice, deeper than the other, but one that still tinkled, like musical chimes, in her hearing.

'Oh, no! No, no – no! Please don't be offended. I am just so taken by surprise I don't know what to think.'

The being swirled her fingers. It excited a medley of lights among the multitude, which, through their interactions, provoked miniature rainbows. 'The First Folk called us frost sprites. But things have much changed since the Age of Innocence. I doubt if their descendents today would recognise us. Not since we hid our existence in the high peaks.'

'The First Folk?'

'Those you call Ursascogans.'

'Scogs?'

'That is a derogatory term that we would rather avoid.'

Eefa, nonplussed, had to bow her head and think some more before she continued. 'I . . . oh, you've surprised me so much I don't know what to think. But from what you say, you have another name for your people?'

The frost sprite was amused. 'Goodness, we are not people! We exist as a core of being about which we construct a carapace of crystal. We alter our carapace to comfort the vision of visitors – at least those we desire to meet. We have a complexity of different orders of sprite being that would make your mind spin.'

Eefa closed her eyes tight shut. This could not be happening. Sometimes in dream states the dream itself tried to persuade you that it was real. This was all so utterly, utterly impossible – as mind-blowing as it was entrancing. Tentatively, she opened her eyes again, as if to test if it had all been an illusion. But the strange being, spiculated by needles of ice, was still confronting her.

'Are you sure that Bird Woman is merely sleeping. She is safe – unhurt?'

'She does not sleep. She sees and hears. It was thought prudent that she be allowed to witness – but not to intercede.'

Eefa blinked several times at that, remembering Bird Woman's words around the fire the night before: *I believe, your question will be answered soon.* It provoked a quickening of her heartbeat. 'I don't pretend to understand all that you say. But I do think that you are lovely, so diaphanous. If what you are saying is true, I would hate to imagine that you were the last of your people.'

'We are not people, as I have already explained. Even so, I appreciate the kindness of your words.'

Eefa sighed, gazing back to the cave where Magio and Quimbre appeared to be sleeping. She must have woken with the very moment of dawn and, in a high-asleep state still, come out into the freezing air. 'Are there many of these, what you called orders of being? I mean, are there others like you?'

'The problem is we can no longer say. We have cut ourselves off from our kind for so long we have lost contact. We have legends, of course, of spring sprites, water sprites, sprites that inhabit the drops of dew that settle over leaves in the morning. Some legends speak of fire sprites that are said to delight in the molten crystals of volcanoes, with their thunderous energies. But we know not who, if any, might have further survived the Chaos.'

Eefa shook her head.

The tiny being embarrassed her by genuflecting before her again. 'I apologise for my arrogance in speaking so wantonly about ourselves. I should remind myself, and you, that there is little time for niceties. You have much to learn in so short a time!'

Eefa had no idea what those words meant. She was still struggling to come to terms with what she had just heard. Around her more and more of the frost sprites were issuing from every crack and crevice, like fireflies dancing in a landscape of glittering starlight.

'I don't understand.'

'Then ask,' came the voice of the tiny being. 'Ask what you will.'

'I've been so uncertain about myself all of my life. I – I never really understood why I was different to everybody else. My life has been so difficult, to be separated from, unable to connect with, other people. It made me think I wasn't real – or that I was in some way being punished. And yet you appear to have expected me. It is really possible that you know something about why I am as I am?'

'You were burdened with invisibility – it was intended to hide your very existence from unfriendly eyes.'

Eefa was startled by this new information – it caused the hackles to rise on the back of her neck.

'What unfriendly eyes?'

'Some you have already discovered – your enemies are many.'

She whirled around, shaking her head. 'Oh, I sense that you wish to be kind to me, but I wish you wouldn't talk in riddles. What's really going on? Why were we brought here, to this place above the clouds? Why won't you tell me your name?'

'We are the Oonaree.'

'But that sounds like a people. It doesn't sound like your name – I mean you in person?'

The tiny being looked back at her, as if surprised. 'My name is complex, since it must carry information of clan and inheritance that would be key to my people but hardly relevant to a stranger.'

'Then simplify it for my sake.'

'You may call me Woll.'

'Thank you, Woll. Do all frost sprite names carry such information?'

'All names have a wealth of meaning – and the meaning can change with the circumstances.'

'How confusing!'

Woll stiffened. 'You are correct. Misunderstandings have arisen from the misinterpretation of names. Even so we, frost sprites do cherish names.'

'You mean, you keep them secret?'

'Certainly. They must be held both sacred and secret when it comes to big folks, like you.'

'Why?'

'The big folks, the very few who know of our existence, do not like us. They fear us because we are small and, to them, so pellucid as to appear invisible.'

'Oh!'

'They also imagine that we are capable of impish behaviour, casting spells and blighting crops, hurting animals and even people.'

'Are you?'

'No. But such have been the rumours, convenient no doubt to your farmers of old, so they could feel free to dispossess us from our natural homelands. Such ill behaviour led to unpleasant encounters in the past. We are peaceful by nature, and rather than enter into confrontation, we flee. In time this forced us into more inclement niches – such as you find us.'

Eefa was staggered at what she had seen, and heard. But despite this she had decided that she already loved the gentle face, so spiculated with icy needles. She felt a strong desire to reach out and touch the minuscule form, but she was afraid that mere contact with her human warmth might inadvertently melt her.

'But what in the world can you find here to eat?'

'We do not consume the flesh of the living, whether of animals or plants. We respect and venerate all life. We carry within our bodies friendly beings that capture the energy of sunlight. We provide them with a temple to inhabit, and they provide us with the sustenance to live.'

'Oh, Woll! How . . . how utterly wonderful! My brother, Magio, would call it superquadruple britzy!'

'We count ourselves fortunate.'

'But how, then, could the Chaos have affected you?'

'We remain exceedingly sensitive to the balances of the world. The Chaos you referred to deeply affected us. We suspect that the much-loved orders of the White Cotton Dew Sprites and the Lilac Berry Dew may even have been . . . extinguished.'

'Oh, I'm so sorry.'

Woll gazed back at her. She hesitated, as if considering what she had to say carefully. Her pale blue eyes regarded Eefa, blinking a little faster. 'This meeting is not about us. It is about you.' Woll hesitated, as if taking time to consider her words. 'I know more of you than you might imagine. Enough to know there has been much in your life that has

been hidden from you. Much, I regret, that as a result of the
necessary secrecy, must have added to the burden of one so
sensitive.'

'I . . . I don't understand.'

Woll drew her two tiny fists to her mouth, provoking a
high-pitched musical tinkling from the icicles that sprouted
from her fingers.

In Eefa's ears, the music was so eerily beautiful it brought
tears to her eyes.

Woll spoke quietly, but insistently. 'You are blessed with
the grace of bringing the torment to an end.'

'What . . . what are you talking about?'

'At the very moment of your birth, we received a sign.'

Eefa was again astonished. 'My birth . . . Oh, what
possible sign?'

'In that same moment the Chaos was at its worst.
Darkness threatened, not merely the world of mortals but also
that of the Undying. They say that the Chaos was provoked
by rebellion among the Undying. Such was the disturbance
that the frost sprites readied for likely annihilation. Many
indeed suffered that terrible fate. We, those of us who were
left, assembled in a single congregation to accept the end
with grace. But then, at the very darkest moment, we saw a
bright new star enter the heavens. A star of hope, as we later
came to realise. And then, we encountered visions . . . Oh,
my dear Eefa, including one most extraordinary vision.'

Eefa was so shocked she took to her feet and gazed about
the frost-frozen landscape of mountain peaks and snow, all
changing in patterns and hues as the sun rose to shine through
it at different angles. She stared at the tiny figure of Woll. This
strange being was clearly wise, and very much older than she
looked. She possessed great knowledge and wisdom. Even as

Eefa attempted to appraise what was happening, the myriad tiny forms were now spreading in a sparkling oval about her.

'Oh, Woll, I know that whatever you've been telling me is important. But I don't really understand. What role am I supposed to play in it?'

'A most vital role! You are the bearer of the Bree Salis.'

This was the term she had just heard on Woll's lips. She recalled the terrifying experience of the strange voice that had emerged from Magio's mouth – the voice that seemed to come from the figure of the old woman, chained to the iron hut on that dreadful beach . . .

A tension clutched at her throat as she pressed Woll. 'What is this thing you talked about? What is the Bree Salis?'

'I cannot explain the Bree Salis. The Lady of the Shore herself must explain, and even then, only when the time is right.'

'The Lady of the Shore?'

'Please don't be afraid – though I would understand why such a burden might appear confusing and frightening. Be comforted that she chose you.'

'The Lady chose me?'

'You were chosen – from the moment of your conception. Thus were you honoured, even as at the same time burdened. The risk that you might be identified was very great. Your invisibility was vital. Such was your peril, even as a babe-in-arms. There would have been no hiding your precious role from the prying eyes of the enemy among the Undying had you been visible.'

Eefa's felt so dizzy she had to sit down in the hoar frost. 'You're speaking in riddles. Why won't you explain all of this – this thing you call the Bree Salis – this Lady you speak of?'

'I think you already know who I speak of.'

She did – it had been lurking in her mind throughout this conversation. 'The old woman – the old woman on that awful beach?'

'The one who was, and always will be our blessed Lady of the Shore.'

'Who is she?'

'The most beautiful, the kindest goddess of them all.'

'Goddess!'

'Yes.'

'How am I expected to understand? I know nothing about goddesses.'

'But you do. You have already met her.'

'The old woman . . . the old woman in chains on the sea shore?'

'Yes.'

'I know nothing about her. What happened to her? Why is she being punished in this way?'

'I cannot explain. Soon I hope to lead you to her, though the way will be perilous. But first you must be advised as to what to expect.'

'No, no . . . no!'

Eefa didn't think she could take any more adventure, danger to her life. How could this be happening to her? She appeared to have no control over anything any more. She was caught up in a bewilderment of change, the world of ice spiralling in her senses, and the myriad upturned faces of the frost sprites drifting away from her, in her half dream, all now metamorphosing into a blinding brightness of dawn.

She forced herself to retract from this conversation. She clenched tight shut her eyes again. She thought, *I'm waking from a dream. I must be. This just appears to be real. It cannot be real. I am still only half awake, more like three quarters asleep.*

She wished she were herself an enchantress, so she could cast away all of her recent experience into the land of dreams. But when she re-opened her eyes, the frost sprites, and with them the unbelievable magnitude of what was being put upon her shoulders, refused to go away.

*I . . . oh, please let me go!*

In a moment, as if by the wave of a conjuror's wand, she heard the susurration of waves on shingle. She issued a muted whine of terror as she found herself gazing at the figure, seated cross-legged on the stony beach before the brooding shack of rusting iron. Now she was so very close to it, she saw that there were no windows, no entries or exits, just massive unyielding walls. The rusting hut of adamantine iron crouched there, monstrously unmoving, a brooding horror.

She waited, paralysed with fear.

'*Would it help you, Eefa, if you were granted more explanation?*' The voice was one she recognised: it was the kindly old woman.

Eefa whispered, 'Yes.' She wanted to say more but the words were choked back in her throat.

'*Your disbelief is reasonable. So I shall explain. For a transgression of love was I condemned for all of eternity to this fate.*'

'For a . . . a transgression?'

'*I betrayed the One who now rules the world of the Undying. When love turns to its opposite, it can be more vengeful than mere hate.*'

Eefa felt utterly out of her depth.

'Are you the being the frost sprites spoke of? The Lady of the Shore?'

'*I am.*'

'Then why can't you stop this . . . stop this being . . . from doing these terrible things to you?'

*'Once I loved him, with a passion that went beyond reason. In such a passion, I allowed him insight into aspects of power that, had I been less emotion-led, I would have concealed from one so ambitious. As I now realise, he used the intimacy of our courtship to elevate himself to a position of undeserved power.'*

'You were married to him?'

*'Oh, little one – how simply you envision it! Yet you put your finger exactly on the core of my transgression.'*

'All this – all that you have been explaining – is why I had to suffer being invisible all my life?'

*'Once the plan for resurrection was cast – and it involved many echelons of Undying, including those who favour me and those who simply loathe my former lover – the protection of invisibility became a necessity.'*

'Why?'

*'Because it would have drawn unwanted attention to you. If ever our connection were to be exposed, your life would have been imperilled, and with it the possibility of my release.'*

Eefa wasn't altogether sure she understood all this as clearly as she would have liked to. But she was already angry. 'I was not asked to become part of your plan. What if I refused? What if now I walk away from your Bree Salis?'

*'Such a path you, the Chosen One, are free to choose.'*

She hesitated, surprised.

'Am I really free?'

*'Indeed, you are.'*

'How can I be sure?'

*'You may reject the Bree Salis, even though, in so doing, you end all hope.'*

'I don't understand.'

*'It is integral to its very nature that the Bree Salis can only be borne by one whose spirit is pure. Such a spirit must be offered the freedom both to bear it and also to bestow it.'*

Eefa, more confused than ever, said, 'How do I know that you aren't misleading me? You could be playing with words. I don't want to be misled into doing something I shouldn't do.'

*'Your doubts are natural. You will search in your heart for the truth. When you discover it, you will see that the decision really is yours.'*

'But how will I ever find it, this thing you call the Bree Salis?'

The spirit smiled, a weary smile, and Eefa found herself gazing into eyes that were both knowing and weary of it.

*'The Bree Salis will discover you.'*

# THE SPIRIT OF CHANGE

The old woman is exhausted. She has fallen into a slumber, cross-legged in her iron shackles on the rocky shore. But even now she senses an unwonted challenge, an unwelcome approach. From time to time souls have flocked to her over the vastness of time that she has been entombed here on the Beach of Bones. They have come from all over the archipelago they called the Sea of Stars – indeed sometimes from much further afield, from the entire world of Tír itself, spinning through space, and further still, from stranger worlds, drawn to what has become a legend, even a parable, of this old woman chained to her iron prison. Even from among the Undying, some have come to observe, to gloat, to sympathise, to ask for advice . . . She will sometimes answer their question, when questions they ask.

On other occasions she hears voices, individual, sometimes the murmuring of masses. Now, as if in a fell moment, the quiet sky is rent asunder, as if to usher in a gale. The rising wind gathers around her, whipping a mass of flotsam against her seated figure. Furies wheel and spiral in the tormented air. They pour an opalescent liquid over themselves and then set fire to it. She closes her ears to the screaming of their voices . . .

Is this some new torment? A caution? A message of sorts? She does not care to wonder. Such spectres are meaningless, the harbingers of the visitation that follows . . . On this occasion it is a single figure. A child . . . a waif in the form of a girl. She is dressed in rags, torn and stained with pus, the body within them ravaged, her eyes tearful. She trembles as she presumes to speak.

*'Am I dead?'*

The old woman gazes back at her from her manacled position on the shingle. 'The question is irrelevant, since you were never alive.'

The child's eyes widen, their sockets filling with liquid black, maintaining their stare at her.

*'What am I, then? What is to happen to me?'*

*'You are the embodiment of another's wrath, sent to torment me.'*

The old woman closes her eyes, allows grief to overwhelm her spirit. It is a penance of the Undying that there are no true tears to be shed. When she reopens her eyes, the figure persists, now silent before her.

*'Oh, husband!'* she declares. She is suddenly on her feet and in a rage. *'Do you imagine I cannot recognise the nature and purpose of this wretch?'*

The child's figure fades to a shadowy presence.

A voice deep and ragged comes from it. *'There is a saying among the mortals that death is the ultimate redemption.'*

She has no such faith in death. *'Even now you would try to control me. Do you think that I don't know that you watch my every move, harken to my every thought?'*

The presence assumes the cadaverous features of a ghoul, with looming talons, and glaring lemon eyes.

*'Begone, tiresome spirit! 'Do you think I don't know your master, what he is doing to me? Husband, since I know you are listening, I don't care. Thus, crudely, would you attempt to*

*influence me? And, as ever, you fail. Does this not suggest an increasing desperation on your part?'*

Her words must have angered him. She awaits a reply, though she knows there will be none. And yet . . . *'And yet I detect a change in you. I am suspicious of this new determination in you. I sense that you fear the change that is in the wind. I sense that even as you intrude upon my very thoughts, they provoke a fear in you.'*

Silence.

Her eyes turn to gaze once more upon the spectre that has invaded her peace, one that moils and festers within its canker of malice.

*'Begone! Or you will face a wrath more terrible than any your kind might summon in an eternity of woe!'*

೧

The frost sprite queen, Woll, harkens to the wind, to the pattering of falling snow: she is sensitive even to the roar of the distant waves on the sea shore in the far distance, and further to the whisper of the wind that scurries above the waves.

The sea warns her . . .

*'Touch fingers . . .'* The entire order of frost sprites reaches out to touch fingers and thus embrace the totality of her senses.

She has visions of an inhuman being hunting over the nearby ocean, winged and fierce. She reaches out her spirit being until it is poised above that same ocean.

*'Pray with me . . .'*

The entire order prays, and their prayer emboldens her spirit.

She focuses on that hunting being, its ruthless nature, the baleful green eyes, split like a serpent's, the maw with a vicious array of fangs, the talons extended out of thick red scales that extend to claws as large and cruel as an eagle's. Even as it registers her invasion, she harkens to its thoughts . . .

'You – whomsoever you are who is listening. Be warned – I am not one you would dare to sport with.

'Keep touching fingers! Maintain the prayer!'

There is no time to explain further. Time is picking up its skirts and running pell-mell through every sense. Woll reaches out with fingers now hugely elongated by icy spindles. Her spirit being pierces the hard, black cuticle covering the claws, a freezing cold icicle of pain. There is a shock of contact and then an ululating screech as a spiralling body plummets into the depths of the ocean.

'Mistress – you saw?'

'I saw.'

Woll hears the words of the goddess inside her mind. 'How resourceful and brave!'

'What further plan?'

'My tormentor is increasingly suspicious. A conflict is fast approaching. One that will question the precious nature of liberty and truth.'

Woll closes her eyes and gazes out through her gift of her vision, witnessing the rise of strange and terrible forces. Forces that cause her being to tremble and her wings to flutter with unspriteful clamour.

'What must we do? All is in flux.'

'Be not alarmed!'

Her mistress's voice is calm and soothing, but the queen of the frost sprites is not altogether soothed.

'You must make manifest Eefa's destiny.'

'Yes, Mistress. Your will be done.'

'*You are my hope.*'

'*We have long survived in love of you in inclement places.*'

'*You must help her and those who protect her. Guide them through paths that none would imagine possible.*'

'*I shall lead them.*'

'*It will be dangerous for you to leave your icy sanctuary.*'

Woll shivers at the very thought of that. '*Yes.*'

'*Take every precaution.*'

'*If we succumb, we perish knowing that we have served you.*'

'*Do not speak so. You cannot sacrifice your race for my being. Take comfort in knowing that the Bree Salis is manifest.*'

'*As you command, My Lady.*'

'*Yet, beloved sprite, would you do this not out of duty but through love. I do not command. A goddess that merely commands does not merit obedience. In this most auspicious moment do I cherish your faith in me.*'

'*My desire, the desire of all the Oonaree, is to serve you.*'

# THE BREE SALIS

Eefa had been so disturbed and excited by her awake-dream meeting with Woll and the frost sprites, she had rushed back into the cave to waken Magio. There, the twins had burst into an excited chatter. Quimbre, who had been sleeping soundly within the cave, was now shuffling out in a state of confusion to prepare a meagre breakfast. But the twins were too excited to eat. They wrapped themselves up warmly and woke up Bird Woman, who was close to freezing to death in the frost-rimed landscape as a result of her overnight vigil outside the cave. Magio and Eefa busied themselves brushing the coating of frost from their protector's hair and shoulders.

'Tell me more,' Magio demanded of Eefa as they moved to rubbing Bird Woman's hands, still frozen from her night-time vigil, back into life. 'Where are they, then, these magical sprites you've been talking about?'

'I don't know. They seem to be able to appear and disappear when it suits them. But I know they'll be back.'

Magio stared about himself with a dubious expression.

'If you don't believe me, ask Bird Woman. I think she was watching and listening to every word.'

'Is that right?' Magio demanded, still rubbing life back into Bird Woman's reviving hands.

Bird Woman's face lifted to gaze into Magio's with a half smile. 'Strange as it is for me to relate, it is true. I saw it all – the very wonder of it.'

'Tell me about it. Eefa is too excited to explain it properly. It's just not fair! Why wasn't I allowed to see it?'

Bird Woman smiled briefly, though she was still shivering with the return of her circulation. 'Well,' she said, her voice clumsy through her chattering teeth, 'it would appear that our arrival here was indeed anticipated.'

'What does that mean?'

'Here we are, in the Valley of the Raptors. And here, it would seem, you and your sister have been drawn, perhaps from the very moment of your birth.'

Magio's eyebrows were halfway up his brow. 'Eefa – is this true?'

'It looks like it.'

Eefa hardly dared to think of, never mind explain, all she had seen.

'What does that mean?'

'I don't rightly know. I think it has to mean that we were somehow . . . chosen?'

'Chosen?'

'Must you be so dense?'

'Chosen – like picked? Like somebody picked us out?'

'I think so. Oh, Magio, I'm not sure about anything, but I saw such peculiar things. And I was told by the goddess . . .'

'What goddess?'

Eefa told Magio about her strange conversation with the old woman chained to the shack on the stony beach.

'The one who's been coming to us in dreams?'

'Yes.' She hesitated, then, as if suddenly excited by it, she gripped Magio's face with both her hands. 'I think that, for some very special reason, she – the old woman – Woll told me that she is a goddess! Oh, don't look at me like that!

I don't understand anything that is going on any more than you do.'

'But why would some goddess be interested in us?'

'All I know is that she is an Undying. Woll called her "Our Lady of the Shore". She did something wrong. She angered somebody else among the Undying. I think, maybe, the one she was married to. Whatever – it was somebody very powerful and cruel. That terrible place, the beach – the way she was chained to the iron shack – that's her punishment for eternity. But then she told me about the Bree Salis.'

'The Bree Salis?'

'Yes. Will you please let me explain without any more of your questions? The Bree Salis is her salvation. She told me I was chosen to be its bearer. That was why I had to be invisible from the moment of my birth. I had to be invisible so her enemies couldn't find me.'

Magio's eyes were wide and staring. 'I don't believe it.'

'I can't blame you. I struggle to believe it myself. But that's what I was told.'

'It's such a strange story.'

'I can only tell you what she told me. But my guess is that we were both chosen. I don't know why.'

Magio shook his head. 'How do you know? I don't rightly know if this is britzy or jinxy. I can't believe it. It just isn't logical.'

'Things don't have to be logical.'

'Huh!'

She watched him gaze up into a sky of wheeling mist, with occasional glimpses of the purest, palest blue of morning. A fine spindrift of icy snow was still whirling weightlessly around them. It felt so rare, so alive, so intoxicating –

frightening! And yet she could see how Magio was struggling to get to grips with it all.

'Stop feeling sorry for yourself. Don't you know how it has always been for me? What if you had a terrible accident and died? Then nobody would ever have known that I existed. I would have become a lost soul.'

'Don't talk like that!' He had his hands pressed tight about his ears.

She thought, *How close was I to being nobody at all!*

Magio had complained about things being unfair to him, but it had been her plight that had ever been so terribly unfair. She felt herself alive, just like all the visible people did. She felt her heart beating inside her chest. She felt her eyes blink. She felt her lungs move as she breathed the same air that Magio, and everybody else, breathed. They talked about a calamity that had changed the world. But she had suffered her very own calamity, at least as she saw and felt it.

And yet she was changing. She knew about how girls and boys grew up and changed, in some weird way – sometimes, she gathered, it could feel almost suddenly – into men and women. That was a new terror: that it was beginning to happen to her too. She was experiencing weird stuff, stuff she more often than not hated about herself. Like . . . like she was becoming less of the girl, as she had thought herself, into something different. She didn't like it at all.

She couldn't stop herself from crying out to Magio, 'No one other than you will ever look me in the eye. No one will put their arms around me to hug me.'

'At least I care about you.'

'All you care about is adventure.'

'No, Eefa! I really do care about you.'

'Nobody really understands. They don't realise that I have desires, hopes, dreams that you couldn't possibly imagine, or help me with.'

'But I want to understand you. I want to help you, Eefa.'

On impulse, she hugged him, kissed him on the cheek.

Shocked, he stared back at her in silence. It was the first time ever that Eefa had kissed him.

She looked at him excitedly and said, 'Okay. Tell me – what do you want more than anything in the world?'

'I want you to be . . .'

'No – don't talk about me. Talk about yourself!'

He shook his head vehemently. 'That's what I really want. It's what I have always wanted.'

'Oh, Magio, stop. I know you care for me. Think differently. Think why, if I'm to believe the goddess, I am supposed to have some vitally important role that neither of us understands. Think, like, what could possibly be the reason that I must remain invisible. Think of what we both want.'

'You're confusing me. I don't know what you're talking about.'

'Forget about me, the fact I'm invisible. What then would you wish for in all of the world?'

'You mean, like Mum and Dad?'

'Yes.' She hugged him, and he hugged her back, in tears. 'But . . .'

'I know – *I know!*'

'It's impossible.'

'Because they were lost in the Chaos. But what if, maybe, they weren't?'

'You think maybe they weren't?'

'I think that you and I were taken because it suited some great power. But that doesn't necessarily mean that Mum and Dad were lost.'

'You wish?'

'Yes, Magio, I do wish it were true.'

'But do you really hope?'

'I do. Oh, I do! I really do hope so.'

'You know that you are probably – absolutely, probably – wrong.'

'Yes!' The word was less than a whisper. Sitting there, amid the whirling, prickling snowflakes, Eefa felt so deeply anguished in her heart and soul.

જ

Bird Woman, now within the protection of the cave, had wrapped herself in her blanket. By now she was wide awake, listening in to the conversation between brother and sister. It was understandable that they should be feeling tense. She was consumed by a febrile tension herself at the thought that the Bree Salis was approaching. For her there had been no question of sleep. Not that she needed much sleep these days. She had much to reflect upon. And now, overhearing this emotional crisis for Eefa, she deeply sympathised. She, too, had also experienced estrangement. Such was the price of a discovering within oneself a special purpose. But it wasn't always easy to bear. For her, too, it had provoked a great deal of self-analysis and self-questioning. She had thought such rumination far behind her. But now this strange and perilous journey had rekindled both the overwhelming wonder of her special purpose and a deal of all too reasonable doubt. She couldn't help but hug her blanket closer to her shoulders, the whisper on her lips, 'The danger has not entirely gone away.'

They were involved with something that was not merely unknown, but was so vastly bigger and more terrifying than anything she had ever encountered before that it might be beyond being knowable to mortals. People who are consumed with fear will sometimes head by mistake towards the thing that they most fear. She believed that this was the explanation for Eefa and the stone formations on the beach.

'What is it, Bird Woman?'

Magio's voice broke into her thoughts. She had been so wrapped up in herself, she hadn't noticed his coming inside. Goodness! She hadn't given sufficient thought to the fact that he was a twin of Eefa's. He could hardly be regarded as ordinary. And though they were not identical, their faces really did look alike. Only yesterday she had been shocked to hear that Eefa's voice had been silent to Quimbre because Eefa herself had decided so. That was an extraordinary revelation. Eefa was more special – more gifted – than Bird Woman had hitherto realised. And that being so, could it be that Magio was also more special than she had previously considered? Could he be privy to her innermost fears? Had she been muttering to loudly herself, allowing her anxiety to show?

She turned to him. 'It's nothing, Magio – nothing to worry about. But today is likely to be such an important day. Have you not noticed that the pure cold clarity of the air? A clarity that uplifts one's very soul?'

Magio moved to the entrance to look skywards, peering all about him at the gigantic cleft in the mountains, with its multitude of caves. 'No – should I have noticed?'

'Well, of course we're all a little overexcited. Take no notice of me. I'm just thinking aloud. I tend to do that when I'm nervous.'

He frowned. 'Why are you nervous?'

'Oh, dear Magio! I am so nervous. We are so close to the real purpose of your great adventure. I can't even bear to think about what approaches us.'

'What approaches us?'

'You are so young. You have not encountered the cruelty, the ruthlessness, of the powers that rule this world.'

Magio's face creased with a mixture of anxiety and determination. 'I don't care about that. I'll take my chances if it will change things for the better.'

'Bravo! I know, from being close to you throughout this journey, you would swap your visibility for your sister's invisibility if you could, wouldn't you?'

His eyes welled up with tears. 'How did you know?'

'I couldn't have spent so much time with you both without witnessing your love for each other. It has been such a ghastly burden to you both.'

Magio wiped away his tears with the back of his hand. He blurted out, 'I still don't know what we're supposed to be waiting for. This thing that Eefa was told to expect – this Bree Salis!'

She joined him at the entrance. 'Look, Magio. Look up, high, into the sky.'

Magio's face turned skywards again, blinking his eyes to clear them of the residue of tears. Suddenly his eyes opened wide as circles. 'Eagles! Hey – I think I can see eagles!'

Bird Woman smiled. 'It is the Valley of the Raptors.'

He clapped his hands. 'Britzy! Hey – Bird Woman! You've got to tell me what's going on.'

She accompanied him in walking further out into the snowy landscape on somewhat stiff legs, sheltering her eyes with her hands to get a better view of what was happening.

'What's going on? I don't profess to know. Those fast ones, sweeping in and out of the formation, are falcons.'

'I know what falcons look like. I'm talking about the really big ones – the ones really high up in the air. Even that high they look gigantic, with those huge wing spans. They just seem to be floating on thermals, or something.'

Bird Woman appeared somewhat startled when peering up high into the air to where Magio was indicating. 'Yes – indeed I see them!'

'Wow!' Magio shouted out. 'Hey, Eefa – come take a look at this!'

Eefa's voice sounded jittery. She was blinking up into the sky. 'Oh, my goodness, there must be dozens and dozens of them. What are they, Bird Woman?'

Magio interrupted. 'Raptors! Look at how they're circling.'

'So they are!' Bird Woman attempted to calm the twins.

'They don't usually do that together, in some kind of a swarm. Not eagles, or falcons, do they, Bird Woman?'

'No. They don't.'

'What do you reckon?'

'I confess that in all of my life, I have never seen such a sight. Birds have quick and extraordinary instincts. But these really are circling. It's as if they sense some extraordinary focus here in the valley.'

'What focus?'

'A presence that draws them – perhaps.'

'A presence?'

'A presence – or perhaps they sense the need – Birds have an exquisite sense of the balance of things.'

Even as Magio and Eefa stared into the pallid blue morning sky, with its persistent showering of icy spicules of snow, to witness more and more winged shapes invading the sky. There appeared to be very many different birds, judging from the great variety of sizes and wing shapes. They wheeled in extraordinary interactive patterns against the great blanket of purest blue.

Magio demanded, 'But you're Bird Woman. You can communicate with them. Find out what's going on.'

Bird Woman put her hand on both their shoulders as all three stared up as one at the eerie spectacle. 'I don't know. It's so very exciting, even for me. I have never in my life seen the like.'

Eefa spoke in a whisper. 'Perhaps it's something to do with this thing the goddess talked to me about? The Bree Salis?'

'Perhaps it is. But we must remain calm and observe.'

'It's hard not to be scared by it. What are the birds doing? Are they coming for me? Are they going to hurt me?'

Bird Woman squeezed Magio's shoulder a little tighter. 'I sense no threat. I doubt that they intend us harm.'

'Oh, Eefa!' Magio hugged Eefa to him. And for once she didn't resist him. He hugged her so hard, he didn't ever want to let her go.

Bird Woman was still gazing up, perplexed. 'I don't understand any more than you do. From what the Old Woman told you, you were chosen from even before you were born. And because of that you were kept invisible. It was so cruel to make Eefa invisible. But at least we know now that there was a reason behind it.'

'She – the goddess – told me it was to hide me from some terrible enemy.'

'Dear Eefa! What a dreadful burden you have had to bear.'

'I wanted to scream. Every morning when I woke up and nobody, except Magio, knew I existed, I so hated it. I hated everything about it. I hated the fact that I couldn't help Gran, when she needed my help. I thought that the way she treated poor Quimbre so was because I wasn't able to help her like a granddaughter should.'

Magio whispered, 'I was too stupid to understand.'

'No, no, no! If it wasn't for you, Magio, I don't think I could have borne it.'

'Hush, now! Hush – the both of you!'

∽

Eefa gazed up into the strange, ever-changing sky above the Valley of the Raptors. It was now afternoon and that pale blue sky was fissured with silver. But the wheeling raptors had never tired. Instead, their numbers had massively increased, so that in the most packed areas they were dense enough to look like clouds. Even as Eefa gritted her teeth, anxious that even Bird Woman was uncertain as to what was happening, she heard the tinkling sound that told her that the frost sprite queen, Woll, had returned. But this time the tinkling was louder, in some curious way more complex. Second by second, it was expanding into a great orchestra of hundreds, perhaps thousands, of tinkling bells.

She whispered huskily, 'Look, Magio . . . Bird Woman! Oh, look!'

The air around them was also thickening with what appeared to be a very fine powdery snow. But as it fell, it became obvious it wasn't snow. It was a swarm of frost sprites, hordes of them, alighting on every twig, branch and ledge – and even on her own head and shoulders.

'Oh, Woll!' she cried. 'What's going on?'

'My people have come to be with you.'

Eefa spun around to witness how the frost sprites had formed a huge circle around them, with myriad tiny blue eyes watching her as if waiting for something to happen. Eefa felt a powerful hand grip her shoulders. She spun round to see that it was Quimbre, now standing resolutely beside her. He guffawed. 'It seems that, whether through alighting snow, or these fairies, you become truly real to me.'

She reached back to grasp the gnarled fingers of Quimbre's right hand and whispered, 'I think something really important is happening.'

'Yeah? Well now, I'm prepared to believe anything.'

Eefa smiled back into that dusky, battle-scarred face – the face no longer of a frightening pirate, but of a friend.

Magio, meanwhile, was hopping with excitement from foot to foot. 'Now even you've got to believe in magic, Quimbre!'

'Hey, kiddo! I do. It's quite a spectacle to see these ice creatures, but don't you go expecting miracles!'

There was a renewed tinkling music coming from the multitude. It was so beautiful it melted Eefa's heart. It was taken up by others, until, soon, the air was filled with its rapture. Above the rapture, the voice of Woll.

'We have come together – all that remain of the sprites in this blighted world. We welcome the coming of Eefa, herald of the Bree Salis. We equally welcome her twin brother, Magio, and their guides and protectors, Bird Woman and Quimbre.'

Eefa could hear the tinkling exclamations of her companions, of Magio and Bird Woman, of Quimbre . . . Quimbre's whose voice, croaky with emotion, was actually humming some kind of sea shanty under his breath, as if still expecting trouble.

Woll's voice, now serious, intoned, 'We, the Ooonaree, beloved of our Undying Mistress, are entrusted with this most precious secret, a most powerful and holy host of redemption. Only recently have we treasured it! But already the time has come for us to part with it. May the mistress we so treasure be restored through it! We entrust all of our hopes and faith in you, Eefa, chosen of the goddess herself.'

So saying, Woll placed her hands on Eefa's brow. 'You must call upon the forces to make it be.'

'Me! I must do what?'

Bird Woman nodded upwards towards the sky. 'I'm not entirely sure, but I told Magio that they were spiralling around some extraordinary focus. I made the mistake of thinking it must be at ground level. But now I think that focus is up there, at the epicentre of all that circling in the sky.'

'I don't understand.'

Bird Woman shook her head. 'No more do I.'

Woll spoke, as if to mitigate Bird Woman's consternation. 'Truly, only you, Eefa, have the power to call upon the Taloned King.'

'The what?'

'We waste time in words. You must call him!'

'I have no idea what you are talking about. Who is the Taloned King? And even if I did know who he might be, I have no such power.'

'Dear Eefa, you are more powerful than you could possibly imagine. You merely need to open your heart and call upon him in blessed spirit to embrace him.'

∞

Eefa saw that Magio was strenuously shaking his head. He glanced first at Bird Woman and then at Quimbre, and realised, as she had already realised, they were baffled. She, too, was baffled. But she took a deep breath, and thought about what Woll had instructed her. She closed her eyes and thought about it again, realising that only she could do whatever it was that had to be done. With her heart racing, and her lungs panting as if they could no longer get enough air into her chest, she gazed up at the wheeling circles of raptors and she opened up her arms, calling, 'Come! Taloned King! I earnestly beseech you! With all of my heart and soul, I beg you to come!'

The swarms of birds wheeling in the sky continued unchanged. But within the dead centre a winged speck was descending. It grew large very quickly, resembling no bird that Eefa had ever seen. As it neared, she saw that it had no feathers. Its body was scaly – and it was increasingly obvious that it was enormous. It had four taloned limbs instead of the two of eagles. Its eyes, staring down into hers, glowed with a spectral light. And borne in the cradle of its enormous front claws was something small and glowing, something minuscule in size against its enormous bulk, but golden and glittering.

Eefa almost fainted with terror, gazing up at the huge creature's descent; her throat clamped shut, unable to speak.

'Behold,' Woll's tinkling voice invaded her mind. 'Behold the power that is now entrusted to you.'

Entrusted to her! Eefa didn't know what that meant, or what she was supposed to do. She had to force her trembling self to look up at what now confronted her. A creature of leviathan size, one so gigantic that its head, which was immediately above her, blocked out the daylight. Its wings were beating slowly, but the currents of them were scattering frost sprites and snowflakes as if they were caught in a typhoon of winds. Yet, strangely, she wasn't buffeted.

She tried to take it in: this was important. It had to do with what the old woman chained to the iron shack had asked of her. It had to do with liberating her from her imprisonment, punishment – whatever she had attempted to explain to Eefa under such scary circumstances that she had only half understood it. Eefa panted for breath. She stared up and saw scales, massive scales, as brightly coloured as the plumage of the most beautiful birds. The patterns of colours, of greys, and gold, and rosy red, and silver, were so bold and extraordinary that she understood now why the raptors above circled this giant. She saw the huge head, lifted, as if in an effort not to frighten her, with its yellow split eyes, those eyes alone as large as a house, and the terrible jaws with their gargantuan rows of teeth.

*'Do not be frightened of the Dragon King, Eefa! Remember that, through all of that power and terror, he is our friend.'*

The voice of the old woman . . .

She couldn't help thinking, *The Dragon King!*

*'You must be brave in this key moment!'*

But even so, it exhausted all of her reserves of courage to instinctively lift up her hand and then her arms, to hold up her two hands, fingers splayed, without knowing what to expect. She found herself taking possession of a golden oval as large as a coconut that yet appeared no more substantial than mist. She hardly dared to look at it, though even her brief glances suggested whirling, constantly moving skeins of complexity moving within and through one another in a spellbinding mystery. Even now enfolded against her chest, it felt peculiarly weightless within her hands, yet it pulsated through the very essence of her being.

'Is this the Bree Salis?'

Woll's singing voice answered. 'Yes.'

'It feels . . . alive.'

In her hands, the Bree Salis appeared to dim, as if demanding her attention. Instinctively she closed her eyes, and in doing so was enchanted by its invasive presence within her. She was unable to unable to keep her eyes closed. Opening them tentatively, she found herself within a great chamber, perhaps so great it was without dimensions. There was an all-embracing tingling of wonder. Shadows wheeled, beings as fierce as suns moved about her, a sense of knowing so great that to attempt to understand more of it would destroy her mind. Terrified, she closed her eyes to this terrible world.

*You find yourself within the world of the Undying. Alas, it was necessary. Yet even so, the decision is yours.*

The voice of the old woman again: but what decision was she now talking about? Eefa was reminded of their earlier conversation. She had been allowed to choose . . . But she hadn't known what to do.

*You may decide: yes or no. If yes, you must welcome its presence within you. Even so you are yet free to choose.*

'I don't know what I should choose.'

*Whether to support my cause, or not.*

'What if I say no?'

*My torment will continue to eternity.*

Eefa hesitated: but then she welcomed the golden enchantment within her. Immediately she felt it tingling against her skin, the bones of her hands, at the same time diffusing at once through her arms and throat, spreading out in every direction within her being, to reach her heart, her mind.

She whispered, 'Oh, Woll! I . . . I think the Bree Salis is speaking to me. But I cannot understand what it is asking me.'

'It welcomes you. It seeks to comfort you and also to explain its nature.'

'Oh!' Eefa's voice still quivered. 'Oh . . .!' She felt her body lifting off the ground. Her mind was spinning, bedazzled by a medley of voices, by visions.

'I'm terrified by what's happening to me!'

'Be assured, the Bree Salis will not harm you. But you cannot allow it to be so wild within you. You must control it.'

'Control it?' She doubted that she had it in her to control such a powerful and strange thing. 'What in the world is it?'

'The Bree Salis cannot easily be defined. But it might help if you remember how Bird Woman compared it to the everyday wonder of the butterfly.'

Eefa remembered this story explained to her by Bird Woman. The butterfly began life as a lowly caterpillar, feeding on leaves and growing. Such was the nature of life, and the world, for simple beings. Yet then, as if by magic, this mundane existence was transformed. The caterpillar sacrificed its being, enclosing itself within the sheath of the pupa. Here it dissolved away its living being and was reborn as the butterfly, resplendent in its multifaceted eyes, in its beautiful wings.

Eefa tried to force her terrified mind to think about what Woll had told her, gazing up into the sky full of wheeling raptors. 'I – I'm not sure I understand. Am I the caterpillar – or the butterfly?'

'Neither. You are the cocoon.'

'Oh!'

'I can see that you are surprised, shocked. I offer sympathy. In time the Lady of the Shore will, perhaps, be able to explain better than I can. But I'm afraid that we don't have the time to dwell on confusion and even to comfort one another. I must leave you for a short while to allow you to become one with your blessed charge. Time beckons. Your enemies are now our enemies, and they never rest. Soon – within hours – we must journey north from the Valley of the Raptors to your final destination, which you know as the Beach of Bones. It will be a perilous and arduous journey and there will be little respite.'

# LIBERATION

'Ursascogans – blood of my blood!'

King Wirgnatha opened his arms wide. 'We are gathered here, in Ashtree, from all corners of the island in celebration.'

He took several paces to the left. Then he took several paces to the right, pounding the floor of the cobbled square that had once been the civic centre of the capital city of Moon, as if he were testing its ability to bear his weight.

'Our people are emerging from their enforced servitude, from caves and woodland and from tunnels beneath the soil, to enjoy the warmth of sun on their faces.'

A deep rumble of cheering broke out from the gathered thousands. It was the largest gathering of the Ursascogan people in recent history.

'Once the accursed, we, the First Folk, now stand triumphant.'

This evoked another resounding cheer.

'After centuries of ignominy, we demand the light of liberation.'

One among the congregations began to sing, a deep, low dirge of rage that was taken up by others, so, in continuing, it formed a natural choral background to the speech of the king. He waved a hand towards them, as if welcoming it.

'As we all know from the stories of childhood, the First Folk ruled the Age of Beginnings. It was the coming of humans who ended that glorious age. With my leadership, we shall restore our birthright. We shall restore the Age of Wonder and depose the human interlopers.'

A raucous accompanying music was beginning to sound over the multitude that was already singing. A blare of brass. It was punctuated by thunderously deep beats of a single drum, the "thunderclap", borne on the body of an enthusiast who was a giant, even among the Ursascogans. Every beat of the thunderclap shook the very ground with promise of the victory to come.

King Wirgnatha acknowledged the enthusiastic cheers of the many, standing tall and strong, looking about him over the crumbling ruins of human habitation, gesticulating to his left and his right, extolling the gathered Ursascogans from every tribe and smith, filling every square foot of space between the burgeoning trees and the rich proliferation of sunflowers, moonflowers, and starflowers that now decorated the new Ursascogan capital.

'How beautiful it is, now that nature has wrested the wildness back from the controlling and lazy humans!'

The resultant cheers were so long-lasting and deafening that the king was obliged to lift up a hand for silence.

'There comes a time when the enchained must unshackle themselves from the curse that forced them underground. We shall liberate the conquered lands, and in so doing assume the powers that once ruled this island – given to us in our distant past by the holy Undying. We reclaim our entitlement to this land that the undeserving humans called Moon – the land that was home to us, the First Folk, when it was known as Eiluth – Isle of Mists and Sorrows.'

The cheering rose to a thunderous crescendo.

Wirgnatha paced again, to the left, then to the right, all the time with his great head bowed. 'Surely, all assembled

here know that I speak the truth. Eiluth was our birthright.
The humans stole it from us.'

Another ground-shaking cheer.

'But don't imagine that what remains of the human
usurpers will simply hand it over to us. Oh, no!'

This was echoed by an enormous shout, and roaring
from the assembled army of warriors.

'The humans are dangerous. They are cunning. Before the
Chaos they ruled every island of the Sea of Stars. But lately
they have been much reduced in number. They appear lost –
confused. Even so, do not let that lull you to underestimate
them. Such was the mistake of our ancestors. Even after
the Chaos, the humans remain a formidable enemy. Some,
despite the Chaos, will still possess the knowledge of their
weapons of fire. They are still many of them surviving in the
wastelands west of the Sea of Stars. Yet, even now, though
they are reduced in numbers here in Eiluth, and their towns
and cities reduced to impoverishment, they still assume their
former hegemony. They will attempt to subdue us and rule
again if we allow them to do so.'

'No! No! No!' roared the crowds, with a noisy if
ponderously slow drumming of their feet against the stony
floor.

'So, then, may I take it that it is the unanimous will of
the First Folk that we shall, by force of arms, take back what
was once ours?'

The bedlam of roaring, howling, trumpeting and
drumming was more than sufficient answer to his question.
A regiment of warriors, dressed in the resplendent battle
armour of the Warrior Elite, reared back and then hurled
blazing javelins, as big as sapling trees, into the pounding
waves of the nearby ocean.

'Then, my people, let us celebrate our liberation!'

A short time later, he stood, enormously tall and strong, on the rostrum in the old human capital, and he listened to the musicians weave their songs of legendary battles, and he watched the young women dance a sympathetic weave of bodies around the huge weapon of magic that had been gifted to his people by Lustfera. Humming choirs sounded out from the various gatherings of clans, each with its own pride of tradition. There were great differences in clan size, appearance, dress, fierceness of expression, music, song, and dance, yet all strived to be included in the joyful variety of celebration, and with it the patterns of tattooing now proudly displayed in the array of nakedly exposed chests.

The king gazed around himself with jubilation. There was a blaring of the battle trumpets. The sound was deep and low, ear-shattering and magnificent. They signalled the opening of the warrior games.

The cheering of the ordinary folk, unused to comfort or celebration, who made up the majority of the audience for the great melee of music, song, dance, and gladiatorial combat, had now risen to a continuous background crescendo when the elderly wizar, Khakhov, who waited until he got a nod from the king, then ascended the dais. He attempted, with little success, to silence the multitude with a thumping against the floor of his Staff of Wisdom. But then a massive flare of blue-black lightning struck, close by the wizar. This silenced the celebrating masses, provoking a shocked focus on the elderly figure on the dais.

The wizar's voice could not conceal its tremble as he struck his staff once more against the floor, resounding in the now hushed chamber.

'Behold the coming of our saviour – the great Lady of the Undying, Lustfera, who came to aid us in our hour of need. Behold the saviour of the First Folk, the blessed Star of Mourning!'

☙

Lustfera had been observing all, and now, invested in the ethereal light that surrounded her, she manifested before them. Formidable as she might have presented herself, she decided to eschew any rumble of thunder or flash of lightning, choosing merely a rising mist in the centre of the dais. Such was the ominous sense of her arrival, the crowds drew back, allowing her to control the stage.

She had no need to overly impress or frighten these simple beings, rather to enrapture them. The Ursascogans were malleable and predictable – they brooded on past grievances. That was a powerful enough lever for her to manipulate them. With a signal from the king, her arrival was greeted with the deep-throated choir of Ursascogan warriors, who chanted with renewed urgency and vigour. Stars of purplish incandescence wheeled about her resplendent form. She stood tall and fiercely erect, gazing about her. She might readily have appeared more menacing. But it was not appropriate in the circumstances. She must mollify her spirit, and with it, her address, all the better to capture the attention of the multitude. When she spoke, it was with a clear voice, resonant as steel.

'You have heard your king.'

A great cheer erupted from the multitude.

'There can be no failure in this enterprise. The First Folk have been ill-treated in ways beyond reckoning. You have been robbed of all rights and dignity. Your claim to this island cannot be denied.'

Another enormous cheer. It was all so ridiculously easy. She waited for the cheering to abate.

'Your king is right. The humans who have taken the island from you will not simply allow you to take it back.'

'Indeed, they will not.'

She spun around to discover the source of this provocative interruption. She was confronted by the resentful glare of Queen Pittaquera. Who else would have had the temerity to speak!

There was a dissonance of voices from the crowds.

The Star of Mourning lifted a long, sinewy arm, with fingers and thumb widespread, as if to quieten the crowds. "Well, now! Let her Royal Majesty speak. Let us hear what she has to contribute to this assembly."

The queen, undaunted, continued, 'The human enemy has proved resourceful throughout our long and painful history of subjugation. They have confounded us, time after time, in the most ingenious ways. Let us not be carried away with our sense of injustice so to expose ourselves to the peril of a new insurrection.'

Lustfera studied the figure of the queen, the minutiae of her facial expression, the stubborn look in those eyes, the tensing in that posture, all of which told her more than the challenge of the words. Was it possible that the wily queen suspected the true nature of her pact with the stupid king?

*Yes – indeed it now seemed likely.*

It was written in her face and her bearing that she knew that Lustfera intended to usurp the Ursascogans to her purpose.

Lustfera's eyes flashed with irritation.

She spoke, again, in a soft voice. 'It is understandable that even Queen Pittaquera should baulk at the ambition of defeating the humans after centuries of suppression, humiliation and submission. But will the indomitable heart and courage of the Ursascogans not take comfort from the ease with which you wrested the port of Wart from their grasp?'

Pittaquera bunched her lips. She could not deny that victory. 'We should take a just pride in this success. But we should consider also their unpreparedness for the siege. We had the advantage of surprise on our side. Next time they will be better prepared.'

Lustfera looked towards the king, who was already on his feet, bristling with embarrassment and rage. He raised his clenched fist, rattling the battle armour that encased him. 'It was not surprise that won us this victory. We won it with ease through the power and benevolence of our sacred visitor.'

The cheering rose again from the gathered multitude. It almost drowned out the single voice that would not be denied.

Pittaquera replied, 'Who knows the dangers of weaponry of forbidden magic – the magic of brooding darkness? In the deepest reaches of Ursascogan lore the legends decry such magic.'

'Forbidden magic?' Lustfera laughed, a throaty cackle that silenced the multitude and appeared to echo far and wide through the streets and alleyways of the ruined city. But behind the laughter her hackles sprang alert. Was this the seeds of rebellion? What had given such courage to the hitherto timorous wife of the king? A fury rose in her that might have exterminated Pittaquera with a thought. But that would have confounded her plans with these dull-witted beings. Her score with the queen would have to wait. Meanwhile she needed to regain control of this gathering.

Her eyes blazed over the now silent multitude to come to rest on the wizar. Was the old man a loyal servant to the king, or a plotter in league with the queen?

As if sensing her attention, the wizar cleared his throat, readying himself to speak. 'Majesties – My Lady, Lustfera – I find myself placed in a most awkward predicament, whether to support my king and thus confound my equally beloved queen. Or should I, on the contrary, confirm her fears?'

The wizard's words astounded her such that she turned her attentions to the now bristling king.

But it was the queen who once again captured the stage.

'Your Majesty – My lord and husband! I am familiar with the legends, and their warning. Who could deny us the pride and satisfaction in taking ownership of this city, ruined as it is? I well remember that, like every town and city on this island, it was built with our ancestors' toil and sweat. Such a recovery deserves to be celebrated and duly enshrined in legend. Must we bicker among ourselves? Can we not find a route of common assent?'

The blazing eyes of Lustfera swivelled from the queen to further confront the king. She drew satisfaction to see how that monstrous frame trembled under her gaze. She took an even deeper satisfaction at how this would astonish the queen, to see her royal husband humbled so. He, the indomitable Wirgnatha, whose heart was said to be made of annealed iron.

'There will be no compromises with our sacred covenant.' Wirgnatha spoke huskily, as if his throat were dryer than the surrounding desert. 'I would have expected a better support from our beloved queen. But what can one expect of an ageing woman other than fickleness and nail-biting where a dauntless heart is called for! Aye, and a fearless trust in this blessed ally, who gifts the Ursascogan people with the weaponry of conquest?'

Lustfera smiled. His words must have struck Pittaquera like a slap in the face. The Star of Mourning allowed herself a moment of gloating before she hissed to the multitude, 'There speaks your true leader!'

Their roar as one, the deafening thunder of the drums, was answer enough to reassure her that it was time to reveal her true self.

Her present form evaporated. In her place a vortex of darkness rose and spiralled, in the depths of which three serpents with red pits for eyes, coiled about one another in the shape of a giant heart. Splinters of darkness wheeled out of the vortex, like sparks caught in the wind from a bonfire, moving among the terrified multitude, and passing through them, as if testing the living hearts of all present, and discovering any who dared to question the king and his immortal muse.

Her voice penetrated their minds, in a seething rattle of words.

'I, The Star of Mourning, have come among you, leaving the side of my Lord, The One, to devote, at His divine word, what assistance I can to the most deserving First Folk. It was He, my most gracious Lord, who drew my attention to your history of abuse and suffering at the hands of the haughty humans.'

Queen Pittaquera shrank into the background of her own courtiers, by turns astonished, frightened, and bewildered at the terrifying vision now confronting them.

Up to this point she had thought her husband arrogant, vilely cruel, but caring of their people and imbued with the potential of a great leader. She no longer thought so. She feared that he was something approaching anathema. She now thought he was very unlikely to liberate the long-suffering Ursascogans to liberty and happiness, but condemn them to a new servitude. And glancing in the direction of the elderly wizar, and seeing the look of horror on his face, she thought that she was not alone in that conclusion.

The being of darkness spoke again, in that strange rattle of a voice: 'No more lies!'

There was a hesitation for a second or two, but it was followed by a heavy murmuring of agreement.

'For generations beyond count you have waited for a redeemer. Your king, Wirgnatha, is that redeemer. He was destined to inherit the mantle heralded in the age-old legends – he is the redeemer of the First Folk. The queen surely spoke true when she feared that it will not be easy to defeat the human interloper. They are indeed cunning. They have weapons of fire that you do not possess. But they do not have the power and magic to deal with the bounty I shall bring to battle. I, the Star of Mourning, will alter the balance in your favour. Have I not done so already, with the gift of the Leviathan of legend, which made short work of restoring Wart to its builders? With my help, you will go on to take control of this island, restoring Eiluth to its founder folk.'

Her words were greeted by a resounding cheer. Huge bare feet were pounding the cobbles of the square, and extending back into the ruined streets.

'But it will not stop there. From this small start, I shall help you, and your indomitable king, Wirgnatha, to conquer the entire Sea of Stars.'

# The Crystal Staircase

Eefa whispered, 'I'm changing!'

She had suffered episodes of faintness and light-headedness since accepting the Bree Salis. It felt as is something – a force that felt enormously powerful – had entered her. She had felt it surge through every tissue and organ, as if infusing her entire physical being. It had happened in such a rush that she hadn't really had sufficient time to take in what the . . . the possession, if that was the right word for it . . . was really doing to her. 'Oh, help me, please, Bird Woman!'

'I'm here, Eefa. I'm always by your side!'

Bird Woman stood back, with her hands resting firmly on Eefa's slender shoulders, bolstering her courage. 'Please do not worry. All will be well. Change can be so very terrifying, even though such processes of change are integral to us – integral to life itself.'

Eefa found it difficult to grasp those complex ideas. She couldn't stop herself from trembling. 'I don't understand.'

They were walking through the snowy mountainous landscape to some place in the Valley of the Raptors where Bird Woman had been instructed to lead Eefa and Magio. Quimbre, as mistrustful as ever, had gone on ahead to scout out the land, and keep an eye out for any sign of threat.

'You are maturing. You and Magio both. It is only natural that you should be uncertain. Such maturation can be very confusing, bewildering. It isn't just the Bree Salis. I have observed subtle changes in you, and in Magio, during this journey. Puberty is a strange state, one as I well recall that we have no control over. Surely your grandmother must have explained this to you?'

'Gran . . . oh, poor Gran . . . she was struggling from day to day just to keep me and Magio fed and clothed.'

'You are growing up – developing. Your body, your being, is changing to that of a young woman – as Magio is becoming a young man.'

Tears dimmed Eefa's eyes. She squeezed them shut. At that moment Magio's hand enclosed hers. They clenched each other's hands.

She and Magio – they had both been so excited to enter this world above the clouds, the extraordinary Valley of the Raptors, where flocks of eagles and falcons were still circling in the sky. They had both been keen to explore it further. But the frost sprite, Woll, had persuaded them not to. They hadn't even had time to spend a single day further exploring the valley. Their purpose here was done. Time, Woll now insisted, was too precious to lose even a single day. Why couldn't it all have been a wonderful adventure, such as Magio had been hoping for? Why must there be some monstrous beings searching for them, hunting them down? Eefa had only gradually come to realise that there was something more complex and dangerous going on, and not just the changes of growing up that Bird Woman was suggesting.

She whispered to Magio, 'I've been given the Bree Salis so I can somehow take it to the old woman we see in our dreams. But what am I supposed to do? Nobody has explained to me who she is, or where she is, or how I am supposed to give it to her when, if ever, I get to meet her.'

'Don't look at me.' Magio was fidgeting restlessly all the while he was walking. 'There's nothing we can do except wait for Woll to return.'

'And just when will that be?'

'Soon, would be my hope. Woll seems to be in such a hurry.'

Eefa could see from his face that he left unsaid what he was likely really thinking, which was exactly what Eefa herself was thinking. It wasn't over. When last they had seen him, the man who was hunting them had taken a terrible battering from the Scog sentry. Surely that beating had put an end to his pursuit? But what if he had somehow recovered? What if he was now waiting for them below the mountain?

She said, 'How do we know that we can trust Woll to help us? How do we know who to trust any more?'

Magio shook his head. 'I know. I feel the same. But we have no choice.'

She sighed, unable to sit still. 'I can't just wait for something to happen. I need to know what is to become of me.'

Magio shivered. 'Let's face it, we couldn't have predicted anything that has happened to us on this journey. And you know what that tells me?'

'What?'

'We're not meant to know. We are not meant to predict a single thing that is going to happen to us.'

Eefa was silent for several moments thinking about that. 'And what are we supposed to do in the meantime?'

He shrugged. 'We worry and fret.'

Eefa stared at Magio. She stared directly into his eyes. In doing so, she realised that he was already an inch or two taller than her. He must be growing faster than her. Was Magio changing too? He wasn't just taller. He was leaner than when they had set out from Warren. He had lost his puppy fat and become more bony, gangling.

Her head dropped. 'Oh, Magio!' She didn't know what to say, so she wheeled away, confused. And then, suddenly, she saw the burly figure of Quimbre up ahead, waiting for them. 'Hey, watch your step, kiddo – and you too, Eefa.'

Eefa was startled but also delighted; it was the first time he had called out her name.

Bird Woman pressed him. 'What is it?'

'Come and look for yourselves! But approach it warily, and watch your step as you get close.'

All three of them found themselves on the edge of a great hole in the rocks, through which they glimpsed a precipitous drop.

Woll appeared, fluttering some eighteen inches or so in front of Eefa's face, and those opalescent blue eyes held hers in a probing confrontation. 'Do not be frightened. It is a secret tunnel where, in distant times, the molten rock discovered a release, to descend over the distant lands even as it created the sacred mountain.'

'I . . . I don't understand.'

'My friend, Eefa! Bree Salis bearer! You must trust me – trust the frost sprites – to be your guides.'

Eefa hesitated, attempting to think. 'What are you implying? Are you saying we must somehow go down this hole?'

'A hole might become a staircase.'

Eefa peered down into the stygian depths with sceptical eyes.

'Allow me to illuminate.'

As swarms of glowing frost sprites entered the darkness, Eefa could make out what appeared to be a spiral of dark and grimy steps that ran around the perimeter of the hole. Her heart raced. She spun round to make certain that Bird Woman was still there to protect her. Her breath caught in her throat at the thought of descending those steps into that dark tunnel.

'I'm terrified I'll fall.'

Woll smiled. 'You will not fall. Our light will illuminate your journey at every step. And do not forget that you have the protection of the Lady of the Shore!'

After an hour or so of preparation, during which they packed their backpacks and weapons, Quimbre volunteered to take the lead, with Eefa and Magio following on behind him. Eefa and Magio followed behind him as they began to descend what appeared to be a vast staircase of ancient stone. The steps were black with dust and cold as ice. Bird Woman followed on close behind them, her protective presence, as with Quimbre's lead in front, comforting every tentative step of descent. A fiery stream of frost sprites illuminated the way, swirling and flowing in waves overhead and around them, providing their personal clusters of fairy lights. At every step, Eefa was aware of the strangeness within her being that marked the sacred burden she was carrying, a burden that weighed nothing at all, a tiny puff of golden vapour, and yet it felt like the most ominous weight about her heart.

The spiral staircase appeared to be never-ending, their presence, amid the twinkling glow of magical light, utterly swallowed up by the stygian gloom that yawned at their feet, mile after mile of dank steps, leading down from the Valley of the Raptors, and returning them to the coastal plains.

The repetitive steps, the steady, monotonous rhythm of it, hypnotised Eefa's mind so that after many hours of descent she was only half aware of the journey. She had fallen into a daydream of automatic stepping, with her mind lost in anxious musing only to be jerked back to awareness by a roar from Quimbre down below. Magio had taken hold of her hand with an arresting tightness. He called out, 'Halt – everybody!'

'What is it, Quimbre?'

'The staircase is sundered up ahead. You must stop where you are. Take not another step!'

In fact, both Magio and Eefa could see now for themselves, through the bright illumination as the frost sprites gathered about the calamity. Part of the ancient staircase had been torn from the tunnel wall, leaving little more than fragments of steps hovering over a bottomless void.

Magio moaned, 'Oh, now we're done for!'

'Perhaps not so!' There was a twinkle in Woll's frost-rimmed eyes, a tinkling laugh upon her lips. 'We are not so easily confounded. The problem is serious, but it may yet be resolved – and in its resolution you, dear Magio, will discover a secret that will make this an adventure of legend.'

'What do you mean?'

Eefa gazed about her, and above and below her. There were minuscule glints from the dark steps, where the scratching of passing feet had exposed chinks of glittering surface below the black coverings of dust. Clearly there was more to the vast winding staircase than first appeared.

'The steps – they're not carved out of rock?'

'Indeed, they are not!'

'Oh, Woll – you're teasing us! What does it mean?'

'A secret very well kept, up to now!' Woll laughed her lovely tinkling chimes of a laugh. 'A secret that has long been kept from your kind, and indeed must certainly be kept by you for evermore. I must have your word – both of you.'

'You have it!' Magio now exploded with curiosity.

'The staircase is not the construction of the frost sprites.'

Magio hesitated, his face a mixture of belief and doubt. 'So – are you saying that it was what – some work of magic?'

'In a manner of speaking.'

Eefa interrupted. 'I don't understand.'

'You might, if you brushed away the dirt and dust of ages from the very step you are standing upon.'

Eefa did so. She shuffled her right boot over the thick layer of dust and dirt on the shelf where she stood and then further wiped the smooth surface with her spit and bare hands to witness glints and gleams of rainbow-hued light.

'Oh, Magio!'

They both knelt down on the step to spit and rub it even cleaner.

'Oh, my goodness – it's crystal!'

Woll, who was gambolling overhead in what seemed excited figures of eight, alighted on the emerging glittering surface. 'Yes, it is!'

'The whole enormous staircase?'

'Yes.' Eefa had never seen Woll look so twinklingly gleeful.

'But how?'

'As I began to explain, this is not the construction of frost sprites. This is the construction of our sister race, the stone sprites.'

'Stone sprites?'

'Sprites that create invest their living spirits with the crystals of stone as we do with the crystals of frost and ice.'

The very idea of a race of stone sprites excited Eefa. She blinked repeatedly in wonder. 'Woll – do tell me truthfully – are there races of sprites that inhabit all manner of . . . well, of what is crystalline in nature?'

'That, dear Eefa, is the secret I now entrust to your confidence.'

Magio clapped his hands. 'Britzy!'

Woll fluttered her wings in excitement. 'Britzy indeed, dear Magio!'

Magio laughed and then he jabbed his fist in the air, as if raised against the invisible sky above.

Woll sighed. 'We should not allow wonder to overcome common sense. Here we find ourselves in a difficult position, one in which we must beg charity.' So, saying, Woll fluttered her wings, rising up into the tunnel above them. 'I, Woll, Queen of the Frost Sprites, must now beg favour of my distant but hallowed relative, Queen of the Stone Sprites, to repair this broken staircase.'

'But where are they?' Magio couldn't contain his impatience. 'Surely they can't be skulking down here in the depths?'

'Oh, believe me, stone sprites are infinitely capable of skulking in deep and dark places!' Woll waved aside his questions. Her tiny body became transfixed, her position in the air above them held perfectly still, through the blur of tiny wings fluttering, and her eyes firmly shut.

Eefa and Magio listened with bated breath to what rose to a tinkling chorus that must, presumably, be some sort of communal communication from the multitude of frost sprites, a summons for charity addressed to . . . to whatever in the world constituted their distant relatives, the stone sprites.

There was a silence lasting for several long minutes as the summons ended. Even Magio was compelled to hold his tongue and be patient, all eyes on the closed eyes of the tiny Woll, her transfixed figure aglow in the air above them, the solemn expression on that tiny perfect face that bade them wait. And then, when they thought there would be no reply, they heard an answering chorus, not a tinkling of frosted crystals, but something lower pitched, like the grinding of rounded pebbles of beach stones rolling over one another . . .

*'We hear . . . we listen . . . You are our cousins. But it has been aeons since we last met. Forgive us if we hesitate to engage upon this new creation. First, we must confirm the authority of the sororal request.'*

Woll's face became very serious indeed. *'If I might be allowed to speak my relevant thoughts aloud: it has been so long since such distant cousins communicated, and that makes it hard to remember the observances . . .'* Her eyes remained closed, her mouth sufficiently ajar to whisper. Then she appeared to summon up strange words, words that seemed imbued with the susurrations of nature, the cries of birds . . . Magio and Eefa listened in thrilled silence as this conversation, which sounded like a conversation between orchestras of tiny bells and lowing counterpoint, went on for what appeared to be far too long. And then, with astonishing abruptness, it ended.

'Woll?' Eefa whispered.

'We are graced with their co-operation. Though it was never really in doubt. The stone sprites just love to make a formal occasion of such confluences.'

'They'll restore the steps?'

'So, we have agreed.'

'You are wonderful!'

'They also wish you both well in your endeavour.'

'Thank you!'

'Well – it isn't me you should thank. But I shall duly thank them for you.'

Then they were silenced by the intrusion of sudden groaning noises arising from the tunnel in the vicinity of the broken steps.

Woll whispered to them, 'It would be wise to observe their creations carefully, and comment loudly on their precision and efficiency – just in case we ever need their assistance again.'

'Oh!'

Woll laughed at Magio's worried expression, then waved a finger. 'Try not to question. Best to just let them complete what must be done without interruption. But you may watch them.'

Eefa shook her head. It wasn't easy for Magio to keep his mouth shut. But at least he did so for the moment, watching as constellations of tiny glowing figures poured into the gap in the staircase, each figure bearing a tiny glowing crystal. He continued to watch, wide-eyed, as little by little, they recreated the missing steps. But these steps looked nothing like the dark and grimy cylindrical staircase above them.

'What's going on?'

'Hisst!'

Eefa grabbed Magio's shoulder, both to quiet and to comfort him.

'What's going on here?'

'Do what Woll told you to. Don't ask questions. Just look!'

They both stared at the reforming steps in amazement as the glowing crystals crackled and hissed, before, in a flowing exudation, they took the perfect shapes of the missing steps.

'They're beautiful!' Magio exclaimed.

Woll appeared to actually blink.

'Yes, they are!' Eefa added her voice of praise.

Woll hovered before them, her wings beating to the blur of movement that was necessary to hold her perfectly still. 'The stone sprites insist on perfection of individual crystals and absolute accuracy of placement of crystal upon crystal.'

Magio spoke, his voice suddenly subdued. 'But . . . oh, britzy, britzy, britzy! They're not ordinary crystals, are they?'

'No, they are not.'

Eefa agreed with Magio. 'The steps – oh, Woll! The steps are actually made out of diamonds?'

'Yes. The stone sprites insist on making use of the most apposite crystals drawn from stone. In this instance the most enduring crystal for steps that are designed to last for many thousands of years are diamonds.'

Magio's face wore a look of exaltation. 'All those thousands of steps we descended . . .'

'Yes.'

'Wow!' Magio appeared to be lost for words for several moments. But then he had a powerful intuition. 'Woll – how old are you, the sprites? I have the feeling you are older than I could imagine.'

'Magio – we the sprite folk are older than you could possibly imagine.'

༒

After the restoration of the damaged staircase, the descent was so fast and problem free that they had to rest at intervals to allow their tired limbs to recover and their minds to sleep.

On their journey Eefa and Magio were surprised to discover that they had to pass through many natural chambers in the rock, from some so small they were through with a few dozen strides, to caverns vaster than any room Magio had ever encountered, and fascinating in their secrets. It would appear that he and Woll had struck up a tentative friendship of sorts, though it might also have been more that she felt that he, perhaps more than Eefa, needed closer protection. Magio, who had become increasingly tired, had lost all sense of time on this descent through mile after mile of rock, so he didn't know if it was day or night outside the tunnels and caverns.

Magio would only retain the vaguest recollection of the latter part of their descent through the seemingly interminable diamond staircase. He vaguely recollected strange images, no doubt some playful chiming communications between the sprites, coupled with delightful scents, songs of longing, sprinklings of delight in what, in retrospect, felt like dreams of pure magic. He would have loved to retain every single memory. But he had the suspicion that the entrancement was not designed to last. All was already fading from his memory as the company, in an exhausted state, arrived at the portal leading out into the lowland marshes. They were greeted by a vista of luxuriant forest trees, from which dangled some kind of golden fungus growths. It was accompanied by the most wonderful feeling of escape as he felt his exhausted body slide with blissful lack of caring, so he was sitting, straggle-legged on the soft earthen ground, ready for sleep.

Already Woll and her frost sprites were readying to leave.

Magio heard his sister's calm and certain voice, soft and full of wonder, her face illuminated by the light of the fluttering figure of the sprite that had been so caring and helpful to them in the Sacred Mountains.

'You look so young,' Eefa said. 'Don't you age, like humans?'

'We do not age.'

Magio struggled to clear his stupefied mind to climb to his feet to gaze up at them in astonishment. 'Does that mean you don't die?'

'Not through age, as you do. Yet if I were to openly accompany you on your journey, I would surely wither – my crystals would melt away so there would be no trace to say that I had ever been.'

'Must we say goodbye, here, then?'

'Oh, my newfound human friends, dearest Eefa and Magio, take care in this perilous journey. Though we cannot accompany you in physical form, we shall accompany you in spirit.'

'We're so reassured to hear that!' Eefa said.

Magio's eyes were falling shut as he heard the tinkling wonder of Woll's laugh, even as she, and all of her people, faded and then vanished.

# Dead Eyes

Kull was moving stealthily through a vile forest embedded in mud. He had made numerous false steps, steps his former self would have judged clumsy, and so he was now soaked from head to toe and encased in the stinking effluvium. There was something resentful, evil, about this landscape that the seasoned hunter sensed in his very bones. If this place could speak it would whisper, '*Stranger – what are you doing here? We have ways of dealing with strangers here.*'

He shrugged the thought off.

The quarry had come down from the mountain. This was no great calculation on his part. He had been instructed by the purchaser of his hunt that this would likely be the case. He was instructed to find them here. There were questions that should trouble him with this hunt. But his recent experiences made him wary of asking questions. The quarry must be somewhere close. He could sense them, almost smell them, taste them. So why were his instincts telling him to beware?

He was beginning to think that, maybe, he had been duped by that magnificently attractive, if daunting, female with the emerald eyes.

'Bastos Kull be tricked,' he whispered to himself. 'Tricked by that scheming witch!'

She had bewitched him with that small mountain of gold on his ale-wet counter – made him abandon his normal caution. Now Kull stopped his long-limbed loping, feeling slightly dizzy, as if some kind of blanket was closing down over his senses, dismissing such negative thoughts. It was as if his mind were being invaded by the will of another, an alien mind, that forbade his cursing what had proved a disastrous hunt. He had lost two out of three of his beloved gals.

Now his instincts bade caution.

There was a part of his mind that questioned everything about what he was now undertaking. It was true that this hunt was unlike any he had experienced before. The memories of what had gone before were so terrible that he had constructed a wall in his mind to block them off. Yet still there was this weasel voice inside his head that insisted that when things went this wrong, you had to take a step back and think.

There was also a stirring fear in him that warned him that he didn't really want to do that. The fact was, he didn't know what to think.

'Hsst!' he whispered to his one remaining gal. 'Maw, what we got to do here is to use us cunning.'

There was a movement, just out of his vision. It arrested his careful plod across the soft mud between the trees.

'At bay!'

The hound stopped its pursuit, frozen. He looked all about himself again, cursing the pallid light under the dense canopy of branches.

'Careful!!'

He pressed on again, with the hound pressing her wet nose against the ground to follow what appeared to be a scent.

A foetid wind whipped against his cheeks.

Maw's nose had led him into this coastal valley of strange, exceedingly lofty trees. He had no reason to doubt her scent. Every tree appeared to be the same, with their branches interlacing a good hundred feet above the ground, with such leaves and pattern of bark as he had never seen before. The forest was fertile with bright red fruit the size of coconuts. But there was an overwhelming stink – the stink of charnel.

'Cautious now, gal!'

This place was, as he was coming to realise, a natural orchard of sorts. Hence the big fat fruit, bright red – too big, too red . . .

Maw sensed something. She was growling at the spindly trunks. All of a sudden, a fruit detached and fell to the ground, bursting open, its carmine flesh flowing over the sandy soil, exciting swarms of ants. The hound howled, as if crazy with excitement.

'What the devil's got into you?'

She looked up at him, and her eyes made him shiver. Those weren't Maw's eyes. She should have been looking at him with big brown loving eyes. But the eyes regarding him were glowering pits of red. And it wasn't only Maw who had changed. Kull knew that he, too, was different. He no longer needed to rest or sleep. There was no hunger in him any more. He didn't dare to look at his own reflection in a glass or still water, afeared of what he might see.

He shook such thoughts from his head.

What was it about this stinking fruit? He looked about him at the trees, which promised too much. He dipped a finger into the pulp of the fruit.

'No – can't be!'

But now he sniffed at it, tasted it, it smelled it. Blood! The fruit was gore apples – something he had heard of but had never seen before. Now he looked more carefully about himself, there were cobwebs among the branches, massive cobwebs, with strands as thick as twine, spread out in huge nets.

'We got to get us out of here!'

Kull was ready for running, but Maw was stood there, hackles up, growling. Kull heard a disturbing sound. A humming, like hornets, somewhere overhead. He was getting the very worst feelings about this place. 'Here, gal!' He spun about himself, grabbing at the pelt of his hound. 'To me, now!'

But Maw was driven mad by the stink of rotting meat that was coming out of the gory fruit. She tore free of his grip and began to gobble up the bloody pith. That humming sound – it was getting louder. Kull rocked back on his heels to peer up into the foliage. That was where the humming sound was coming from.

Maw was growling. Within a moment or two, she was howling. But it wasn't Maw's howl he heard. It was something darker, a screaming sort of sound that caused him to grit his teeth and lower his head to his chest. There was a plop upon the ground at his feet, and then another.

He knelt on one knee and patted Maw's head. Those furnace eyes lifted up to his. 'What is it, gal? What's going on?'

There was no answering whine. The hound wasn't Maw any more. He got back up to his feet. He hefted the axe out of its back holster. As he did so a thought entered his head, unbidden: *Death never comes without a reason.*

What in a demon's curse did that mean?

He whirled in a circle, with his axe extended. 'It better watch out, whoever, or whatever it be!'

But still the same thought returned, and once back inside his head, it whirled around and around in his mind: *Death never comes without a reason.*

He froze in his circling. What reason then? He lifted his head and glared once more at the interlaced branches high overhead. What was the nature of this threat?

He had hunted down soldiers – warriors – themselves experienced in war. He had hunted entire exalted families, whose existence was considered redundant by more powerful enemies. He had hunted politicians, housewives, counsellors of the faith. He, Bastos Kull, had been the paid instrument of vendettas far beyond Moon—beyond even the Sea of Stars. He had terminated the haughty high-born with the same skill and ruthlessness he had hunted down outlaws. That was why contracts of every sort had come his way. But now the thought whispered inside his head that maybe he, rather than the hunted, was the quarry here.

Cursing and spitting his way out of yet another pit of mud, he heard that same insistent voice: *Stranger! What bewitchment brought you here?*

He blew the phlegm and mud out of his nostrils between finger and thumb.

Whose voice was it? What was going on? Things didn't make no sense.

'What the devil? We be caught up in some kind of haunting?'

Bastos Kull prided himself on the fact he didn't fear ghosts. He prided himself on the fact he didn't fear no spirits, or goblins, or spectres of any nature or portent. But still he just couldn't shake off the fact that he mayhaps he should be afeared here. Had he truly blundered into a haunted land?

He refused to believe it.

All the same, the fear refused to go away. A strange new vision crept into his mind: a desolate beach, with some kind of hut, a refuge of some sort that appeared to be built out of rusting iron plates. There appeared to be no entrance, no windows.

There was a figure there – on that desolate beach. It looked like that same figure was watching him . . .

A shiver ran through him.

He shrugged it off, forcing himself to continue the hunt, closing his mind to such disturbing thoughts. If spirits existed, he doubted that any such haunting spirit, however powerful, would survive a face-to-face encounter with the spirit that had commanded him to conduct this hunt.

And yet still there were other thoughts, thoughts encouraged by his own rising sense of uncertainty, that he didn't want to consider. He waved them away, wiping mud from his eyes and forcing his legs to stride on.

*Bewitched us, she did! Bewitched by that lying schemer!*

'No – begone!'

*But we knows it now, doesn't us? There wasn't ever no mountain of gold!*

He saw her again, the strange female being sitting cross-legged on the Beach of Bones, an old woman with the tormented eyes. Them tormented eyes were looking straight at him.

He held his hands over his ears. 'Get outa me head, witch! Get outa me mind!'

His ma, Ellumbra, had cherished an icon of her angry god. It had been painted onto a slab of oak in bright colours. Before she beat him with it, she would kiss the icon and call upon it, imploring it to make all the more hurtful the beating.

Ellumbra had been an enormous woman. She was head and shoulders taller than any man in their village. She had cut into the skin of his chest with a sharpened flint and rubbed in charcoal from the fire to tattoo the symbol of her clan, the clan that her Scog father had belonged to. He, Bastos Kull, was a quarter Scog. It was a curse and a half that he had gone to great lengths to conceal throughout his life. But that same curse had given him size, and strength, and instincts better than any human. And those same instincts were now raising the hackles on his neck.

*What in bloody slaughter's a-going on here?*

There was a pattern to the sounds he was picking up in the air about him. Some things – from the sounds he judged that there were surely many of them – were closing in on him. Whatever they were, they surely were not human. Their movements were more stealthy than human feet. And their high-pitched whispered chittering was in no language that he had encountered. He could thank the Ursascogan bit of him for the fact he sensed things that no human could possibly have caught a hold of. He pressed on beneath the high dark canopy, glimpsing a pallid light and followed Maw's lead in heading towards it. He was staring ahead into a moonlit bay that should be like any other of the thousands of bays that surrounded Moon.

A feeling suddenly stopped him dead. 'Here, Maw!'

The hound was stationary, her flanks atremble.

Kull listened hard. He sensed in his very soul that hunters of a different kind had followed his every step. Did they think to fool him into dropping his guard? None alive was more familiar with the hunt than Bastos Kull.

Maw growled again, deep in her throat.

He spun round. Took up a fighting stance. The axe was clasped aloft in his right hand. 'Come on! Um would look death in the face? Come then. Gaze into them dead eyes of us hound. Come – um been a haunting us a good hour or two. Come get to the close if um dare. Close in for the kill!'

Maw was still growling, staring up into the trees.

Kull looked up. Things were falling down, slow-falling like snowflakes, from on high. But these weren't the blood red fruits. These were shapes of black floating gently on . . . well, it looked like threads of silk. They looked eerily beautiful. They snowflaked down out of the canopy in a mesmerising display. In seconds they were all about them.

Maw was howling.

Kull tensed. He focused on the balls that were now close to reaching them. They had a furry covering, like coarse black hair. One brushed his arm as it passed him by and in doing so it exploded. He stared at the nature of what the explosion revealed, astonished. It opened up into a hairy ugliness of fangs and claws. A gigantic spider, fully two feet wide, with eight gangly legs and what looked like six or maybe more blood-red eyes. He only belatedly noticed how his arm was stinging and bleeding from the contact and now the vile thing was rushing at him with vicious mouth parts dribbling venom. He cut it into two with his axe.

'Maw – flee!'

He was flailing with his axe as more and more of the giant spiders floated down and landed about him. There were hundreds of them. His axe was moving with lightning speed and accuracy, cleaving the balls in two while still in the air, before they could open up on the ground. But there were far too many of them. He couldn't possibly kill them all.

Maw was squealing.

Kull spun round and saw that numerous of the monsters were attacking her. He throttled the spider that was biting into the hound's throat with his bare hands. He ripped two more apart, where they were biting into her back. He bit the head off another and ripped the rest off her, trampling them underfoot.

'Get them fangs off me gal!'

But they had injected their venom into her. He saw it in the dimming of her eyes. He felt it, too, in the numbness spreading from the bleeding holes where the side-to-side jaws had chewed on his arm.

'We got to keep going!'

Bastos Kull had his dagger in his left hand to support the axe in his right. He was cleaving through a spitting, clawing, biting morass of spiders, while encouraging his hound to keep up.

He heard Maw's whine.

Turning around, he saw her covered in the biting monsters and he swept them off her with an axing frenzy.

'C'mon, gal!'

But it was no good. She was already weakened by their poisons.

It was a stupid thing to do, but he shoved the dagger back into his belt. He grabbed the nape of Maw's neck and he continued to hack his way through the tide of monsters, kicking and biting whenever possible, until, with his skin ensheathed in his own blood, and with his own heart faltering from the venom, his feet felt the waves of the tide.

The monsters held back, a foreshore black with the multitude of them, at the limit of the waves.

So – it seemed they didn't like salt water.

Kull felt half dead, but also exultant. The sun was setting in the sky in front of him and the moon was already visible. The vision filled him with a deep, archaic joy. But then he heard Maw's piteous whine.

She was still dangling from his left hand by the scruff of her neck. He hauled her up, then cradled her in his arms. It provoked a thunderous hissing from the huge gathering of black furry bodies just yards away, filling the entire bay. Kull saw that the last of his gals was dying. The red fire was dimming in her eyes and her face was more like her old self. His darling Maw. His dearest gal.

He hugged her to him. He hugged her there, in the to and fro of the tide, and he kept on hugging her until she gave up the ghost. Then, in the moonlight, he turned back to the beach, with its twinkling of so many spider eyes, and he spat at them.

'Filthy spawn – ya won't get my gal!'

He just couldn't let her go. He waited all through the long night as the tide changed and slowly declined and then rose again about him, coming up to his knees and then halfway to his hips. His darling Maw was dead and gone. It was time to let her go, but he couldn't make himself do so. He hugged her dead body to him, ignoring the waves.

'Do you remember the time, when us first took you back to us bar, and us made a playpen for you and your sisters? You was the runt of the litter. I should've put you in a bag with a rock and thrown you into the river. But then you looked at us with those big brown eyes and growled. It was the way you growled. Bastos knew then you wasn't no weakling. Not in spirit. Reminded us of the many times ma said that she should've weighed us down with a stone and drowned us. But in me mind right then I knew that you was me special darling.

It was that stupid world what didn't like you, any more than it liked old Bastos from the start. That stupid world would've liked you dead. Only Bastos spited it and saved you. And you didn't disappoint us. You might have been the runt but you was also the bravest. You was ever me bootiful gal.'

Time went by. By the time the moon was fully risen, the water was now rising about Kull's chest. The spiders were still gathered hungrily on the beach, but he disappointed them still by carrying Maw's body out with him as, with his weapons secured, he swam into the deeper waters of the bay. There, with a gentle opening of his hand, he released the body of the last of his gals, to be taken not by vicious spiders but the kindness of the ocean.

His heart was transfixed with grief. His breath came in shuddering gasps as he turned his face to the dappled surface and saw there, in his reflection, the twin orbs of red that were his eyes. Well now – he had nothing left but his work. And his work was not done. He felt a powerful urge within him to avenge his losses. Turning to follow the course of the shore, he swam northwards, looking for a place to land beyond the spider-infested forests.

# Shadow Vale

A swarm of purple moths flick-flacked against them as they crossed a wide, fast-flowing river in moonlight. Even as Quimbre shovelled mud over the fire to extinguish the embers, Bird Woman had insisted that they wait for night. Then she had further insisted that they wait for the moon to be hidden behind a scud of cloud before they set out on a hastily constructed raft of reeds, tethered together with strips of bark from the birches that proliferated here. Quimbre had stripped off his clothes and swum across the fast-moving river so he could tether a line to a tree on the other side. Now they hauled on the line, as fast as possible, to gain the cover of a grey murk of forest on the other side. Eefa and Magio couldn't understand the need for such caution any more. Their hunter had been pulverised by the Scog sentry. There was no more howling in their wake. They just wanted to run, as quickly as possible, to wherever they needed to go. But Bird Woman insisted that they remain vigilant.

'We should take the opportunity to rest!' Bird Woman raised her face, as if sniffing at the night air, as Eefa and Magio settled down, nice and dry in their blankets.

They woke to find they were within the edge of a forest of pine trees, growing on a pale sandy soil. But now that soil worried Bird Woman, who thought that its soft dry nature would make tracking easier. But who, the twins wondered, could possibly be tracking them any more? A full hot sun was breasting the horizon, promising that the day would be bright and warm.

Magio asked her, 'Was there any howling in the night?'

Bird Woman, who was cooking a breakfast of gull eggs, shook her head. 'The night was silent.'

'Surely – !'

'Surely nothing, Magio. We may not be immediately threatened. But we should not be lulled into thinking we are safe.'

'Why not?'

'We have seen the implacable determination of the one who hunted us. And so much depends on your safety. We still need to be extraordinarily careful.'

'But we saw what happened to him. The Scog sentinel . . .'

'Even so. We can hope, but cannot be sure, that he is dead. Even then it would be foolish to imagine that he was alone in his quest.'

'But why are we of any importance to him?' Eefa's voice was filled with her own undimmed sense of anxiety.

Bird Woman shook her head. 'I don't know, Eefa. Only that you have endured much already. And now your burden has increased.'

They crossed a smaller river tributary, cut with streams, trudging the pebbled stream beds amid the thick knots of roots of trees. Bird Woman would stop every so often and lift her face to the sky, her nostrils dilated, ever sniffing the air. Magio watched her, but saw from her expression that she detected nothing imminent. There was no howling to raise the hackles on their necks. No threat at all since they had said their goodbyes to Woll and her sprites at the exit from the crystal staircase.

'We've done it.' He reached out and took hold of Eefa's hand. 'We've got rid of that terrible man and his hounds.'

Eefa did her best to squeeze his hand back. 'Hush, Magio. We mustn't grow overconfident. Remember Bird Woman's warning.'

Her squeezing his hand brought back Magio's embarrassment of being a kid, but also such wonderful memories of Quimbre's yarn-telling. The games they would play. Tales of being chased through storms at sea by haunted ships manned with dead crews, who rattled their chains in the dark. Quimbre teaching them cunning card tricks, or best of all, the dagger trick, where you surrendered your dagger, with the hilt turned towards the foe, then flipped it in the air and lunged with the hilt now caught in your other hand and the blade in the belly of the foe before he knew it. Quimbre had a multitude of such tales and tricks. Like how to slip out of the bonds of an enemy who had captured you and tied you up.

How Magio had loved to watch Quimbre's dusky face grinning back at him through his moustache. 'They like to tie your wrists behind your back, like this – you see?'

Magio would allow himself to be tied, sitting or lying on the ground, with his hands behind his back.

'Now look where your hands and wrists are close to. The seam of your trousers in the nick of your bum.'

Magio, now, as in his memories, was nodding. He liked to imagine, from the delight with which Quimbre enjoyed the telling, that Quimbre himself had been captured and tied this way and had escaped through the very same trick.

'Look, see – let's say I'm all tied up. But maybe if I was to hide a sliver of cutting wire in those trousers' seam. Go ahead. Tie me good with that leather thong. And now watch old Quimbre perform the trick!'

In mere seconds, Quimbre was free, his hands cut loose, the same hands now freeing his ankles. And with a bound he was free.

'Now – your turn, kiddo . . .'

*Kiddo!*

Quimbre's pet name for him ever since he could remember!

જ

Magio was awake-dreaming. He was standing, bare-footed, on the familiar rock, that first delightful step onto the beach in Warren. He was waiting for something to happen, something that he sensed, overwhelmingly, was important. As he broke cover of the pine trees, he saw something strange in the moonlit sand ahead of him. It glowed in the dark landscape of the bay like a fallen star. Some trick of the moonlight, perhaps a piece of glass or crystal. He approached it cautiously, determined to investigate it.

Gingerly, he stood before it. He had expected it to melt away, as tricks of light usually did when you got close to them. But this shiny thing refused to disappear. He hesitated. Bird Woman's repeated warnings were now uppermost in his mind. They had come across terrifying entities and tricks during this journey, and this might well be another. He fell onto his knees in the sand so he could examine it more closely. The thing was silvery, and somehow changing its shape even as he examined it. It expanded, then contracted, its surface becoming even shinier, reflecting the moonlight like a mirror, then it metamorphosed to a capricious being, with glowing tentacles extending in every direction.

'What are you?' he whispered.

It appeared to be studying him back.

He felt an overwhelming impulse to pick it up. Tentatively, he reached out to touch it with the tips of his fingers. There was a reassuring frisson, as if a kitten or a pup had responded to his brushing its fur. He took hold of it, held it up above his head in both hands, to get a better notion of the shape of it against the moonlight.

'Are you some kind of a spawn?'

In the yarns Gran used to regale them with, magical spawns were the start of just about anything. It wouldn't be difficult for a demon or a wight to make itself appear small, even to become as weightless as this curious object. Even as he thought along these lines, the thing extended a lengthy head, on an even more extended neck, and four spindly legs. It was as if it had read his mind. It certainly wasn't a demon. In fact, it really was coming to resemble a partly coiled dragon. A very tiny and twisty dragon! Without quite realising what he was doing, he had taken it into his arms. There was no weight to it at all. As he embraced its awkward shape to his breast, the sound of the sea entered his mind, his consciousness, his being. Magio felt strangely uplifted, exalted, his senses filled with elation.

He had to tell somebody about his discovery. He didn't care for the moment exactly what it really could be. It was enough that he treasured it, wrapping it in his shirt, and running all the way home to show Gran what he had discovered. But when he rushed into the living room, she wasn't there. He searched the entire house at a run, but there was no sign of her – no sign of anybody else at home. He ended up in the yard, a stupid place to search for Gran, since she never went there because the surface was uneven and with her stroke, she was bound to trip. A woman appeared before him, as if by magic. A woman-being might be a more accurate term to describe her. She was as diaphanous as a ghost. Yet she wasn't like he would have imagined a ghost. Her hair was salt-grimed and windblown. She had injuries and scars all over her body, as if night creatures had been feeding on her flesh.

*'You have something precious – a thing you discovered?'*

'Who are you?'

*'You know who I am – you have visited me so often in your dreams.'*

'You're the old woman – the old woman chained on that terrible beach?'

*'Alas, I cannot manifest in this time and place.'*

'What is it? What's really going on? I can't make head nor tail of what's happening.'

She placed a slim cold finger against his lips.

*'Ask no more questions. Show me your treasure.'*

He held the strange thing aloft.

*'It is beautiful. I can see why you would treasure it. Make sure you do not lose it when you are compelled to run.'*

'Why must I run?'

*'Even in the respite of dream there is peril on your tail. You should not have lit the fire. In these dark lands, even though you extinguished it, you provided a beacon. The peril has marked your fire and will surely find you.'*

Their conversation was interrupted by the first faint infusions of light in the sky that heralded daybreak.

The light of day caused his senses to shimmer. Things became confused. The strange vision wavered. Magio heard what he imagined to be whispered words, but they were barely audible against the crashing roar of the incoming sea.

*'You and Eefa must make haste to the appointed place . . .'*

Magio was immediately awake. Fear rose in him. He threw off his blanket and stared about himself to where Eefa and Quimbre were fast asleep.

What did the strange woman's words mean?

He remembered the dragon spawn. Was it just a dream? Had he lost it when the dream faded? Panic overwhelmed him until he registered its weightless presence, still clutched to his breast in his white-knuckled hands. A sweat of relief broke out over his goosepimpled skin.

What was going on?

It seemed to Magio that he had somehow been given this strange gift in his sleep – but at the same time he had received a warning. He must wake the others up. He must do so immediately. He was shaking Eefa's shoulder, then Quimbre's.

'The hunter – he's not dead. He's onto us!'

'How do you know?' Eefa cried, terrified.

'I know – I just know.'

A pandemonium of movement was sweeping through the rough shelter. Clothes were thrown on, backpacks mounted. Bird Woman's head was poking into the shelter, alerted by the commotion of voices. 'What's wrong?'

Magio shouted, 'I was woken by a dream. A spirit spoke to me. She warned me that we are in great danger.'

'How?'

'We should never have lit the fire,' Magio said, issuing out of the shelter and peering around in the false dawn.

They all stiffened with shock as a new howling fell upon their ears. But this was a very different sound from before. This was an anguished roar, diminishing to a drawn-out wail. It seemed to come from somewhere much too close. A howling that came from a dreadful human throat, one that hungered for their blood.

Quimbre was attempting to break camp, but Bird Woman put her hand on his. 'Forget that! All of you, forget the backpacks. We must abandon everything other than weapons of protection. We must flee this spot!'

There was no time for Magio to explain his discovery. Already they were running at full pelt. He felt Quimbre's hand pat his sweat-soaked head. 'Run, kiddo. Run with the Bird Woman. Do what you can to protect your sister.'

'What about you?'

'Quimbre is the cunning fox. A fox that will lay a false trail so this hunter will end up discovering a cliff of rock, or the salty ocean.'

Magio's voice was already breathless. 'We can't abandon you.'

'You're not abandoning me – I'm giving you a chance. I lit the fire that has drawn the enemy to us. Go now – run like the wind!'

Magio ran. Barely half dressed, the only thing he carried in his hands was the weightless spawn he had discovered in his dream. Even so, he couldn't stop himself from looking back over his shoulder at Quimbre, who was calmly loading his flintlock pistol. His cutlass was dangling loosely from his belt. A thrill of fright caused Magio's heart to somersault inside his chest.

# The Haunted Chyme

'There can be no more rests, no more sleep!'

Bird Woman was talking to Eefa and Magio, even as they were still running. 'I had thought to circle around it, and approach the Beach of Bones from the north coast. But there is no longer time for such circumambulation. We are obliged to approach it head on, through the perilous region known as the Chyme. But fear not! I shall guide and protect you.'

Those were supposed to be comforting words.

Neither Magio not Eefa felt comforted. But they accepted what Bird Woman had to say. All they could do was to hurry on. Both were seasoned runners. But now what had once been their competitive pleasure was the one thing that was keeping them alive. Eefa was suffused by the Bree Salis and Magio sensed that the burden of it was somehow slowing her down, so that she tended to fall behind. Concerned about his sister, he fell back to support her, though he couldn't possibly imagine how a magical thing, that weighed close to nothing at all, could slow down Eefa, who was normally so full of energy. Soon perhaps they might need to give Eefa more of a helping hand.

The Bree Salis also appeared to draw strange forces around them. Magio had a suspicion of this and, at times, he suspected it might even be attracting even stranger beings. As the company made its hurried way into the narrow crescent that was the northern extremity of Moon, the wind and weather changed. They had arrived into a misty valley filled with toadstools of every variety and hue. Here the very light appeared to become whimsical. Shadows of startling colours flitted about them, like fish gliding about the clefts and hollows of a coral reef.

In an unexpected tunnel of darkness, Magio worried about the dragon spawn he had discovered in what had appeared to be a dream. He pressed his hand against his shirt, to discover that it had attached itself to the underlying skin of his chest. This so startled him that his legs faltered. He felt the press of Bird Woman's hand against the small of his back. 'Do not stop running. We must not permit ourselves to be beguiled.'

*To be beguiled . . .*

Speeding up again, he reached out for Eefa's hand. He found it for the briefest of moments . . . or he thought it was her hand. But how could he be sure of what he was feeling here, in such deceptive shadows and visions?

'Hey, Evie!' He was so frightened he couldn't help calling out his childish name for her. 'I can't really see you any more.'

'Oh, Gio!' It was truly her voice, but sounding so lost and distant from him it frightened him.

'Bird Woman . . .!'

'You must not slow! Keep running! Ignore all distractions. If you stop, you lay yourself open to danger. The path we follow remains true.'

'But how do we know what direction is true?'

'Trust your instincts!'

At times it felt to Magio that he was ploughing through ocean shallows, surrounded by the brilliant arabesques of the shore spray. But he remembered the words of the spirit emissary – and he clung to the treasure he had found.

'Help me, Bird Woman! I'm truly lost.'

Then a familiar whisper, *'Fear not! We are here to guide you.'*

'Woll? Is it really you this time?'

*'Did I not assure you that we would accompany you in spirit?'*

'Yes – oh, dear Woll – yes you did.'

But was this truly their friend, Woll? Bird Woman had cautioned them not to be taken in by malign misdirections.

*'I have been obliged to abandon my aurora of crystals. But if you but close your eyes, you might discover a guiding star.'*

Magio did so. He closed his eyes and saw a pinpoint of blue light – the same blue as he recalled of Woll's eyes back in the Valley of the Raptors.

'I see you – I see your star.'

*'Good. We are approaching a pass that even frost sprites fear to travel through.'*

'Why do you fear it?'

*'The Beach of Bones is not really of this world. You would not find it on any map, since it is within the in-between world, known as Dromenon. It is forbidden for mortals to enter. The Undying who imprisoned the Lady of the Shore there has made it into an inescapable prison. All approaches to the Beach of Bones are warded with dark magic and the most perilous traps. These very labyrinths we now tread are exceedingly ancient. We are approaching the most perilous aspect of our journey, known as the Cavern of the Spirits.'*

'What are you saying? This place is haunted?'

*'The Cavern has long served as a sepulchre. I have only ever passed through it on a single occasion, but I confess that even I fear it now as I feared it that first time. We will encounter the spirits of departed beings.'*

'Departed beings?' Eefa murmured, her steps pounding by his side.

'Ghosts!' Magio murmured. 'The ghosts of the dead!'

Woll contradicted him. *'Ghosts they may be. But do not treat the past as dead. It is ever present to them. Do not be beguiled by their whispers.'*

'Will they see me?'

*'They are sure to gather about you as you pass.'*

'Why?'

*'Because there are seers among them who will sense something of the importance of your mission.'*

Magio slowed in his running, turning from side to side to gaze into the bewildering shadows that surrounded him. He felt more puzzled than ever by Woll's words. His head was addled with increasing confusion.

'How can the past still live? Why would these ghosts care anything about what's happening now in the present?'

*'The present gives meaning to the past.'*

Her words caused Magio to think back to his last sight of Quimbre. He hated the fact that they had abandoned him to fight alone. He wished, with all of his heart, that he had stayed to fight with him. It provoked a heavy anguish in his heart.

'Ooohhh!'

Magio had fallen onto his knees.

*'What you sense is the proximity of death. You must get back onto your feet and continue running.'*

Magio didn't think it was anything to do with the closeness of death. It was conscience – the fact he had run away and let Quimbre give his life to save them. It was extremely difficult, racked by such shame, for Magio to climb back onto his feet. His muscles felt juddery.

*'You must be strong. We shall guide you.'*

Magio felt a shock of relief as he heard Eefa call out his name, then felt her arm about his shoulders. 'Come on, Gio! Race you!'

He laughed, a somewhat hysterical laugh. But he was running again, and, somehow, still clasping his dragon spawn thing to his breast.

'I don't understand anything of this any more.'

'I don't think we're intended to understand,' Eefa whispered into his ear. 'Oh, Woll! You are supposed to be our friend. Why are you tormenting him?'

'I am not tormenting Magio. He is consumed by grief of his own making. Even so, such is his attraction, he gathers the past about him. It clings to him. It seeks to bind him here forever.'

Bird Woman had joined them, with a hand on each of their shoulders. 'You are both exhausted. Perhaps, though I am loath to say so, we should pause for a few minutes or two and allow you to rest.'

Woll countered, *'If you do it will increase the danger.'*

'Nevertheless, I think we should rest for a very short while. Magio and Eefa are too exhausted to carry on. We must take the risk.'

*'Very well. The frost sprites will encircle you while you do so. We shall do what we can to mitigate the danger.'*

Magio had thrown himself down spreadeagled on the ground, hating himself for what he had done. 'But surely even if the spirits of the past are drawn to me, they can't see Eefa? She'll be as invisible as ever.'

*'I'm afraid that they can see her altogether clearly. Is she not a spirit, like them? Indeed, I fear that, now we have slowed*

*our passage, they might redirect their attentions to Eefa and the
burden she bears.'*

'Oh, jinxy!' Magio gripped his head between his two
hands and yanked at his hair. 'What's going to happen?'

*'We will do all we can to protect you both. Remember that
Eefa is unique, she and her burden. We cannot predict what will
happen.'*

'Jinxy! Jinxy! Jinxy!'

*'I'm sorry, Magio. But the Cavern of the Spirits is the price
we must pay to make possible the undoing of a terrible wrong.'*

'Please don't apologise to us.' Eefa spoke softly. 'Magio
and I know the risks you and your people have taken to
protect us. We are very grateful for all you have done, and for
your protection on every step of this way.'

'How soon to this cavern?' Magio said, his voice jittery.

*'I'm afraid we are already here.'*

Magio stared ahead, dumbstruck, as the glowing bodies
of the sprites spread out, as if diffusing their light into an
ocean.

'I thought it would be a cave – a gigantic cave.'

*'Not quite. Perhaps it began as such, but it has been much
weathered over the ages of its existence.'*

Magio's first instinct was one of delight. A vast hollow,
something that had once been a cave, and what was left of
it still full of mysteries to explore. Immediately he felt Eefa's
hand tug at his sleeve. Then her two hands gripped his left
wrist, so he couldn't follow his instincts and run helter-
skelter into the strange promise of it. There were cries of
astonishment up ahead from Bird Woman.

'Come, Eefa! Look – *look!*'

'I can see it.'

They had arrived at a face carved in a pillar that must once have been an enormous stalagmite, carved into a playful landscape of clouds and eagles.

Magio squealed, 'It's brilliant!'

Eefa tugged at his hand. 'Remember Woll's warning.'

But despite that warning he was struggling to break free of Eefa's hand, desperate to run ahead and explore. Then, with a terrifying shriek, a disembodied face swept by them, a bald head, a face shrunken to a skull, skin pallid as the moon, with eyes as black as midnight. That spectre halted Magio in his attempted rush. It was so horrible it stopped him dead.

They held onto each other, hardly daring to move.

Woll's voice sounded in their heads. '*We must press ahead. Do not halt. The last thing you should do here is to fall back and find yourselves alone.*'

Magio's heart was beating much too fast for comfort. He took a firm grip of Eefa's hand and they hurried on, following the pinpoints of light that marked the guide of the sprites. But now the hollow had become so vast that their company resembled a small boat lost in an ocean. They were passing between what appeared to be the ruins of an entire city, with alien-looking temples, and arcades, and squares. Yet who in their right minds would construct such a city within what had once been a gigantic cavern?

Woll barked, '*Quickly – put your fingers in your ears.*'

They did so without question.

Moments later they heard the suppressed murmur of myriad voices. The murmurs grew until they became a deafening thunder.

When the thundering receded, Woll urged then back to action. '*Now,*' Woll bade them, '*do not run, but keep walking briskly. Let me lead you. Meanwhile, it would be wise to close your eyes.'*

Magio kept his fingers in his ears, but he could not resist peeping through his almost closed lids. He wished he hadn't. All around them, from every angle, side to side, and from above and below, skeletal arms were reaching out as if to take hold of them.

Eefa's elbow jabbed into his side. 'Shut your eyes, this instant!'

'Oh, jinxy to the millionth degree!'

Woll shrieked inside his head. *'You must do as Eefa tells you. Have you the slightest idea of how great a danger your sister might face here?'*

Magio was alarmed at the notion that Eefa might be harmed because he had not fully closed his eyes. He admitted to himself now that opening his eyes had been a mistake. A grim-faced Bird Woman had taken a firm grip of his free wrist and was forcing their way through a morass of dreadful spectres. He glimpsed beings with the sucking faces of bats, others as tall as giants, with elongated skulls and mouths filled with sharp teeth like those of crocodiles, fluttering in between vicious hordes of winged forms that resembled the goblins of Gran's most frightening fairy tales.

Magio could hardly breathe through his fright. His heartbeat had risen into his throat. A peculiar feeling of burning weakness was sweeping over him. He wondered if, for the first time in his life, he was going to faint.

'What are they? What do they want from us?'

*'Is it not obvious? The Bree Salis offers resurrection.'*

'Oh, no!'

*'Please close your eyes and keep a tight hold of your sister's hand while we lead you through. We must escape this place.'*

Magio and Eefa were running pell-mell through a devastated landscape of petrified trees rooted to a soil that was dry as dust. They ran and ran until at last they were forced to stop. Their lungs were bursting, their legs trembling from exhaustion. Eefa, her hands pressed against her thighs, forced the words from her mouth.

'Maybe we should ask Bird Woman to explain?'

They both turned to the woman who had stopped running alongside them. They looked up into her wrinkled, leathery face, her dark brown eyes.

Magio, still gasping for breath, asked her, 'What's really going on? Why does the whole world want to hurt us?'

'Oh, Magio, I confess that I am as bewildered as you are.'

He pressed her. 'But you came to look for us. You must know something.'

'All I can tell you is my own strange and disturbing story. I'm not sure we have the time for it.'

'We're exhausted. We're going nowhere right now.'

Bird Woman settled on the dusty ground, then invited them to join her. When they did so, she put an arm around each of their shoulders.

'It began in the most ordinary of fashions. I only ever knew one parent, since my mother died giving birth to me. My father was devoted to me. When I was very small, I was constantly afraid of losing him too. It was he who first introduced me to the study of birds.'

Magio said, 'Why were you so afraid of losing your father?'

'When I was very young, I remember how dangerous the world appeared. It was during the Chaos. People simply vanished, never to be seen or heard of again. I took to climbing out of my bed at night and creeping out into the dark. Incongruous as it might seem, I felt safer out there in the dark than in my bed. I grew wild – feral is the word. I added my own experiences to what my beloved father had taught me. My father was himself ill, but he lived on, at least for long enough to permit me to learn how to survive. I learnt how to creep and to peep. I became one with the rustling of the brush and the birdsong in the air.'

Bird Woman closed her eyes and she took some long slow breaths, and then she reopened her eyes and nodded. 'I survived the Chaos. But then I came to realize that I had learnt a more valuable lesson than mere survival. I could travel through places that were forbidden, to detect and then keep track of those who were a threat to me.'

'What happened to your father?'

'I knew we had to go – leave the village where I was born. The Chaos was coming our way. One night, there was a loud knocking on our cabin door, fiery brands thrown through windows . . .'

'Oh, no!'

'I'm afraid so, Magio.'

'What did you do?'

'We both knew we had to run. But my father was too old to run. And all that was dear to him was there in that small cabin. He told me I must go. Much as I hated to leave him, I realised that I had to run if I were to survive.'

Magio shook his head. He felt Eefa grip his hand.

'I knew the wilderness. It made it surprisingly easy for me to lose myself out there. And so I ran.' Bird Woman hugged them. 'I have been running ever since.'

'Eefa and I will protect you.'

She laughed, a gentle laugh. 'Thank you, Magio. But you are hardly capable of protecting yourselves.'

'We have magic, even though we don't yet know how to use it.'

'Yes – oh, indeed you do.'

Eefa's eyes welled up with tears. 'But we didn't save Quimbre. We just abandoned him.'

Then, all of a sudden, they heard a distant but terrible sound, that inhuman howling of their pursuer, followed by what had to be the roaring din of battle.

Magio exclaimed, 'Poor Quimbre!'

Bird Woman did not reply.

The half light was soft and misty, and Magio felt bathed in its phosphorescence. His nostrils were filled by an ozone smell, which suggested they must be close to the sea.

Woll's voice interrupted his reflections. *There's a storm coming.*

Bird Woman agreed. 'Yes. Perhaps it may help conceal our scent. We must hurry on again – before the storm makes it too difficult to run.'

Magio shook his head. 'No! I'm done with running.'

As he felt Bird Woman's fingers grip his own with a fierce, almost frantic grip, there was a distant boom of thunder. Then he felt the absence of Eefa's fingers in his other hand. Magio immediately jumped to his feet.

'She's gone – Eefa!' He spun all around, searching for her, overwhelmed with panic. 'Where is she? Eefa's been taken!'

Magio found himself running on feet that were numbed with shock. As he ran, his head was turning and turning, searching every possible direction, peering through what was now a falling curtain of rain.

Bird Woman's voice followed him, though he wasn't certain whether it was in his ears or in his mind. 'You must stop thinking about Quimbre. He is wily and experienced.

He will divert our pursuer – and in doing so give us a little time.'

Bird Woman was close behind him, calling to him. 'Stop running, Magio! We must organise – search together for her!'

Magio took no notice. His ears were startled by another almighty crack of thunder. He continued to run. As he did so there was another roar in the distance. This time it sounded like Quimbre's roar. It was followed by more of that awful howling. Then a screeching so dreadful it made him want to block off his ears. He ran in what he thought was the direction of the roars and howls, ignoring the voice of Bird Woman, who was calling on him to stop running. When at last he slowed, in the still pouring rain, Magio realised that Eefa was nowhere to be seen.

Magio called out her name. 'Eefa – *Eefa!* Where are you? I can't see you. I . . . I can't even feel your presence.'

He knew now – he knew it instinctively – that she had gone back to save Quimbre. Panic consumed him. Eefa had gone back alone. He, through his cowardice, had let her and Quimbre down. The sense of his own worthlessness was overwhelming. He trembled all over. He found himself calling on the old woman, who seemed so knowledgeable and powerful, to do something . . . do something magical to save his beloved sister.

# Such a Frail Chrysalis

She moves through the cooling night air like a puff of smoke in the moonlight. She will visit the places and the living things that interest her, ever wondering, ever observing. Her senses are preternaturally acute. She hears the bird calls as an orchestra replete with symphonic mystery. For her, human time does not exist, but rather past and present are equally amenable. She revisits the boy sleeping in the loft bedroom, reached through a ladder, with his collection of shells and spiky sea urchins and five-armed starfish and the twisty piece of driftwood hung up on the wall over the head of his bed. She explores his dreams back then . . . In what is less than a moment, the entirety of his existence has passed through her mind. She digests this even as she roams the evolution of his immature spirit, discovering a love of nature, and the exaltation of wild adventure.

In such a frail chrysalis must hope be born!

Anger consumes her for a moment. This has unfortunate effects on the world around her, a metamorphosis of the elements into violent movements of air, and most tellingly of all, of ocean. Storms rage. Fish huddle into shoals among the frenzy of seaweeds under the waves. The same frenzy causes myriad gulls to take to the air, cawing in protest, eyes eager in expectation of damaged bodies. As quickly as it rose, her anger settles. She climbs cumbersomely to her feet, the rusting chains chafing at pre-existing sores, grinding and rattling. She stretches, and her all-black eyes survey the landscape. She bends her head and grinds her teeth.

*I am become impatient of destiny.*

She has suffered extraordinary indignity for time beyond measure. Few have cared, few have dared to care. The few who cared have lacked the power to free her. But the omens are changing. Could it be that all is about to change? What was once a pipe-dream is now a possibility, though still hugely threatened. She stares up directly into the bright yellow moon.

She lifts up her manacled arms and laughs into the tormented sky. '*Change is coming. You sense it now. But you cannot stop it. You cannot protect even your benighted self from it.*'

## 'I HAVE ALREADY TAKEN MEASURES TO FRUSTRATE IT – AND YOU!'

His voice – his thunderous voice again! A fury devours her. It is as if the elements have gone berserk, rain, snow, storm, lightning . . . The One can no longer suppress her fury, which has been building for aeons. No more can he make malignant use of the strands that held this world of pain together. If only she can keep calm in the hurricane that is now gathering about her, her hair welcoming it, blowing to the four winds, her being exultant with the destructive forces of it.

She makes a calculated decision to retract her rage, careful not to reveal too much. He might undo her yet through her dependency on mortals.

*I must desist!*

She, who has suffered mind-numbing torment for aeons, must think more clearly. Something extraordinary is happening. His very presence, his brooding silence, provokes her wariness.

*Passion . . . passion was ever a weakness in me . . .*

He waits a moment or two, and when she fails to reply he speaks again.

*'THOUGH YOU AFFECT TO HIDE IT, I SENSE
SOMETHING IMMINENT ABOUT A BOY . . .
AND AN INVISIBLE GIRL!'*

The sense of danger rises exponentially in her. Has she been careless? Oh, how the urge to protect Magio and Eefa rises in her. But even to think of them would now be perilous. She is silent.

In the half-light of dawn, she observes a new day dawning over the ocean. Her mind is momentarily distracted by the awareness that Magio is deeply disturbed. He could not know, he could not possibly know, what needs to be done.

She buries all thoughts in a wanton confusion. But she is unable to suppress her hopes her fears . . .

*Heed him! Heed the boy! The Bree Salis is beckoning . . .*

She abandons her own tormented thoughts, aware now that the boy is calling to her. She refocuses her mind so she can hear Magio's impassioned calling to her. 'Help me! Help me save Eefa!'

In that same moment he appears before her, lost in the abyss of Dromenon, his mind reaching out in all directions, calling for her.

'Won't anybody help me?'

*'I am here, dearest Magio. What is it? What so imperils you?'*

How forlorn he appears, trembling with fear, gazing up at her from such a distance, and there is such panic in his face and voice. 'Eefa is gone. She's run back to help Quimbre. She's in terrible danger. Please help me – help me save Eefa.'

'*Where is she gone? What is happening?*'

'We were coming to you, to the Beach of Bones. But then we were warned that we were in danger. I ran, together with Eefa and Bird Woman. But Quimbre stayed back. I knew he must be fighting the hunter so we could escape. Quimbre is brave, but he's an old man. He can't beat the monster we saw at the root of the mountains. And now Eefa has disappeared. I think she's gone back to save Quimbre.'

'*Dearest child!*'

'I can't bear it. I must try to save Eefa – save them both.'

His words shock her. The Bree Salis is compromised. This is a calamity none had heralded. But in gazing at his anxious figure, she senses the secret he is clutching to his breast . . .

'*Calm yourself, Magio. You cannot think clearly when your wits are scattered with panic. There is something you're not telling me. A secret lurks close to you – something you mentioned when, in spirit form, I came to warn you that your enemy was nigh upon you.*'

'What secret?'

'*You told me of your discovery. That treasure you now clutch to your breast like life itself.*'

'I don't rightly know what it is. I found it in my awake-dream . . . shining like a fallen star, half-buried on the beach.'

'*Show me!*'

He holds it out to her, his hands shaking with fright. 'It was smoky and silvery, and ever-changing, just sort of hovering in the air. Then it sent out tentacles. I've never seen anything like it.'

'*It didn't frighten you then?*'

'It did . . . at least at first. I didn't know what it was or why it was there. But there's something really beautiful about it.'

How extraordinary the youth appears: how sensitive his nature seems, even though he is unaware of his gifts.

*'Have you considered that, perhaps, the answer to your present need lies with what you have discovered? Could it be possible that it placed itself in your path for the express purpose of being found by you?'*

'Why would it?'

The old woman laughs softly. *'Tell me what you felt when first you held your discovery in your hands.'*

'I felt a sense of wonder . . . exhilaration.'

It is difficult for her to stay patient with Magio. So much is at stake. But she quells her impatience and speaks soothingly. *'It might help if you put your discovery close to your heart, and explain your need to it.'*

'I don't understand.'

*'Merely do it!'*

She watches as Magio brings his discovery, with its slippery changing shape, against his chest, and he urges it to save Eefa and Quimbre. His face is extremely sceptical and he is immediately disappointed.

'It hasn't done anything.'

Patience again . . . Patience, patience, patience! She is dealing with mortals, in this case a very young and inexperienced mortal.

*'Perhaps you didn't pay sufficient attention to its reply?'*

'I didn't hear any reply.'

*'Try again. Try to listen with more than your ears. Listen with all of your heart, with all of your hopes, with all of your being . . .'*

With a sigh of resignation, Magio presses his discovery against his breast again, focusing all of his thoughts and hopes upon it, embracing its strange twisty curves and

shapes, curling every fibre of his senses, his very spirit about
its strangeness.

'Oh, I think – yahoo, I do – I feel something.'

*'What did you feel?'*

'It . . . it feels like . . . like a sigh.'

*'Oh, glorious boy!'*

'What does it mean?'

*'It is your genie, Magio – the part that was taken from you
at birth as visibility was taken from your sister. Embrace it, as a
released prisoner would embrace his freedom. Set free your heart
. . . set free your spirit!'*

'I . . . Oh . . . *Ooohhh!'*

*'You are discovering your true nature – your true destiny,
Magio!'*

Magio's voice is a little blurry with tears of joy. 'What is
my destiny?'

*'Do you imagine that your sister was the only one to be
touched by magic?'*

'Magic?'

*'Magic indeed, such as would hardly be sufficient gratitude
for such a blithe spirit as yours. You are no ordinary mortal,
any more than your twin sister, Eefa. Were you not born from
the same womb? Was it not you who first discovered me and my
plight, finding a way through dreams?'*

'I don't understand.'

*'Oh, dearest Magio! It was ever present in your name.
Now you are reunited, it will guide your journey through the
Shadowlands.'*

'What journey?'

*'Now, in this moment of great danger for Eefa and Quimbre,
it is appropriate that you discover your true destiny. It will
seem strange, thrilling, perhaps even terrifying at first, as your*

*genie seeks consummation with your physical self. It will probe intimacies in ways you have never experienced before, all the while being ready to guide and instruct you.'*

'Oooh!'

# Juniper and Baccy

Quimbre flicked his head to one side. It brought a searing pain in his neck that caused him to clench his eyes shut for moment. 'Would you mind, warrior to warrior? I'm dying for my last puff of baccy.'

Kull, seated comfortably on a rock, studied him back contemplatively. He stuffed what was left of his captive's baccy into his own pipe, then lit it with a burning ember, puffing contentedly into his captive's sweat-soaked face.

Quimbre thought, *Go ahead – enjoy your victory! Take your time to smoke the last pipeful – give the kiddos more time to escape!*

That final encounter had been the most bruising of his life. Fought out on a precipitous forest slope, there had been no quarter asked and no quarter given. Neither had had the opportunity for the discharge of more than a single weapon. Both his flintlock and his enemy's steel-tipped arrow had found their mark, so they had both ended up wounded. But the arrow had only taken Quimbre in the shoulder. His ball had taken his enemy dead in the centre of his chest. Even now he could see the bloody mark. What was more, he had seen with his own eyes the spout of blood from the place that surely marked the hunter's heart. It was a killer shot that had floored his opponent for a full half minute. It made no sense that, within that same short time, his captor had climbed back onto his feet and they had ended up in a punching,

kicking, gouging, biting melee. Quimbre had fought –
valiantly was hardly the word since he had used every trick in
his devious book – but his opponent was younger, bigger and
vastly stronger than he was. How could the brute, without
armour, have survived what should have been a fatal shot?

Quimbre was now coughing from the irritation of the
smoke blown into his face by his tormentor, which added to
the pain in his broken ribs. It was just another humiliation.
But he had no cause for complaint. He'd have done the
same if the situation were reversed. No point in pretending
anything other than the rank loathing that hung in the air
between them. He had ended up hurt. Besides the flesh
wounds of biting, gouging, punching and kicking, Quimbre
had lost several teeth. His jaw was stiff, though he could
move it gingerly from side to side. Several of his fingers were
not so lucky, and the same applied to his left collarbone and
those lancinating ribs below it on the same side.

The empty pipe now tossed onto the fire, his enemy
took to his feet, so that he towered over Quimbre in gloating
appraisal. 'You put up a good fight.'

There was a strange red glow in the centre of those amber
eyes now looking down at Quimbre.

'Not good enough.'

Sudden his captor lunged. He struck Quimbre a bruising
kick in the face, leaving him stunned, spitting even more
blood.

'That was for me gals, Fang and Claw!'

Quimbre blinked in an attempt to shake the dizziness
brought on by the kick from his head. 'So,' he whispered to
himself, 'it comes to this.' At any moment now he expected
his captor to slit his throat. Yet no matter how hopeless it
seemed, he renewed his struggle, even with broken fingers,

to find the blade hidden in the back seam of his trousers. The giant figure loomed over him, that scarred face savouring the intent of finishing him off. But then Kull appeared to hesitate, as if some kind of struggle was going on within him that yet held him back. He surprised Quimbre when he squatted down in the dirt to confront him again.

'You be a dead man. Only Bastos Kull decides how and when.' Kull grinned. 'But you got me interested by that warrior to warrior stuff.' He grinned to see the expression in Quimbre's startled face. 'I be curious to know what warrior I got me here?'

'Well now!' Quimbre spat out a gobbet of bloody saliva. 'There's a question and a half!'

Kull squeezed Quimbre's broken collar bone again, causing him to groan aloud. 'None plays the fool with Bastos Kull.'

Quimbre winced. 'You really want to hear my story?'

'Mmmm!' His captor took a swig of what was left of Quimbre's juniper.

'The truth is I got a bit soft in the head. Found myself a family.'

His captor shrugged again.

Quimbre couldn't believe that the brute was allowing him to play for more time for Magio and Eefa to escape. He would have been happy to spin out the yarn for a night and a day. 'Had to be something to do with the chaos. The sea went crazy,' he said. 'A maelstrom the like of which I have never witnessed in decades of sailing the Sea of Stars. Not a single one of my fleet survived.'

His captor chuckled. 'Don't look likes ya had much luck.'

Quimbre shrugged, one-shouldered.

Kull seemed to like Quimbre's story. Either that or he had some reason of his own for wanting him to keep on spinning it out. Quimbre was happy to do so. Having downed what was left of the juniper juice, his captor belched in Quimbre's face.

'You spin a good tale, old pirate. Tell me more – your name?'

'Quimbre.'

'Just that?'

'Yeah – just that!'

His captor's strange red-glowing eyes turned from Quimbre to root through what was left of his back pack.

'I like the cutlass. Would make a pretty trophy. Maybe I puts it up besides your head. The blade a Quimbre – pirate captain who loses his head and his fleet!'

Quimbre ignored his captor's mockery. He cursed the broken fingers that were delaying his finding the blade in the seam of his trousers. The fact was he should still have won that fight. He had figured out a plan, and his plan had appeared to be working. He had drawn the ogre out onto a ledge of rock overlooking a wild rocky estuary, with the foaming abyss far below. He had timed the single flintlock ball to perfection. He had hit the target. Kull shouldn't be alive. Even then, seeing the monster rise back up out of what should have been certain death, Quimbre had fallen back onto the all-is-lost position of wrapping his arms around the monster, then hurling them both over the ledge and onto the rocks below. But his captor, despite the ball to his heart, and the bruising encounter with the rocks, had an endurance unlike any Quimbre had ever encountered – that plus the cunning to go with it. Quimbre needed to beware that cunning all the more. Surely by now he had given the kiddos more than time enough to escape? But instinct bade Quimbre to remain cautious and keep on spinning out time with such a terrible foe.

'Nice baccy – nice juniper!'

'Self-grown – and my own distillation.'

'You interest Bastos Kull. Takes a villain to appreciate another villain. But it won't save you when Lovely Lady arrives.'

'What Lovely Lady is that?'

Kull grinned. 'You'll see! You and me, we just got us a few minutes more to play games afore she gets here.'

Kull's words puzzled Quimbre. Everything about his captor was a puzzle. Why was this monstrous creature even bothering to keep him alive? There was no need for pretence. Quimbre needed to know what he was talking about. Was this anticipated arrival of the Lovely Lady a threat to the kiddos? He lifted his head up slowly, like someone beaten to exhaustion, someone who accepted he was defeated.

'Like you said, fellow warriors!'

'Yeah?'

'You the hunter – me the pirate.'

His captor laughed. 'Your head'll make a great trophy!'

'Yes – I guess it will. I was the best pirate in all of the Sea of Stars. Started from nothing, but I gathered my own fleet.'

His captor shrugged. 'Must have been some storm, huh!'

'Yeah!' Quimbre hissed with relief, at last discovering the blade hidden in the stitching of his trousers. But now he must somehow find some way of making use of it with those same broken fingers.

'It was as if the ocean had gone berserk. At the end of the madness I found myself washed ashore on the beach at Warren, more dead than alive. Nothing but the rags on my back. I found myself wandering the decrepit little excuse for a town called Warren, looking for food to steal. I just hung around the ruined streets until I found a shack that, through some miracle, had remained intact. There was a walled-off yard. I just fell into an exhausted stupor in the log pile. I woke in the dark of night to find a wrinkled old woman poking at me with her stick, holding a lantern in her other hand. She demanded to know who I was and what was I doing there. That was how I met Gran.'

'Gran?'

'The most cussed old witch you were ever likely to meet. I told her I was a ship-wrecked sailor.'

'She swallow that?'

'Of course not.'

'Not for one second.'

The ogre bellowed with laughter and he poked a fat tongue around the rim of the upended juniper bottle to lick away the last few drops.

'So you connived to lie some more?'

'I didn't bother.'

'No?'

'I was too jiggered to make the effort.'

'So – why not kill the old witch?'

'I will admit that I thought about it. I still had my flintlock and cutlass. But for some reason I didn't. Maybe I was just too blown away by the loss of my fleet. Then time just drifted by. And the funny thing was she never told me to go. Just kept on lashing me with her tongue.'

'Me – I'd a strangled her. Took what I wanted.'

'Perhaps an earlier version of me would too. But time went by. I expected, day after day, that she would tell me to go. But she never did.'

'She didn't figure you as a pirate?'

'Oh, she figured that right away. And yet still she never told me to go. That first night, when she let me sleep in the yard, I knew, right away, that my story didn't fool her. She knew what I was. She'd call me a pirate to my face. But she never told me to go.'

'Stubborn old hag, huh!'

'Yeah!'

'But it still don't explain you. A pirate on the Sea of Stars! And now here you are, settling down in a shack and growing juniper and baccy?'

'Why would I bother trying my hand at roving again? All that I had achieved, my beautiful fleet, was on the bottom of the ocean.'

His captor stared at Quimbre for a lengthy moment. Then he stared up into the night sky. Quimbre wondered if there was some reason he was looking into the sky.

'So, what now?'

'We wait.'

'For this Lovely Lady who is coming?' Quimbre had somehow managed to get his thumb curled around the blade behind his back.

Kull's red eyes turned to gaze into Quimbre's. And as he did so, Quimbre had the strangest feeling – as if the ogre was himself afraid. What could be so terrifying about this Lovely Lady that such a brute as Bastos Kull feared her?

Quimbre's mouth was dry as dust. He licked at his cracked lips to help him speak. 'I have shared my story with you. I'd be intrigued to hear your own. How did you come to be the great hunter?'

He wouldn't have been surprised to receive a second kick in his face. But the ogre lifted his eyebrows, as if amused by the question. 'Like you, I learnt from an old witch – but with me it wasn't me gran but me dear old ma.'

'She was a hunter?'

'Hah, hah – haaaahhhh!' Kull laughed so hard it brought tears to his eyes.

'No?'

'Her passion was to beat me. She would find any excuse. Her bare fists, when I was small. But as I grew – and I grew pretty fast – she found other ways.'

'Why – why did your mother beat you?'

Kull shrugged. 'Never bothered to explain. Maybe I reminded her of me absent father. He beat her, raped her, and so on – or so she said.'

'She blamed you for him?'

His captor laughed, as if highly delighted. 'When she branded me with that poker, when I was five years old, the old bitch said I was only three quarters human, and the only good quarter was Scog.'

Quimbre's eyes widened. But now he looked afresh at Kull, he saw the Scog in him.

'She took things out on you?'

'How you think I got these scars?'

His captor's face had once again turned to the sky, peering this way and that, as if searching for something.

The very notion that Kull was a quarter Scog explained his enormous size and strength. It might also explain something that had puzzled Quimbre. There were some very strange tattoos decorating his captor's brawny chest, amateurish-looking tattoos . . . and now he looked at them more closely they looked more branded into the skin rather than etched with a tattooist's needle.

'How did you cope with it – the beatings?'

'I'd get lost. At first it was by accident. Later I got lost
for longer. Learnt how to survive out there in the wilds of
Aytini.'

'Sounds like a tough childhood.'

'Mmmhhhh!' Kull was studying the sky again.

By now Quimbre was frantically attempting to figure out
what was really going on. What could the brute be planning?
He was the most resourceful and cunning enemy Quimbre
had ever encountered.

His captor returned his attentions to Quimbre. 'You
could learn a deal from watching them creatures in the wild.'

'That's how you became a hunter?'

'I – Bastos Kull – took my lessons from them whose
instinct is to hunt so they can survive.'

Even as Quimbre was reappraising Kull, he spun around.
At first Quimbre thought it was to lunge at him. Those red-
glowing eyes were terrifying when they focused on you. But
he wasn't the focus of those eyes. Kull was staring around
them, in a circle, sniffing at the air. It reminded Quimbre of
the way a cat or a dog searches for a scent. And then Quimbre
noticed that even Kull's ears appeared to twitch and turn, as
if searching for sounds.

Kull was still talking, half-whispering, as he continued to
spin his head, nostrils twitching. 'By the time I was fourteen
years, I'd had enough of her beatings. Had this dream – every
night the same dream. I was the legendary hunter – that one
who's supposed to roam the skies.'

Quimbre had to keep him talking. 'What was your
quarry?'

'All that moved.'

There was something else going on here, something
secretive. Kull would never bother to tell a prisoner his own

history. The ogre was playing games, attempting to distract Quimbre with the aim of putting him off his guard. It surely had something to do with the increasing tendency for Kull to raise his face into the air and sniff and harken. What then was Kull hoping to discover?

Quimbre writhed his body, his spine, his limbs, in an attempt to cut through his bonds, ignoring the pain that wracked his shoulder, his ribs, his broken fingers . . . ignoring the pain when the blade cut into his own skin.

'How did you deal with your mother?'

'I nurtured my grievance, all the while growing bigger, stronger, learning the cunning I would need.'

'The tormenting never stopped?'

Kull laughed, shaking his head.

'But your mother – she must have figured that, one day, you'd get bigger, would overpower her and take the whip, or the rod, or the glowing poker, out of her hands and use it on her?'

Kull snorted. 'Course she figured that. She figures she's gotto kill me afore I get full grown. So I figures to watch her closely, just like a hunter would. All the while testing my strength in fighting back. Used a trick I saw with the beasts in the forest. Pretended to be injured – weaker than I was. I saw how that pleased her, me dear old ma. Thinks she knows me, she does. Thinks she has the measure of me. And there's me, all the time making plans, testing weapons of wood, and iron, weapons I'd whittle and beat into shape, all by myself. And then, one day, when she's beating the living daylights out of me with a rod of iron, I takes the rod from her, and breaks the arm that wields it . . .' Kull's face took on a look of rapture. 'You should've seen the look on her face.'

'And then what?' Quimbre was staring up into those red-glowing eyes, appalled.

Kull giggled, like a little boy. 'I tell her – go ahead, Ma – run!'

The monster laughed, that terrible roar of a laugh again. He laughed, and laughed, and laughed . . . as if the memory were etched into his very soul.

'Your hunted your own mother?'

Kull wasn't listening to Quimbre any more. Those nostrils were elevated, sniffing at the ambient air again, his ears twitching, his every sense heightened with interest at something those nostrils and ears were detecting.

Suddenly those nostrils flared.

# CAPTURED

Invisible to the two men, Eefa hesitated on the edge of the scene before getting even closer to them. She crouched down low, having astonished herself with how readily she had followed Quimbre's trail from where he had abandoned them in the confusion of fleeing their overnight camp to a place above a yawning cliff where she found signs of a desperate struggle, Quimbre's smashed-up musket, and scatters of blood. Right now, she was so terrified of the huge man who was holding him captive, she hardly dared to breathe. This was the remorseless hunter, with his baying hounds, who had chased them all the way north from Warren. In the flickering firelight, she could make out that Quimbre was still alive, even though he was clearly bleeding and injured, seated in the dirt with his hands tethered behind his back. She had gathered, from their conversation, that some terrible fate was approaching. At any moment the hunter might take it into his head to cut Quimbre's throat from ear to ear.

*Oh, help me! Help me, Woll – help me anyone who can hear my thoughts! Help me find some way of saving Quimbre!*

Why was she crouching and hiding? The hunter could not see her. Yet so terrified was she of him that she had removed her boots in coming here, and now it took all of her courage to stand up at the edge of the firelight and remain confident that he couldn't see her. Step by faltering step, she drew closer to Quimbre, entering the full light from the fire, all the while prepared to flee if necessary. She stared at the glowering face of the hunter, gazed at those protuberant amber eyes which appeared to reflect the glow of the fire. There was no shock of realisation. He really couldn't see her. She held still for several seconds, taking slow breaths and waiting for her faltering heartbeat to slow down.

A voice was entering her mind, unbidden.

*'You have little time if you must rescue the mortal you care about.'*

She replied, mind to mind, *'Who are you?'*

*'You know me as the Lady of the Shore. I come in answer to your plea.'*

*'What are you? You cannot be human?'*

*'I am the reason you have been burdened with invisibility since birth.'*

*'Why . . . oh, why?'*

*'It was ever necessary to both our purposes. For you to bear the Bree Salis to me, it was essential to keep you safe.'*

*'Keep me safe from what? From whom?'*

*'My enemies are powerful beyond your imagination. They would have hunted you down and destroyed you – as here and now they strive. Why do you think this conversation goes unheard beyond our company? Meanwhile, time is pressing. You have risked all for the love of a companion. Yet your courage has placed you, and the Bree Salis itself, in imminent peril'.*

Eefa stared around herself at the situation she was facing. *The Bree Salis in imminent peril?* Her heart faltered again as she took a few steps closer to Quimbre. She stared down at his broken figure. She appraised the stout leather thongs that tethered his ankles and wrists, and further tethered his limbs to his neck, binding him into a cruel and awkward hog-tie. She saw how the skin of his hands and fingers was scratched and bleeding, the nails broken. Several fingers were so bent, they must also be broken. She crept around so she could examine him from the front. His face was bruised, one eye close to shut. Blood was trickling out of the left corner of his mouth, where teeth had also been broken.

*Poor Quimbre!*

She turned her attention to his captor, who looked even more gigantic this close, as tall, sitting in the dirt, as a medium-sized man would be standing fully erect. His bearded face was criss-crossed with scars under a beetling brow. Strangest of all were his eyes, which really did appear to glow red from their very depths, as if lit by two deep-seated flames. Even as she watched him, that heavy head was slowly turning here and there, as if apprehensive – those capacious nostrils flared. She shivered to see the great axe that straddled his back and the two heavy daggers that lay in a sheath by his knapsack. If only she could take one of those to Quimbre, she could cut his bonds and help him escape.

She was so terrified that she couldn't bear to think of the danger. Holding her breath, she went down onto all fours and crept behind the hunter's back. Reaching out with a trembling hand, she curled her fingers around the hilt of a dagger, silently inching it out of its scabbard. In that heart-pounding slow-motion of terror, she saw Quimbre's face tense, his eyes widened on the moving dagger. There could be no panicky giving in now. In the same slow motion, she withdrew the heavy weapon completely out of its sheath and clasped it within her two hands. But in that same awful moment, she heard the sudden whip of the hunter's arm, and she felt the snap of one huge hand around both of her wrists, enclosing them, and the hilt, in a crushing clasp.

'What we got us here?'

Eefa twisted and turned, but it was no good. The hunter was on his feet, her wrists tight-clasped in his huge hand, lifting her body high into the air as if she weighed no more than a feather. Those terrible eyes were peering all about her, those nostrils sniffing close to her skin. Then a deafening roar of triumph.

'Got ya – invisible imp!'

She swooned with terror.

'I was told to watch out for an invisible brat such as you. Never has Bastos Kull hunted an invisible quarry before. I scarcely believed it. Even me bootiful gals struggled to pick up your scent. But now I got you.'

'Let me go, you monster!'

'Ah – it squeaks!'

'Oh, Quimbre!'

'I'm sorry, kiddo! I guessed he was holding back, waiting for some reason. I didn't know what for. But now I know that I underestimated him.'

'He shouldn't be able to smell me, or take hold of me!'

'He's just been telling me that he's a quarter Scog.' Quimbre sounded grief-stricken. 'Remember the Scogs back in Warren.'

Eefa recalled the circle of Scogs that had surrounded her and Magio in Warren. They had somehow detected her presence.

Kull boomed with laugher. 'Scogs can smell better than a hound. It's true. I could smell you, imp, from the moment you came into my camp.'

Quimbre's voice was husky with emotion. 'She's worthless to you, Kull. Let her go. I'm the one you want.'

'Oo wants you, old man, other than dead? But My Lady will be tickled pink when I presents her with this prey.'

'She's a child – of no use to you or your mistress.'

'Wrong, wrong – a thousand times wrong! She has ever been my main quarry in this hunt. The Mistress will reward me with a bucket full of Scog gold. Foolish girlie – you make a stupid attempt to save the old pirate, and end up saving Bastos Kull!'

'No!' Quimbre roared, though still tethered, attempting to climb to his feet, his throat bulging with his attempt to rip apart his bonds. 'Please – I beg you!'

Kull laughed from the depths of his belly. 'Me old ma – she surely taught me the usefulness of mercy.'

'Your mother was a sadist.'

Kull laughed, towering over the bound figure of Quimbre. 'Her name was Ellumbra. Burned it into me chest with a red-hot poker, so as I'd know who owned me. It's still there. The reason you can't read it is cause it's Scog. Me ma taught me a few lessons what has proved most useful in me life. There is no mercy. A lesson that might have served this imp better than come to rescue you.'

Her captor abruptly fell silent, his gaze fixed on some point in the night sky where a disturbance was rippling through the starry darkness. Something was approaching. Eefa saw a strange cloud rippling through the dark. It was unlike any cloud she had ever seen before, a malevolently angry shape, as if three serpents were writhing within one another, brimming at the very tip of an invading darkness. Eefa saw Kull's eyes protrude further out of his eyelids, and glow brighter. Her heart recoiled from the ominous feeling of that approaching cloud. She felt her captor's grip release her wrists. But she was not free to run. A rising vortex was encircling her, a force of dark magic, paralysing her limbs. Moment by moment, she sensed the tightening of its hold on her, as if she had been seized within the closing coils of that trio of serpents.

'Help me!' Eefa screamed.

$\infty$

The voice of the Lady of the Shore spoke urgently within Magio's mind. *'We must act quickly. Eefa faces the gravest danger.'*

Magio cried, 'You must save her!'

*'Perhaps it is your sister who might save you – and me?'*

'I don't understand.'

*'You must call her to you.'*

'I . . . I don't understand. She isn't here. How can I call her?'

The voice now sounded urgent. *'Do not question me. Merely call her.'*

'How . . .' Magio flopped onto the beach, bewildered. 'Oh, Eefa! I don't know what I'm expected to do.'

*'Merely call her . . . '*

But what did that mean? 'Should I shout out her name? Am I to think about her, think that I am calling her?' Magio had no idea what it meant.

*'Are you not twins?'*

So, what did that imply? The fact that they were twins? He recalled the closeness he had always felt with Eefa, how they had sensed things so similarly, how they had, on occasion, even shared their dreams.

*'Time is running out!'*

Magio flopped down on the pebbly beach. He clenched shut his eyes. He blotted out all sense of where he was, all notion of the wind in his ears, the feel of the breeze on his skin, the ozone smell of the sea in his nostrils. He enveloped himself in a cocoon of unfeeling, unseeing, unhearing, then, in the tiniest whisper, he spoke her name.

'Eefa!'

He heard what might be the vaguest squeak of a reply. But it could have been no more than the wind.

'Eefa! This time he roared her name, expressing every fibre of his being into the shout.

*'Oh, Magio! How are we talking to one another?'*

*'I think we must be talking mind to mind. The Lady of the Shore is making it possible. Where are you? What's happening?'*

*'I'm trapped. I'm a prisoner of the same monster who has captured Quimbre. I can't abandon him. The monster plans to kill him. He's waiting for something to arrive before he will do it. But I fear it's going to be horrible.'*

*'Be brave. We're trying to save you.'*

*'How . . .?'*

*'I haven't figured that yet.'*

Magio desperately wanted to hug his sister. But she wasn't there to hug. The voice of the old woman was soothing in his mind.

*'Be brave, Magio. There is so little time. The darkness is closing even as you chatter among yourselves.'*

Magio scratched at his shoulder, as if to reassure himself he was still real. But there was a rising sense in him that didn't feel real at all. It was the old woman. She was doing something he didn't understand. She was gazing into the sky, as if calling on the heavens. But then a strange sound, like a distant thunder, responded. And then she was speaking words that had no meaning to him. Yet even he sensed that these were words of power, words of magic, maybe, that Magio couldn't interpret.

'What's going on?'

'*There are conflicting forces fighting for supremacy.*'

'We must save Eefa.'

'*You must fight for her!*'

'How?'

'*Set free your genie – set it free to call upon the one who bore the Bree Salis to you in the Valley of the Raptors.*'

The world about them was becoming stranger than ever. The wind was so biting and hard it made it almost impossible to speak to each other. The daylight was weirdly flickering. The beach before them was no longer real. Magio hugged his treasure to his breast. He closed all of his senses, all of his being around it and willed it to become part of him. And then he felt the wonder of approaching magic enter his body, his heart and soul . . . the thrill of its consummation within him, being for being.

**୯ଛ**

Out of the corner of her eye Eefa saw how Quimbre was somehow breaking free of his bonds. He was pulling a blade from somewhere behind his back and approaching the heedless figure of their captor. But Quimbre couldn't possibly help her now. The growing power of the approaching darkness was already immense, tearing her off her feet and lifting her, her whole body spinning, beginning to rise up into its maw.

'*No time left. Seize the moment, Magio!*'

She heard that gentle voice again: the voice of the old woman who called herself the Lady of the Sea. She heard Magio's confused reply:

'*How? Oh, please help me!*'

The darkness was invading her body. It was drowning her senses, her spirit, in its ravening maw.

'*Remember – the Bree Salis!*'

It was too late. Her heart, her entire being, was enveloped in darkness.

'*Remember . . . Remember . . .*' Her mind focused on the single word. She focused with all of her might on her paralysed lips, forced them to fashion the whisper, 'The Bree . . . the Bree Salis . . .'

An inhuman screech from overhead. In that screech Eefa sensed a weakening of the hold of the darkness upon her. 'Yes,' she whispered. 'I . . . I remember. I remember what I am carrying. I am carrying the Bree Salis.'

'*Allow it to expand within you, beloved Eefa!*'

She did as she was bidden. She opened her heart to what she knew must be there, allowing the golden light to flood her being. Immediately she felt stronger, no longer terrified.

'*I'm coming for you!*'

Magio! That surely was Magio's voice. She couldn't believe that she heard Magio's voice inside her head.

He said it again, '*I'm coming for you, Eefa!*'

How could Magio be coming for her?

It was all so confusing. Even so, she felt able to take a deep breath, feeling the same confidence expand into heart, her blood, to diffuse into every morsel of her being. As she lifted her head, things looked different. The light, the ground, the sky: all appeared unreal.

She gazed about her, just as Quimbre was stabbing their captor in the back of his neck with what appeared to be a long sliver of a blade. She saw the look of astonishment that came over the face of their tormentor, even as he was falling into the embers of the fire.

'Eefa – come on!'

Quimbre's voice . . . But it was a struggle to return to normal consciousness. Quimbre was looking about him, as if trying to locate her. 'Come on – you know I can't see you when you make yourself invisible. We need to run.'

But she could see from his numerous injuries that he was in no fit state to run. He was merely thinking of her, attempting to encourage her to escape. She had no intention of abandoning Quimbre a second time.

There were yet more ripples in the night sky, a second cloud approaching, the sound of giant wings beating. A gigantic shadow was blotting out the stars. It was crashing through the branches of the surrounding trees. Bolts of lightning appeared to erupt from its passage.

Magio cried, 'Come on, Eefa – Quimbre!'

Neither could move with the shock of what confronted them.

The giant dragon that had bequeathed the Bree Salis to Eefa in the Valley of the Raptors was swooping down on them. Its yellow eyes had become blazing orbs of gold, and its great wings were tearing apart the air with a deafening thunder.

'Come on!' Magio's cried again.

Eefa stared up to glimpse what must be Magio's face looking down at her, from somewhere high above, in the region of the dragon's neck.

'Magio!'

He shouted back, 'It's going to be all right. That's provided I can instruct the dragon to pick you up without crushing you. Oh jinxy! I think, maybe, I might be able to tell it to grab you both.'

Eefa was too bewildered to reply. Scared out of her wits, and trembling from head to foot, she bent herself into a foetal curve just as she felt the talons of the dragon close about her and, all in a single sweep, hoisted her aloft.

She managed a single word. 'Quimbre?'

Magio's gleefully responded, 'We've got him too!'

Her thoughts were going around and around in her head as she was being whisked aloft into the vastness of the starry sky.

'Yeeee-haaaahhh!'

Magio's idiotic cry celebrated his great adventure.

Her head was so confused she didn't know what to think. She was conscious of being borne through a whirlwind of place and time, with flashes and intimations of things she didn't understand, perhaps would never understand. At some stage in a confusing journey, Bird Woman's voice entered her head. 'The Beach of Bones does not exist in your sense of space and time.'

Eefa heard Magio exclaim, 'Britzy!'

Bird Woman must have been picked up too. It was fortunate that dragons, unlike eagles, had four and not two taloned feet.

Magio was calling out, 'Hey, Quimbre – you okay?'

'I'm alive, kiddo. Though I don't know how!'

'Britzy, britzy – a million times britzy!'

It was a stupid word, but she supposed it was as good a word as any in the circumstances. Eefa bit her teeth together and forced herself to uncurl from her terrified posture. 'Bird Woman – I don't know how Magio got us out of there. I don't even know where we are headed.'

Bird Woman said, 'There is a place – an island – north of here. It is aptly named Woe. No sailor would dare to head there, not in his right mind. It is said to be haunted by ghouls and demons.'

Quimbre joined the conversation. 'She is right. We sailors are familiar with such a place. It is fearful bad luck to be blown off course there. It is said to be a graveyard of ships.'

Bird Woman added, 'If we assume that the Beach of Bones you have visited in your awake dreams is at the interface between this world and Dromenon – I couldn't think of a more appropriate place for that interface than the Isle of Woe.'

'What are you suggesting, Bird Woman?'

'Your primary task remains unfulfilled.'

'I don't understand!'

'You are the bearer of the Bree Salis. You must fulfil your destiny – you can only do so on the Beach of Bones.'

Eefa brought wrapped her arms and hands about herself and she clenched her eyes shut. 'Magio – you heard what Bird Woman said?'

'Yeah. I heard. Can I ask everyone, you, Eefa, Bird Woman, and you too, Quimbre – are we all agreed? Am I to instruct the dragon to take us to the Isle of Woe?'

Eefa waited for confirmation from Bird Woman, and then Quimbre, before she too murmured, 'Yes, Magio – we are all agreed.'

'Yeeee-haaaahhh!'

# THE BEACH OF BONES

Eefa was relieved to return to solid ground after her flight within the terrifying grip of the dragon. She expected Magio and Bird Woman and Quimbre to join her. But she found herself alone. There had always been so much she did not understand, and this was merely another puzzle added to the great many that had baffled her throughout their flight from Warren. She was back in what seemed like early morning in what at first seemed a familiar place: that lonely beach by the abandoned watch tower – the beach with the radiating lines of stones.

Her ears were deafened by a screaming wind that attempted to drown out the voice that was insisting on communicating with her inside her own mind. '*Do not fear, brave one. Your brother and your two companions are nearby, and for the moment they are safe.*'

'Where am I?'

'*Dromenon is an in-between world, one that both separates and connects the world of mortals and the Undying.*'

'Why have you brought me here?'

'*You are the bearer of my liberation. In this you are under no duress or obligation. You must choose to save me or condemn me to my eternity of woe.*'

Eefa could not see the old woman, but she was aware of her ethereal presence as if it were one with the entire landscape.

'I know who you are. You are the Lady of the Shore, chained to the terrible iron shack in Magio's and my awake-dreams.'

*'Indeed I am.'*

'Who did that cruel thing to you? Why are you imprisoned like this in such a terrible place?'

*'A sentence was passed on me long ago. A dread enchantment cast by a jealous and angry husband. He had long tired of me and decided that he would abandon me. Then, when I turned to one more caring, that same husband, in his infinite cruelty, created this punishment for me, deeming it to last to eternity.'*

'That's horrible,' Eefa said.

*'For aeons have I been searching for a way to undo the spell. But it was deeply woven, and enmeshed with adamantine malice. Even so, I was never entirely abandoned. I have allies among the Undying. It was these allies who helped me create the Bree Salis, which, if the fates are willing, may prove my liberation.'*

'But why – why was I chosen to play a part in this liberation? And why must my part demand that I must be invisible?'

*'Your questions are reasonable. But I cannot answer all of them in this moment. You must trust me when I tell you that it would not be safe for me to explain all at this juncture.'*

Eefa blinked away the tears that were rising into her eyes. 'There's so much I need to know – to understand.'

*'My sweet brave girl, we have very little time for such conversation. Their search for you, that proved so frightening and distressing, has not ended. Any moment now it is likely to spread to Dromenon.'*

'What must I do?' Eefa asked, panicking.

'*You must find me – in the flesh. Do so, I beg you, before my enraged husband discovers what I am planning. You must enter Dromenon.*'

Eefa turned, and in doing so, she saw that the beach had changed. It had become altogether more arid than it had appeared moments before. There was no sand, merely bare rock and stones. It, too, was cut through by radiating lines. But these lines were not piled up monuments of stone such as led her on the beach below the tower; these were walls made up of bones, bleached white bones, vast in number and frighteningly compacted and intertwined with one another. This was a beach conspired to crush one's heart and soul. But she couldn't stand still and stare at it. She must hurry, just as the voice of the Lady of the Shore had urged her. Already she was running, haring between the walls of bones, which were surely directing her to whatever horror lay at the dead centre of their radiating compass. And running, with her limbs trembling as she ran, and with her thoughts now all of a muddle in her head, she heard a new whisper.

'*Do you feel it – do you sense the power of the Bree Salis within you, Eefa!*'

She searched for it, even as she was running. She found it so quickly it was as if it had found her. Immediately a new strength flowed through her and empowered her, making her body lighter than air, her legs as fleet as a gazelle's. She steeled herself for the horror ahead, even before she could see it. She anticipated iron . . . the hard, unfeeling coldness of iron . . . and now, running on, she caught her first real glimpse of it, the monstrosity of heavy rusting plates of iron.

This close to it the very bleakness of it overwhelmed her senses.

It was gargantuan – much vaster than she would have anticipated. It could not possibly be a building that anyone, or creature, could take shelter in. Running closer still to it, it just grew larger and larger, towering above the landscape of the beach. There was an implacable cruelty about it, a sense of irredeemable hate, brooding at the dead centre of the radiating walls of bones. As Eefa drew closer to the shack, a strange idea crept into her mind, a curious idea even to think about. The idea was somehow captured in a single terrible word . . . *fate*. The iron monstrosity was meant to symbolise fate – the fate of the goddess who had been chained to it for all of eternity. Even as Eefa realised the horror of what she was witnessing, her ears were buffeted by the rising wind that rattled a hail of pebbles against her running figure. It was as if the very elements objected to her approaching this monstrosity.

Though it terrified her, she was unable to take her eyes from it, as it loomed larger and larger. What she had thought of as a shack now towered high over her, so tall the roof was above the clouds. She was now close enough to touch it, her tentative fingers registering the adamantine solidity of the rusting slabs of iron that comprised it. They made an impression in her mind of utter hopelessness. She felt foolish in pressing her face up close to it, as if she must sniff the rusting metal to make absolutely sure it was real. Her hand hammered against its ungiving surface, which was as solid as a mountain, eliciting no answering reverberation.

The iron monstrosity was terrifyingly real. But she could see no trace of the Lady of the Shore, in her manacled constraints.

Anxiety rose in Eefa's heart. Had she made a mistake coming into Dromenon on her own? Why wasn't Bird

Woman here to advise her? The rising terror bade her run away. But her limbs felt weak and she doubted she could run. She backed away, her bare feet bruised by the stony ground.

Then the world appeared to change. The line of the horizon appeared to become alive in a glitter of fine blue light that extended inwards all the way to the beach, with its radiating walls and iron prison, as if to illuminate the monstrous landscape in a revelatory light. And then the wind rose further until it seemed to be developing into a localised hurricane.

'Oh, no!' She brought her fist to her mouth.

The voice invaded her mind, a voice gentle as the wind, but insistent.

*'We have so little time left, Eefa!'*

She was down on her knees, hugging her arms close to her chest to withstand the wind. It tore at her ears. Her heartbeat was swelling up out of her chest and into her throat. And there, where there had been mere emptiness moments ago, a figure now huddled against the sheer cliff face of iron, its ankles manacled and chained to it, its face rising slowly from its fallen position against its chest. Eefa saw that it resembled the woman from her dreams, but this figure could not possibly be human. She was gazing at a giantess, her face and body eaten away in places, as if it had long been food for the crabs and sea creatures that even now appeared to be crawling within her flesh, creeping in and out of holes and tunnels within her abdomen. There were similar holes in the flesh of her chest where the ribs were exposed, holes even in her head where her very skull was exposed.

*'Thus ruined do you see me, brave Eefa! I am sorry to so shock your senses. But perhaps now at last you understand?'*

She took a deep breath, then found the strength to climb back onto her feet, and to attempt to run away. She managed what might have been fifty yards before her muscles wilted.

*'Am I so loathsome you would run from me?'*

That was wrong: it felt so deeply wrong, that Eefa turned back to confront the shackled goddess.

Her vision was once again blurred with her own tears. 'Oh, I am sorry – but it's so horrifying to see you treated this way.'

*'I understand.'*

'You are truly she? You're the old woman who has haunted our dreams?'

*'Yes.'*

Despite her evident torment, the old woman's voice was strangely calming in Eefa's mind.

*'The chaos of war came to the world of the Undying. I was but a minor deity in such arenas of power, contented to care for and be venerated by the creatures that inhabit the oceans. Sailors and fisher people would plead for my blessing. One of great charm, but even greater cunning, captured my heart. He became my husband. And once my husband, he proved darkly possessive, taking pleasure in tormenting me. He abused my good position of trust to befriend a being of enchantment, one of the greatest powers in our world, and, as with me, once within the embrace of his false friendship, betrayed the enchanter to usurp his powers. So, the Chaos, borne of his greed, came among the Undying.'*

'Was that what brought the catastrophe down on our world, including Moon?'

*'All was so thrown out of balance in the world of the Undying, it was inevitable the resultant chaos would manifest through Dromenon into the world of mortals.'*

'But you – how did you become so horribly imprisoned?'

*'My realm – a realm I loved – was the seashore. It was of little or no concern to my nemesis. But to consolidate his power, after he had stolen the secrets of enchantment, he took to him a usurper for a lover, one from a similar mould to his own dark heart. Her name is Lustfera, The Star of Mourning. But an Undying can only take to him, or her, a replacement spouse with the consent of the former spouse. This I would never consent to. He tormented me by imprisoning me within the world I had once ruled and still held dear to my heart. I could escape only through consent to his new union with his terrible new bride. Refuse him and I was condemned to this barren prison, without hope of salvation.'*

'Why didn't you just give in?'

*'An eternity of anguish is a terrible price for obstinacy, which is true. You might think me simply jealous or obstinate. Yet I knew that if I once agreed, such a union of two dark powers would not be satisfied with simply ruling with wisdom and restraint. Terrible would be the consequences of their potential for ruthlessness and cruelty in the world of the Undying – and it would surely extend to your mortal world of Tír.'*

'Oh, Lady of the Shore, I feel so sorry for you,' Eefa said, overwhelmed. 'I so want to help you. I really do – I want to help you fight this horrible sentence. But this thing I am carrying – the Bree Salis – what is it? How will it cure you?'

*'Being an Undying, I cannot die. This made it all the more dreadful that the enchantment was designed to be eternal. Over the vastness of time I searched for an escape from such a sentence and found none. Not until Woll, Queen of the Ooonaree, suggested a possibility so rare and wonderful that, I strongly suspect, my enemy would never have considered it.'*

'What possibility?'

'That my soul spirit could be reincarnated. Oh, there were ancient legends of metamorphosis amid the Undying, but none really understood them. Woll and her people are truly knowledgeable in the ancient lore. She would appear to be one of the few who understand what such a mystical change might involve. It begs a question, Eefa. Can a spiritual being be reborn with a new spirit? Woll persuaded me through showing me how such rebirth exists, indeed is commonplace, amid the world of the mortals.'

Eefa exclaimed, 'The butterfly!'

'Yes – indeed.'

'But you're no butterfly.'

'Indeed, I am not. But nevertheless the idea provoked much thought among my friends in the Undying. There would appear to be little in the way of enchantments that deal with reincarnation among the gods. But when Woll drew my attention to it, I discovered that the reincarnation of the butterfly requires a somnolent form known as a chrysalis. You are my chrysalis, Eefa.'

'But I'm just human.'

'Yes indeed. But you are more than just human. You are loving and caring to your twin brother. And your heart is pure.'

'I may not be so nice and innocent as you think.'

The goddess smiled. 'You are sufficiently pure, as all that I have seen of you has amply confirmed. And you have another quality of equal importance. My dreadful enchantment was cast for the soul spirit of an Undying. Transferred to the soul spirit of a mortal it was rendered impotent.'

'You transferred your soul spirit, cast with its terrible enchantment, to me – in the Bree Salis?'

'Exactly!'

Eefa didn't know what to think. 'But it could have done something terrible to me!'

*There was risk, I cannot deny it. I protected you by making you invisible, and by recruiting Bird Woman and the frost sprites to aid you. It was selfish and cruel on my part to use you in this way, but I was faced with such a terrible alternative. There were risks for us both, Eefa, I do admit. And I heartily apologise for exposing you to those risks. But I hope you will understand that I had no alternative option to free myself. And now I would be pleased if you would transfer the Bree Salis back to me. Only then will I know if my soul spirit will be reborn free of torment.'*

Eefa shuddered at the dangers she, Magio, Quimbre and Bird Woman had faced on their journey here. But now she understood the horror of the goddess's plight, she bore no resentment towards her. 'You said there was no more time. Then show me how to transfer the Bree Salis to you right away!'

The giant figure appeared to smile. *'What a wonder you are! We cannot embrace and share our beings. Were we to do so, I would consume you, body and spirit. I love you too dearly for that. There are others who will lift the burden from you without injury – friends who have also come to love you while aiding your journey to me.'*

'Woll – you must mean Woll, and the frost sprites?'

*'That was ever their role in protecting and accompanying you to this dreaded destination.'*

The air was suddenly full of pinpoints of silvery light. They filled Eefa's vision like an all-embracing cloud, wheeling and spiralling about her in a playful frenzy. At the same time Woll's words penetrated her mind. *'Please trust me, as I have long trusted you.'*

'I do trust you!'

'*Then let the sacred reunion take place!*'

'I'm still scared.'

'*There is no need to be frightened. You – Eefa – you and your brother, Magio, have gained a powerful ally in me. My gratitude, if such a wonderful rescue comes to fruition, will be your reward.*'

The goddess laughed, a wonderful sound, causing the frost sprites to wheel and circle in rapture about them. They began to change their colours to assume all shades of the rainbow. They whirled and assumed the delightful shapes, and forms of the creatures that inhabited the oceans, wheeling in spirals within spirals, as if performing some graceful dance of initiation.

'*They will not hurt you as they enter and penetrate you.*'

She thought, *Penetrate me!* Eefa took a deep breath and then said, 'Go ahead. But I can't pretend I'm not frightened.'

'*Please do not be alarmed as you feel the consummation.*'

It was happening. Eefa felt the sting as the tiny star that was Woll penetrated her breast, felt her move within her. Then more and more of the frost sprites began to invade her being, like a warm and gentle rain. She attempted to stiffen her trembling legs at the knees, to force her spine to full erectness.

'Oh!' she cried, 'Ooooohhhh! What's happening to me?'

'*Be brave! We are releasing you from the burden you have so bravely borne for our Lady of the Shore.*'

Her skin prickled at the myriad points of entry, as if exposed to the most extreme cold. The same prickling cold was running through her, being borne by her heart and then her blood to every cell of her being. The peculiar feelings within her terrified her, but she was equally thrilled. She was filling up with such extraordinary feelings of mixed anguish and delight that she was close to swooning. Then she saw what she presumed was the tiny star of Woll leading the frost sprites back out of her. But this Woll was a tiny golden star. All the wheeling stars that followed her formed a coruscating golden cloud, the gold of the Bree Salis. The cloud wheeled around the tormented figure of the giantess that was still chained to the iron shack. They were already flowing into her enormous frame.

The daylight appeared to change again. The sky lightened, the air warmed. The storm clouds that had accompanied the hurricane of wind evaporated in mere minutes so that the blue sunlight of a summer morning emerged. The terrible beach, and the pounding sea beyond it – everything was changing.

But Eefa was no longer interested in sky or weather. The old woman had metamorphosed before her eyes. That horribly injured body was melting away. What emerged was utterly transformed. She was emerging as a youthful woman, with skin devoid of blemish, with eyes the cerulean of a midsummer sky, and hair as golden as corn. She was too radiant to be anything but a goddess.

Eefa was so astonished she had lost her voice: she simply stared in a mixture of wonder, her heart pounding with uncertainty as to what was to happen next. Those cerulean eyes now lifted into the sky, as if seeing far beyond anything that Eefa could see. And then, as if by another miracle, she heard Magio's voice . . . She heard how his voice was trembling, as if he had shared her vision of the change in the old woman. But he was stronger than she was in this astonishing moment. He was insistent where she would not have dared to be so forthright in addressing the emerging goddess. 'Now you must do it, Lady of the Shore! You must keep your promise to Eefa.'

The beautiful youthful goddess smiled down at him. '*It is so wonderful to see how you so love your sister.*'

'It wasn't fair, what you did to her, the burden you put on her. Now you must keep your word to her. Make my sister real.'

'*Is this your desire, Eefa?*'

'Oh, yes!'

'*You have proved my saviours – both sister and brother. I have a reciprocal duty to you. Yet I should caution you that the conflict that underscored it is not over.*'

'What do you mean?'

'*Forces of rage, of retribution and conquest, have been released. Once opened, this box of serpents cannot simply be resealed.*'

'But you can stop this now – you're a goddess!'

'*Dear Magio. Have you not yet realised that there are others, some equally powerful as me, some even more powerful, each with their own selfish motives?*'

'Then we can't win.'

'*Oh, let your and my brave hearts not quail so easily. For half of eternity it seemed that I was alone. Yet goodness eventually prevailed in the shape of you blessed two. Now we are three . . .*'

'Four,' the roar of Quimbre corrected her.

'*Bravely spoken, man of the sea. So, given the many wrecks, some of which might be made seaworthy, you are the agent of Eefa's and Magio's escape from Moon.*'

'Five!' Bird Woman added her voice.

'*So, resolute Magio, does your army grow in number even as we speak?*'

'Six.'

'*Ah! My heart grieves me if I am to lose this one!*' The towering goddess lifted Eefa from the ground and held her within the cocoon of her hands. '*I wondered when that pipsqueak would speak.*'

Eefa's gaze lifted to those enormous beautiful eyes now reflecting her own upturned face, and beyond it the arid desert of beach, and further still the pulsating, devouringly alive sea.

'*You heard?*'

'Yes,' she spoke little above a whisper, knowing how dear was this companion to the goddess. 'It was Woll's voice.'

'*Woll indeed. And now I rather imagine that she too has a bargain she would strike with me on your behalf. But first she must present this bargain to you and obtain your acceptance before she dares to present it.*'

'*Yes, I have!*'

Eefa recognised that same voice of her frost sprite friend. 'Please, Woll, tell me what it is you are thinking?'

'*I want, as your brother rightly demands, that you be freed from your cloak of invisibility.*'

Eefa blinked several times. But she waited, knowing there must be more.

'*But I want also to strike a bargain with My Lady of the Shore that you keep the option of becoming invisible when it might be helpful to you.*'

Eefa was astonished. She would never have thought of such a bargain. 'Why? Why do you want this?'

'*Think! What if the need for invisibility became important for you in a fell moment, as when you helped save Quimbre's life? What is there to lose? After all, it might make a gift of what was formerly a burden.*'

Eefa thought hard about that. And then she saw what Woll was suggesting was eminently practical and sensible.

'I – if you wouldn't mind, My Lady – I agree with Woll.'

*'Then so be it. Even though it means I must part with the spirit I so cherish. Yet I gladly sacrifice this as my gift to my redeemer.'*

Eefa was astonished to see the single golden star re-emerge from the body of the goddess and spiral around herself. There was a familiar playfulness about it that gladdened her heart. She closed her eyes and took a deep breath and inhaled it within herself with a strange new joy.

'Thank you, My Lady!'

*'It is I who should be thanking you. But now I would caution you that your work is done here on Moon. The enemies who troubled you will have no further interest in you for now, certainly not if you depart this island speedily. Go, each of you, where your heart desires. Take advantage of the fact that there is a sailor among you, and a young rascal in search of adventure. Go! Try to keep yourselves out of trouble while sailing the Sea of Stars, where, I'm sure, there will be adventures a plenty for Magio to discover.'*

## Other Swift titles by Frank P. Ryan

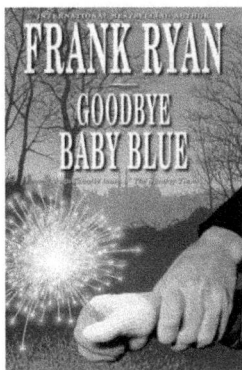

On a chill November day in Sheffield, Bobby Stephens, an eight-year-old boy is kidnapped. As the hunt proceeds, the paucity of evidence becomes alarming. Woodings feels personally involved: his own son, Gerry, is of the same age as Bobby. And Woodings' marriage is on the rocks. Then a bizarre note arrives, addressed to Margaret Stephens . . . and the murders begin.

This is the book that was glowingly reviewed in The Sunday Times as "magnificently tense". With his perceptive eye for background and character, Frank Ryan has created a thriller masterpiece. In a violent cat-and-mouse game, Woodings finds himself no longer the hunter but the hunted, his own life in constant danger as he begins to unravel a monstrous and terrifying secret with roots that spread far from the North of England and reach back into the turbulent sixties.

*Category: Thriller; Pages 336; PRICE £6.99;*
*B-format paperback.*

More at  www.swiftpublishers.com and www.frankpryan.com

In the Middle East Apache gunships attack an agricultural station in the desert. In Thirless, Arizona, cactus grower MayEllen Reickhardt is waiting to meet her friend, Lucille Cordoba. They plan to visit the annual convention in Phoenix. They won't make it.

At an ecology station in the southern Mojave, Ake Johansson is carrying a roll of computer printout back to his office from the mainframe in the lab. The printout is alarming. In Atlanta CDC-based Will grant is woken from sleep by a call from an ITU doctor at the Thirless Memorial Hospital. 'Well, I'm telling you that this is a very strange case. We've already sent you specimens. I certainly hope you can help us.' They don't know it yet but it is already too late. Something extraordinary, something very frightening indeed, is emerging - and their lives will never be the same again.

Once again, Frank P. Ryan has created a thriller masterpiece that will have you on the very edge of your seat throughout.

*Category: Thriller; Pages 411; PRICE £7.99; B-format paperback.*
*More at  www.swiftpublishers.com and www.frankpryan.com*

Lightning Source UK Ltd.
Milton Keynes UK
UKHW011519190819
348225UK00001B/183/P